THE HUSH

ALSO BY JOHN HART

Redemption Road

Iron House

The Last Child

Down River

The King of Lies

THE HUSH

JOHN HART

ST. MARTIN'S PRESS NEW YORK

THIS IS A WORK OF FICTION. ALL OF THE CHARACTERS, ORGANIZATIONS, AND EVENTS PORTRAYED IN THIS NOVEL ARE EITHER PRODUCTS OF THE AUTHOR'S IMAGINATION OR ARE USED FICTITIOUSLY.

 For information, address St. Martin's Press, 175 Fifth Avenue, New York, N.Y. 10010.

www.stmartins.com

Designed by Omar Chapa

The Library of Congress Cataloging-in-Publication Data is available upon request.

ISBN 978-1-250-01230-2 (hardcover)
ISBN 978-1-250-18495-5 (signed edition)
ISBN 978-1-250-20049-5 (international, sold outside the U.S., subject to rights availability)
ISBN 978-1-250-01229-6 (ebook)

First Edition: February 2018

10 9 8 7 6 5 4 3 2 1

For Saylor and Sophie—because there is such magic in the world, and such strong hearts to hold it

ACKNOWLEDGMENTS

This book was delightful to write and bring to market, and I'd like to thank all the publishing professionals involved—the design team, production team, sales force, publicity team, editorial group, marketing team, publishers, all of you. Your work, as always, makes the difference. Mary Hart and James Randolph were kind enough to guide me in questions of the law. Both are consummate professionals. Any mistakes in the book are either intentional in order to further the story or entirely my own fault. Pete Wolverton and Jennifer Donovan deserve a special note of thanks, as do my writer friends here in town, John, Corban, and Inman. Esther Newberg gave early reads, and was invaluable, as always. Thanks as well to David Woronoff, Emlyn Koster, Melanie Soles, Leslie and Robert Ketner, and Bob and Anne Brinson. Erik Ellsweig and Jay Kirkpatrick continue their grand tradition of support, so a warm shout-out to them as well. A special note of appreciation goes to my friend John Grisham, who helped me launch the book in such a meaningful way—I owe you one, John. Warmest thanks, of course, to my parents, siblings, children, and in-laws, who've always been there to support, encourage, and keep me humble. You guys are the best. Other friends make life a joy, so to Neal and Chris and Rick—thanks for bringing the metal. As always, final thanks go to my lovely wife, Katie, who walks the path beside me and makes it all so fun.

THE HUSH

CHAPTER ONE

Johnny woke in the crook of a tree under a diamond-studded sky. The hammock around him was worn nylon, and the great oak a hundred feet tall. Even at sixty feet, its trunk was thicker than Johnny, its branches bent but strong. Johnny knew every one of those branches by feel: the worn spots from his feet and hands, the way they leaned out from the trunk and split like fingers. He could climb the tree in total blackness, find his way past the hammock to smaller branches that bent beneath his weight. From there he could see the moon and the forest, the swamp that rolled off to the south. This was his place—six thousand acres—and he knew every stream and hill, every dark pool and secret glade.

He didn't always sleep in the tree. There was a cabin, but it felt heavy at times. He'd built it himself, so it wasn't the shape or size of it that pushed him, like a wind, to the ancient tree on its splintered hill. It wasn't the dreams or memories or any dark thing others might suspect. Johnny came for the views, and for the way they connected him to the land he owned. The tree grew from a knob of stone and soil that rose from the swamp to join a span of similar hills that cut a line between the wetlands and the thin-soiled higher ground that notched into the far, north corner of Raven County. From the hammock's crook he could see beyond the swamp and across the river. Climb another thirty feet, and he could see a glint of light that was the tallest building in town. That was eighteen miles in a straight line, thirty-seven if you had to drive. Roads this far north were twisted and crumbled, and that was fine with Johnny. He didn't care for people on his land, and had fired once on hunters too antagonistic to leave when asked politely. He didn't plan to hit them—they'd be dead if he had—but black bear had a special place in Johnny's heart, and two mothers had been killed with cubs still in the den. Because of that, he marked the borders and tracked hunters, in particular, with sleepless determination. Police, of course, didn't see it his way, and neither did the courts. After the shooting, there'd been a few months in jail and a firestorm of media. That was because reporters never forgot, and to most he was still the same dark-eyed child they'd made famous ten years earlier.

But Johnny didn't care if people thought him dangerous or strange. It hurt to see the worry on his parents' faces, of course. They wanted him in the city and between four walls, but deep down they understood how life had lifted him from the dark pages of his youth and brought him to this special place. And it *was* special. He could taste it on the breeze, see it in a sky so heavy with stars, it made his eyes water to look up and marvel at the relentless depth of it. Beneath all that pure, white light was a purple forest that moved with a rhythm as familiar, now, as the beat of Johnny's heart.

This place.

His life.

Leaving the hammock, he let his hands and feet find their way to the smallest branches that would still take his weight. The trunk was thin so high, the horizon a purple line darker than the rest. He studied the canopy, then moved up the tree until the trunk was small enough to cup with both hands, and then with only one. It was dangerous to climb so high, but Johnny had a reason.

He was looking for fire.

There'd been fires in the wood before: campfires and lightning strikes; a burn, once, from a hunter's dropped cigarette. Fires like this were different because Johnny, the next day, couldn't find a trace of them, not a charred twig or a burnt blade.

And he'd looked hard.

The first time it happened was just like this: a cloudless sky and a whisker of smoke. He'd gone higher for a better look and seen a glimmer halfway up a distant hill that was two down in the line of peaks that ran north and west. Three sides of that hill sloped gently beneath a layer of pine and scrub; the side facing Johnny was a slab of weathered stone. Near its base, boulders littered an area the size of a city block, and from that ruin the rest of it rose: sheer walls and slopes of scree, then more piled stone and knuckles of trees before the final wall of broken granite pushed free. That's where the fires were, somewhere on that weather-beaten face.

In three years he'd seen the fire eleven different times. This was the twelfth, and Johnny took his time watching it. Paths ran between the boulders and up the shattered face, but the paths crossed and doubled back and petered out. It was easy to get turned around, so he gauged angles and approaches. He pictured the route he would take, and when he left the tree, he did it quick and sure, dropping the last eight feet and rising at the run. He was barefoot in cutoff jeans and no shirt, but his soles were hard as leather and his eyes sharp from years in dark woods. And this night wasn't close to dark. Stars speckled the sky, and from beyond the river a half-moon rose. Even then, most would find it hard to move at such speed, but when Johnny ran, it was for real.

And he was running hard.

A footpath took him to the river, and when the water spread, he followed a ridge that carried him to the second hill and up it in a hard, fast climb. At the top he paused, looking for smoke. The wind was right, and for a moment he thought he was too late, that the fire was dead and whoever built it, gone. It had happened before—a sudden void of scent—and when it did happen, he wanted to throw caution to the wind and run blind, if that's what it took. The fire was a riddle, its builder a ghost. But life in the forest taught lessons beyond readiness and speed. Patience had its place, as did stealth and simple faith, and Johnny trusted his senses.

The fire builder was no ghost.

The smoke came again in the final valley, a downdraft that tasted of wood ash and charred resin. Creeping to the edge of the trees, Johnny studied the open ground and boulders tumbled like flung houses against the root of the hill. Paths ran between them, and in places they touched to form cathedral vaults. Beyond the boulders, the trails were narrow and twisted, and Johnny let his eyes move up and down the dark lines they cut through trees and scree and along the foot of the lower face. Other trails showed higher up, but they were faint in the moonlight, and not so much paths as ledges. Johnny looked for fire on the face, but couldn't find it.

Halfway up, he thought, *nearer the east side than the west.*

Problem was, the fire seemed to move. Last month it was higher up and farther west; the one before that, dead center above a rockslide shaped like an inverted V.

Crossing a final stretch of broken ground, Johnny took the main draw through the boulders. Side trails split off three times before stone met above his head, and the path narrowed. When it got tight, Johnny angled his shoulders and trailed fingers over the walls, feeling a vellum of fur and fine hairs left over the years by bear, coyote, and deer. Once around a final bend, the stone rose up to form a secret place that might have been there, unchanged, since the dawn of man. Johnny peered up a narrow chimney and saw a slash of pale stars. After that, he followed the right-hand trail, twisting up the slope as boulders dropped away. He was on a ridgeline beneath a final belt of woods. Still no sign of fire.

"All right, then."

He worked through the trees to a slope of scree at the base of the cliff. Rock shifted as he climbed, and twice he fell. After ten minutes he peered down, dizzy from a sense of sudden *wrongness.* There was too much space beneath him, too much purple stone and empty air. Looking again, he saw a notch in the tree line that should be beneath him, but had somehow shifted left. It felt as if he'd gone blank and climbed a hundred yards without knowing it. Leaning out, he tried to determine exactly where he was. Higher than he should be, and farther right.

No problem, he thought.

But that was not true. The slope was too steep, the scree as slippery as scales piled one atop the other. A hundred feet up was a stand of scrub oaks and pine. Beyond that, a footpath followed the base of the lower cliff and led to a series of ledges that twisted upward to the final cliff beyond. Johnny was too high and too far right, pinned on a section of slope he avoided exactly because it was so dangerous. He told himself it was a simple mistake, that he'd rushed the climb, that things looked different in the false light of 4 A.M. He said it twice, but didn't believe it. He'd been up the face seven times with no problem.

Now this.

Moving with care, Johnny tried to work his way off the pitch. He looked for the largest stones, the most stable holds. Twelve feet across, his foot slipped, and twenty feet of stone disappeared beneath him. Johnny felt it go, then was gone, too, the sound like a freight train as he saw the fall in his mind: hundreds of feet, near vertical, then trees and boulders, an avalanche of scree heavy enough to bury him alive.

But Johnny didn't die.

Fifty feet down, he slammed to a stop, bruised and bloodied and half buried. It took time to think through the hurt and figure out if the chance yet remained to die. The hill above was swept clean. Around him, loose stone mounded against a two-foot lip of solid rock, beneath which was a drop long and steep enough to kill most any man alive. Johnny looked left and right, and that's how close it was—a foot or so, or maybe inches.

Dawn was a blush in the trees by the time Johnny limped to the small, square cabin and let himself inside. His bed took up space near the stone fireplace, and he fell into it, hurting. When he woke, it was three hours later. After dropping his clothes in a corner, he went to the creek to wash off dust and blood. He bandaged the worst of the cuts, then pulled on jeans, boots, and a shirt. At the door, he checked his face in a four-inch mirror. The eyes that stared back were as still as glass, and so unflinching that few people looked into them for very long. At twenty-three, Johnny didn't smile without reason or waste time on people he found insincere. How often could he hear the same questions?

How are you, son?

Are you holding up okay?

For ten years he'd endured one version or another of the same pointless phrase, knowing, as he did, that people sought the darker currents that ran beneath.

What did you see in those terrible places?

How messed up are you, really?

Those were the people who risked the darkness of Johnny's eyes, those who asked the questions and looked deep, hoping for a glimpse of the boy he'd been, the glimmer of wildness and war paint and fire.

Thirty minutes later, Johnny left the cabin, pushing south into the swamp, and from there across tendons of dry ground until he reached the ruins of a settlement once owned by freed slaves and their descendants. Most of the structures were rotted and fallen, but a few buildings still stood. When people asked about Hush Arbor, this was the place they meant: the cemetery, the old houses, the hanging tree. Few understood how large it really was.

Unlocking one of the sheds, Johnny backed out a truck that was white and dented and a half century old. From there, it was two miles to a metal gate. Once through it, he merged onto a state road and turned up the radio, scrolling past gospel and talk radio and local sports. Near the bottom of the dial he found the classical station out of Davidson College, and listened to that as hills spread out and the city rose. Johnny knew every street corner and neighborhood, every monument and cobbled drive and twist of asphalt. In three hundred years, Raven County had seen its share of loss and conflict. Sons had gone to war, and died. There'd been riots, depression; parts of the city had burned.

Johnny drove past the courthouse and stopped at a light, watching how people held hands and laughed and admired their reflections in the burnished glass. A block later he angled to the curb where the old hardware store touched the sidewalk and women gathered to look at potted plants and tomatoes and wooden trays stacked with beans and corn and peaches. Nobody noticed Johnny until he stepped from the truck; and when it started, it started small. A young woman blinked, and another one noticed. By the time Johnny edged past, four of them were staring. Maybe it was the way he looked, or his history with the town. Whatever the case, Johnny kept to himself as he pushed through the door and made eye contact with the old man behind the glass-topped counter at the rear of the store.

"Johnny Merrimon. Good morning to you."

"Daniel. Morning."

"Sorry about the welcoming committee." Daniel dipped his head at the front window. "But two of them are pretty enough, and about your age. Maybe you shouldn't rush past so quick and determined."

Johnny nodded, but didn't respond. It wasn't that he didn't like a pretty girl—he did—but Johnny would never leave Hush Arbor, and few women were interested in life without power or phone or running water. Daniel didn't seem to know or care. He waved at the ladies beyond the glass, then put his eighty-watt smile back on Johnny. "So, young Mr. Merrimon. What can I do for you this fine day?"

"Just the ammunition."

"Got a new four-wheeler out back. I can offer a good deal."

"All I need are the cartridges."

"Fair enough. I like a man who knows his own mind." The old man unlocked the counter and removed a twenty-count box of .270 Winchester. "Twelve gauge, too?"

"Same as always."

"Bird shot, then. Number seven."

Daniel put two boxes on the glass, and a tuft of white hair rose at the crown of his head. "What else?"

"That'll do it."

Johnny paid the exact amount from long habit, and had both boxes in his hand before Daniel spoke again. "Your mother asks about you, you know." Johnny stopped, half turned. "She knows you come here, and that it's a monthly thing. Now, I know it's not my business—"

"It's not."

Daniel held up both hands, his head moving side to side. "I know that, son, and I'm not the kind to interfere—I hope you can accept that about me—but she comes here asking about you, and damn it . . ." The old man broke off, struggling. "You should really call your mother."

"Did she ask you to tell me that?"

"No, she didn't. But I've known you since you were six, and you've never been the selfish kind of boy."

Johnny put the boxes down. He didn't mean to sound angry, but did. "We have a good thing here, Daniel. Don't you think?"

"Yes, but—"

"Most of what I spend in town I spend in your store. It's not much, I know, just cartridges and salt, fishing gear and tools. I come here because you're local and you're nice, and because I enjoy it. I really do. We smile and talk rifles. You ask what I do up in all that wilderness, and I give you the best answers I can. A joke between us is not a rare thing, either."

"Johnny, listen—"

"I don't come here for advice about girls or my mother." It was the hardest voice, the darkest eyes. It wasn't fair to unload on Daniel, but Johnny lacked the will to walk it back. "Look, I'll see you next month, okay?"

"Sure, Johnny." The old man nodded, but kept his eyes down and his mouth bent. "Next month."

Johnny pushed his way from the store, not looking at the women still gathered on the sidewalk. He settled into the truck, closed his eyes, and wrapped his fingers around the wheel.

Shit.

He was forgetting; he could feel it. Forgetting how to relate, to be a part of . . . this.

Johnny opened his eyes and looked at the old man and his store, at the stretch of sidewalk and traffic, the pretty girls who still looked his way and giggled and whispered and stared. One of them was Daniel's granddaughter, who was twenty-two and pretty as a picture. The old man had tried to set them up once, six months ago.

Johnny had forgotten that, too.

So Johnny made a choice, and it wasn't an easy one. In spite of what the shopkeeper said, selfishness had nothing to do with Johnny's long absences from his mother's side. When she looked at her son's face, she saw the daughter, killed young, and the husband who'd died trying to save her. Johnny knew that truth because he faced it every time he chose to confront a mirror.

This is how my father stood.

This is how my sister would appear.

That all made sense, but Johnny was forgetting, too—not just how to live a normal life, but also the sound of Alyssa's voice, the secret looks only a twin could understand. The past walked beside him as a shadow might, and every day that shadow stretched and thinned, the memories of childhood and family and how good it all had been. Johnny feared that when enough days had passed, the shadow would fade and pale until it was simply gone. Johnny dreaded that day more than anything else, so in the end, he did what the old man said.

He went to see his mother.

Katherine Hunt lived with her second husband in a small house behind a picket fence. Two blocks from the library and the original courthouse, it filled a shaded lot on the corner of Jackson Street and Bank. It had a good porch, good neighbors. Pulling to the curb, Johnny studied the bright windows, the gleaming paint.

"Are you staking out the place?"

Johnny's stepfather came around a boxbush the size of a small car. He wore blue jeans and leather gloves, was dragging a tarp full of lawn clippings.

"Aren't you supposed to be out catching bad guys?"

"No bad guys today." Clyde Hunt dropped the tarp and opened a gate in the fence. He was in his fifties and fit, and wore his hair short. Clyde leaned on the passenger door, then dropped an eyelid and pushed a hand through the open window. "How are you, son? It's been too long." The big detective leaned closer, squinting. "Goddamn, Johnny. What happened to you?"

"It was nothing. Just. You know . . ."

Johnny retrieved the hand, but couldn't stop his stepfather from looking more closely with those cop eyes of his. He saw the abrasions and the scratches, the way Johnny sat with one shoulder rolled inward.

"Step out of the truck, Johnny."

"I just came to see Mom—"

"Your mother's not here. Come on, now, son. Step out of the vehicle."

Johnny thought about it, then switched off the engine and stepped from the truck. Clyde peeled off the leather gloves and watched him onto the sidewalk.

"You look a little busted up. What happened?"

"Nothin'."

"Doesn't look like nothing. Is it the ribs?"

"Why would you ask that?"

"Don't bullshit me, son. I saw the way you were sitting, the way you walk. You don't think I've had cracked ribs before? Come on, now. Let me see." Johnny looked the length of the street, then lifted the shirt on one side. Clyde whistled low. "Goddamn, son. That's a hell of a lot of damage. Was it a fight?"

"A fall."

Clyde studied Johnny's face, and the doubt was hard to hide. There'd been fights before: trespassers, the two hunters, the four months in jail. Johnny was stubborn, and rarely backed down. It caused problems. "Come inside, I'll patch you up."

Johnny lowered his shirt. "That's not necessary."

"It wasn't a suggestion."

Accustomed to obeyed orders, the big cop turned without looking back. Johnny watched him for three steps, then trailed him up the gravel walk and onto the shaded porch. Inside, they followed a broad hall to the master bath.

"Take off the shirt. Sit." Clyde pointed at a stool in front of a sink and mirror. Johnny shrugged off the shirt and kept his eyes down as his stepfather rustled in a cabinet for hydrogen peroxide, ointment, and adhesive bandages. When he straightened, he stood for long seconds, watching Johnny stare at the floor, the wall, his hands. "Your mother does the same thing sometimes. Not as much as she used to, but it still happens."

"What are you talking about?"

Clyde sat, and his voice was softer. "The way she gathers herself before facing the mirror. It's just in the mornings, really, and just for a second or two."

"I don't know what you mean."

"Don't you?"

Johnny faced the mirror and in his reflection saw the face of a dead twin. "Next week it will be ten years since we found her."

"Thursday, I know."

"Do you ever talk about it?"

"With your mother? Sometimes. Not like we used to."

Johnny looked away from the mirror. "Where is she?" he finally asked.

"Your mother's at the coast with some lady friends, and it's a good thing, too. She'd have a heart attack if she saw your back like this."

"It's bad?"

"You haven't looked?"

Johnny shook his head.

"Go on, then."

Johnny twisted on the stool, saw bruises and dried blood and ripped skin.

"You've bled through the shirt," Clyde told him. "I'll give you another one."

"Thank you."

"This next part's going to hurt." He palpated the ribs, the spine. "Just hold still." Johnny did, but it was hard. "All right. I don't think any ribs are broken. Cracked, maybe. Definitely bruised."

"Are we finished?"

"Not yet." The cleanup took another ten minutes. When it was done, Clyde pulled a shirt from the closet and tossed it to Johnny. "You could probably use a few stitches, but the butterfly bandages should do the job if you take it easy for a few days. No pulling, all right? Don't chop any wood or climb that damn tree." Johnny shrugged into the shirt. Clyde leaned against the wall. "Do you want to talk about it?"

"It was just a fall. A careless mistake."

"I've seen you make mistakes. None of them have ever been careless."

"This one was. Just stupid, really."

"What about life in general? You doing okay?"

"Yeah, I'm fine."

"How about money?"

"The money's fine, too."

"How is that possible, Johnny? You don't work. You don't have plans to work."

"Dad's life insurance—"

"Your father's life insurance, right. Let's talk about that. You got a hundred thousand from the insurance company when you were thirteen. By the time you turned eighteen, it grew to what, about one-twenty? How much have you spent on lawyers? All of it?"

"I'm fine, Clyde. Really."

"We're here for you, son. Let us help you."

"I said I don't need money."

"Only because you live on berries and roots and snakes . . ."

"It's not like that, and you know it."

"Okay, you have a garden. That's nice. What if you couldn't hunt or plant? What if you'd cracked your spine instead of a few ribs? What if that great swamp just swallowed you whole?"

"It didn't. It won't."

"You can't live like this forever."

"Says who?" Johnny stood. "Listen, I appreciate the bandages and all, but I have to go."

Johnny pushed into the hall, but Clyde caught him before he got to the front door. "Come on, Johnny. Wait, wait, wait." Johnny did, just a second. But it was enough for Clyde to turn him, wrap him gently. "We just love you, son. We miss you and we worry." He stepped back, but kept his hands on Johnny's shoulders. "There's no judgment here. Look at me, all right." Johnny did, and felt the anger ebb. "Anything you need: if you want to come home, if you need money."

"Listen, Clyde—"

"You want to go, I know. I can see that, too. It's always Hush Arbor, always the land. Just tell me one thing before you leave. Help me understand."

"What?"

"Why do you love it so much?"

He meant the silence and the swamp, the lonely hills and endless trees. On the surface it was a simple question, but Johnny's past had branded him in a way few could ignore: the things he'd believed and leaned upon, the way he'd searched so long for his sister. If Johnny spoke now, of magic, they'd think him confused or insane or trapped, somehow, in the delusions of a difficult past. Without living it, no one could grasp the truth of Hush Arbor.

Johnny wouldn't want them to if they could.

CHAPTER TWO

The lawyer's office occupied the top three floors of a nine-story building downtown. The building itself was the second tallest in Raven County, and from the top-floor lobby Johnny could see the courthouse and jail, the banks and people and redbrick sidewalks. Bright metal winked on the street, and Johnny felt heat through the glass as he stepped closer and looked into the distance where houses showed beneath a canopy of trees.

"Excuse me, sir? May I help you?"

The receptionist was as polished as the marble floor. Her smile seemed real enough, but it was clear she was unused to clients in faded jeans and scuffed boots. "I'm here to see Jack Cross."

"I'm sorry. Who?"

"Jack Cross. He's one of your attorneys."

"I don't think so."

"He started this week."

"Sir, I would know—"

"Fifth from the top, thirty-third from the bottom." Johnny dipped his head toward the directory on the far wall. "Thirty-seven lawyers. My friend is your newest."

The woman glanced left, and for a moment her head tilted. "I'm sorry. Have you been here before?"

"First time."

"How did you . . . ?" She pointed at the list of lawyers and lifted an eyebrow to finish the question.

"How did I see my friend's name?"

"And count the number of attorneys in this firm?"

"I have very good eyes."

"Apparently."

"He's on the seventh floor. May I go down?"

"Give me a minute to sort this out. Would you like anything while you wait?"

"I'm fine."

"Just a moment, then."

Johnny watched her walk away, noted the fitted skirt and expensive shoes. He noticed subtler things, too. Beneath the perfume, she smelled of coffee and toner and men's aftershave. A single nail was bitten to the quick. A few moments later she was back. "I'm sorry for the confusion," she said. "We do have a Jack Cross who joined the firm this week. I'm not sure how I missed his arrival, but I did. He's in our bankruptcy division. Seventh floor, as you said."

"May I go down?"

"He's in court with one of our partners. May I take a message?"

Johnny blinked, unsure why his best friend's presence in court was so unexpected. He was a lawyer, after all. It's why Johnny had come. "I'd like to leave a note."

"I'm happy to deliver it."

"May I leave it on his desk? He's an old friend, and it's personal."

"Of course." The receptionist pressed fingers against the skin beneath her neck, and left fine, pale ovals when she lifted them. "Seventh floor. Ask for Sandy. She handles clerical for the new associates."

Johnny took the stairs down, and found Sandy, who was everything the receptionist was not. Frenetic. Mussed. Charmless. "Mr. Cross is not here."

"Yes, you've said as much."

Johnny followed her from one hall to the next, stopping each time she pushed into a cubicle or office to dole out files and hard advice.

You signed in the wrong place!

This is for Judge Ford, not Judge Randolph. Pay attention!

After the fourth office, she rounded on Johnny, smoothing gray hair behind an ear. "I'm sorry. What's your name again?"

"Merrimon. Johnny."

A moment's confusion clouded her features. She'd heard the name, but couldn't place it. "Are you a friend? Family?"

"I'm a client."

"Mr. Cross doesn't have clients yet."

"Then, I'll be his first."

She remained unconvinced. Around her, keyboards rattled and clicked. Other assistants pushed other papers. No one looked up twice. "I'm more than able to deliver a message."

"I'd prefer to do it myself."

"Is there a problem of some sort?"

"Not at all. I'd like to see his office if I may, and I'd like the note to be front and center when he returns from court."

"And your name is Johnny Merrimon?"

The name still tickled something deep. Johnny saw it in the eyes, the pursed lips.

"Why does that sound familiar?"

"I have no idea."

She worked the angles, concerned that, despite appearances, the scruffy young man taking up her time might just be important, somehow. It took three seconds. When the decision broke, it went Johnny's way. "I can't leave you alone in an attorney's office."

The office was better than Johnny expected. Double windows looked down on the courthouse and the park beside it. Framed diplomas hung on the wall. The furniture was expensive and new.

"This is it. There's paper on the desk."

Johnny took his time because no one had expected much from the small, lost boy with the bad left arm. Jack had seen a girl die, and lied about the whys of it. He'd served time in juvenile incarceration, and spent more time than most in the shadow of Johnny Merrimon. But Jack didn't end up where people thought he would. He wasn't in prison or working at a car wash, wasn't a drunk or strung out or ruined in some other way. Johnny thought that deserved a moment's appreciation, so he ran a finger along rowed books, then lifted a photograph from the desk. It was the only one in the office: two boys at the river—Johnny and Jack, like brothers.

"Anytime now would be fine."

The gray-haired woman was frustrated and tense, but Johnny kept his eyes on the picture of the boys. They were shirtless and grinning, both of them burned as brown as dirt. Behind them the river looked as motionless as stone, and beyond that was only shadow. It seemed as if the sun shone on the boys alone, and in some ways it had. There were no secrets between friends that age, and the differences were small: X-Men or Avengers, stickball or bat. Johnny could blink and taste his first beer, drunk warm on a flat rock in the center of the same river. Jack had stolen it from his father, and wanted to share it with Johnny. *Boys to men,* he'd said. *First beer . . .*

"Sir, I really must insist."

Johnny gave it another second, then put the photo down. Squaring a legal pad in the center of the desk, he wrote his note in broad strokes. When he straightened, the woman read it without hesitation or shame.

I'm proud of you, Jack. You did it.

Now do the right thing or I break that pussy arm for real.

She read it twice, and a flush built in her neck. "Mr. Cross cannot help his deformity."

"I'm aware of that."

"Is this some kind of joke?"

Johnny offered the first real smile since he'd left the lobby upstairs. "Just make sure he sees it."

An hour later the city was a glint in the rearview mirror. A bag rode the seat beside Johnny, and in it were the other things he needed from town: shampoo and cigars, hard cheese and brown liquor. Johnny pictured what was coming, and the smile stayed with him as he rolled through the trees and beside black water. In the clearing, he drove past a burnt shack and the old kitchen, standing alone. After parking in the same shed, Johnny left the truck and turned for the web of trails that would carry him through the swamp and into the hills on the other side. The route took him beside the cemetery and past forty-five markers, most of them ancient. Beneath an oak tree that was massive and gnarled, the oldest of the stones were small and unmarked. Johnny dreamed of them more often than he liked.

Hanged slaves under a hanging tree . . .

That was county history, and dark.

It was family history, too.

The walk to the cabin took thirty minutes, but for anyone else would be longer. A wrong step, and the mud would suck off your shoes. Another moment's inattention, and you might not get out alive. Water moccasin. Copperhead. It was part of the reason he'd chosen to build the cabin where he had. No road led in from the north, east, or west. Beyond his property line was another forty thousand undeveloped acres, most of it state forest or game lands. It was possible to hike in—there were trails—but the old slave settlement was the closest you could get by car. To go from there to high ground meant crossing the swamp, and few had the stomach for it. It wasn't just the snakes and mud. Trails turned around and faded and died. It was easy to get lost.

Not that it was all mud and black water. Land rose up in places to support hardwoods, never timbered. Five acres or thirty, the islands broke from the swamp like the back of some great creature, half-submerged. Between them, the trail grew spongy and slick and, in some places, was no more than a succession of hummocks. The cabin itself rode a finger of land jutting in from the hills to the north. A fifty-foot rock face backstopped the glade, the face of it like a bronze shield as sunlight stained the cabin yellow. It was a beautiful place, and Johnny kept its secret close. His parents had been twice, but didn't care for the wild lands in the north of the county. Only one other person had ever seen the cabin. He'd helped Johnny pick the spot, helped him build it.

Johnny glanced at the sun, then checked his watch.

He laughed aloud, thinking of Jack in the middle of all that swamp.

"Damn it! God . . . bless. Fuck."

Jack went down in the mud for the third time. It's not that he didn't know the trail—he did—it's just that he wasn't Tarzan or Doc Savage or any other purely fictional character who chose to live in the ass end of a jungle.

"Johnny . . ."

His feet went out again.

"Damn it . . ."

Breathing heavily, Jack dragged himself up and moved with care. He was still in his suit, the pants tucked into tall boots. The tie was off, but the jacket carried the same mud stains as the seat of his pants. He cursed again, wondering why mosquitoes loved him so much, yet found Johnny Merrimon somehow distasteful.

"You like this, don't you?" He was muttering now, switchgrass sawing at his hands as he pulled himself through the mud. "Probably watching me right now. Sitting in some tree . . ."

A foot broke loose with a sucking noise, and Jack worked along the trail, staying where the grass was tall and tufted. He'd known Johnny since they were seven, and even now, after so many years, struggled with the idea that his best friend owned all this.

Don't know why he'd want to . . .

Just mud and bugs and . . .

Jack crested the last hump of dry ground before water stretched away and the sun sank low enough to paint it all with perfect color: the orange water and distant hills, the trees and green earth and sun-kissed granite. In that light he saw Hush Arbor as his friend did, as he'd seen it himself when they first crossed the swamp. They'd been fourteen at the time, a couple of kids with no business so deep in the wild. But they'd come nonetheless; they'd stood in the same place and seen the same view.

"Jesus Christ." Jack palmed sweat from his eyes, still breathing hard. "How could I ever forget?"

By six forty, Johnny had everything ready. A camp table and chairs stood on hard-packed dirt at the edge of the glade. Bourbon was on the table. Enamel plates held cheese and smoked venison; a nine-pound catfish was ready for the spit. The cigars were more than he could afford, but they didn't screw around with cigars, he and Jack. That was a promise they'd made a long time ago.

Cheap booze, cheap cigars . . .

They'd go hungry first.

It was a silly promise, a boy's boast; but they'd lived by it since high school, and Johnny would not be the one to break the streak.

Stretching out his legs, Johnny laced his fingers behind his head and closed his eyes, smiling. The air was warm; a light breeze moved.

In the swamp, Jack went down again.

The trail firmed at last, and Jack slowed as open water fell away and sycamores and cypress leaned out, close enough to touch. He wanted this part to go right, so he moved quietly through the twig rush and scrub.

Just this once . . .

He ghosted onto dry land, the cabin a wink through the trees. Johnny sat at a table beyond the ferns, barefoot in faded jeans with both eyes closed and his face tilted to the sun. His hair was longer than the last time, and for an instant Jack felt the old jealousy. Johnny was angular and strong, and had the kind of face that even men looked at twice. He wasn't movie-star handsome, but *striking* was too small a word. With the tan and dark eyes, he looked like a hero from old stories, the kind who fought with swords and got the girls.

Jack's gaze fell briefly to his own misshapen arm. Hanging from his left shoulder, it looked like the castoff from a ten-year-old boy. The suit sleeve swallowed it; even the fingers were too small. It's how people had known him, growing up. *Oh yeah, the kid with the screwed-up arm.* Only Johnny understood that talking about it made it a nonissue, that joking was even better.

And Johnny was close now, legs stretched out, eyes still closed. Jack stopped under the last tree and bounced a pebble on his palm. The throw had to be just right—not in the face and no blood, but hard enough to sting like a mother. That's how it had been since they were kids.

Who was quietest?

Who had the better arm?

He smoothed a thumb across the stone, and Johnny spoke as the good arm went back.

"Don't do it."

"Goddamn it, Johnny." Jack lowered his arm, not surprised but genuinely bothered. "How do you do that? You do it every time. It's not right."

Johnny opened a single eye. "You make a lot of noise."

"Does raising my arm make a lot of noise?"

Johnny got to his feet and lifted the bottle of bourbon. "Don't worry about it. Come on. Have a drink. You look like you could use it."

Jack stepped from the shadows, still troubled by the unnatural way Johnny seemed to always know. The sound of footsteps, sure. Cracked twigs and sucking mud. Jack could see that. How did Johnny know the very second he was about to throw?

Every time, Jack thought, but could be more specific than that.

Seventeen times in the last three years.

Before that, Jack could catch him unaware at least half the time; and that had been the pattern since childhood. Sometimes Johnny saw it coming. Sometimes he didn't.

So what was different now?

Stepping into the clearing, Jack took in the table and the food and his friend's sharp grin. The eyes were intense but bright, his hair wavy and unkempt and long enough to brush the collar of his shirt.

"Jack Cross, Attorney-at-Law." Johnny moved into the ferns, gave Jack a hard squeeze. "Goddamn, I'm proud of you."

Jack returned the pressure, then stepped back, embarrassed. Johnny rarely showed affection, and its expression touched Jack's heart in complicated ways. "Thanks, Johnny. It's been a long road."

That was a bitter truth, and both of them knew it. Jack had clawed from a ruined childhood in the space of six months, and Johnny was one of the few who understood the engine that drove such rapid, irreversible change. Guilt. Regret. Juvenile incarceration.

"Welcome," he said. "Sit, sit."

Johnny gestured at the table, and Jack took a chair as Johnny poured bourbon and passed a glass.

"Bright lights and better days. I'm glad you came."

Jack touched Johnny's glass with his own. "Did I have a choice?"

"Always," Johnny said; but there really was no choice. Twice a month they met for dinner, once at Jack's and then here. That was the pattern, and neither of them broke it. "Why the suit?" Johnny asked.

"Huh?"

Johnny sat across the table. He swirled bourbon in the glass and pointed with a finger. "Why didn't you change clothes?"

"Court ran late. I didn't have time to go home, and wasn't about to be caught in that swamp after sunset. I'd get so lost, not even you could find me."

"Ah, you'd manage."

Jack sipped, and looked uncomfortable. Lies always made him uncomfortable.

"So." Johnny leaned back in the chair. "Court."

The comment sounded innocent, but Jack wasn't fooled. "Okay, fine. Your stepfather called and asked me to stop by the house before coming here. He had a lot to say; it took some time."

"Let me guess. He's worried about me."

"He says you showed up black and blue and cut halfway to the bone, that you could have died alone in this place." Jack held up a thumb and forefinger. "He said that far as he could tell, it was about this close, that you were busted up and bleeding and that you'd damn near broken your back."

"Do I look that bad?"

Johnny swirled bourbon in the glass, and Jack frowned because Johnny appeared to be fine. The smile was easy and amused, one eyebrow slightly raised. "Clyde wants me to convince you to move back home, or to town, at least. He says this has gone on long enough. He says your mother—"

"Don't bring my mother into this."

Jack refused to back down. "He says your mother has nightmares of losing another child. That it's affecting her happiness."

"She only *thinks* she wants me close. You've seen how it is when she looks at me."

"Maybe."

"You know it's true."

"It's time to come home, Johnny."

"You think you can convince me?"

"I think you need my help, and that because of that you should listen to me more than you might normally do."

Something moved in Johnny's eyes, and it was stark and dangerous and quick. "Are you blackmailing me?"

"Do you need my help or not?"

Johnny put down the glass, and the hard eyes softened. "Maybe."

"Is that why you showed up at my office, unannounced? Why you frightened and offended my assistant? Because *maybe* you need my help?"

Johnny rolled his shoulders. "I was just messing around."

"She wanted to call the police."

"Come on . . ."

"You threatened to break my arm, Johnny. She said, and I quote: 'He's the single most intense man I've ever met.' She's met a lot of men, Johnny. Judges. CEOs. Whatever you said or did, you worried her."

"That's ridiculous. You're my best friend."

"I know that. She doesn't."

"What do you want from me, Jack? What do you want me to say?"

"I want you to be honest."

"Aren't I always?"

"Not about this place. Not all of it."

Johnny stared off at darkened trees and distant water. "Will you help me or not?"

Jack considered the contradiction so evident in his friend. Johnny was the most independent soul Jack had ever known, but his need showed; it showed in the stiff shoulders and unmoving gaze, in the unnatural stillness. "How broke are you?"

Johnny shrugged again, swallowed bourbon and dragged up a shadow of a smile. "Too broke to hire another lawyer."

"Is any of it left?"

He meant the insurance money, so Johnny dug into his pocket and tossed a sheaf of bills on the table. Jack picked it up, put it back down.

"That's three hundred dollars."

"Three hundred and seven."

"What about the rest of it?"

"Lawyers."

"All of it."

"Yep."

"Jesus, Johnny, you do have other options."

"Don't tell me to sell land."

"You own six thousand acres."

"I won't sell it, Jack. Not an acre. Not half an acre."

"I hear what you're saying, but the math is simple. You can do nothing and risk losing all of this, or you can sell a thousand acres to save the other five. Even at fire sale prices, you'd have enough money to hire another lawyer. Hell, hire three. You'd have money in the bank and still be the fourth-largest landowner in the state of North Carolina."

"All that law school, and that's your best advice? To sell?"

"Yes."

"Why?" Johnny put down his glass, the black eyes flashing. "To be drained and timbered? So some rich banker can bring his friends out to four-wheel and trophy-hunt and disrespect everything I love about this place?"

The despair and anger were hard to watch. Johnny inherited the land on his eighteenth birthday, but other people had claims, too, and those claims had merit. Johnny won on the merits at trial, but the risks on appeal were legitimate. To keep the land, he needed a heavy hitter from one of the big firms. That meant five hundred an hour, maybe even six.

"This was my family's land, Jack, the last of it that hasn't been chopped up and sold off and ruined. I won't let it go without a fight."

"Okay, let's forget the appeal for a moment. How will you live without money? What if you get hurt and can't hunt? What about gasoline? Property taxes? Medical care?"

"All I need is a lawyer."

"I'm five days into the job, for God's sake! You need appellate work at the highest level."

"You're capable enough."

"How can you say that?"

"Because you finished college in three years and law school in two. Plus you're my only friend."

"That's not fair."

"It's what I have."

"Goddamn it." Jack walked to the edge of the ferns and showed Johnny his back. "Can we just drink?" he said. "Can we drink bourbon and eat catfish and worry, tomorrow, about the rest of it?"

"You owe me, Jack." The words came as carefully as metal drawn from an unhealed wound. "I've never let the memories come between us, not in ten years. I've kept you out of that, kept it separate."

"I know you have."

"No one else can help me."

Jack nodded, five good digits on the glass, the small ones curled white. "The stakes are big, Johnny. Your land, your life." He gestured at all of it. The forest. The water. "I'm not sure I want that on my head."

"Are you scared?" Johnny asked.

"Are you kidding? I'm terrified."

Terrified was a big word between young men, and in the space behind it, Johnny showed a twist of a smile and sudden, startling sympathy. "Then don't worry about it," he said. "Tomorrow's problem."

"Are you sure?"

"Of course I am. Sit. Drink."

Jack did as he was told, and Johnny topped off the glass.

Jack drank that down, too.

It was dead quiet when Jack woke alone in the cabin. He bolted up, heart pounding.

What had woken him?

He didn't know, but felt horribly afraid, a scraping in his mind like nails on glass.

Was it a dream?

His feet touched the bare floor, and when he stood, the dizziness pressed him sideways. He leaned on the wall, but it was not enough to steady him. He tugged his shirt, bent at the waist. When he straightened, he felt his way to a chair by the window and fell into it, one hand on his chest, sweat slick on his face and neck. Pale light spilled onto the table, but all else was shadowed and gray: the corners and low places, the dead space beneath his chair. Looking through the glass, he saw mist in the trees, the weak light of a false dawn.

"Johnny?"

Opening the door, he stepped into a world so still, it looked painted. No insects called; the frogs were silent. A dozen steps carried him to a trail through the ferns, and then to a place beneath the trees. It was dimmer there, and cooler. Beyond him was the swamp, the smell of black mud and rot. Going there made no sense, but dreams never did, and this felt like a dream: the silver haze, the sense of choking. He wanted to wake in his own bed, but the mist was thinning and someone stood at the edge of the swamp.

Johnny?

He didn't know if the word escaped his lips or not. Sound died in the mist, and Johnny was unmoving. He stood in black water, shirtless in jeans that were wet from the knees down. The muscles of his shoulders rolled and twitched, and Jack hugged himself as he stopped at the water's edge to watch his friend stare into a silence so complete, it seemed as if the swamp itself were holding its breath.

"What are you doing, man?" No response or movement. "Johnny?"

"Do you see it?"

Jack followed his friend's gaze; saw water and darkness and, far out, an island. "What do you mean?"

Johnny pointed into the swamp. "Don't you see?"

"There's nothing there. Come on, man."

But Johnny didn't answer, and the arm stayed up. Looking again, Jack saw switchgrass and trees and, somewhere behind all that, a swell of light that was a rising moon. Jack stepped into the water to look at Johnny's eyes, which were glazed and barely open. "Johnny, man. Hey. You okay?"

Jack touched his shoulder, and Johnny blinked once. "Jack," he said. "What's happening?"

"I think you're sleepwalking."

"It's cold."

Johnny wasn't wrong about that. His lips were blue, his skin like ice. Even Jack felt it: the chill, dense air with no business in the damp and heat of an August swamp. "Do you remember how you got here?"

Johnny said nothing.

"You were talking to me. Do you remember that?"

Johnny blinked again, and it was half speed. He dragged fingers across his eyes as if to strip off cobwebs.

"All right." Jack took Johnny's arm. "You're dreaming, man, that's all. Let's get you back to the cabin."

Johnny resisted at first, then drew a foot from the mud and turned for the shore. He allowed himself to be led, and for that instant Jack believed his own lie, that chance alone had brought them both to the edge of the swamp. But with every step, it felt more like a falsehood. The world was hushed and heavy, the air as cold as something dead. That wasn't an exaggeration. The temperature was falling by the second, Jack's breath a sudden plume. "The cabin," he said, and it was like a prayer. Because a deeper fear was descending with the cold—he felt it in his skin and along his spine, a prickling as if some dreadful thing was close. "Come on, Johnny." Jack pulled hard, but his friend was rooted like a stump in the mud, pointing again as, beyond him, a hollow place appeared in the mist. It looked like no specific thing, but hung shapeless and still against the rising moon. Looking at it, Jack couldn't describe what he felt, but it was as if all the cold and fear radiated out from that dull splotch of empty air.

"Do you see it?" Johnny said.

But Jack was pulling harder. He wanted light and heat, to be anywhere but this damn swamp. "Damn it, Johnny! Come on!" He added his small arm to the strong, broke one foot free and then the other. They moved slowly at first, then faster, dark water splashing, feet dragging in the mud. Jack was first from the water, and Johnny followed. He stumbled into the ferns, and when his feet touched ground, the cold and terror broke.

Crickets called from the trees.

Frogs, in the reeds, were singing.

Jack got Johnny to the cabin, but his friend moved as if held up by strings; dropped in the bed as if those strings were suddenly cut. Jack left him and checked the windows, the door. A breeze moved the trees outside. The mist was lifting.

What just happened?

Already, the memory was fading, fear lifting like the mist. Jack looked at the mud between his toes. That was real. So was the blood on his hands and feet, the scratches from where he'd fallen and run and fallen again. There was no lock on the door, so he wedged it tight and sat against it with his back braced. When dawn broke he checked Johnny and the windows. Ten minutes later he opened the door and stepped outside. His watch said 6:25. The light was watery, the morning hot and getting hotter.

Why did that feel strange?

The memories were there, but fragmented. He recalled air like ice, the fog of his breath.

Jack peered through the trees and followed the trail to the swamp. The soil was damp under his feet. He touched a tree, and that, too, felt like the memory of a dream.

At the water's edge, he tried to hold the images that troubled him, but the more he squeezed, the more elusive they seemed. He'd stood on this very ground. So had Johnny.

Why had they been so afraid?

The more he worked the question, the more it disturbed him. *Fear* was not even the right word. He'd been *terrified*.

Looking at the swamp now, it was hard to believe. Everything appeared soft in the morning light, the islands distant, the waters dappled.

Had they really come to this place?

Jack stood for a long time, but like every dream he'd ever had, the images faded until only glimmers remained.

Was it a nightmare or was it real?

When Jack returned to the cabin, he found Johnny feeding twigs into the coals of last night's fire. "Good morning, Counselor. Coffee in five."

Jack hesitated, watching his friend for a sign that he remembered anything about last night. His attention fixed on the fire, Johnny looked as he had on a hundred other mornings, half asleep and relaxed. He built the fire up, put an old coffeepot on the grate. "There's bread," he said. "I'll make bacon in a bit."

"You feel all right, Johnny?"

"You kidding? I feel great."

He poked at the coals, rubbed his cheek and left a smudge of soot. He'd not yet looked up, so Jack took a chair across the fire. "How'd you sleep?"

"Deep and sound."

"Johnny, look at me." Johnny did. "You went to sleep last night in the tree. You woke in the cabin."

Johnny's eyes glazed for a moment; then he shrugged. "Sleepwalking, I guess. It happens."

"That doesn't scare you?"

"I'm here," he said. "I'm fine."

"You remember nothing about last night?"

"We stayed up late. We drank too much."

"What else?"

"We talked about your dad in prison, your mom in that shit-box trailer. You told me how it feels to practice law. You fell down once, taking a leak."

"That wasn't funny."

"Yeah, it was."

Johnny laughed again, but Jack was still serious. "That's it? That's all?"

"Of course that's not all." Johnny stopped poking at the fire. "We finished the manchego before the bourbon. You liked the catfish, but thought you'd swallowed a bone. We smoked cigars, told jokes, solved the riddles of the universe. It was dinner, Jack, like every other dinner we've ever had out here."

"What about after?"

"There was no after. I went to bed. I woke up. Here we are."

Jack stopped pushing. Two minutes later he made up his mind. "Listen, I'm going to get out of here."

"What? Seriously?"

Jack stood and smoothed palms across his thighs. "I'm not feeling it."

"Okay. Well, shit." Johnny stood, too. "You want me to walk you out?"

"No, I'm good."

Jack found his boots and pulled them on. Johnny watched, conflicted. Days like this meant something to both of them. Normally they fished or hunted or shot skeet; breakfast was always a big deal. Johnny opened his mouth twice before he finally spoke. "About the lawyer business—"

"It's not that."

"Then, why are you leaving?"

Jack picked up his jacket and looked across the clearing. He'd never fully understood Johnny's desire to live in this place, but if he chose to live as a hermit, it was Jack's place to be there for him. Part of that stemmed from childhood and mutual obligation; part of it was that they lived as brothers. That meant they trusted, supported, accepted. But today was different, and Jack felt the change as surely as he smelled coffee on the morning air.

Johnny was lying.

By the time Jack returned to the small apartment he kept above a bakery downtown, his suspicion had only grown. Something in Johnny's laugh, and in the way his eyes moved. With the door locked and lights off, Jack pulled off muddy clothes, lay on the bed, and considered the very real chance his best friend was a liar. The thought troubled him, and Jack chewed on it for a long time, hating it; but it was in dreams that a more disturbing truth found him. He stood in black water, and in the wan light Johnny was shirtless beside him. His eyes were half-closed, his hands turned up as if to catch a falling rain. Everything was real: the water on his shins, the cold air and fear. Jack watched Johnny point, but was afraid to look.

Do you see?

Jack didn't see; didn't want to.

Jack . . .

Jack looked that time, but not where Johnny pointed. He looked at eyes glazed black and muscles that gathered and twitched. Maybe Johnny was afraid. Maybe he was like Jack.

Tell me what you see.

But the fear was too real, and Jack too ashamed. He closed his eyes, and when they opened, he was awake in an apartment that smelled of bread baking. The sky outside was dim, the sheets twisted and damp.

"It's not possible."

But it was.

Johnny's stepfather had spoken to Jack of injuries from a fall, of bruises black as ink and cuts so deep, they went halfway to the bone. That's why he'd called Jack in the first place, because Johnny had fallen and almost died. With the bourbon and the mist, Jack had forgotten, but not now. He wanted to deny the sudden truth, but blinked and saw Johnny, as he'd been last night, and not just in the dream. He was shirtless and still and flawless.

There wasn't a mark on him.

CHAPTER THREE

That night—for the second night in a row—Jack drank more than he should. It started with a six-pack and ended with a liquor bottle on the parapet that circled the roof of his building. He was angry with himself and frightened, staring north to where storm clouds broke above the distant swamp. Even here he felt the dampness of it, the electrical charge. The storm was moving for the city, and he thought he might remain where he stood, to let it lift him up or flatten him against the roof. The thought was illogical, but Jack had begun to doubt reality and, because of that, himself. Awareness and focus were the levers he'd used to break the prison of childhood fears. What remained when he no longer knew his own mind?

"Damn it, Johnny."

Jack lifted the bottle and swallowed liquor that burned all the way down. He was a lawyer now, and grown. It wasn't supposed to be like this.

He drank again, choking. Beneath him were movement and light, the sounds of the city on Saturday night. It was late, and he should be asleep. That's what new associates did. They slept and worked and fed the machine. Since Alyssa's death, it's all Jack had ever wanted, a life of rationality and resolve. That's what the law was, and what it was designed to make of people. He could hear the professors now:

Fact and law and precedent . . .

Jack laughed, and the sound frightened him because there was no rationality in it. It sounded broken and wild, and that's exactly how childhood with Johnny had ended, not in quietness and time, but in a sudden rush of secrets and death and superstitious dread. That's what Jack knew of precedent. He could share the thought with Johnny, and Johnny would nod because they'd walked the road together: Alyssa's disappearance and the long search, her body, when they found it, all the others who'd died and suffered in the year she'd been gone. Johnny would say, *Yes, I remember,* and *Yes, there is a line between good and evil.* But people could walk the same road and see different things. In the years since childhood, Johnny had taken the pragmatic view that people were cruel and selfish and base. Jack recognized that, too—it's why the law mattered—but his need for order ran more deeply than even Johnny understood; because Jack had learned different things on that road, and not all of them were rational and real. Where Johnny chose to see cause and effect, Jack saw the hand of God, and of the devil himself. That wasn't hyperbole or false belief; he knew it like he knew his bones: that the world ran shadowed and deep, that evil was real and had a face. Because of that, Jack sought order, solidity, control.

But there were no such things.

Not if what happened in the swamp was real.

It was an ugly thought, and heavy inside him. He told himself he was foolish, but didn't believe it; said Johnny was telling the truth but didn't believe that, either. Something happened in that godforsaken swamp, and Jack could not drink the conviction away. So he watched the storm instead, urging it on, thinking it might be strong enough to sweep the roof clean of dust and heat and worry. But the storm turned east before it reached the city. It flickered yellow and spit rain, grew small and left him where he stood. Jack watched it roll away, and by the time the sky was empty, so was the bottle.

When he woke a few hours later, the light outside was gray. That was a habit born of college and law school: early to rise and early to work. Few days offered hours to waste, and Jack knew the value of concerted effort. He'd finished Wake Forest University first in his class and Duke Law at number two. He could have gone big city, big salary; but Jack wanted to prove something to the place that shit all over his childhood.

Besides, Johnny was here.

Rolling in the bed, he lifted his watch from the table and squinted through bloody eyes. Six seventeen. He'd overslept.

"Lovely."

It was Sunday morning, but that didn't matter. Being a lawyer worked best if you were a partner, and that didn't come easily or cheap. Nine years, he'd been told—that's what it normally took to make partner. Jack planned to do it in five, so he'd made a deal with himself. Two Saturdays a month, he'd spend with Johnny. The other days he'd work, and not just any kind of work. He'd work the way he had in law school. Fifteen-hour days. Sixteen if he ate at his desk.

By six fifty he was showered and dressed. The walk to the office took eight minutes, and he stopped on the way to pick up coffee and a bagel. The building was empty, but Jack didn't mind. He liked the quiet halls and the cleaned, processed smell. At his desk, he sipped coffee and considered the practice he'd chosen to join. The firm was medium-sized but highly regarded. Raven County was a small market, but the firm drew clients from all over the South. That kind of accomplishment took time and effort, and hard, smart lawyers. Even now, there was talk of expansion—an office in Charlotte, maybe, and then another in Raleigh. After that, anything could happen. Washington. Atlanta.

Jack moved to the window and stared east. The prison was too far away to see, but he pictured it there, and in it, his father. Did that have something to do with his decision to stay in Raven County? He asked the same question about his mother, knowing she'd be at church already or at home on folded knees. She lived in an old trailer under a dead tree, and blamed Jack for everything wrong in her life. Because of that, her prayers were the spiteful kind, and other believers saw that in her. They'd tried to change her and failed, pushed her from one church to the next, each one a little poorer, a little more desperate. Last Jack heard, she attended service under a canvas tent pitched on a bald spot by the river. The preacher came from southern Alabama, and was prone to long bouts of caterwauling and sweat. Beyond that, Jack didn't really know or care. The man could be a revivalist, a snake handler, or a charlatan. It was all the same to Jack, who believed that God—when he chose—connected to people in a very personal manner.

Sometimes that was okay.

At times it hurt like hell.

Jack gave himself another minute to dwell on sin and the past, then got to work. And when Jack worked, it was in a state of total concentration. Sounds dulled; surroundings blurred. He worked a single file for five hours. Filings. Briefs. Deposition summaries. The hangover hurt, but he powered through it. This was what he did, and where he thrived. Details. Strategy. Minutiae. He worked through lunch, and by two, there were others in the building. He heard muted conversations, a ding in the hall as the elevator rose and fell. Jack stood, once, to stretch his back, and watched a car pull into the lot below. It was long and silver, and when its door opened, a woman stepped out. The angle did funny things, but Jack knew she was petite and pretty and dangerously smart. Her name was Leslie Green, a partner with expensive clothes and the sharpest, prettiest eyes Jack had ever seen. He watched her to the building, and lost her at the door.

After that, he tried to work, but read the same paragraph six times without absorbing a word. He made a seventh try, but knew the signs. His mind was twisted around a different axle, and that was Johnny's fault.

"Well, goddamn."

Jack considered options for about ten seconds, and in the elevator pushed the button for three.

The appellate division was on three.

So was Leslie Green.

He thought about her as the elevator dropped. It's not that he disliked her—she was probably a fine person—but on three occasions she'd cornered him, and each time wanted the same thing: Johnny's life, the story.

She wanted to know if it was true.

The first time it happened, she'd come to Jack's office and been blunt about it. She had the book in her hand and a smile on her face.

Leslie Green, she'd said. *Partner. Appellate Division. Are you the same Jack Cross that's in this book?*

She'd tilted the book so he could see the jacket, and her face reflected the same hunger he'd seen so many times before. People got turned on by the story—the tragedy and violence, the remarkable tales of Johnny as a child. The photographs didn't hurt, either. He'd been striking even at thirteen, what with the cheekbones and jet-black hair and wild, dark eyes. The most famous picture was taken in a half-wrecked car in front of the hospital, and showed him streaked with blood and ash and berry juice. He was small behind the wheel, his arm still clutched by the girl he'd saved. He'd been cut a dozen times, his chest sliced open. Dull marks striped his face. Feathers and rattles and copperhead skulls hung from leather thongs around his neck. The papers called him *the wild Indian, the warrior, the little chief.* Some said Johnny was unhinged, a danger. Others thought he was the bravest child ever to come through Raven County. When Johnny's sister went missing, he'd spent a year looking. He'd tracked pedophiles and killers, gone alone to places so dangerous, even cops feared to go. By the time it was over, he'd found not only his sister, but the remains of seven more victims besides, including his own father. In the process, he'd exposed a ring of kidnappers and killers, gone into the wilds with an escaped convict, and done what the police could not. The story was a sensation, and the networks carried it coast to coast. For a while there was talk of a movie. The book had been inevitable. It came out on a Tuesday, and spent three years on the bestseller lists. Even then, no one knew the full story, not the reporters or the cops, not even the guy who wrote the book. Nearly a decade had passed, and Johnny carried his secrets the same as Jack, quietly and heavily. They didn't talk about how things happened or why they survived. The unanswered questions were even bigger.

So, Jack was used to interest from outsiders. Even in college and law school, people put it together: Jack's name and his hometown, the old stories and the stunted arm. It was the book that did it. People loved true crime, and the book made every "best of" list ever published. That kept the story front and center, and with the ten-year anniversary fast approaching, the publisher was going back to print, planning a big push. They'd asked Jack to be a part of that, and Jack guessed they were looking for Johnny, too. They wanted a tour, interviews, talk shows. They sensed a bigger story, same as everyone else; wanted reasons behind the feathers and rattles and skulls, the details of what happened when Johnny and Jack went deep in the swamp and came out with a killer half-dead in the back of a truck. It was part of Jack's life, for good or ill. So when Leslie Green appeared in his door, Jack had leaned back in the chair, looked her in those pretty eyes and told the smallest truth he possibly could.

Yeah, he said. *That's me in the book.*

She'd sat opposite his desk, crossed lovely legs, and offered a smile designed to bend the will of men. *Tell me everything,* she'd said; but Jack had not. The truth she wanted belonged to Johnny and Jack and no one else. She didn't like his answer or the flat, unafraid way he offered it. She'd left angry, and on two other occasions cornered him with the same questions. That made three times in Jack's first week at the firm. Three times he'd angered a partner.

Not a good start, he thought.

And worse now.

Lights were off on the third floor, and every office door closed but one. It was the corner office all the way down, Leslie's office. She looked up when Jack knocked, and frowned for an instant before one corner of her mouth twisted the other way. "Do you have a minute?" Jack asked.

"I guess that depends."

"May I?"

Jack gestured, and she dipped her chin. "Sit."

Jack did, and Leslie studied his face, the suit, the small fingers curled tight in the hollow of his sleeve. She took her time, and Jack endured it. She was more than pretty, he thought, midthirties with ivory skin and blond hair. She had a tattoo on her wrist, a chip on her shoulder, and had made partner in seven years. She was brilliant, hardworking, and cold, and Jack wondered what she saw from across the desk, thinking it was the bad arm and ill-fitting suit, the boy from the book, grown older.

"It caused quite a stir," she said, "when people in this firm realized who you were. The hiring committee didn't tell us the new associate was famous."

"I'm not famous."

"Your friend certainly is."

The smile notched a quarter-inch higher, and Jack added *unyielding* to the list of her attributes. "I want you to take a case," he said. "Pro bono."

"I choose my own cases."

"I understand that."

"Is there some reason, then, that you're wasting my time?"

"I need an appellate lawyer," Jack said. "A good one."

She laughed at that, and leaned forward. "Bless your heart and get the hell out."

"If you'll just listen—"

"Please. I gave you three chances to be my friend."

"Leslie—"

"It's Ms. Green, actually. Now, go on." She pointed. "Get out of my chair. Leave."

Jack had no intention of doing either. He let his gaze wander the room, and found the book on a shelf behind her desk, its spine cracked, the cover well thumbed. Johnny had groupies; Jack knew that. Many were disturbed—the kind who wrote fan letters to Charles Manson—but not all of them. Some were moved by Johnny's courage, others by the tragedy of his youth or the undeniable love he felt for his sister. Many were girls when it happened, but grown now and full of questions about this wild-eyed boy who'd captured the country's imagination for so well and so long. They wondered what he looked like as a man, and what he'd become. Then there were those who understood what the feathers meant. They'd read the chapters on Indian lore and vision quests; they felt powerless in life, and wondered in their quiet but desperate way if young Johnny Merrimon had found some kind of key. How else the win over such dangerous men? How else the fame and glory?

"Would it change things," Jack asked, "if I told you the client was Johnny Merrimon?"

"You're joking."

"Are you interested?"

"That depends."

"On?"

"Two things. What kind of case is it?"

"You know about his land?"

"Only that he has a lot of it."

"In the 1850s his family owned forty thousand acres up north in the county. Picture the vineyards outside of town, every subdivision built on that side in the past twenty years. His ancestors owned more of this state than just about anyone alive."

"That's in the book. I read it."

"Then you know about Hush Arbor."

"I know slaves worshipped there in secret, that some of them settled there after the Civil War."

"Before the war, actually. It's Johnny's land now: six thousand acres, half of it swamp, the other half dry but stony and hard to reach. In the 1850s, Johnny's ancestor freed a slave and gave him the entire six thousand acres. Isaac Freemantle. The first freed slave in Raven County. That's in the book, too."

"I remember the chapter. John Pendleton Merrimon stared down a lynch mob with a gun in one hand and a Bible in the other. What the book doesn't say is why he cared enough in the first place."

"I'm not sure anyone knows."

"What about Johnny?"

"If he does, he's never told me."

Leslie sharpened her gaze, debating, measuring. "What does this have to do with an appellate case?"

"The deed conveying Hush Arbor to Isaac Freemantle had a reversionary clause returning the land to the Merrimon family when and if the last male Freemantle died. That happened ten years ago, and the land went to Johnny. A female descendant of Isaac Freemantle challenged the transfer—Luana Freemantle, a great-niece of some sort. She tried to take ownership, but Johnny won at trial. She's challenging on appeal."

"On what grounds?"

"I haven't read the filings. I don't know."

"You're his friend. Why not?"

"Because I *am* his friend—"

"And you don't want to be responsible for losing his land. You'll have to be tougher than that if you want to make partner at this firm. I've seen your transcripts, your application packet. You're smart enough. Take the case yourself."

"I can't."

Her lips twisted again, and Jack knew she saw all the way through him: the amount of risk and Johnny's need, the nightmare fear that Jack would fail the only person in the world he loved.

"Will you help or not?"

She laced her fingers, seeming to enjoy the control. "I said there were two things."

"Okay."

"I have friends who've seen him around town, your friend Johnny. He's a ghost, yes, but they've seen him at the hardware store, the grocery, late in the day, driving that old truck on Main Street. They text each other when it happens. A 'sighting,' they call it. So enlighten me, Mr. Cross. This young man about whom my friends speak so much—is he as remarkable as they tell me?"

"I beg your pardon?"

"Handsome, yes—but a rule-breaker, too, and unlike other men. If it's true, I'll take the case."

"Why would any of that make a difference?"

"I do appellate work and corporate law." She leaned away, cool and collected. "How many men like that do I see in a day?"

CHAPTER FOUR

The next five days passed swiftly for Johnny. He slept in the tree, and woke rested. There were no fires or signs of fires, no sleepwalking or confusion. It was only September, but winter was out there like a line of cloud, and Johnny knew how quickly the good months would pass. Nights would chill; the leaves fall. Winter would come hard to Hush Arbor, and Johnny was too broke to buy anything but flour and salt and dried pasta. He wasn't worried, though. The garden was twice its normal size, and he spent long days canning tomatoes and peas and beans. He ground corn for tortillas, and salted fish on long racks. Deer season opened soon, and meat would never be a problem. Nevertheless, he double-checked his stockpile of seeds, turned compost once a day, and planned the winter garden.

Then there was the matter of firewood. Six cords were already seasoned in a shed behind the cabin, but he'd need wood for the next season, too. So Johnny spent long days with a chain saw and an ax. He took dead trees when he could find them, preferably oak or ash, something hard. The blade work was a pleasure. Hauling tons of wood over broken ground, not so much. He strapped wood to his back and carried it as a mule might—uphill and down, back and forth through mud and over streams. By noon on the fifth day, he knew Jack was close. He tracked his progress from one island to the next, then through the last bit of open swamp. At the clearing he circled to Johnny's blind side, ducking under branches and placing his feet with care. When his arm went back, Johnny smiled to himself and said, "Don't do it."

Jack stepped from the trees and pushed the pebble into a pocket. "It scares me how you do that."

Johnny leaned the ax against a stump and dusted his hands. "It's your smell."

"Bullshit."

"You've been wearing the same aftershave since you were nineteen. Six months ago you switched to a scented detergent. The question is, how could I *not* smell you coming?" Johnny smiled, but Jack looked unhappy, even miserable. "What are you doing here, Jack? Our next dinner's not for nine days, and it's at your place."

"We need to talk."

"All right. Let's talk." Johnny pulled his shirt from a branch and led his friend to the camp chairs beyond the cabin.

When he sat, Jack stayed on his feet. He looked at the cabin and firewood, the blue sky and racks of salted fish. He considered his friend for a long second, then said, "You know something, I think I'd rather fish."

Johnny blinked once, then went into the cabin and came back with spinning rods and a tackle box. He led Jack to the water, loaded gear into an aluminum johnboat, and shipped the oars. "Are you coming?" Jack clambered in and sat very still as Johnny rowed them over deep water and toward the nearest island. When they were close, he angled the skiff to follow the line between deep water and the shallows. "What do you want to catch?" he asked.

"Doesn't matter."

Johnny rigged a line for Jack and pointed. "Cast for the shadow, right there along that line." He held out the rod, but Jack's eyes were on the dried mud in the bottom of the skiff. Johnny lowered the rod. "Do you want to talk, after all?"

"Not yet."

"Then here."

Jack took the rod and watched Johnny throw out a line. On the second cast, he hooked a largemouth bass and reeled it in. "Seven pounds."

Johnny held it so sun glinted on its scales, then threaded a stringer through its gills and lowered it back into the water. "You fishing or not?"

Jack tossed out a lure, but the cast had a desultory air. Fishing in silence, Johnny caught another bass, a redfin pickerel. "You're casting too far right," he said. "Aim ten feet off that stump; let the lure settle. Give it fifteen seconds, then bring it in slowly." Jack stared, dead-eyed, at Johnny's face. "Go on." Johnny pointed. "Ten feet off the stump. Trust me."

Jack frowned and let the line fly. He gave it fifteen seconds, and the bass hit on the first tick of the reel. The strike was enormous: a silver-green flash and a ten-inch wave of water. The fish stripped twenty feet of line off the reel before Jack got it under control. Even then it took five minutes to land it. "There you go." Johnny lifted the fish, which fought in his grip. "Twelve pounds, at least."

"Let it go. I don't want it."

"Are you serious?"

"I said put it back."

Johnny lowered the fish over the side, watched water swirl as it powered deep and down. "Okay, Jack. What's the problem?"

"This." Jack raised his voice, spread his arms. "All of it. How you know I'm coming, and how, even with your back turned, you know I'm about to throw a rock. How you catch fish like they want to be caught. And that." He stabbed a finger at the water. "That damn fish. 'Ten feet off the stump. Fifteen seconds.' In my whole life, I've never even seen a twelve-pound bass. For God's sake, the state record is only fifteen."

Johnny studied his friend's face. He was sweating and pale and breathing hard. "Are you finished?"

"Where are the bruises?"

"What?"

"Clyde said you were black and blue, cut half to the bone in a dozen places."

"It was never that bad."

"So, he's a liar?"

"I believe the word is 'hyperbolic.'"

Jack shook his head, still unhappy. "What are you doing out here,

Johnny? Why do you live like this? Why are you passionate about this place?"

"Because I own it. Because it was my family's."

"That's not enough."

"Just 'cause, then."

"That's your answer?"

"Yeah, just 'cause." It was an angry response, but Johnny let it stand. "Can we just fish?" He said, "Can we just fish and tell jokes and do like we always do?"

"No, we can't."

"Is this because of Friday night?"

"Of course it's because of Friday night! Jesus Christ, Johnny! How can you even ask such a stupid question?"

"So I walked in my sleep . . ."

"It's not just that."

"Look, it happens sometimes. . . ."

"How many times?"

"Three."

"I don't believe you."

"Okay, fine—seven or eight." Johnny put his own rod down. "Sometimes I go to sleep and wake up elsewhere."

"Like where?"

"The cabin once or twice. Sometimes, the woods."

"How about in the swamp?"

"What do you mean, 'in' it?"

"I mean *in it*. How often do you find yourself standing in the middle of this goddamn swamp?"

Johnny leaned away from his friend. The anger was real, but so were the hurt and the worry.

"Do you know how hard it was for me to come here?" Jack asked. "When I close my eyes, I see you in this swamp. I see mist and my breath. I still feel the wrongness and the cold. Something happened, Johnny, and it was something bad."

"What, then? Tell me."

"I don't know." Jack laughed darkly and made a motion with his fingers. "It's a glimmer."

"Then why are we talking about it? Let's fish. Let's have a drink."

"I'm scared, Johnny. Do you understand? It's broad daylight, and I'm terrified."

"Jack, come on—"

"This isn't a 'come on' kind of thing. You're the best friend I've ever had, but something happened here that I don't understand."

"Jack—"

"Take me to shore."

Jack pointed at the island, and Johnny rowed him to the trailhead on its northern edge. The boat slid into the weeds, and Johnny sat in silence because he had no idea what to say. Hush Arbor was his life, and Jack his only friend. When, finally, he opened his mouth, Jack cut him off with a raised hand. "Give me a second, all right?"

"Yeah, Jack. Sure. Whatever you need."

Johnny watched the struggle on his friend's face. Jack was torn and uncertain and honestly afraid. When he moved, it seemed to be with great reluctance, shifting on the seat to pull a business card from his back pocket. It was rumpled, one corner folded. Jack stared at it for long seconds, then sighed deeply and held it out. "This is for you."

Johnny took the card. "What is it?"

"Leslie Green, an appellate lawyer. She's good."

"I don't have money for a lawyer."

"She'll do it pro bono. You need to make an appointment, though, this week or next. I wouldn't let it wait."

Johnny tilted the card, and his eyebrows drew together. "Why would she take my case for free?"

"Just smile a lot, and try to look pretty."

Jack stepped out of the skiff, but Johnny stayed where he was. "Why are you helping me?"

"You know why."

Johnny looked away because the debt between them had always been an unspoken thing. "Thanks, Jack. It means a lot."

"Don't thank me, and don't remind me. Meet with her. Handle the case. I don't want to know anything about it. I hate this enough as it is."

"Okay." Johnny pushed the card into his back pocket. "You want me to walk you out?"

"I know the way."

"Are we still on for dinner?"

"Next week. My place."

"About this lawyer. She's good?"

"Yeah." Jack said it sadly. "She really is."

Watching Jack fade into the woods, Johnny tried to remember what had happened to scare his friend so badly, but most of it was a blur. He recalled sensations, flickers of thought. Jack called them glimmers, and Johnny thought it a good word. What did he actually remember?

Distance and cold.

A void with him at its center.

Johnny couldn't deny the problem. He rose from sleep and wandered the forest, and because of that he understood his friend's concern. It hadn't happened seven times or eight, but twenty times, at least. Sometimes he woke at the water's edge or on some distant hill. Other times, he rose from bed to find mud on his feet, knowing as he did that it had happened yet again. Occasionally, a restless memory stirred, some furtive image. But even those passed when the sun rose. Besides, there was something else in the night, and it wasn't frightful or cruel or unfeeling. That was the thing Jack would never understand about Hush Arbor.

The magic of it.

The power.

Rowing back to the distant shore, Johnny unshipped the oars and flipped the boat. Moving through the trees, he noticed insects in the leaf litter, a flutter of wings in a hollow tree. The sounds were crystal clear, the images exquisite. Twenty yards later he stopped and tilted his head, hearing ripples on water and kits in a den beyond the hill. A fox was moving through the forest a quarter mile to the east. It scraped beneath a cedar, dropped into a gully, and left prints in earth that smelled of red clay. Tilting his head the other way, Johnny heard scales on bark and knew, without looking, that a copperhead was uncurling beneath a log ten feet away. Not a hognose or a canebrake.

A copperhead.

A female.

He watched it appear on the trail, then slip into grass and whisper away.

It came and went, this *awareness*. On strong days he could lie in his hammock and hear beavers chew a willow tree two miles down the second creek. He knew if birds were hatching and where, if ants in the dirt thought a storm was coming. When an animal moved in the woods, Johnny knew, without seeing, if it was a coyote or a mink, a marsh rabbit or a bobcat or a long-tailed weasel. When the awareness flickered, he felt half-blind, but even then could track a bear in total darkness. The awareness disappeared in its entirety only when Johnny left Hush Arbor, and even then, the loss was not a hard line. It began to fade when he closed the gate, weakened further when he reached the first blacktop. After that it diminished with time, until an hour later the line snapped and he was as unfeeling as everyone else.

Opening his eyes, Johnny stared at the glint of water through the trees. He knew where to find the swamp darters and the bullhead, the eel and the perch and the bowfin. When turtles broke the surface, he knew instinctively whether they were stinkpots or sliders or any one of a dozen others. It was a glimpse of shell, the pattern of ripples, a thousand tiny things. But it was more than that, too.

When Johnny was near the swamp, he knew.

He just, simply *knew*.

CHAPTER FIVE

The lawyer agreed to meet on Tuesday at one o'clock. When it was time to go, Johnny combed his hair, put on clean jeans and a shirt with a collar. His plan was simple.

Meet the woman.

Make sure she'd help.

He had no illusions about the stakes involved. Jack couldn't take the case, or wouldn't. Johnny was broke. That made the sit-down with Leslie Green the most important meeting of his life. Even so, Johnny hated leaving the Hush; he hated to leave it unprotected, but more than that he disliked the feeling of physical disentanglement, of a thread drawn through some secret organ. His awareness dulled as he passed the gate, but for another ten miles he could still feel the difference between healthy trees and those dying from the inside out. He could sense movement in the grass, life around him. Then it was subdivisions and lawn mowers and concrete.

After that it faded fast.

At the tall building downtown, the lawyer made him wait. Five minutes became fifteen, and Johnny sat unmoving beside a pale-skinned man who drummed his fingers on the side of a polished shoe. When the receptionist called Johnny's name, he followed her through double doors and into a warren of halls and cubicles and offices.

"Ms. Green apologizes for the delay. As you can see, people get busy around here." The comment appeared meaningless, but enough awareness remained for Johnny to divine the deeper truth. She disliked the frayed cuffs, the rime of mud on his shoes. "This is her office."

She stopped at a closed door, and Johnny sensed movement beyond it: fingers on fabric, a sudden flush. The receptionist opened the door and moved aside. "Ms. Green," she said. "Your one o'clock is here."

Johnny stepped through the door, and stopped. Behind her desk, the lawyer was ivory-skinned and finely dressed, her eyes bright under eyebrows arched to elegant perfection.

"Mr. Merrimon. Welcome. My name is Leslie Green." She offered a hand, and Johnny took it. "Sit, please." She indicated a chair, then sat behind the desk. "Jack Cross tells me you need an appellate lawyer. He also says you can't meet my fee."

"Ah. Straight to the point."

Johnny smiled, but it was not returned. "I bill my time in six-minute increments. What some consider blunt, I consider efficient."

"Then, yes. Jack is right."

"Yet you own six thousand acres, unencumbered."

"Think of me as land-poor."

"A not-uncommon situation. My parents were much the same way."

"Farmers?"

"Ranchers. Texas." The bright eyes lingered on his lips, the line of his jaw. "You could sell land to meet the fee."

"That will never happen."

The hardness was there. He couldn't hide it. Strangely, the lawyer seemed to like it. Heat built in her skin. The pupils dilated. But she wasn't angry, he thought. Not the way she was leaning forward, not the way she was staring.

"Why should I help you?"

"I was under the impression you'd already agreed to take my case."

"Not yet, no."

"Then why am I here?"

She shrugged. "Mr. Cross is a colleague. Consider this a courtesy."

That was not entirely true. Johnny could tell that, too. "Very well. What can I do to convince you?"

"Do you understand why Luana Freemantle filed the appeal?"

"I won at trial. She doesn't like it."

"I mean the legal framework of her appeal, the nuances. Do you understand the foundation on which she's built the appeal?"

"You've read the brief?"

"And transcripts of the trial. This meeting may be a courtesy, but I would never take it unprepared. Besides, the case holds a certain interest."

"Such as?"

The lawyer crossed her legs, showed a flash of knee. "Trial courts find fact, Mr. Merrimon, while appellate courts consider errors of law. You maintained ownership of Hush Arbor because the original conveyance stipulated that title to the land would return to the Merrimon family when and if the last male Freemantle died. Levi Freemantle was the last male of his line, and he died ten years ago. Those are the facts established at trial. Without obvious errors of law, Mrs. Freemantle has been forced to appeal on the grounds of public policy, equity, gender inequality. Those are compelling issues, and likely to be argued before the State Supreme Court. Perhaps that helps you understand my interest."

"Do you agree with Ms. Freemantle's arguments?"

"You ask that, why? Because I'm female?"

"Partly."

"Are you interviewing me, Mr. Merrimon? That's not how this works."

"Public policy. Gender inequality. I just wonder how dedicated to my case you could possibly be."

"Your ancestor's beliefs were a product of the time. In 1853, men owned ninety-nine percent of all real property in the country. That's a simple fact. What matters now is the law and its theoretical underpinnings. Courts are loath to reinterpret the plain language of any conveyance, but it happens if equity and public policy demand it. In that case, you would need dedicated counsel."

"You can maintain that dedication?"

"I'm a professional."

"Other women might take issue."

"And notoriety brings its own reward, especially in the practice of law. I'm not above a headline if it helps the cause."

She still appeared cool and in control, but makeup couldn't hide the pulse at her throat, the smell of overwarm skin. Johnny wanted to think it was the argument—the back and forth—but she'd been like that since the moment he walked in.

"Do I factor into your thoughts on notoriety?"

"Personally, you mean?" She laced her fingers and spoke as if the answer were a foregone conclusion. "A law practice is a business like any other. That requires me to think about reputation, perception. There's nothing inherently wrong with media attention."

"And you'll get more of it because of who I am."

She ignored the obvious anger.

"Television. Newspapers. Books. Right or wrong, the community has certain perceptions about you. In my experience, there is rarely such a thing as bad publicity. I'm speaking honestly here so there'll be no illusion as to motive. I don't do anything for free."

Johnny's jaw hardened. "I won't discuss my sister or what happened ten years ago."

"Levi Freemantle died in your mother's house. What happened ten years ago is relevant to your case."

"I won't discuss my sister or her disappearance, nor will I discuss my portrayal in the media. Things were said about me, yes. Some considered what I did newsworthy. The photographs were . . . provocative."

"As were things left unsaid. Your continued silence has led to speculation, and that has kept your name in the media. Is it true you turned down a movie offer?"

Johnny stood.

"Mr. Merrimon—"

"Levi Freemantle is dead. The facts are settled. You've said as much yourself. As for Hollywood, no, no one has offered money for my story. Had it happened, I would have turned it down."

Johnny's anger was now impossible to hide. He looked at the dilated pupils, the damp lips. Too many people were drawn to the road he'd walked as a boy, to suffering and dark places, the flowers of childhood, ruined.

"My interest is purely professional."

"I somehow doubt that."

"Mr. Merrimon, please."

"The book is there, on your shelf." Johnny watched the lawyer turn toward the bookcase behind her. She stopped halfway. "Under the file," he said. "Half-hidden."

"How did you—?"

"I won't talk about my sister or how I found her or about the people who died along the way. Let me make that plain."

"Very well." The lawyer cleared her throat and leaned closer to the desk. "Let's talk about this instead."

She laid out a photograph. In it, Johnny's hair was shorter. He was unsmiling, wearing orange. "That's a booking photo," he said. "From two years ago."

"William Boyd and Randall Parks. They claimed that you tried to kill them."

Johnny sat, and measured his words. "If I'd wanted them dead, they'd be dead. My intention was to frighten them."

She removed another sheaf of photographs. They showed a campsite in disarray, personal items shot through with a large-caliber weapon. Canteens. A camp stove. The stock of a rifle. "Do you always hit the things at which you shoot?"

Johnny said nothing, but in his mind he heard men screaming and the crash of a .270 Winchester, the action slick and fast as he'd pumped round after round into tent poles and weapons and gear.

"You could have been charged with attempted murder."

"They were killing bear out of season."

The lawyer leaned back and pursed her lips. She was looking at the angles now, all business. "William Boyd is a wealthy man."

"If you're worried about representing me, let me put your mind at ease. Boyd lives in New York. He only comes here to hunt."

"The lodge, yes. I know about that. What's your relationship with Mr. Boyd today?"

"He has a restraining order against me."

"Have you ever violated it?"

"Not yet."

The lawyer pursed her lips once more, dissatisfied. "The district attorney could have locked you up and thrown away the key. Instead, he offered you a misdemeanor plea and a four-month sentence. Can you tell me why he did that?"

"Perhaps you should ask Mr. Boyd."

"Do you actually want my help, Mr. Merrimon?"

"Yes."

"Then understand my position. You're visible, unpredictable, and demonstrably violent. Notoriety is one thing, criminality something entirely different. I need to know that you'll not be shooting at billionaire hedge fund managers from New York. If you can't promise that, I can't help you."

"I pinky-swear."

She lifted an eyebrow; waited.

"Fine," Johnny said. "I won't shoot at any billionaire hedge fund managers."

The lawyer studied him for long seconds, then rose from the desk and moved to a window. Johnny guessed she was thirty-three or -four, an educated woman used to being taken seriously.

"Why did he do it?" she asked.

"What?"

She leaned against the windowsill. "Your ancestor owned forty thousand acres of Raven County. He was one of the wealthiest men in the state, yet he freed a hundred slaves and gave one of them six thousand acres. The decision cost him his land, his fortune, his place in society. Yet none of the history books say why he did it."

"I don't know what to tell you."

"No family stories?"

"None I'm willing to share."

She tensed minutely, a hint of anger. "Then later, perhaps."

"That depends."

The lawyer did not respond. Her fingers found a chain at her throat.

"Will you help me or not?" Johnny asked.

"I'll think about it. You can call me next week."

She kept her face neutral, and Johnny watched it for a long moment. He wanted a sign, some kind of hint.

But Johnny was too long from the swamp.

He couldn't read her.

After Johnny left her office, Leslie let the façade break, slumping in her chair to blow out a slow and steady breath. She'd known attractive men her whole life, and dated more than her fair share of them. Yet there was something about this Johnny Merrimon—her friends were right about that. Was it the looks? The brown eyes and stillness? Or was it, indeed, his history, what a friend once called *the dark celebrity of the surreal*? Leslie had dated famous men before: the football player in Charlotte, the senator in D.C. Those men had worn celebrity like a suit of clothes, and maybe that was the difference. Johnny wanted none of it. He was wild-haired and rough and unapologetic.

"Joyce." Leslie buzzed her assistant through the intercom.

"Yes."

"Will you bring me the rainmaker file on William Boyd?"

"Of course. Two minutes."

Leslie drummed her fingers as she waited. Like any ambitious firm, this one was made up of partners who knew it was better to work smart than hard. That meant bringing in the big clients, the million-dollar retainers. Files were kept on the best prospects, and William Boyd was one of them. He ran a nine-billion-dollar hedge fund from his offices on Wall Street. The fund paid its New York attorneys nine hundred dollars an hour. His own income was rumored to be thirty million dollars a year.

When Joyce returned from the short walk to central filing, her hands were empty. "The William Boyd file was signed out three days ago."

"By whom?"

"Jack Cross. Would you like me to track it down?"

Leslie thought about it for half a second. "No thank you, Joyce. I'll take care of it."

Leslie waited for her assistant to leave, then slipped into a blazer and took the elevator to seven. Bankruptcy law was a big part of what the firm did, but she preferred working with winners, so generally stayed clear of the seventh floor. This was a different issue, though, and it wasn't just about Johnny Merrimon.

Leaving the marbled lobby she followed the hallways until they began to narrow, at which point she cut through the center of the building, twisting between the cubicles and file rooms until she reached a stretch of decent offices. Putting her head in the first door, she said, "Jack Cross?"

An attorney she recognized but whose name she forgot pointed deeper into the bankruptcy section. "Sixth door down, two before the corner."

When she reached Jack Cross's office, she didn't bother knocking. "Where is it?"

Jack was hunched over the desk, hair rumpled, a yellow highlighter between his fingers. "What?"

"Rainmaker files are for partners. You have no business with the William Boyd file."

"I'm sorry. I didn't know."

"Every associate knows. It's part of the orientation. The file."

She held out a hand, and Jack turned for the credenza behind his desk. When he handed over the file, he appeared contrite. "I'm not trying to land him as a client."

Leslie felt a flutter of humor at the idea of a first-year associate trying to convince a man like William Boyd to trust him with anything more serious than a parking ticket. She knew why Jack had the file. "You showed this to your friend." Jack said nothing. "Johnny Merrimon was just here. Did you show it to him?"

"It's not really confidential."

"It's proprietary."

Leslie had not been through the file for several years, but knew it held more than could easily be found in the public domain. Rainmaker files contained the usual newspaper clippings, interviews, and business filings, but they also contained proprietary financial estimates, research into political affiliations, social connections, marital status. Was the prospect moral or immoral? Did he have mistresses, bad habits, vindictive ex-partners? If a prospective client was big enough, the firm had been known to use private investigators, paid informants, forensic accountants. Nothing illegal was done to accumulate the information and nothing illegal would ever be done once it was in hand. But being a rainmaker took work, and knowledge was power.

Leslie held up the file. "I could have you fired for this."

"Please don't."

Leslie took the chair opposite the desk, not quite so angry as she pretended. Six different partners had tried to land William Boyd, and she knew it would never happen. He used the top firm in New York, and considered anything else provincial. He came to Raven County only to hunt on a nineteen-hundred-acre preserve that used to be part of the Merrimon estate. There was a lodge on it, she knew, and when Boyd was there, he kept it full of clients and dead animals and, usually, young women. You couldn't swing a cat in Raven County without hitting a pretty young thing with some story or other about wine from France and pale men from the big city.

Ignoring Jack for the moment, Leslie flipped through the file to see if anything had changed since the last time she saw it. Boyd was forty-two and single. A graduate of Yale and Wharton, he had an ex-wife who came from California money. Vineyards, apparently. Napa. Sonoma. Photographs showed Boyd in various settings, his offices on Wall Street, a mansion in Connecticut. The financials had been recently updated. His fund now ran thirteen billion dollars, and required a minimum investment of twenty million. His income last year was twice that amount. Halfway through the file, Leslie came across a tax map showing the preserve and its place in the county. The northern corner of it was less than a mile from the southern edge of Hush Arbor. She snapped the file closed. "I assume Mr. Merrimon came here before his meeting with me."

"Listen, Leslie—"

"What did he want with this?"

She held up the file, and Jack swallowed in a dry throat. "He was just, you know. Curious."

"None of this convinces me to help either you or your friend."

"I understand that."

"Is he still angry with Mr. Boyd?"

"You mean *actively angry*?"

"Don't play games with me, Cross. I may yet fire you." The young attorney leaned away from the threat, but Leslie wasn't going to fire him—she didn't have the power. "Why did Johnny shoot at Boyd? The real reason."

"He told you about the bear cubs."

"It can't be as simple as that."

"Johnny had tracked Boyd before, a couple times at least. Deer. Bear. Bobcat. The killing was indiscriminate. There'd been confrontations in the past."

"Violent?"

"Close enough."

"He could have gone to the police."

"That's not really Johnny's style."

Leslie tapped the file against her knee, thinking of pro bono cases and billion-dollar hedge funds. "Can you drive a stick with that arm?"

Jack looked confused, but nodded.

"Good." She tossed keys on the desk. "Because you're driving."

Leslie read through the rest of the file as Jack drove. Boyd was five-ten and handsome—not Johnny Merrimon handsome, but decent enough. He played golf and squash, but hunting seemed to be his passion. Africa. The Far East. If something could be killed for sport, chances were good he'd killed it.

"How do you know he's even in town?"

Jack's words were the first uttered in five minutes. Leslie cut her eyes left. He looked uncomfortable behind the wheel of a machine as aggressively styled as her Jaguar XKR. His good arm worked the stick through the gears; his bad one barely reached the wheel. "I don't," she said. "But if you want me to help your friend, I need both sides of the story."

She didn't mention that the day could still go two ways. Either she got to know Johnny Merrimon or she brought in the largest client of her career. According to the file, William Boyd's hedge fund had paid twelve million in legal fees the previous fiscal year. Ten percent of that business would make her a senior partner. Twenty would make her a rock star.

"Is your friend really that good with a rifle?"

"He is."

"He could have been charged with attempted murder. You know that, right?"

Jack clenched his jaw, downshifted through a curve and accelerated onto an open stretch of blacktop.

Leslie smiled at his discomfiture. "When I asked him about the misdemeanor plea, he refused to speculate on the reasons it was offered. I should think that with Boyd's wealth and influence, he could have your friend buried *under* the jail. Any idea why that didn't happen?"

Jack shrugged. "It would have meant a trial. No way a man like William Boyd would let Johnny take the stand."

"Why not?"

"Because he wet his pants when Johnny opened fire, and because he had a sack full of bloody hides, killed out of season. He's a public figure. The media would have crucified him."

Leslie tried to imagine being shot at in the woods. "Do you think your friend got off too easily?"

"Not at all."

"You sound like a defense lawyer."

"They were five weeks old," Jack said.

"What?"

"The cubs left to starve. They were only five weeks old."

Once they turned onto the property, the drive to the lodge was two miles long. It followed a stream before twisting to the top of a flattop hill that offered views the length of the valley. Everything around them was manicured: the grass, the hedgerows, the climbing ivy. The lodge itself was built of oak and stone and cedar. It rambled beneath ancient trees, commanded the hilltop. Beside it was a ten-car garage, and on the tarmac, a

Range Rover and a silver Audi. As impressive as it all was, Leslie ignored it when she stepped from the car. "This is unbelievable."

She meant the long valley and the plunging views. The stream glinted silver on the valley floor. Distant hills rose on the horizon, the trees like shadow, the granite hard and yellow in the afternoon light. "That's Hush Arbor," Jack said. "The first rows of hills and three thousand acres beneath them. The river spills from the highlands, then feeds the swamp before running another hundred miles to the Atlantic."

"What about this property?"

"From the road, it stretches north another mile or two. The lodge is about dead center."

Leslie glanced at the house with its slate roof and stone columns and covered porch. "I see why he sighted the lodge here. This hilltop is spectacular." Jack looked away, and she sensed something unspoken. "What?"

"This is where the original mansion stood. Johnny's ancestors are buried just there, through the trees."

"You're kidding me." Jack gestured with his chin, and Leslie saw hints of granite and marble and twisted vine. "I'm starting to understand why Johnny took those shots."

"It wasn't like that."

"Yeah, right. Come on."

On the porch, double doors rose ten feet from bluestone floors. Leslie reached for an iron knocker, but the right-side door swung open before she could touch it, and a woman appeared. She was in her midforties, with a pleasant face and a soft figure squeezed into denim jeans and a flannel shirt. "May I help you?"

Leslie took the lead, stepping closer. "Hi. I'm Leslie Green. This is my associate Jack Cross. It's an unscheduled visit, I know, but we were hoping for a moment of Mr. Boyd's time. We're not selling anything and we don't bite."

She put on a smile to seal the deal, but the woman inside needed no enticement. "Absolutely," she said. "I'm Martha Goodman. Cook. Housekeeper. I do pretty much everything." She held out a hand, and Leslie and Jack shook it. "We don't get a lot of visitors out here, and frankly, I'm happy for the distraction. Come in, please. Mr. Boyd is here somewhere."

Inside, the ceiling rose to an immense vault. The central support was a tree trunk covered with hand-carved hunting scenes.

"Amazing, isn't it?" The housekeeper touched it gently. "The woodcarvers came from Poland. It took three of them nine weeks just to carve this one post." She gestured at the ceiling. "The rafters took another year."

Almost as thick as the post, the rafters stretched thirty feet from the central peak to each side of the room. The walls beneath them were hung with trophies from around the world. Leslie recognized antelope and kudu and water buffalo. A stuffed grizzly rose from a mount beside the fireplace. Elephant tusks framed a door that led deeper into the house.

"Give me a minute to find him," Martha said. "I believe he's in the gun room. In the meantime, make yourselves at home."

She left, and Jack ran a hand along one of the tusks by the door. The ivory was yellowed and smooth, the tusk eight feet long. Leslie asked, "What do you think about all this?"

"An eight-foot shaft of ivory? I think he's compensating."

Jack stepped between the tusks and moved into a hallway that ran past a broad staircase and other doors. Warm rugs lent color to the wood. Portraits covered the wall, beside muskets and spears and antique crossbows.

Leslie said, "This guy's not kidding around."

Jack nudged a partially open door. The room beyond was rich, its leather chairs as soft and brown as poured honey, the desk a monument of wood and tooled leather. A fireplace broke the right-hand wall, its mantel lined with photographs of Boyd with lion and elk and what appeared to be a dead rhino. On the wall above the mantel hung the largest mounted deer's head Jack had ever seen. It was obviously very old, the glass eyes cloudy, the antlers as thick as Jack's good arm and six feet wide from tip to tip. Jack counted eighteen points, the symmetry perfect. At the base of its throat was a tarnished plaque. Jack stepped closer and read aloud.

" 'A Lord of the Forest, shot through the heart by Randolph Boyd, age fourteen, in the winter of 1931.' "

"Do you hunt?"

The voice came from the door, and the man was unhappy. Jack recognized Boyd from the photographs, but Leslie spoke first. "I hope you don't mind. Martha said to make ourselves at home."

"Martha should know better. This room is off-limits."

"Mr. Boyd—"

"I asked if you hunt."

He was looking at Jack, his eyes blue and unforgiving. Jack thought carefully before answering. "No." He held up his bad arm to support the claim. "I don't hunt."

"Do you know what that is you're looking at?"

"I assume it's a deer of some sort."

Boyd studied Jack from top to bottom, returning to the bad arm, and nodding once as the tension broke. "My grandfather killed that deer in 1931. He was a boy in Illinois. They say whitetail grow large in that part of the world, that it's due to the harshness of the winters or something in the gene pool. Do you know anything about Illinois deer?" Jack shook his head, and Boyd relaxed further. "You're Johnny Merrimon's friend."

"You recognize me?"

"Mr. Merrimon fired eleven shots at my camp and almost killed me. I saw you at the preliminary hearing."

"That was two years ago."

"Then I'll confess to having seen you somewhere else. I'm William Boyd." They shook hands. "And you are Leslie Green. I'm familiar with your firm."

"You are?" Leslie shook the same hand, surprised. "May I ask why?"

"Honestly, it's about him." He pointed at Jack. "More specifically, it's about his friend's land."

"Why would you care about Hush Arbor?" Jack asked.

Boyd lifted an eyebrow. "Ah," he said. "Your friend didn't tell you."

"Tell me what?"

"Come. Sit." Boyd indicated the leather chairs. "Would you like anything to drink? Water? Wine? Something stronger?" Both declined. Boyd went to a sideboard and poured liquor from a decanter. "I apologize for my anger a moment ago." Boyd gestured vaguely at the door, the mounted deer's head. "This is a private space. I rarely allow visitors."

Leslie said, "We should have stayed where Martha left us."

Boyd shrugged as if the topic were already closed. "A question, then, if I may."

"Of course."

"Do you represent Johnny Merrimon in some capacity?"

"I'm considering taking his case on appeal."

"Of course. The trial court's decision to quiet title in Mr. Merrimon's favor."

"You know about that?"

"Yes, of course. Will you help him?"

"I've not decided yet."

Boyd perched on the edge of the desk. "Has he approached you about some other matter? Mentioned my name, perhaps?"

Leslie said, "He has not."

Jack interrupted. "I'm not sure I'm comfortable with this discussion. You may not consider Johnny a client, but I do."

"Has he paid you?" Leslie asked. "Signed anything?"

"Leslie, listen—"

"Patience, please." Boyd waved Jack down. "You're protective of your friend. I respect that. Believe it or not, I'm trying to help him. I'd like to help you, too, for that matter."

"In what capacity?"

"I wish to buy your friend's land. He refuses to sell. I would compensate anyone able to persuade him. You're his friend and advisor. Thirty million is a fair price. You should tell him that."

Jack almost choked. "Thirty million dollars?"

"My fourth offer in six months. I've sent other lawyers, even a few locals. It's hard to find him, but not impossible. He does leave the swamp from time to time."

Jack was still struggling. Johnny owned three pairs of pants, a single pair of decent shoes. "Thirty million dollars?"

"The offer is more than fair."

"It's ten times what it's worth."

"I consider worth subjective, and would pay you well to convince your friend of that." Boyd smiled behind the glass. "What does a partner make in a year? I'll double it." He looked at Leslie. "For both of you."

Without asking, Jack crossed the room and poured a drink.

Thirty million dollars . . .

What the hell???

"It's a good offer," Boyd said. "Mr. Merrimon could lose the land on appeal. Better he take the money now, and allow me to assume the litigation risk. Ms. Green, I would happily engage your services to manage any appeal. My lawyers in New York bill nine hundred dollars an hour. I can offer you the same."

"That's very generous," Leslie managed.

"Just stop a minute." Jack's back was turned, but Boyd was paying close attention. Even Leslie seemed to realize that the moment hinged on Jack. "Johnny took eleven shots at you. He threatened to shoot you in the throat if you ever returned."

"Sticks and stones, Mr. Cross. Tell me, Ms. Green, what does a partner in your firm make?"

Leslie opened her mouth, but Jack spoke first. "Nobody pays ten times market value."

"Are you sure of that, Mr. Cross? My net worth is north of a billion. Forgive my bluntness, but there it is. If I want something, I buy it. That includes the willing assistance of qualified people. I'll pay three years' salary plus any litigation expenses related to the appeal."

"Perhaps if I understood why it's worth so much to you."

"Ah, I see. You fear that my sole intent is to deprive a man I dislike of the thing he values most dearly. Let me assuage your worry. Come this way. You, too, Ms. Green."

He led them down the hall to a windowless room full of long guns racked on velvet and stained wood. Jack touched one gun, then another. Purdey. Holland & Holland. Most of them cost more than he'd make in a year.

"Do you know guns?" Boyd asked.

"No," Jack lied. "Not really."

"Hunting is my passion. It's why I bought this place and built the lodge. I entertain clients here from all over the world: real estate developers, Saudi sheikhs, actors, Texas oilmen. I consider it a business expense. Problem is, it's only nineteen hundred acres. Here." He indicated a topographical map on the wall. "This is Hush Arbor. See how large it is? Six thousand acres plus access to the state game lands beyond." He indicated a vast swath of green on the map. "Three farms fill the space between your friend's land and mine. Two, I've already acquired, and the third is under contract. When that sale closes, I'll own thirty-four hundred acres contiguous to Hush Arbor."

"And you want to own it all."

"Nine thousand four hundred acres is big, even by Texas standards. Add the game lands to the north, and we're talking something close to fifty thousand accessible acres."

"Forty-nine thousand four hundred and twelve."

"There you go." Boyd lifted both arms. "You know the land, you know the numbers." He tried for a smile, but Jack didn't buy it. He didn't buy any of it. "It's thirty million dollars, son. Do you still think I plan to hurt your friend?"

"What exactly do you want from me?"

"I want you to convince him."

"He won't sell."

"Come, Mr. Cross. Two more years, and he'll lose it for unpaid taxes. Your friend is broke. His mother has a few dollars, but not enough. His stepfather is a cop with seventy-eight grand in an IRA and twice as much debt on the mortgage. You're his only friend, and while I'm sure you're a fine lawyer, you also carry ninety-seven thousand dollars in law school debt." Jack's mouth fell open. Boyd was unblinking. "Private investigators," he said. "Surprisingly inexpensive."

"That's it, then?" Jack hid the anger. "I get Johnny to sell and you make me rich?"

"I want the land. Cost is secondary."

"Why?"

"I've already told you why. Bobcat and bear, deer and geese and quail."

"Why Raven County?" Jack asked. "You live in Connecticut, you work in New York."

"It's an easy flight."

"That's it?"

"Land in a place like this is cheap, even at five thousand an acre." There was an edge to him now, something close to an open taunt. "Let's call it four years' earnings if you help me." He looked at Leslie that time. "What does a partner in your firm make?"

In the car, Jack drove and kept his mouth shut. He worked the car hard, pushing through the gears. "You're angry," Leslie said. "I understand."

Third gear. Fourth. "He's a liar."

"Perhaps."

Jack shook his head. He had no doubt.

"We should talk about his offer."

"What's there to talk about? We can't represent Johnny if the firm represents Boyd. It's a conflict."

"That's not your decision to make."

"Actually, it is. Do you think Boyd would hire the firm if I weren't part of the deal?" Jack was uncompromising, but didn't care. He felt played. Leslie was part of that. "How did you even know he would be there?"

"I didn't. It was a gamble."

"Pretty damn convenient."

"Come on, Cross. You can't really be upset about this. Your best friend lives in a swamp. How's that working out for him?"

Jack chewed on the words, thinking Leslie had somehow sensed his newfound fear of the swamp, this concern he had for Johnny. In the end, only one truth mattered. "Johnny knows his own mind. It's not my choice."

"Whether it is or not, you should consider the offer more carefully. Convincing Johnny to sell is the smartest thing you could do for all of us. Thirty million for him. Another two for each of us."

"Two million dollars?"

"Conservatively."

The number stunned Jack. His salary was sixty thousand a year, and he'd fought hard to get that much. "Boyd is a liar."

"Why do you keep saying that?"

"His grandfather didn't grow up in Illinois. Randolph Boyd was born here. He spent his life in Raven County until he died, at twenty-one, in World War Two. The family history is in the file."

Jack pointed at the rainmaker file, but Leslie didn't pick it up. "You're talking about the kid who shot the deer in 1931? Who cares? We all lie. Jesus, Cross."

She was right. Jack told lies when necessary, but that didn't change the way he felt. "Boyd said he came here because land is cheap and it's an easy flight from New York. He never mentioned that his grandfather lived in Raven County or that his father was born here. Why would he leave that out?"

"Maybe it's unimportant. Maybe he doesn't care."

Leslie wanted to believe, and Jack didn't blame her. It was big money, easy money. Whatever interest she had in Johnny would pale beside that kind of payout. Problem was, she needed Jack to make the payout happen. He thought she'd move gently at first, use soft words and logic, those pretty eyes and a hand on his arm. Eventually, she'd let more of the anger show. When that failed, she'd rally the partners to force his hand. Jack wondered if they'd use the carrot or the stick. All he knew for certain was anger and worry and a creeping sense of the utterly surreal. Because it wasn't Boyd's simple lie that twisted knots of disbelief into the walls of Jack's chest, nor was it the risk of threats or joblessness or the very real possibility of failing his best and only friend. Boyd had told not one lie but two, and the second one was so big, Jack had no idea what to do with it.

"Slow down," Leslie said.

Jack didn't.

"Damn it, Cross."

Jack drove faster. He wanted out of the car—needed to think—and it wasn't about the job or Johnny or the anger building like a storm in the eyes of the pretty woman beside him. Jack had spread his own lies, too. Bad arm or not, he'd grown up the child of a cop and a son of the South. He'd known guns since he could walk, just as he'd known hunters and hunting and all the creatures of the wild. And that was the biggest problem of all. Because whatever circumstances led to the shooting of a deer in 1931, it didn't happen the way William Boyd said. A bullet to the heart, yes, that much Jack believed. But nothing else Boyd said could be true. The great head on his wall rode a neck as thick as a grizzly's and carried antlers so broad and gleaming, they were like nothing Jack had ever seen. And that alone put the lie in Boyd's story, for nothing so magnificent had ever been shot in Illinois or Wisconsin or in any other place else on God's earth that Jack could imagine.

Deer like that were not supposed to exist.

CHAPTER SIX

William Boyd stood on the porch and watched the car fall away. It crossed the creek, crested the second hill and was gone. Even then, he stood for long minutes and held himself with care.

If he saw Martha, he'd hit her.

He was that angry.

Replaying the visit in his mind, he grew convinced that he'd hidden the worry and the rage. If the lawyers had seen them they'd wonder at their cause, and wonder led to questions. William Boyd disliked questions. If forced to answer them, he'd prefer to do so in New York or Washington, not on the bitter edge of some pissant town. Beyond that simple concealment, he'd also developed a decent idea of the types of people he would be forced to deal with. Jack Cross was as he'd expected: intelligent, devoted to his friend, depressingly earnest. Leslie, too, failed to surprise. She was a player, and for a moment he considered it—the tight skirt, the blond hair.

"Martha!"

She was close. He could smell the perfume.

"Yes."

Turning, he found her in the open door. "Walk with me." He pushed past her, and she trailed behind. At the door to his private study, he stopped. "What have I told you about this room?"

"No one is to go inside without your express permission."

"And yet?"

"It was an accident, Mr. Boyd. I went looking for you. I didn't think—"

"Need I lock doors in my own home?"

"No, sir, of course not."

"Visitors are to be instructed. Am I clear? Tell them where to wait, and make sure they do so."

"Yes, sir."

"Where is Mr. Kirkpatrick?"

"He was in the gym earlier. I believe he's returned to his room."

"Find out if he's showered and dressed. If so, ask him to join me in the study."

"Do you mean—?"

"Yes, this study. Go on, now."

She left, and Boyd poured another drink at the sideboard. Sitting at the desk, he sipped thirty-year scotch and replayed what he knew of James Kirkpatrick, a coal-country billionaire grown rough working the mountains and coves of West Virginia. He liked to fight and hunt and make money, and because of that Boyd actually liked the man. But that's not why he was here. Kirkpatrick was looking for the right place to park two hundred million dollars, and William Boyd wanted the account. That took work and convincing. They'd hunted buffalo in Africa, tiger on the subcontinent. They'd been drunk and shared secrets and chased girls fresh out of college.

Now they were here.

Boyd swirled liquor in the glass, and did the math in his head: 2 percent management fee plus 20 percent of any profits.

"Definitely worth the risk."

"Are you talking about me?"

"Jesus, James." Boyd rose and let a smile touch his face. "How does someone as big as you get to be so damn quiet?"

"That doesn't answer my question."

Kirkpatrick crossed the room. He was fifty-five and stood six-three, his shoulders heavy and broad, his hands scarred over wrists as wide as other men's ankles. Gray bristles covered his head and cheeks, so that his eyes, in the center, seemed brighter than they otherwise might. Boyd waited until he sat, then went to the sideboard, poured another scotch, and handed it over. "I was talking about the hunt."

"Are you worried?"

"Not really."

"What's his name again?"

"Johnny Merrimon. We'll handle him."

"The last time you took a client near Johnny Merrimon, he shot up your camp and damn near killed you."

"It's worth the risk. Cheers."

They clinked glasses, and Boyd sat. They were friends in a loose sense, but Kirkpatrick understood the dance. "How's the market?"

"I don't follow the markets when I hunt. I have people for that."

Kirkpatrick grunted because he felt the same way. Hire well. Delegate. He waited a long minute, then spoke without actually looking at the giant deer head on the wall. "So that's it?"

"It is."

"Six months, William. That's how long you've made me wait."

Boyd shrugged. "I only show it to a special few."

"May I?"

"It's why we're here."

Kirkpatrick put down his glass and they crossed the room, Kirkpatrick in front. He moved steadily, but Boyd sensed the disbelief. He'd brought two potential clients to this place. All of them had the same reaction.

"May I touch it?"

"Gently," Boyd said. "It's very old."

The big hand reached out, fingers on coarse fur at the base of the animal's neck. "All this time. I thought you were lying, exaggerating." His voice thickened. "Jesus. I've never seen anything like this. Never heard of it." He turned finally. "Your grandfather shot this here?"

"It's a special place."

"Are there others like it?"

"I thought you'd never ask."

Boyd led Kirkpatrick through an arched doorway into a second room at the rear of the study. There was a bookshelf, two chairs, a leather sofa. Photographs and maps covered two walls. On a third hung the largest bear hide Kirkpatrick had ever seen. "What in the name of God . . ."

"I took that bear the same day the Merrimon kid shot up my camp."

"It's not possible. This is . . . It's . . . This is enormous."

Boyd didn't share the rest of the story: that they'd actually killed two bear that day, and that the second hide hung proudly on a wall of his newest client's. "Remarkable, isn't it?"

" 'Remarkable'? My God, man. This . . ." Kirkpatrick spread his palms as if to capture some intangible thing. "This is inexplicable. It's extraordinary. These animals. How do you explain it?"

"I can't."

"What about your grandfather?"

"That's him." Boyd lifted a framed newspaper clipping from the wall and showed it to Kirkpatrick. The headline read: LOST BOY RETURNED TO MOTHER. Beneath it was a photograph, and in it, the boy was black-eyed and gaunt, with bandaged hands and dark splotches on his cheeks. Behind him, snow drifted against an unpainted shack. His mother, beside him, was unsmiling.

Kirkpatrick pointed at the boy's face. "Is that frostbite?"

"They say it was the coldest winter in a hundred years."

"And the deer?"

"My grandfather was lost in the swamp for three days. When they found him, the deer was dead at his feet, the gun frozen to a tree beside him."

Kirkpatrick tilted the picture, leaned closer. "What happened to him?"

Boyd shrugged. "He went hunting with two friends. The friends came home after a day and a night. My grandfather didn't. It took a hundred people two days to find him."

"Tell me the story."

Boyd smiled. "The story is for clients."

"So, it's like that?"

Boyd shrugged, and did not apologize. "My grandfather never spoke of what happened in the swamp. After they found him, he barely spoke at all: a word here or there, a little more when he finally married." From the bookshelf, Boyd removed a leather journal that was old and stained and battered. He took a chair and Kirkpatrick took the other. "This is his journal."

"Written after the swamp?"

"Yes."

"May I see it?"

"I want a decision first."

"Two hundred million is a lot of money."

"Investments, hunting, the journal. Life matters, my friend, as do the people with whom we share it."

Kirkpatrick studied Boyd's face, then the newspaper clipping. The frame was mahogany, the glass polished. There was something about the boy, the starkness of the old photograph. "His hair is white."

"I know."

"Why?"

"Something to do with what happened in the swamp. That's how it was when they found him."

Kirkpatrick drummed his fingers; stared at the journal on the arm of Boyd's chair. "How many others know the story?"

"Other than me, you would be the third."

"The other two?"

"Clients now. You'd like them."

Kirkpatrick rose from the chair and walked along the photographs that covered two walls. Old and faded, they showed the white-haired boy at different ages. A teenager. A young man. In one, he leaned on a plow behind a mule. In another, he stood beside a plain-faced girl in a flower-print dress. She was smiling; he wasn't. In all the pictures, he remained thin and unhappy. He never filled out; the eyes never changed. The most recent photograph showed him in the uniform of an army private. A date scratched in the corner said the picture was taken in March of 1942.

"My grandfather died on Omaha Beach; never got off the sand. This was in his pocket when it happened." Boyd pressed a palm on the journal. "He wrote about the swamp the night before they stormed the beach. It's almost as if he knew."

"What? That he would die?"

"I think he wanted the story known, at least to his wife."

"The battlefield confession of a traumatized halfmute. Hardly the most convincing document."

"Yet the pages speak for themselves."

Boyd placed the journal on a small table, and Kirkpatrick stopped pacing. "Two hundred million dollars?"

"It's a fair start."

Kirkpatrick sat, and the stare between them held. Big men. Big money. The outcome, though, had never been in doubt, not in this room in this place, not with a dead man's journal bloodstained and closed tight on the table beside them.

"It better be a damn good story."

CHAPTER SEVEN

1931
A Lord of the Forest

Like many boys in that bitter time, Randolph Boyd knew cold and hunger better than he should. The old folks blamed the economy or the Great War or what people still called the Crash of '29, but none of that meant a thing to Randolph or his two best friends or any other county boys whose houses seemed emptier than most. Course, there were plenty of boys without fathers—that was the thing about war—but it was harder for Randolph than it was for Charlie down the road, whose father won a medal before he died, or for Herbert, whose father took a bullet clean while fighting with the French at the Somme. Randolph's father came home alive, but it was still the war that killed him. A German bullet took half his face in October of 1918, three weeks before it all ended and other fathers came home without their jaws shot off and hurt so deep in the marrow, no kind of love could touch it.

But that's how it was for Randolph's father. The pretty wife couldn't make a difference, nor could the parents, proud but wounded. Not even the son too young and innocent to recognize the horror of his father's face could smile bright enough to lift the shadows from those haunted eyes. According to Herbert, who'd heard it from his mother, the homecoming lasted three months before the rifle came out from under the bed that husband and wife tried so hard to use as it had once been used. *But what woman could kiss a face like that?* That had come from Herbert's mother, too, whispered in the dark of a sleepover when she thought the boys long since down for the night. Randolph was nine when she'd said it, and even now, five years later, it hurt to think that the ultimate failing had belonged to his mother, an uncomplaining woman who'd chopped wood and carried ice until her face was as sunken as any warship torpedoed in that horrible war. Looking at her now, Randolph thought: *She's only thirty-one.* But she looked half-dead in the gray light by the cold stove, her hands bony and thin as she crinkled paper and fed kindling and tried to light a match without shaking.

"Let me do it."

Randolph took the matches and lit the paper. The old clock on the mantel said it was 4:55 in the morning. Outside, a hard snow ticked on the glass window.

"I'll make breakfast for you before you go."

His mother pushed herself up and clanked around in the empty cupboards. She'd said *breakfast* but meant flour and lard and the last scrapings of bacon grease.

"They'll be here any second," Randolph said.

"Well, they're not here yet."

She ignored the impatience etched on the boy's face, and he peered once more through the window before sitting at the small table set with two-tined forks and scratched metal plates. His father's chair was long removed, so it was just the two chairs now. Against his mother's was propped the same Springfield rifle his father had fought with in the war, and used twelve years ago to take apart the rest of his skull. Randolph could shoot it better than most. He'd won competitions at the county fair and, two years ago, brought home a thirty-pound turkey after outshooting the mayor himself. He'd handled the rifle since he was seven, and broke it down one more time to check the action. Metallic sounds rang in the kitchen, and the smell of gun oil rose. Working the bolt a final time, he fed in the last five bullets he owned and put the gun against the wall, looking at his mother as he did so. A year ago she'd have told him to work on the rifle someplace else, but cold air and hunger weighed her down.

She was starving, Randolph thought.

They both were.

"Here you go, son." She spooned mush onto the plate. "Eat it while it's hot."

"You're not having any?"

"Not really hungry."

The smile that cracked her face was as worn and forced as anything Randolph had ever seen. He looked at her eyes instead. There was life there, and love. What sat on his plate was the last food in the house. "Eat a little bit," he said. "Just so I don't worry."

"Okay, baby. Maybe a little."

She sat beside him, and they ate from the same plate. The mush was black in places, but that was the good part, the burnt grease. Leaving the last black bite on the plate, Randolph pushed it across the table. "I'm full," he said, and stood before she could argue.

"Is it time?" she asked.

"Don't you hear it?"

"What?"

"The squeak in Herbert's left boot."

"You can really hear that? I don't . . ." She stopped when she saw the smile on his face. "You're funning me."

"Just a little." He lifted the rifle and kissed her cheek. "I'll meet them at the end of the drive. You eat that last bit." He pointed at the burnt mush, and saw that she was crying. "I'll be fine," he said. "Herbert and Charlie will be with me. We have guns."

"You know what they say about that place."

Her eyes glistened in the dim light, and in the silence behind her words, the snow ticked harder on the glass. "Those colored folks are nice enough, Momma. I don't think they'd hurt us."

"I'm not talking about the colored folks, and you know it."

"We need food."

"I know we do. But do you have to hunt there?"

She sat straighter, and some of the old steel showed. Randolph wanted to give her a better answer, but they both knew the truth. "County's hunted out," he said. "Even the rabbits are getting scarce, and you know what they say about rabbits." He thought the joke might lift another smile, or that she'd scold him for teenage impertinence. But she was too hungry for that, and too afraid. "It's not just us," he said. "We have to think of others, too."

He meant Charlie and Herbert, old friends with families equally starved. It was the same across most of the county—joblessness and poverty, the bitter winter that refused to end.

"People have gone lost in that swamp," she said. "Some have come back half-mad and ruined, and those that weren't are still frightened of shadows and filled with crazy stories."

"I know," he said. "But that won't be me."

"Promise me you'll be careful."

"I will."

She took one of his hands with both of hers. Even with the fire and cooking, her skin was cold. "Stay clear of the coloreds," she said. "Watch for thin ice."

"Everything's frozen solid. There is no thin ice."

He thought the logic would help, but fresh tears glittered in the seams of her face. "Charlie gets lost," she reminded him. "He gets turned around and confused, and Herbert can't shoot straight, so you stay behind him or well off to the side."

"I know. I'll take care of them."

"One more thing." She reached into an apron pocket and pressed a brass lighter into his hand. "It was your daddy's from the war, and I know he valued it." She smoothed her son's jacket, pulled it tight across his chest. "I filled it in town last week, thinking maybe it was time you have it. He was a good man, your father. But for the war and what it did to him, he'd have never left us like this. I want you to believe me when I say that. Can you do that for me? Can you trust me when I say it's true? That he was a good man?"

Randolph studied the metal cylinder in his hand. It was newly polished, but scratched and dented and old. He had vague memories of the lighter, or maybe they were memories of a dream he'd once had. Whatever the case, he could picture his father near the end, how he'd sit before the fire with the lighter in one hand and a knitted scarf drawn across the ruin of his face. He'd turn the lighter in long fingers and watch firelight in the metal. He'd prized it more likely than not—Randolph thought his mother was right about that—but whatever places those flickers took the old man—whatever memories they conjured—none of it stopped him from kneeling on a rock by the creek and blowing off the crown of his skull.

In the yard, Randolph rolled his collar against the snow, then walked to the drive and looked back at the house. Small and unpainted, it was the same color as the snow and sludge, the old barn and frozen metal. Wind took smoke as it left the chimney, and Randolph raised a hand to his mother, who was small behind the frosted glass. She waved in return, and he watched her through the snow, feeling it settle on his shoulders, the brim of his hat. Two months' wind had piled drifts against the house, and against the old car, rusted solid. Randolph lifted his hand higher, then made for the road, knowing that if he lingered, his mother would stay by the glass until the fire burned out and the kitchen went cold.

Tucking his chin into a scarf, Randolph moved quietly through the snow. A pack rode his back, and in it was a tarp and blankets and sheets of waxed canvas to wrap chunks of meat and keep the blood from dripping. The rifle weighed on his left shoulder, muzzle down to keep out the snow. At the road's edge, he looked back a final time, but the house had faded into the fuzz of winter, and that was just as well. Herbert and Charlie were waiting, and the picture was all kinds of wrong.

"That's it?" Randolph said. "That's all you've got?"

He pointed at Charlie, who was a small boy, and easily offended. In his father's waxed jacket, he looked even smaller, a quick-thinking but careless boy with a narrow face and dull brown eyes. "I can make it work," he said. "You know I can."

"Give it to me."

Randolph took the boy's rifle, looked it up and down, and handed it back in disgust. "It's the .22. You brought a peashooter."

"You don't think I know that? Jeez."

"What are you planning to kill with it, a squirrel?"

Charlie slung the rifle, but didn't back down. "Dad sleeps with the carbine by his bed. You know how his eyes pop open at the slightest noise. He'll be mad enough I took his jacket and his canteen. If he'd caught me light-fingered on his favorite gun, he'd have belted me black and blue, and then where would you be?"

The boy was right. Jax Carter was known for his temper, and had once beaten a man half to death over a jostled coffee, and that was outside the Baptist church on a Sunday morning. The borrowed jacket would cause Charlie problems. The gun might have gotten him killed.

"Besides," Charlie said. "Look at this poor bastard."

He pointed at Herbert, who carried a canteen, a near-empty pack, and nothing else.

"What about it?" Randolph said. "Where's the twelve gauge?"

Herbert stayed cool in the heat of Randolph's obvious frustration. Randolph was older, but they were the same size, and dead even in a fight. Over the years, they'd dusted up once or twice, but at the bottom of things were almost brothers. They'd been born two weeks apart in the same hospital, had the same steady hands and blue eyes and heavy-boned limbs. Randolph was stronger maybe, but Herbert was smarter, and everybody knew it. Teachers. Parents. It was the way he studied the world, the calm voice and level gaze. "No shells," he said. "No point in bringing a gun with no shells."

Randolph couldn't argue with that. Shotgun shells were scarce as money, and those who had extra traded them like gold coins. He'd seen one shell buy wool mittens, a tub of butter, and a pair of used spectacles. Without shells you couldn't hunt, and without hunting it was hard to eat. Randolph himself was down to five cartridges for the Springfield, and after they were used up, he didn't know what he'd do. At night he prayed for springtime and summer crops and some kind of job. He could write and do his numbers and was as strong as any grown man in twenty miles. But jobs were like shotgun shells and rabbits and candy bars.

Charlie stomped his feet in the snow. "Are we really doing this?"

Randolph glanced at the house, hoping that his mother was too far away to see the .22, the missing scattergun. She would worry if she saw, but it was too late to call anything off. He raised his shoulders; spoke plain. "Everything else is hunted bare."

"That may be true, but Willis Dred and his son still went missing in that damn swamp. There's still those boys, sitting in the windows at the crazy house and drooling down their shirts."

Randolph understood everything Charlie said. People had gone missing, yes, and people came back changed. In town, they talked about the colored folks and the deep pools and the mud like quicksand. Slaves had been hanged in those woods eighty years back, and there were some who thought angry spirits haunted the swamp from one side of it to the other. Why else did Willis Dred and his boy go missing? Why else did the Miller boys go in for five days, then come out speechless and drooling? Everybody had a theory, but the truth was that nobody knew the truth at all. Maybe there were deer in the swamp and maybe not, maybe Willis Dred killed himself in despair and took his son with him, maybe those Miller boys were already crazy and just looking for an excuse to show the world. Randolph had thought about it long and hard, and found those explanations as likely as any others. People were superstitious and stupid. Besides, there was a simpler truth.

"My mother's liable to be dead in another month, and Herbert's folks are the same. How 'bout you, Charlie? How's your momma? Fat and happy feasting on ham biscuits?" The stare held, then broke in Randolph's favor. He rolled his shoulders, adjusted the rifle. "We don't have a choice, not one of us."

The walk out seemed farther in the snow. It dragged at their feet, muffled sound. Fence lines were barely visible, as were the last three houses, as dim and gray as the one they'd left behind. All three boys lived in the northern neck of the county, on the final bit of decent dirt before the road ended and the swamp spread out to push against the distant hills. It was the poor part of the county, and only those who lived in it understood the reasons for any kind of pride. To folks in town, they were hardscrabble and ignorant. The coloreds, the poor whites—it was all the same to those who had fathers and cars and warm houses. Randolph understood his place in the scheme of things, but like others brought by choice or circumstance to the northern wilds of Raven County, he took pride in his place and in the people who shared it. They were rough and uncomplaining, and considered the town folk soft, what with their electricity and iceboxes and store-bought meat. If jealousy informed part of Randolph's character, he chose to ignore it. He had friends, his mother. Besides, people in town were hungry, too. That was the great equalizer.

This terrible thing.

Whatever it was that ruined the whole damn country.

That brutal truth was hard to miss, even so far out. Great fortunes had failed; men in northern cities had leapt from high windows. For a long time it was just talk, but after that came misery, as if waves had rolled out from New York and drowned all the good in the land. Money disappeared. Storefronts closed. A few in town remained flush, but lines were blurring, and to Randolph that was fine. Let *them* sleep in the frost and wake to burnt mush.

For a moment, the emotion warmed him, and he realized that—yeah—maybe he was jealous. He was only fourteen but had lost two adult teeth. *Scurvy,* they called it, which was just a fancy word for "starving." The thought weighed him down for long minutes, but faded when they reached the end of the road. Ahead was the track that led to Hush Arbor, where freed slaves and their descendants had lived since 1853. Randolph had seen it once when his mother went there to trade needles and thread for honey and extra seeds. Those who lived there spoke in a way that was hard to understand. They lived in a cluster of unpainted shacks, but had gardens, a church, a smokehouse. They'd been open enough, but those were better days, the time *before.* Trust was rare now, and lately—on the few times he'd seen coloreds on the road or in the woods that bordered the swamp—they'd stayed distant and watched with lowered lids. Randolph understood that, too. Take care of your own. Stay tight. He felt it now with Charlie and Herbert.

"How should we do this?"

Charlie asked the question on each boy's mind. The track led to Hush Arbor, and no one who lived there would take kindly to white boys hunting the swamp. To the east was the river. They could turn right, cut through two miles of woods, and follow it north. Eventually, though, it would turn back to Hush Arbor. Randolph looked that way, then turned left. To the west lay the ruins of the Merrimon Plantation. The house had burned in 1854, but the foundation stones were plain, as was the well, the fallen barn, the shadowed outlines where slave quarters had once stood. It was the longer route into the deep swamp, but when Randolph started walking, the other boys fell in beside him. Another mile took them past the ruins, and Randolph led them through fields to the woods' edge, then north. They followed the tree line for another three miles, and when the last hill trended down, Randolph felt hard, slick ice beneath the snow. It was the low ground, the bitter edge of the swamp that covered more than fifty square miles. Beyond it and east was the river and more open ground. To the north was nothing but forest and stone and wind.

"I'm freezing."

Randolph looked left, and frowned. There was a whine in Charlie's voice that put his teeth on edge. "It's winter," Randolph said. "Winter is cold."

"Naw, man, it's more than that. Just looking in there is making my balls pull up."

He meant the place where forest met swamp, and the boys stared long into it. The trees were bare and gray, the snow between them drifted so that ice, in places, made dull black streaks on the forest floor. This was the edge of the swamp, and still civilized. Farther in, the brush thickened until, at times, it made solid walls of thorn and vine. In warmer months, the firm ground disappeared, the mud and still water forming a maze so twisted, most any man alive could get lost. The boys had poked their heads in over the years: a little fishing, plinking at squirrels. Those had been brief flirtations—a dance around the edge—and the swamp had danced back. They'd seen bobcats and coral snakes, a bear once, glimpsed through the brambles. That had been the purpose, the whole point; but this felt different. They weren't here for the thrills or escape. They were as desperate as boys could be, the swamp so vast, stark, and empty, it made each of them feel small by comparison. Randolph studied each boy's face in turn. Charlie was clearly frightened, all his normal bluster scrubbed away as he shifted foot to foot and used a crusted glove to wipe his running nose. Herbert looked steady, his gaze resolved if not filled with the usual faith. "Herbert?"

Randolph put the question to his friend because he didn't want to be the only one responsible. Snow was falling more heavily, the temperature dropping as they stood. After three hours' walking, they were already half-frozen, and Randolph knew it could get worse. Wind was picking up, and the swamp loomed like a bad story. Randolph thought of missing men and boys struck dumb, a weight of questions, suddenly real. But if Herbert felt the same sense of reckoning, he declined to show anything but the easy smile for which he was known. He tilted his face to the snow and let it land on his cheeks. "Fine day for a walk," he said; and that was it. Randolph nodded once, and stepped under the trees. A moment later his friends followed.

By two o'clock, worry wrapped them like a frozen blanket. They'd found no life, no signs of life. Other than the wind and the sound of their own steps, the swamp was as quiet as a grave.

"It's not natural." Charlie said the same thing for the fifth time. "We should have seen something by now."

His words sank into the snow, and nobody answered. By Randolph's best guess, they were three miles into the swamp, maybe seven miles from home as the crow flew. They'd covered more ground than that, though, crisscrossing north and south, bending through the silent swamp in search of a sign. They should have seen something by then. Charlie was right. Even in the hunted-out parts of the county, they'd have seen some sort of tracks or droppings.

"There's not a goddamn thing."

"Button it, Charlie."

But staying quiet was not Charlie's strong suit. Every few minutes, the words came tripping out.

Mother . . .

Shit.

Not a damn thing . . .

Randolph didn't worry until the words actually stopped. Ten minutes into the silence, he finally looked back. "Where is Charlie?"

Herbert stood still, two feet away. Behind them, trees closed as if to shut out the light, and only then did Randolph realize how late it was.

Almost dark.

How did he miss it?

"Herbert?" A glaze covered Herbert's eyes. His lips were blue and parted. Ice hung from bits of hair where they showed beneath his hat. Randolph squeezed his arm, but Herbert only blinked. "Jesus. Stay here. Don't move. I mean it."

Randolph looked back after twenty feet, unwilling to admit the unease he suddenly felt. Charlie was missing. Herbert wasn't right. On top of that, the gray light was thickening to blue. It should be four o'clock, tops, but this felt like six, like light remained only because the snow held it.

"Charlie!"

He called out as he followed their tracks back through the snow. Nothing looked familiar. The trees were broader and denser and blacker. Snow had filled their tracks—though not completely—and the prints were black, too. There was no sound but his breath and the hush of snow.

He found Charlie after a quarter mile. He stood beneath a leaning oak, both arms at his sides and his mouth hanging slack. Snow mounded his shoulders and hat, and like Herbert, he was staring at nothing.

"Charlie, Jesus." Randolph stopped beside his friend, but Charlie only blinked. Randolph followed the stare; saw trees and shadows and falling snow. His rifle was frozen against a log at his feet. Randolph bent to break it free, and felt cold steel through his gloves. "What are you doing, man? Come on."

His friend blinked as if he'd been lost in some far place. His voice came, small. "I'm dying."

"No, you're not."

"I'm freezing, Randolph. I can't feel my legs."

Charlie's speech was slow and slurred. Randolph guessed it's 'cause his lips were frozen, too. He pushed the rifle at his friend's chest. "Just stay close, all right. I'll take care of you."

"I really can't move."

"Yes, you can. Come on."

Randolph dragged his friend into motion. He stumbled at first, but Randolph caught him, and after that he seemed better. He was talking to himself again, the lips as blue as ice, but moving. Randolph stayed close as they trudged along the broken trail. Charlie fell twice, and when he got up ran a frozen glove across his eyes. It was almost full night when they reached Herbert, who was sitting in the snow with his back against a tree. "Get up. You'll freeze." Herbert didn't move. Charlie settled to his knees five feet away. "Shit."

Randolph knew nothing for sure except they'd *all* freeze if he didn't get a fire going. He'd planned to do it an hour before sunset: get the tarp up, build the fire. In five minutes, it'd be too dark to see his hands in front of his face.

Two hours.

That's what he'd lost.

"Stay here, the both of you."

Working fast, Randolph gathered as much dead wood as he could find. It was slick with snow, but not rotten. Birch trees grew thick in the swamp, and he stripped off bark in sheets, piling it by his pack and covering it as he crashed through the brush and picked up more wood. He didn't need much at first, just enough to get it started, enough to see. Kicking at snow, he drove his boot down to bare earth and scraped an area large enough for a fire. Neither friend looked at him or offered to help. Charlie was shaking where he sat.

Randolph fumbled at his pocket, but his fingers were thick and slow. The glove came off in his teeth, and he tried again, working heavy buttons until he got the pocket open. Inside were matches and a fire starter he'd made from wood shavings, kerosene, and candle scrapings. A ball the size of a peach, it lit quickly and burned hot, with lots of black smoke and spurts of blue. Randolph fed bark into the flames, then added twigs and bits of thicker wood. The wood sizzled and spit, but eventually dried enough to burn well. He added more, cupping his hands over the heat. When the fire was strong enough, he strung the tarp from tree trunks, giving them a space out of the falling snow. That done, he scraped away more snow, put down blankets, and got his friends closer to the flames. They could barely move; neither spoke. "I'll be right back."

Leaving the warmth, Randolph pushed into the gloom and gathered more wood. It took a long time, but he wanted a big fire, and needed enough wood to last the night. When it was done, he could barely move. The mercury was still falling. Ten degrees, he guessed. Maybe less.

"Please, no wind."

That part worked in his favor. Snow fell heavily, but straight down. Clumps of it dropped from the tarp and high branches, landing like whispers in the darkness around them.

Randolph pushed close to the fire, holding out his hands and watching his friends in the dancing light. They looked better, with color in their lips, and eyes that weren't so blank and staring. It was Herbert who spoke first. "That was strange."

"What?"

Randolph wanted more, but Herbert shook his head. Charlie glanced up, but looked away fast. He pulled off his gloves and stretched his fingers toward the fire.

"Charlie?"

"I'm freezing is all, and that's all I know."

There was a lie in there somewhere. Randolph heard it in his voice; saw it in the flick of his eyes. "That's it? That's all you've got?"

Herbert said, "The cold, I guess."

And Charlie agreed too fast. "Yeah," he said. "The cold."

Randolph stared out past the fire. Full dark had come to the swamp, and he thought about how close it had been. They could have been caught out, separated and lost. He'd spent a hundred nights in the woods, a hundred nights in all kinds of seasons. Randolph Boyd didn't get caught out. Neither did Herbert or Charlie.

Did we really lose two hours?

"Anybody hungry?"

Herbert asked the question, and Randolph saw Charlie start. Everyone was hungry, and Randolph knew that every pack was as empty as his. Blankets and waxed canvas—he'd checked. They'd hoped to be eating venison by now, with grease on their faces and every belly full. "Don't joke, okay. I've seen the inside of your pack."

Herbert reached inside his jacket and removed a sheath of jerky wrapped in weeks-old butcher's paper. "From my mom," he said. "The last of it."

Randolph's mouth flooded with saliva. He'd not had meat in three weeks. "Are you sure?"

Herbert took a piece of jerky and passed the package. There was not much, but it was hard and salted, and it was meat. The boys ate in silence. Blankets steamed as frozen earth melted beneath them.

"Tomorrow," Charlie said. "We'll kill something tomorrow."

No one had the will to reply.

Snowfall thickened beyond the fire.

The morning broke cold but clear, and Randolph was up before anyone else. He stood by the fire and watched light filter through the trees. Best he could tell, they were on a spit of land with frozen swamp on three sides. There was a feeling of emptiness beyond the trees, a quiet and simple vastness. Snow had fallen most of the night, and it lay deeply around the camp.

Randolph added wood to the fire, then wrapped a blanket around his shoulders and threaded between the trees until he reached the edge of a great, flat plain that he knew was frozen water buried beneath the snow. Pools of deep water dotted the swamp in places, and this was one of them, a half mile at its widest, with snow shaded at the far edge and a cool, pale yellow where the early sun touched it. He looked for tracks in the light, but the skin of snow was unbroken. It was so still, he heard air in his throat; so cold, the breath plumed.

When he woke his friends, no one spoke of lost time or hard questions. The jerky was gone and it was a long day and they were already hungry. Packing the camp in silence, Randolph kicked snow on the fire and checked the rifle from long habit. Everyone understood the same truth: They had to find meat today. Otherwise, they'd starve or freeze or go home empty-handed.

"Ready?"

Herbert nodded, and the boys fell into the same order as before: Randolph in front, then Herbert, then Charlie. That meant Randolph had to work the hardest. Snow rose to his thighs, and breaking the trail was exhausting work. The swamp was his idea, though, and his plan. He led them due east because the heart of the swamp was in that direction.

"What about the Freemantles?" Charlie asked.

Randolph said nothing. He was breathing too hard.

"Come on, man. What about the coloreds?"

"I figure we're north by two miles, and still a good ways west." Randolph gestured vaguely. "If we don't see anything by noon, we'll head farther north. Either way, we'll stay clear."

"That makes for a long trip home," Herbert said.

"There's food here somewhere. There has to be."

They stopped at the edge of the same, flat plain. "You sure it's frozen?" Charlie asked.

"It's frozen."

"How can you know?"

It was a stupid question, so Randolph studied the boy who'd asked it. Charlie looked sunken in his father's coat. His cheekbones were blades under the skin, his lips drawn back as he shook in the cold. Beside him, Herbert looked just as drawn and pale and frightened. "Anybody who wants to turn back, now's the time."

Each boy kept his eyes down, and no one mentioned the day before—how they'd lost each other in the gloom and damn-near frozen—but it was with them all the same: the knowing of it, the feeling of *wrong.*

"Charlie?"

Charlie shook his head.

"Herbert?"

"Talking won't put meat on the table."

"So we hunt," Randolph said. "We get it done."

The moment held, but no one said another word. And when Randolph started walking, the other boys did, too. They moved across the frozen pool and into the woods. An hour later, Charlie was muttering to himself again.

Nothing . . .

A whole bunch of goddamn nothing . . .

By midmorning it looked like Charlie was right. Randolph stumbled again, and knew it was the hunger.

Herbert asked, "How far have we gone?"

"Three miles, maybe four."

But it was hard to know. Every step was a battle. The sun was high, but the temperature hovered in single digits. The snow seemed deeper. Randolph couldn't feel his feet.

"Let me lead."

Herbert had offered before. This time Randolph let him, and though it was agreed, no one moved. The boys bent at the waist. Charlie hung on Herbert's shoulder. "Just take a minute. Everybody take a minute."

Charlie nodded, and tried to drink. The water in his canteen was frozen solid.

"Well, shit."

"A few more hours," Randolph said. "We'll find something." Charlie nodded again, but around them the stillness was aching in its perfection. "East." Randolph pointed. "We'll go another mile, then make the turn north."

He motioned, and they fell into the new order: Herbert breaking trail, Randolph at the rear.

The day got colder.

Nothing moved.

A hundred yards later Charlie said, "Do you feel it?" The words were light, a scrape. "That weight. Do you feel it?"

"It's nothing," Randolph said; but he felt it, too. It had been building all day, slow at first, and now unmistakable. Everything was heavy. The sunlight. The air. They pushed through a deeper drift and moved beneath a wall of trees. A half mile later the day was only heavier. Herbert stumbled and fell. He was slow to rise. The other boys helped him. "It's okay," he said. "I'm okay." But his skin was powder blue, his eyes half-closed where tears had spilled out and frozen. They needed food and a fire. "Does this look right to you?"

His breath rattled as he straightened and tilted his head to better see with the half-shut eyes. Randolph didn't get it, but then he did. All around them trees rose, barren and bent. Not one cast a shadow.

Charlie said, "What the—?"

"Hush for a minute."

"Don't hush me, Randolph. Jesus Christ. What the hell, man?"

His mouth opened again, but Randolph spoke over him. "Just walk, Charlie. All right? Come on. One step at a time. Keep your eyes open."

They pushed on, but every boy felt the difference. There was malice in the air, a sense of movement glimpsed and then gone. Randolph saw it like a haze at the corner of his eye, a gray flicker. But every time he snapped his head right or left, there was nothing but wood and snow and blinding light. They stumbled on, driving through deep snow until sweat sheeted and froze and sheeted again. Charlie talked all the time now, the words too quiet to hear anything but the pace of them. Fast. Unceasing. He was falling like the rest of them, almost running at times. Randolph knew they should slow—that exhaustion would take them—but nameless fear drove them to harder effort. Herbert pushed through another drift. They dropped into a gully, clambered up the other side. And all the while it paced them, this *thing*, this *awareness*. Randolph wasn't the only one who sensed it. Herbert's head was snapping left and right. Charlie's, too. And every minute they seemed to move faster, breathe harder. They broke from the trees and found a windswept clearing, an island in the distance. The snow was shallow on the ice, and in unspoken accord, all three boys broke into a run, holding each other as they stumbled. They felt the same thing; Randolph knew it. Something was out there, and it wanted them gone.

"There," Herbert said. "Trees."

No one argued when he angled for the closest cover. They were naked on the ice, wind-blind in a sudden gust. In the trees, Randolph took the lead. He bent away from the lake, beating through vines and brambles and scrub. He wanted away from the pressure; followed the path of least resistance. A gap here. A low place there. He slid into the shelter of a giant spruce, but pushed out the other side just as fast.

It was out there.

It was coming.

Panic was a nail in his heart. He felt the pressure, the pain. He fell against a tree, and took skin from his face. No one slowed. No one broke ranks. Single file, they ran through woods and snow until suddenly Randolph stopped at a broken trail.

Footprints.

More than a single set.

Randolph made the decision on his own, turning left to follow the tracks. Whatever made them was human, and that meant help maybe, and maybe food. The path was easier, and pressure lifted when he turned onto it. They moved more quickly, fell less. Randolph led his friends between trees and over frozen creeks. At a small clearing he drew up fast and hard. His heart was in his throat. He felt sick. Herbert and Charlie stumbled to a halt beside him, and stared at the same impossible sight.

A dead fire.

An old campsite.

Charlie said, "Is that . . . ?"

He never finished; didn't need to. The truth was plain enough.

It was their fire.

Their campsite.

"But how?"

They'd walked due east for miles. The campsite should be behind them. Hours back. Lost.

"It's not possible." Charlie was shaking in the big coat, his skin as translucent gray as the frozen sweat that hung in his hair. "Randolph?" He wanted an explanation; Randolph didn't have it. "Tell me how this is possible." When Randolph showed his eyes—just as frightened and lost—Charlie shook his head twice, then threw up a gush of thin bile. "No," he said. "This is not possible."

But somehow it was.

A straight line had become a circle.

They spent the rest of the day huddled around a fire so large, it raged. Words were few, and when they came, they died awkwardly and quick. No boy wanted to confront the horror of his own fears. Charlie's stomach continued to clench, though nothing remained to purge. Herbert stared, unceasing, at the fire. His lips moved in silence, and the shapes they made formed the name of his mother, over and over, a prayer or an apology. Randolph didn't know. He played the day in his mind: the walk out, the sun on his face. It seemed innocent, at first.

They were friends.

There was hope.

When did it get so god-awful, seriously scary?

Randolph risked a glance at his friends across the fire. Charlie lay huddled on his side, his knees drawn up beneath the blanket. He was shaking; every muscle bound tight. Herbert stared into the fire, his eyes as restless as his lips. They were terrified, all of them.

The only real conversation had been an argument. Herbert and Charlie had wanted to leave immediately, to turn back to the trail and follow it all the way home.

To what? Randolph had argued. *A starving family? A slow death?*

Better than dying here, they'd said.

Better than freezing.

What no one mentioned was the one truth they could not ignore. They were frozen half to death. No one had the strength. That alone had tipped the argument in Randolph's favor. They would warm themselves, and then decide. It was four o'clock when Herbert finally spoke aloud.

"I'm sorry, Randolph. I'm not staying here."

Charlie struggled up, already nodding. "Amen, brother. Let's get the hell out. Come with us, Randolph." Randolph said nothing. "Please, man. Please don't make me beg."

Randolph pictured his mother in a cold kitchen. She stood at the window, watching a frozen yard. Behind her, every cupboard was bare. "Go ahead," he told them. "I can't."

"Don't be a hero, man." Herbert leaned closer, his elbows on his knees. "You felt it out there, same as us. You feel it out there now."

"I don't know what I feel."

"That's a lie," Charlie said. "You were as white-faced and shit-scared as the rest of us. Whatever that thing is, it's real."

"What *thing*? I don't see any *thing*."

"Lie to yourself, then. That's fine. But people die here. They die or disappear or go insane. It's not a story anymore, it's real: the Dreds, the Miller boys."

"You won't get out before dark."

"Close enough." Herbert rose, and tossed a blanket over his shoulders. "Anything is better than this. Charlie, you coming?"

"Damn straight."

Randolph watched them go, and felt as if his courage were a string that trailed behind them, a line dragged through the snow and drawn, frozen, from his chest. Each step they took pulled out heat and heart, so that by the time they reached the trail's first bend, Randolph wanted to run, calling behind them. But he could not move at all. He watched his friends pause where a sour gum pushed against the trail and turned it south. Charlie raised a gloved hand that glinted with ice and frozen snot, and for an instant there was communion between them, a look from Charlie that said: *Careful, brother, we love you.* At that moment Randolph wanted more than ever to rise and follow, to make them understand or somehow make them stay. He felt it clearly now, this risk of going separate ways. It was adrenaline and pure terror, a need deep inside to shout and say *Yes, I feel it* and *Yes, it's real.* Because whatever the force that tracked them, it gathered unseen in the gloom beneath the trees. It watched and was torn. Follow the two or stay with the one? Hate and indecision filled the air like a keening, barely heard. But it penetrated, deep and sharp, so that Randolph covered his ears and opened his mouth as if to relieve the pressure. He was frozen, terrified, dying. He tried to call out, but the icy glove fell, and his friends, at last, turned south. It was terrible, that hollowness, and for an instant Randolph was simply bereft. But pressure mounted by the second: pain in his head, a piercing.

Randolph rolled into a ball and covered his ears. Embers popped in the fire. A coal landed in the snow and sizzled. He was almost in the fire, but it was cold, so cold. Randolph thought he was keening, too, but knew nothing for sure. Pressure mounted, a wail in his mind as knifelike as wind through a mountain pass. He wanted to die, and that was real: the weight, the utter dread. He kicked out, thrashed in the snow.

And like that, everything broke.

The keening ceased; his head cleared.

Randolph clawed to his knees, and under the damp wool and heavy coat was shaking like a beaten child. Breath was glass in his throat. No strength. His head hung, and he stared at empty woods.

No Charlie or Herbert.

Nothing.

Randolph blinked, and in dull pain a thought came, unbidden: that whatever moved between the trees had made its choice, and the choice was to follow Randolph's friends.

Herbert felt it come at the same moment as Charlie. He stumbled once, looked back, and saw wild fear all over Charlie's face.

"Just go, man, go!"

Charlie flung out an arm as he shouted, and Herbert needed no urging. Fear was a wind at his back, and everything was as clear as water: footprints and black branches, striations in the bark as he crashed between the trees.

"Come on, man!"

Herbert risked a glance and saw the same gray flicker. It paced them from behind and to the right. It was a blur, a trick of light. They were a half mile from the fire, hours from the edge of the swamp. They fell into a creek bed, slipped on ice and frozen mud.

"Do you see it?"

"I don't need to see it."

"What about Randolph?"

"Randolph made his choice. Come on!"

Herbert hauled Charlie up the bank and dragged him through the snow. Five minutes became ten, then fifteen. "It's following us."

"Not following." Charlie gasped out the words. "Herding."

He was right, and Herbert knew it. Whatever it was, it kept them on the trail and moving fast. If they slowed, the pressure mounted. If they drifted, it turned them right or left. After an hour, Charlie said, "I have to stop. I can't . . ."

"Yes, you can."

But he couldn't, not for long. He fell a dozen times as the day died and purple light bled from the trees. Herbert dragged him, and then carried him. Fifty yards, another mile. He fell himself, and the wail that rose on still air robbed the last of his warmth. "What do you want? What?" He shouted, "Tell me what!"

He was bawling and screaming, firing blindly with the .22 until the hammer dropped on an empty chamber. Then he was up, and Charlie was on his shoulders, as loose and lifeless as a murdered dog. Herbert pushed harder, and the light faded. He didn't want to be in the swamp, not in the cold and black, not at night. But daylight ended and stars appeared. He could have dropped his friend—he thought about it—but in the end, he didn't slow. He struck trees and bloodied his face, stumbled on long-frozen feet. And all the while, Charlie was muttering: "It's coming, man. It's coming."

"Shut up."

"I think I see it. . . ."

If he did or not, they never knew for sure. Herbert blasted through a tangle of vine and found open land beneath a prickling of stars.

They were out; they'd made it.

He managed a hundred feet, then dropped to his knees as a final sound welled from the swamp behind them. Not words, he thought, and nothing kind. But it was familiar, like a knife was familiar.

Laughter, Herbert thought.

Whatever it is, it's laughing.

Randolph didn't move for thirty minutes, thinking that if he did, it might sense him and return. The cowardice shamed him, but it was the hunger that made him stir. On his feet, he felt dizzy and near hallucinatory. The sun was less dim, and the day not so bitter. Shadows stretched where none had been before. Turning at a sound, he saw a rabbit as white as the snow and less fearful than any he'd ever seen. It rose on hind legs, sniffing, and Randolph was so stunned by the sight, he could only stare, thinking: *Life! There is life here after all!* By the time he remembered the rifle at his feet, the rabbit had returned to all fours and disappeared under a thicket. Even then, Randolph didn't move. Birds flitted in the trees, and all around him were the tracks of deer and fox and smaller things. Some of the tracks were fresh, and others half-filled with snow.

The effect on Randolph was a weakness beyond that of emptiness and aching ribs. Leaving the fire, he stumbled along the freshest tracks. Deer, he thought, and recent. He touched a print, and it collapsed at the edges. Above him, a squirrel chittered, and Randolph felt superstitious dread so sudden and intense, he shook even harder.

Did some dark magic make this life appear?

Or had something darker concealed it?

In the end he didn't care, and that, too, was because of the hunger. It drove him a mile and then another—and he scraped at his eyes as if cobwebs covered them. Even then, blackness pushed in from the edges. He saw his mother in the kitchen, his father by the fire with half his face shot off. For a long time he felt the fire and was warm; but his father stared, and the light in those eyes was as unforgiving as iron on a winter's night. *Why do you live?* they seemed to say. *Why are you whole when I am this ruined thing?* Randolph wanted to argue, but ice filled his mouth, and his father receded into a long, grim hall, growing smaller until the hall collapsed into a fuzz of white and gray and dull orange light. Randolph blinked, but the fuzz remained. He blinked again, and realized he was facedown in a drift, that his mouth was full of snow and that one eye was frozen shut.

How long?

The sun was a bulge beyond the trees, and somewhere he'd lost a glove, so that skin peeled from his fingers when he pulled the rifle free. He cried as it happened, and snow gusted from the drift, hard pellets against his face. Cradling the ruined hand, Randolph dragged himself to a clearing where a stream spilled from a stone face, and had long ago frozen into a waterfall of dull crystal. It showed dimly in the gloaming, and at the high place from which it descended stood the most splendid animal Randolph had ever seen. Its coat shone, and its antlers rose, magnificent. It stood in profile, and from a single eye looked down with what the boy would swear to be patience. For even as Randolph leveled the rifle with his raw left hand and tried to find the trigger with the numb fingers of his right, the deer stood with the same steadiness Randolph sought at the bottom of a shooter's breath. And when the final instant came—the boy trembling, the deer pinned on iron sights—the animal's brown eye rolled up and closed, and Randolph squeezed the trigger.

The deer fell where it stood.

It folded at the knees, rolled sideways, and tumbled down the wall of ice. For an instant a leg twitched, and then it was dead.

Randolph slogged to its side—amazed—but there was no time to wonder at the size of it. Night was falling. He couldn't feel his hands or feet. Fumbling out a knife, Randolph unzipped the animal's stomach and warmed his hands in its guts until his fingers would bend enough to pull the offal out. Everything inside the cavity was massive, too. Stomach. Intestines. A heart the size of his head. With the carcass stripped, he cut a chunk from the liver and ate it raw. Blood smeared his face and ran onto his clothes, but it didn't matter. The meat was hot and salty with blood, and by the time the madness of his hunger passed, it was full dark. Randolph built a fire, and made it large. There was movement in the forest, and it frightened him. Eyes caught the light and threw it back. They moved, circling, then winked out at once; and in their absence a pressure grew.

"No, no, no."

Randolph seized the rifle; pressed his back against the still-warm carcass.

He was not alone in the clearing.

Not even close.

CHAPTER EIGHT

By the time William Boyd finished the story, his guest was sitting fully erect with both hands on his knees and the drink, untouched, beside him. He was a restless man, and Boyd found the stillness gratifying, a hunter's stillness.

"That can't be true," Kirkpatrick said.

"I filled in some color, yes, but otherwise relayed the story as it's written."

"What about the rest of it? What about the end?"

"See for yourself."

Boyd handed over the journal, and Kirkpatrick riffled the pages, moving quickly to the back. He spread the leather covers, ran his fingers down the spine. "Pages have been removed."

"Torn out," Boyd said. "Sometime before the journal came into my possession."

Kirkpatrick inspected the journal more closely. The handwriting was crude, the pages rippled and stained. Randolph Boyd's name was inscribed inside the front cover, along with the words *June 5, 1944, 29th Infantry Division, at sea*. "Fiction," he said. "Drunken ramblings."

"His friends were known to tell a similar story. No one believed them, of course."

"Because they were children, and frightened and half-starved."

"Yet some things remain incontrovertible," Boyd said. "My grandfather *was* found, white-haired, beside a frozen stream; the deer, in all its glory, *was* dead beside him. Those are facts, my friend, and undeniable."

Boyd gestured through the arched door, and both men walked to stand beneath the dusty remains of the once-magnificent creature. The eyes were glass, but the remainder was as it must have been on that frozen day in 1931: the dense coat and massive neck, the antlers thick as a man's arm and six feet from tip to tip. Boyd gave his guest time because he knew exactly what the big man was feeling: excitement and distrust, but above all the need to discover and see, and hopefully kill something equally grand. In the end, he had no choice but to accept.

"Tomorrow, then?"

"Not quite," Boyd said. "There are papers to sign, funds to wire. You may want to consult with your lawyers."

"But after that we hunt?"

"The day after tomorrow, yes." Boyd offered his guest the untouched drink. "Bright and early, we hunt."

CHAPTER NINE

After his meeting with Leslie, Johnny spent the rest of the day alone. He gathered more wood, did some work on the cabin, and went to bed with little appetite. From the top of the tree, he watched the heavens open like a flower. The moon settled, disappeared; and the stars emerged in infinite glory. He watched them long enough to feel the earth spin, and when he closed his eyes, it was all about the sound of wind. It moved over stone and through the trees, licked off the water and carried its smell. This was the Hush, and it was his, and he didn't worry about the how of it or the why. He felt it like tissue and bone, like blood in his veins. Drift long enough, and it was hard to tell where he ended and the Hush began.

If there was a price, it came in dreams.

The first time Johnny woke, the dream followed him up, and it was the same dream he'd had a hundred times. He was on horseback beneath a tree, and a fire burned in the darkness beyond the branches. The ground was bare dirt beaten flat. The other white men were gone. Only the slaves remained, and they wept beneath men who swung dead at the end of thick ropes, their bodies beaten and cut and mud-stained and bloody. From his place on the horse, Johnny watched the women and children, the men ashamed of their fear. He felt the heat of all those hot, slick bodies—ninety-seven slaves—and when they looked at the girl, their fear was so keen, it rose to religious awe. She was tiny, the girl, seventeen or eighteen, black-skinned and fierce and less than a hundred pounds. She spread her arms, and the slaves stumbled left and right, crowding at last beneath the dead men and the branch from which they hung. For long seconds, she stared them down, the fire orange on her skin, the black eyes unforgiving. She spread her arms as if to hold the moment, then turned at last to Johnny and grinned as if she owned him, too.

Her hands and face were bloody.

So was the knife in her hand.

The dream had come slowly at first, then more often: the same men on the same ropes, the fierceness and fear and the small, dark feet. What disturbed Johnny most was how vividly he saw the tree.

Slaves had died there.

That was real.

When Johnny slept again, it was in the last, black hours before the dawn. He woke later to a still-dark forest and an edge of sun. He wanted to visit the old settlement; see the ancient tree. It rose from the same earth, and though it was lightning-struck and half-broken, the hanging branch still stretched over dirt where nothing green ever grew. When Johnny dreamed of it, it was often like this. He woke thinking, *maybe*. Maybe if he touched the tree, the bare earth, or if he knelt by the small stones where the hanged slaves had been buried in that brutal, hot summer of 1853.

He had so many questions.

Leaving the hammock, Johnny bathed in a creek, then put on clean clothes and ate breakfast. At the old settlement he stopped in the clearing because that's where the sense of Hush Arbor lingered most. He'd counted the shacks once, finding the ruins of eighteen. Beyond the last of them, the clearing pinched out and a trail led to a cemetery in a second clearing, deep in the trees. The wall around it was old stone, and beyond it were forty-five markers. Johnny opened the gate and went again to the hanging tree that grew in a rear corner. Its trunk was black and gnarled, its thickest limbs larger than most other trees. Lightning strikes had stripped bark and killed parts of it, but the hanging branch still spread above three poor stones and earth so devoid of life, it looked swept. How many times had Johnny stood there? How many times had he dreamed? Closing his eyes, he saw dead men and flames and a bloody knife. He could feel the terror of the crowd.

But who would fear a child?

Kneeling by the stones, Johnny spread his fingers and felt a dead spot in the land that wasn't right. Sap rose in the trees, and he felt it, same with the birds and beetles, the crawling vines and the flowers that followed the sun. But there was nothing beneath the tree to feel. The stones were small and unmarked. The dirt was simply dirt.

Brushing off his knees, Johnny looked up at streaks of bare, white wood. He told himself it was just a tree, just an old, half-dead, giant, scary-looking tree; but even on bright days, he didn't believe it. The dream was too real to be a dream. It was too personal, too hot.

Turning away, Johnny backtracked through the cut and into the clearing. He passed a barn and a shed, then went inside the old church. It was easy to forget that people had lived here, and Johnny wondered if they'd felt what he felt, or if the gift was uniquely his.

"You shouldn't be in here."

Johnny turned, disbelieving. A woman stood in the open door, and sunlight haloed the shape of her. It took a moment to find his voice. "I own this place."

"Not really," she said. "And only for now."

She was young and slender, his age, maybe, dressed in jeans, a T-shirt, and boots. She stepped out of the sun, and Johnny knew her. He felt the sudden resentment. "What are you doing here?" he asked.

"I come all the time."

"I would know if you did."

She shrugged, and the weight of her silence struck Johnny like a fist. He'd not sensed her presence until she spoke: not the sound of her, not the feel.

"Do you know who I am?" she asked.

"You're Luana Freemantle's daughter, Cree. I saw you at trial."

"Then you know I have as much a claim on this place as you."

"The courts disagree."

She shrugged again. "My ancestors lived here for two hundred years.

They worshipped in this church." Cree moved deeper into the room; touched a sconce, a stone baptismal. "You don't belong."

"But you do?"

"I guess we'll find out, won't we?"

She stopped near the door, looking up at his face. She had narrow shoulders, dark hair and skin. "Have you been watching me?" Johnny asked.

"You don't matter." She was dismissive. "You don't belong here."

"But you do?"

She shrugged yet again, and Johnny felt something from her then, a flicker of doubt, the first he'd seen. "You grew up in Charlotte." He pushed a little. "Your mother was Levi Freemantle's second cousin, a distant relative at best. No appeal will change that."

"Maybe not, but I spent my childhood here with my grandmother and great-aunts, and everyone who still remained. I know the history of this place in a way you never will, the stories of my family. You should return the land to those who love it most."

"All six thousand acres?"

"Of course."

Johnny felt her again, and the insight, this time, was like a bright flash. "Does the name William Boyd mean anything to you?" Her confidence failed as truth moved on her face. "He's paying your legal bills, isn't he? Jesus. What's the plan? He funds the lawsuit and buys the land if you win?"

"I'm not going to talk about this."

"I'm right, aren't I?"

"Not about me."

She stepped outside, and Johnny followed. "It's just money to you, isn't it?"

"No. Never."

"This land has been in my family since 1694, a land grant older than the country itself. That's history. That's what matters."

She spun on a heel, so fierce and suddenly angry, Johnny stepped back. "Are your people buried here?" she demanded.

"That way." Johnny pointed. "Four miles."

"Well, mine are buried right there." She stabbed a finger at the cemetery, and Johnny noticed, with shock, that tears had filled her eyes. "My grandmother, who raised me, my aunts and uncles, my great-grandmother, who was like a saint. You can't keep me away."

"You can visit anytime you want. I just like to know who's on my land. That's all. Who's on it and why."

The girl blinked away tears, and looked younger than he'd thought, twenty maybe, or maybe less. "Why do you go to the tree?"

"You were watching me?"

"I've seen you there three times."

"No reason," Johnny lied. "The history, I guess."

"You mean the hanging." She said it harshly. "I suppose we share that, too."

She was right about that. His ancestor was there that night; so was hers. They'd seen the fire, the swinging bodies.

Did they see a small girl with a bloody knife?

"I should go," she said.

"Do you have a car?"

"I hitched to the crossroads. After that, I walked."

"Why did you ask about the tree?"

"I shouldn't have."

She turned away, but he caught up near a charred mound where an old house had burned. "Please. I'd like to know."

"Why?"

"I don't know. It just matters."

"Very well." Sweat shone on her skin, and her eyes were still. "I see you when I dream."

"What?"

"Firelight and dead bodies." She grew solemn and quiet. "I see you at the tree and I wake afraid."

Cree left then, her feet light and quick on trails she still remembered. She'd not lived at Hush Arbor for twelve years—not since she was seven—but the fear was nothing new. Her earliest memory was of the hanging tree and her great-grandmother's folded skin.

I want you to touch it. . . . The old woman guided her hand to the bark and pressed it there. *This is history. This is life.* She was blind and toothless, the lines on her face like ripples in the mud that made the river. *Forget what your mother taught you. This is where it began. This is who we are.*

The girl tried to lean away from the tree, but the woman was strong and patient. She pressed the girl's hand until the bark made it hurt.

Pain is part of it. Let the pain go.

The girl tried, but didn't know how.

Do you believe in your mother's god? Let him go, too.

The girl was confused. Didn't everyone believe?

Why did your mother give you to me?

Because she has a new husband, the girl said, *and because she doesn't want me anymore.*

She was always selfish, your mother, selfish and wrong and too big for the place that birthed her out. You let that go, too. She kissed the girl's head. *Now, close your eyes and tell me what you see.*

I see blackness.

Blackness is good, your blackness and mine. What else?

Nothing, the girl said, and thought it was over then.

It wasn't.

Fingers held her wrist, and a small, bright knife split the skin of her palm. The girl screamed; but the old woman was like a stone, the dead eyes white and hard, the mouth a bitter line. She pressed the bloodied palm against the tree. *This is who we are. Say it.* The girl was crying. The woman pressed harder. *This is history. This is life. Say it now.* The girl said the words, and the old woman smiled. *It's done,* she said. *You're one of us.*

Why did you do that?

Because pain has always been the price.

The girl sucked blood from her palm, and saw other women then: her grandmother and great-aunt, the shadows of others, long dead.

For four years Cree had lived in the Hush, and knew parts of it as she knew her own face. There were long days and secret places, a million ways for a child loose in the woods to find amusement. But the sunny days were only part of it, and the old women taught her early to fear the cold ones and the long nights, to stay close if the wind disappeared or the sky filled with strange light. There were other people, too, but they stayed clear of the old women, and looked at the girl with something like fear. That was about blood and dark prayers, the dread of ancient things.

But her life was the old women.

They lived together in a one-room shack, the four of them alone at the edge of the clearing. Parts of that life were terrifying, but she slept well, pressed between the old women in the old bed. If she woke or was restless, they'd tell stories of slave ships and war, of an ancient kingdom, high on the side of a great mountain. Life was a tapestry, they said, and the girl a mighty thread. They would teach her the weave of it, but only when she was ready. In the meantime she learned rituals and shapes in the dust, strange words and blood and the small, bright knife, always the knife. Pale scars covered the old women from head to toe, and sadness filled them, even when they smiled. The girl understood now that they'd been dying the whole time, that their way of life had been dying, too.

But still, they scoured the deep woods. Cold or hot, it didn't matter. They searched if they were healthy or tired or sick. The girl never knew what they sought, but they wandered the Hush, and were the only ones to do so, unafraid. The few others who remained tended scraps of garden and fished the nearby waters. None ventured to the deep swamp or the faraway hills. When the girl asked if she could help, they'd explained it to her. *It is a thing we do, and that women before us have done. Your time may come, but only when you are older and wiser and very strong.*

It was a good life for a child, but destined to end. Her great-grandmother died first, then her grandmother two years after that, and her great-aunt six months later. When the girl's mother finally came to take her home, it was the first time they'd seen each other in four years. They drove to a big city and a tall building with a pool that smelled nothing like the swamp. The new husband was nice enough, but the girl used words he couldn't understand, and that bothered him. She'd listen to the arguments at night, his voice angry, her mother's pleading. The girl spoke up when she could, but in the end, they broke her. They took her to church and a therapist, and scolded her when she cut her skin or danced at sunrise or spoke the strange words. It wasn't until she was nine that she saw the same scars on her mother's arms and legs.

"I'm sorry," her mother said. "I shouldn't have sent you there."

"I want to go back."

"You'll never go there again."

But the girl dreamed.

She dreamed of old women and the Hush, and even now it was like paint on canvas. She paused once, and looked back at the white man who owned the land but knew nothing that was real. He stood before a slat-sided building and thought it a church, when it was not a church at all.

Not the gentle kind, at least.

Not the kind he meant.

It took Cree two hours to reach the crossroads, and from there she caught a ride that took her south and west to the city. Her mother opened the door before the key could turn, and the lines of her frown were sour. "You went again, didn't you?"

Cree pushed past; threw down a bag. "I didn't do anything wrong."

"That place is money for us and nothing more."

"So you say."

"Did you go to the tree?"

"Maybe."

"The church?"

"The white man was there."

"Johnny Merrimon? Did he see you?"

Cree turned down the hall that led to her room. Other than her mother's breathing, it was quiet in the small apartment. The second husband was gone. So were the third and the fourth.

"Don't walk away when I'm talking to you."

But Cree did. She closed her bedroom door, and locked it. Her mother wanted to sell the Hush. The girl wanted its secrets.

It was an old argument.

CHAPTER TEN

For five years, Johnny's life in the Hush had been defined by fundamental immersion. A dawn sky was a meal, a step in the river a swim. But the girl had walked within eight feet of the place he'd sat, and he'd not felt a thing. That scared and angered him. He was possessive. He admitted it.

Could he actually lose the Hush?

Returning to the cabin, he read the pleadings three more times. The stack of papers was thick, the text so dense, it could have been a foreign language. Tossing them on the bed, Johnny went outside. He needed perspective, and could think of only one place to go that wasn't in the city. A long walk through the hills took him to an open-air bar that leaned beneath a sycamore tree on the bank of the river three miles north of the swamp. More shed than actual building, the place was old like the county was old, a slat-sided, unpainted sprawl with views across the river and into the hills. A single room had windows and a plank floor; the rest of it was a tin roof and dirt and not much else. Johnny loved it because—except for his whiteness—no one looked at him twice. Of course, the whiteness thing took a while to sort out. This far north, the only things thriving were resentment, poverty, and a few small farms that still survived from the sharecropper years. A handful of businesses struggled nearby—a grocery, a one-pump station—but the swamp pushed in from the south and state game lands from the west and north, effectively inoculating the small corner of Raven County from anything remotely similar to progress. But that's why Johnny loved it.

No air-conditioning.

No asphalt.

The first time Johnny emerged from the woods, people had stopped talking, stopped drinking. A dozen people had stared at him as if at a ghost, and Johnny thought that made sense. There was nothing behind him but fifty square miles of swamp and woods. He was young. He was white. Johnny had ignored the stares, though, threading between tables and chairs until he was in the single room and the old bar was hard beneath his elbows. The man behind it was tall and heavy-shouldered. He wore a faded shirt and blue jeans stained with pig blood and grease. "I think maybe you're lost."

"I'm never lost." Johnny put a twenty on the bar, and the bartender glanced at it.

"Where are you from?"

"That way."

He pointed, and there'd come a moment where it could have gone either way. The bartender held the stare, then looked across the room and met every eye out there. It took a minute, maybe more. When the bartender shrugged, people went back to talking, and he dug a beer from a metal chest behind the bar. "You got a name?"

"Johnny."

The beer hit wood. "Might want to step lightly," he'd said; and that was it, which was good.

Johnny was seventeen at the time.

No kind of legal.

Now it was different. Johnny was a regular; he was an outcast and one of them, the white guy who lived as poor as anyone else and wasn't scared to share a bottle. "Leon." Johnny nodded at the big bartender. "How we doing?"

"No complaints."

Johnny leaned on the bar. It was twenty minutes after four o'clock. Outside, two of the tables were taken. Leon put a Red Stripe on the bar, and Johnny said, "Make it a bourbon back." The big man upended a shot glass and sloshed in an ounce of Jim Beam. "And one for you," Johnny said.

"All right." Leon poured another shot and clinked his glass against Johnny's. "Things unseen."

It was a traditional toast at the old bar, and had nothing to do with ghosts or spirits. A single bridge connected Leon's place to the world beyond the river. That made Leon's a good place to do most anything illegal. Moonshine. Stolen cigarettes. If it wasn't drug- or gang-related, Leon would facilitate almost anything. He took a cut for his troubles, and it would stay that way so long as things remained under the radar.

"A question," Johnny said; and Leon nodded cautiously. In six years Johnny had never asked a question. "The swamp."

"What about it?"

"What can you tell me about the people who used to live there?"

"We don't talk about that." The big man leaned on the bar. "Bad juju."

"Seriously?"

He nodded solemnly, and Johnny hid the surprise behind a sip of beer. Leon lived hard and didn't seem the superstitious type.

"Why do you believe that?"

Leon drummed his fingers and looked beyond Johnny to the river, the forest. His unhappiness was plain. So was the conflict. "Do you know why I served you the first day you came here?"

"No."

"I was curious."

"About what?"

"About anybody that walked into my place from that side of the bar." Leon pointed at the wilderness, then took a towel from the sink and began wiping down the bar. "How old do you think I am?"

"Fifty?"

"Fifty-seven," Leon said. "And a man can learn a lot in that many years. Some things he sees himself, and others he hears about from people he trusts. My father was like that. A smart man. Cautious. He ran this place his whole life. I grew up here."

"What's your point?"

"Most people tend to use the bridge." Leon tilted his head, and Johnny glanced at the rusted, one-car bridge. "No one's ever come here from the other side. No roads that way. No houses or people or reason to be there." He refilled his glass and drank the liquor down. "No one goes in the swamp. That's what my old man taught me. No one goes in and no one talks about it."

"Because it's bad juju?"

"You're too ignorant to use that word." Leon poured another shot. "And too damn white by far."

For the next ten minutes Johnny nursed the beer, thinking of the Hush, the girl at the church, William Boyd. Johnny knew why he wanted the land. He'd trespassed there a half-dozen times, and Johnny had tracked him, once, for three days. He'd stayed back during the daylight hours, but come close at night, hoping to divine some deeper truth. Much of what made Hush Arbor special remained a mystery to Johnny, even now. Maybe Boyd knew something more, some kind of *reason*. But the talks, at night, were of trophies and size and how a hunt was like business. They wanted the blood, the win, and always the trophy.

"Leon." Johnny lifted the empty bottle, and the big man fished another from the chest. "Can I use your phone?"

Leon stripped the cap with an opener the size of his fist. "You don't have your cell?"

"Is there even reception out here?" The big man grunted and moved a phone onto the bar. It was black and old and dense as a rock. "Rotary. Nice."

"Just keep it short."

Leon moved down the bar.

Johnny dialed his best friend's cell.

Jack took the call in a crowded hallway outside the ninth-floor conference room. The air was cold. He was sweating. "This is not a good time, Johnny."

"I want you to meet me at Leon's."

Jack moved out of the crowd; found a quiet spot by a plate glass window with views of the city. "They hate me at Leon's."

"They hate the suit and the German car. There's a difference."

Jack licked dry lips and looked at the door to the conference room. Leslie was inside. So was every partner in the firm. "Listen, when I said this was a bad time—"

"Do you know anything about Luana Freemantle's niece?"

"Her niece? What?"

"Never mind. We'll talk when you get here."

"About the timing . . ."

"Just come when you can. I'll wait."

The line went dead, and Jack stared at the phone in his hand. As friends, they were almost never out of sync. But Johnny's single-mindedness had this rare effect.

Jack was frustrated.

And he was angry.

"Jack, are you ready?" Leslie Green broke the plane of the door and moved to Jack's side.

"I don't think so."

"Just listen to them," she said. "Think about tomorrow, the next twenty years of your life. This doesn't have to be a problem."

"It feels like one."

"Trust me. They don't bite."

Inside the conference room, a mahogany table stretched twenty feet across an expensive rug. Nine partners sat at one end of the table. Leslie pointed at Jack's chair, which sat alone at the other end. "Seriously?" Jack said.

"It's just how it's done."

Jack sat; drew his chair close to the table.

"Are you comfortable, Mr. Cross?"

That was Michael Adkins, the senior partner. A broad man with silver hair, his fingers were flat on the table surface, his suit charcoal gray and immaculate. In forty years before the bar, he'd won eight-figure verdicts, taught law school, argued before the Supreme Court. Looking at him made Jack feel like an associate in his second week of practice. "I'm very comfortable. Thank you."

"Since time is money for all of us, I'll cut to the chase. You're friends with Johnny Merrimon. We understand that. We understand there's history there. Childhood. Similar backgrounds. The, ah . . . unpleasantness involving his sister and your brother." Adkins lifted a hand, and every partner nodded in silent accord. "Ms. Green also informs us that Mr. Merrimon has asked for your help in an appellate matter. Under no circumstances are you to offer that help. Mr. Merrimon is not a client of the firm. He will never be a client. Are we clear?"

"This is because of William Boyd."

"If Mr. Boyd requires the service of this firm, we intend to provide it. Having Mr. Merrimon as a client would create needless confusion."

"A conflict of interest."

"Precisely."

Jack glanced at Leslie. She looked away, but not before he saw the glitter in her eyes. "Mr. Merrimon came to me for assistance. I told him I would consider the case."

"Have you done any research?"

"No."

"Started a file? Accepted payment? Rendered any kind of legal opinion?"

"Of course not. He just came to me."

"Have you discussed his matter with any associate or partner of this firm?"

"Ms. Green is aware . . ."

Adkins lifted the same hand and nodded with such calm assurance that words dried up in Jack's mouth. "Ms. Green stands with us on this matter."

"Is that right?"

Jack could no longer hide the anger. Adkins accepted it with a gracious smile. "The law loves a rainmaker, Mr. Cross. Bring in enough business, and nothing is beyond a lawyer's grasp. Money. Power. Prestige." He nodded again, the picture of reason. "We're not asking you to act against your friend's interests. Just speak to him. Make sure he's aware of the truly exceptional nature of Mr. Boyd's offer."

"I'm sure he understands the meaning of thirty million dollars."

"Then your job is doubly simple. Convince your friend. Explain to him that unless he accepts Mr. Boyd's offer, he will face Ms. Freemantle's appeal alone or find the means to hire some other firm. I understand he cannot afford that expense?" He made it a question, but Jack tightened his lips, and Adkins smiled dismissively. "Once Mr. Merrimon understands the nature of his position, perhaps the wisdom of a clean, quick sale will become more obvious."

"Do you require an answer now?"

"We're not unreasonable. Take a few days."

"Very well," Jack said. "I'll think about it."

"Excellent."

"And if tomorrow I choose to help my friend?"

"In that case, Mr. Cross, I believe you'll find solo practice a cold and bitter place."

Jack watched the partners file out, all except Leslie Green. She waited by the door, then touched his arm and held him in the room until they were completely alone. Jack looked at her fingers, then at the wide blue eyes. "I suppose this means you won't be helping my friend."

"The firm has never had a female senior partner. I'd like to be the first."

"And then there's the money."

"There's always the money." Jack looked away, and she trailed her fingers across the fabric of his suit. "Don't go against them, Jack. They'll ruin you. Even if you quit, they'll bury you for spite."

"Good luck landing William Boyd without me. He only cares about the firm because he thinks Johnny will listen to me."

"Just think of the possibilities: all that money, a corner office. You could ask for a partnership, and they'd seriously consider it."

Jack hardened his jaw, but said nothing.

"Listen." Her hand was back on his arm. "I know what Johnny Merrimon means to you, but I can be your friend, too. Boyd will be *our* client. We'll work him together."

"You do appellate work. I do bankruptcy."

"So we'll bring in some other lawyer. All that matters is the relationship. Yours. Mine. Mr. Boyd's."

She pressed into him as she turned to leave, and Jack wondered if she'd meant the touch to be so sensual, thinking she probably had. The perfume of her hair was on his clothing, like a fog.

In the elevator down, Jack ignored the looks he got from paralegals and assistants and, in his office, paced behind a closed door. Leon's was a sixty-minute drive. He had work to do.

"Shit."

More elevator. More strange looks. Heading out of town, he rolled down the windows and opened up the engine, driving north toward the swamp, then east through a world of shimmer and blacktop and faded paint. For a while he was at peace, but the closer he got to Leon's, the more that peace faded. Johnny was an impossible friend, really. The secrecy and demands, the way he always called the shots. It shouldn't be like that anymore. Jack had the job, the prospects, the education. Other than the Hush, what did Johnny have?

Secrets, Jack thought.

And me.

"Shit."

It was becoming his favorite word.

The last turn before Leon's was a left onto a rutted-out dirt track. Jack drove slowly to protect the chassis, but even then he bottomed out over and over.

"I'm not going to say it."

The bridge to Leon's may have been painted once, but was mostly rust and splintered wood, a narrow span over a stretch of river that slowed before tumbling through the hills to fill the swamp below. Jack disliked everything about Leon's. He hated the heat and the bugs, the smoke and cold stares and the smell of roasting pig. The distrust there was old and bitter, and based entirely on the color of his skin. Okay, maybe the car didn't help, and the suit was no bonus. But people disliked him at Leon's, and that was one more reason to be unhappy with Johnny. He sat at a table under a covered porch, lolled there as though he owned the place, feet pushed out in the dirt, one arm over the chair back and a beer in the other hand. He waved once, but Jack was thinking about colors. The building was gray wood on brown dirt, and the cars looked about the same, all red metal and dust and cracked glass. A dozen faces turned Jack's way as he crossed the bridge and parked beside an old truck, locking the car from long habit, and cringing when the alarm chirped.

No one spoke.

Everyone stared.

Under the first roofline, the temperature dropped ten degrees. Jack passed a table; nodded at the two men there, the braless woman in ripped jeans and a worn-out T.

"Excuse me."

He squeezed past the table, dragged a chair from his path, and crossed hard dirt to a second covered area with three tables and a step up onto a plank floor where the bar and more tables showed deep in the shadows. Johnny sat near the back wall. To his right was the river, its water churning under a haze of smoke from the pig cooker out back. Leon loomed behind the bar inside, and a barefoot kid was throwing horseshoes in a sandy pit under the closest trees. The only sounds were cicadas and wind and the clank of metal.

"Hey, Jack, thanks for coming." Johnny knocked on the wall behind his shoulder. "Leon!" he called. "Two more."

Leon took his time. When the beers came, he didn't look at Jack. "You want two more after these, you come inside. Not him. You."

When he was gone, Johnny said, "It's outsiders in general. Don't take it personally."

"It's hard not to. Look at this."

Johnny looked from one table to the next, then down the hill to where old men sat in the shade of a pecan tree, drinking clear liquor from glass jars. "People here have known each other a long time. They'll get used to you."

"Why come here at all?"

"You know why."

Jack did, and felt his anger fade. Johnny could never be himself in town. He was Johnny Merrimon, the kid who'd lost his sister and saved the girl and found all those dead bodies. Jack had tried before to imagine that life. He couldn't. "Why am I here, Johnny? It's a weekday. I have work."

"I met with Leslie Green. I need to know if she'll help me." Jack looked away, and his neck flushed. "I don't like that look."

"She won't help."

"She seemed interested."

"Not anymore."

"But—"

"We saw William Boyd the other day."

"Is that right?"

Johnny stayed cool, and Jack couldn't meet his eyes. "Thirty million dollars, man. Why didn't you tell me he'd offered that kind of money?"

"Because it doesn't matter."

"Bullshit."

"Fifty million. A hundred. I won't sell."

"Then you're stupid, insane, or both. Sell the land. Buy another piece somewhere else."

"I'm sorry, but I can't."

"Thirty million dollars, Johnny. How could you not tell me that?"

Johnny studied the bottle in his hand, then shrugged as any thirteen-year-old boy might. "I didn't think you'd help me if you knew."

"Well, shit." The rest of Jack's anger slipped away. "Boyd offered me money if I convince you to sell."

"Is that right?"

"The firm doesn't want me to represent you. They'll fire me if I do, and blackball me even if I quit. It's why Leslie won't help you. Boyd offered her money, too."

"How much?"

"Two million, plus business for the firm at New York rates. I'd be a rainmaker. They might even make me a partner."

"Two million dollars? Maybe you should take it."

"Don't screw with me, Johnny."

"Money. Job security."

"Don't forget the corner office."

The sarcasm was sharp, but Johnny didn't react to it. He moved to the edge of the porch, looked off toward the Hush. "I have two weeks to answer the appeal."

"I know," Jack said.

"What happens if I don't have a lawyer?"

"You'll probably lose."

Johnny scuffed a boot on the dusty ground. He wore jeans, a faded T-shirt. In spite of the drinking, he was far from drunk. "Will you help me?"

Jack could barely meet his eyes. Johnny had always been the first to sacrifice, to see the path, the first to reluctant manhood. When Jack had failed as a friend, Johnny was the first to smile the reckless smile and, ultimately, forgive. He'd been more father than Jack's father, more brother than any brother God had seen fit to give. In every way that mattered, Johnny Merrimon had defined Jack's childhood. But Jack had clawed his way through poverty, deformity, the ruin inflicted by his crazy parents. He'd worked, unceasing, for a decade, and was two weeks into the only career he'd ever wanted. The partners would ruin that if Jack helped his friend. Even if he started his own practice, they could undercut his fees, poach clients, undermine his efforts in a thousand ways. The only question was one of reach. Could Jack make a go in Charlotte or Raleigh? He didn't want to. He didn't want any of this.

"Jack?"

Johnny kept his voice level, but need deepened his eyes like a long illness. Jack could help him, yes. He could sacrifice his career, his prospects. And if it were that simple, he would. The larger problem was that Jack *wanted* Johnny to sell. Something was wrong in the Hush, and it wrapped his best friend in a blanket of want. That was the sickness Jack saw, that addiction. "I can't help you. I'm sorry."

The words came as a whisper, but Johnny heard them.

"Hey, man. Sure. I get it. You've worked hard. You're successful."

"Just hang on a second, Johnny. Let me think about it a little more. I didn't mean to sound so—"

"No, man. Really. I understand." The pain was in his friend. Abandonment. Betrayal. "I'll get us two more beers. Sit tight." Johnny brushed past Jack, and was inside for a long time. When he came back, a smile was carved on his face, the same hollowness in his eyes. "Here we go. Cold beers. All good."

"Johnny, man, listen. I have debts. Law school was over ninety grand—"

"I said don't sweat it." Johnny clinked his bottle against Jack's. "They need music here, don't you think?" He put the bottle down, couldn't meet Jack's gaze. "Sit tight, all right."

"Johnny . . ."

"I'm going to talk to Leon about some music."

Johnny's chair scraped grooves in the dirt. He stood and turned, but not before Jack saw the redness in his eyes, the sudden, bone-deep paleness under the tan.

Shit.

He drank beer, but didn't taste it.

Shit, shit, shit.

The next hour was brutal. They drank beer, pretended; but Jack's words were a wound between them. Johnny never met his eyes, never looked at his face for more than a second, and, for Jack, that second ached. They'd been friends since first grade, and in all the blackness of that childhood, Johnny had never lost faith or the fire inside. In fact, if Jack had to pick one word to describe his friend, it would be *burning*. Even as a boy, he'd burned. Passion, conviction, certainty.

"Listen, Johnny. Let me think about it."

Johnny shook his head, watched the kid with the horseshoes. "I'll figure something out. Don't sweat it."

"It's just that there are a lot of moving parts. . . ."

Johnny stood to get more beer. "I said don't sweat it."

When he came back, the beer sat untouched for a long time. Night was falling. A skin of mist hung on the river. "Listen, Johnny."

"Yeah, you're right. You should probably go."

"I didn't. I don't—"

"I'll see you in a few days. It's fine. Thanks for coming."

"Are you sure?"

Jack stood. He wanted a look, a nod, anything to stitch up the wound.

But Johnny had nothing.

In town, Jack went to his favorite restaurant and ate a steak that tasted like wood. The wine lacked appeal, as well. So did the pie, the port, the pretty girl who brought the check. When Jack got home, the stairs tilted and his key didn't want to fit the lock. Inside, he kicked off his shoes, threw his jacket at a hook and missed. He replayed the conversation in his mind, the seemingly surreal seconds when his mouth had opened and he'd told his best friend, *No, I can't help you, I'm sorry.*

Johnny's eyes had never been so bloodshot and bright.

Did he go inside to hide actual tears?

It wasn't possible.

Not Johnny.

Pulling off his tie, Jack crossed to the kitchen and played his messages. One was a solicitation. The other was from Leslie. "About today," she said. "We need to talk. Call me when you get this."

It was 9:17. Early enough. Jack found her number on the call log and dialed it. She answered on the first ring. "You're home, good. I'm coming over."

"Leslie—"

"I'm two minutes away."

In the end, it was more like twenty, which gave Jack time to get out of the rumpled suit and into jeans and a T-shirt. Short sleeves showcased the stunted arm, so he rarely wore them around others, but a spark of resentment burned somewhere low in his chest. Johnny was the rock of his life, and Jack had just crapped all over him. Part of that was Leslie's fault. If she wanted to argue, he'd go there, bad arm and all.

He didn't expect her to smell so good.

"Hey, Jack. Thanks for this." In the hall, yellow light made her seem small and very soft. She wore heels under a skirt that fit just right. The spill of her hair made him dizzy. "You don't mind, do you?" She raised a bottle of tequila and two limes. "I feel as if I owe you an apology. I could have handled things better, softened the partners somehow." She dipped her chin, indicating the room beyond. "May I come in?"

Jack mumbled something and she took the room as if she owned it, putting the tequila on the counter, finding glasses, making small talk as she sliced limes and repeated herself with the same, dizzying smile. "I was asking about salt."

"Oh, I'm sorry." Jack stuttered into motion. "Here." He opened a cabinet, handed her the salt.

"Do you like tequila?" She didn't wait for an answer, holding up the bottle instead. "Fortaleza. The best. A friend introduced me to it years ago. Do you know how to do this?" She took a glass and a lime, then licked her hand, poured salt, and showed him how to do it. "Yes. Damn." She clacked the glass on the bar. "Now you." She filled the other glass, and Jack did what she told him to do. Salt. Tequila. Lime. It burned going down, but she poured another. "To the lawyers," she said; and Jack drank.

It happened a few more times, and she did a lot of talking. Nothing about Johnny or William Boyd or even the firm. She touched his bad arm without flinching. She flipped her hair twice, watched him with those impossible eyes and showed a scar on her hip where she'd brushed against fire coral on a free dive off Cabo. Jack struggled, but she was magnetic: the skin, the laugh, the curve of her thigh as she sat beside him, then rose from the sofa to pour another round of shots. Before he knew it, it was midnight and he was blurry and her face was close to his. Jack had never had luck with women. Part of it was the arm and the discomfort born of doubt, and part was born of his mother, who lived in a trailer and saw the devil in all things, including the two of her sons. Blame, too, could be leveled on Jack's father, who'd whelped his boys on honor, effort, and pride, and who was a convict now, ten years into a two-decade stretch. Jack had loved a bright-eyed girl once, but she was a laugh, a twinkle, a sprite; and she'd never cared for him at all. From that hard start, he'd learned to turn inward and run deep.

"Here." Leslie handed him a glass and a lime, and put fingers on his leg. "Go ahead." She smiled as Jack licked salt and grimaced. "Now drink. Now lime." His eyes watered, but she was clapping and laughing, and the sound was music after all the lonesome years. "My turn." A pink tongue touched salt, then she drank, and drew up her legs and curled her perfect toes. The effect was vertiginous. She was soft and small, more smiling girl than partner and boss. "Tell me about Jack Cross." A flush painted her cheeks. One eye was lost in the shadows, but the other gleamed. "College in three years, law school in two. Top of his class."

"Number two," Jack corrected.

"Number two. Still impressive."

Her leg was against his. He was drunk and it was dark and he was swimming. "Is this about Johnny?"

"It's about us," she said. "Don't even say the name." It was a lie, but as soft as everything else. "We're friends, aren't we? Tell me we're friends."

"I think . . . I don't . . ."

The room tilted again, and she was on his lap and kissing him. He smelled tequila and lime and whatever shampoo God had designed to make men weak. "Leslie—"

"Shhh." The shirt came off, and she was bare-skinned beneath it, as pale and perfect as every dream Jack had ever had. "Just tell me we're friends." She kissed him long, moving her hips. "Say we're friends and that friends help friends."

Words passed his lips, but Jack didn't pay attention or care. *How long?* he thought. And in the question of willing women, the answer came as always, and the answer was *never.* This was the first breast, the first real kiss.

"Bedroom," she said, and Jack carried her with the good arm.

"This is about us, right? Just us?"

"Hush," she told him. "No words."

And that sounded good to Jack: forgetfulness and velvet skin, devolution and the long fall. "No words," he said, but in the storm of what followed, he heard Johnny's name not once but twice. It was an exhalation, a prayer; and it was light as sugar on her lips.

When Jack woke, it was to pale light and pain behind his eyes. It was six o'clock, the bed beside him empty. He knew a moment's blankness before memories of the night marched across him in waves: the rush of blood and joy, the awkwardness of inexperience. He saw Leslie, above him, the suspicion of her eyes beneath a waterfall of hair. She'd moved as he'd imagined women might, careful and knowing, then harder, needful, rampant. He thought of all the years he'd been alone, and then of bridges crossed. For a moment he was happy. Then he saw Johnny's face at the bar, heard his name on Leslie's lips.

After that, Jack went back to sleep.

It was a fitful rest, and when he finally went to work, his finger hesitated over the button for Leslie's floor. She'd given a gift but qualified it with another man's name. That twisted Jack up in unexpected ways.

He'd never hated his friend before.

In his office on the seventh floor, Jack counted on work to smooth out the day. He kept the door closed and powered through the sweats and dry mouth and nausea. Every so often, he looked at his phone and at the door.

By afternoon the hangover, too, was a memory, and he considered making the trip down. He wanted to see her eyes, and wondered if she would smile. Maybe they could have dinner. Maybe he'd imagined the name on her lips.

"Pitiful," he said, but couldn't shake the feel of her. He worked until eight, hoping she might appear, then went home, angry at her and at his own stupidity.

If she was thinking of anyone, it was Johnny.

Nevertheless, he paced the apartment. He couldn't eat, didn't want to sleep. His thoughts raced back and forth.

He let his best friend down.

She said Johnny's name.

Leslie's text came at midnight.

Are you awake?

Jack thought for a moment. *Barely,* he typed. *Worked late.*

Thanks for last night.

Something inside Jack broke, relief maybe, or need. All he knew was the flutter. *Would you like to come over?*

A minute passed, and then three. The response was a single word: *Sure.*

Their time that night was different from the last. They didn't drink. She left a light burning. For Jack, it was everything he'd hoped it would be. She was a vision, and patient. She didn't say Johnny's name. "Why are you with me?" he asked.

The clock read two, and she lay in the spill of a single lamp so that light gilded the curves and shadow-stroked the hollow places. "You're a young man," she said. "Young men have lots of energy."

"Don't joke."

"It's just sex. I happen to enjoy it."

"But why me? I'm not particularly handsome. There's . . . you know."

He shifted the bad arm. She laughed and touched his leg. "Would you rather I leave?"

"No."

"Then convince me to stay."

She rose to her knees and Jack, again, was lost. An hour later, they stood at the door. She wore the same heels and a dress shirt, barely buttoned. Jack was physically exhausted. "Can I drive you home?" he asked.

"Such a gentleman, but no. I'm fine."

She kissed him, and Jack took her arm before she could turn away. "I need to know this isn't about Johnny or the case or William Boyd."

"You can ask that even now?"

She meant the bed, the scratches, the ruined sheets.

"Tell me it's not about the money."

She arched an eyebrow, and even that was perfect. "Would you screw me again if I said it was?" She smiled a lawyer's smile because she knew the answer. "Don't look so troubled. We can both get what we want." She took his hand and slipped it into her shirt. "You're happy, I'm happy." Jack looked away, but she cupped his chin. "This doesn't have to be complicated."

But for Jack it was.

She was a user and a taker, and the stink of that guilt was on his skin, too.

The next morning was a Saturday, so he stayed in bed until eight, then took a walk. Afterwards, he showered and spent time at the office. Leslie called twice, but he didn't answer. On Sunday morning he worked again, and didn't see Leslie. Early Monday he went out for breakfast. Even at seven o'clock, the diner was packed and buzzing with excitement. People crowded the tables; they leaned over newspapers and whispered, bright-eyed. One man said, "A billion dollars. Jesus."

He was swollen-faced and unshaven. A man beside him wore a John Deere cap and had so much grease under his nails, it looked as if he'd been digging in a tar pit. "How much is a billion?" he said.

"A thousand million," the fat man said, and a boy dressed for baseball mouthed the words as if he were fake-singing in church.

A thousand million dollars . . .

At the table beside Jack's, an old lady held glasses on her nose as her husband leaned close to see the paper. Similar scenes repeated across the crowded room: housewives in expensive clothes, a state trooper at the counter.

Jack waited for his waitress, then asked about the excitement.

"Haven't you heard?" She pulled a folded paper from her apron and dropped it on the table. "Everybody's talking about it."

She disappeared on narrow hips, and Jack opened the paper to read about the billionaire William Boyd, down from New York and found dead in the Hush.

CHAPTER ELEVEN

The Death of William Boyd

When William Boyd set out to hunt, he kept the joy buried deep. He didn't smile or speak needlessly, and had little patience for those who did. Kirkpatrick believed the same things. Preparation was as personal as prayer and religion: the four o'clock alarm, the ritualistic selection of clothing and weapons and gear, all of it triple-checked and packed to minimize noise. Sound was the killer, as was scent, and both men were acolytes in the church of the hunt. They bathed with special soaps, anointed their rifles with oils designed to be equally scentless. In the gun room, with the air black and still outside, they ate a final meal in equal quiet, the table lit by small lamps, and all else shadowed: the paintings and skins and racked weapons. Silver on china made the only sounds, but the joy showed in neat movements and polished brass and the times their eyes met. They'd known darker mornings in darker places, and there was joy in that, too, in those bindings of trust, respect, and blood.

"It's time."

Boyd fed a final cartridge into his rifle. Across the table, Kirkpatrick stood and shouldered his pack and gun. At the door, the housekeeper handed them coffee in travel mugs. "Three days," Boyd said. "Maybe four."

She frowned. "I wish you'd tell me where you're going."

"You know better than that."

"What if something happens?"

"Risk is part of it. Watch over the house."

"I'll be here when you get back."

He nodded brusquely, feeling the dark charge, the loom of the hunt. It was too early for false dawn, but the sky was peppered with stars. Looking at Kirkpatrick, he said, "I'll need your phone."

"What? Why?"

He was a giant in the gloom, and suddenly angry.

"No one takes a phone but me. It's how this works."

"I just wired two hundred million to your firm."

"That's business, and this is, too. GPS tracking. Photographs. I can't allow it."

"I've already signed your nondisclosure agreement."

"My grandfather almost died finding the place I'm about to take you. It's personal to me. I'm sorry." Kirkpatrick stared into the darkness, one hand white on the strap of his rifle. "Please, James." Boyd held out his hand. "This is no reflection on our long friendship or my feelings of admiration."

"It's bullshit."

"Nevertheless." Kirkpatrick stared at the palm, pale in the gloom. When he handed over the phone, Boyd gave it to the housekeeper, and offered the best smile he had. "She'll keep it safe."

"I suppose you'll blindfold me now."

"No, my friend. Now we hunt." Boyd slung his pack and led Kirkpatrick past the line of expensive vehicles to a mud-spattered truck that showed rust and bare primer. "No one around here looks twice at a twenty-year-old Dodge." Kirkpatrick grunted, and slung his pack into the open bed. Rifles went on the rack in the rear window. Boyd lifted a hand toward his housekeeper. "Four days or less," he said, then drove them down the twisted drive. At the state road, he turned north and gestured at a line of trees, dense beyond the fields. "That's the raw edge of fifty thousand acres. No roads into it. No roads out. To the northeast is another twenty thousand acres owned by a paper company in Main. We'll push in there, go as deep as we can and hike the rest of the way. The country gets rough. It'll take some time."

"Better be worth it."

Boyd said nothing, but his eyes glittered. Kirkpatrick was still angry, but that would pass. What mattered was the nondisclosure agreement he'd signed. Kirkpatrick could never reveal the location of the hunt. More important, he could never buy the land or try to buy it, not through intermediaries, subsidiaries, or any other legal fiction. Penalties for violation of the terms were so enormous, the lawyers had balked. But Kirkpatrick was like Boyd. He hated lawyers; loved the hunt.

Forty minutes in the truck brought them to a dirt track behind a metal gate. It was a hint of earth, a slash in the trees. "Paper company," Boyd said. "Sit tight." After sliding from the truck, he cut the chain, then dragged the gate and pulled the truck through. "Four miles in there's a secondary track running east and south. Close as we can get."

"Why come in from the north?"

"The swamp is not navigable."

"Your grandfather managed."

"In the winter. That's different."

Boyd didn't explain the rest, how the swamp had changed each time he tried from the south, how dry land was there one day and gone the next, how trails had disappeared and turned around, how even the compass had failed. The third time he'd pushed in from the old freed-slave settlement, he became so disoriented, he wandered for days and almost starved. By the time he'd stumbled out, he was filthy and snakebit and bloody. Kirkpatrick didn't need to hear that, so Boyd kept quiet as the world shrank to the cab, the feathered trees, the cones of yellow light. Dropping into four-wheel drive, Boyd powered through one creek, and then another. A gap in the trees showed the first flash of yellow eyes.

Whitetail.

Nothing special.

When the track split, they turned east and south for another two miles. At the edge of a stream, Boyd ran the truck into the understory. "If anybody finds it this far in, it'll be another hunter or some kid out on a four-wheeler." He killed the engine. "Few come this deep."

"Do any go deeper?"

"Not where we're going."

"Why not?"

"Topography, for one. Then there's Johnny Merrimon. Half the rednecks in the county think he's some kind of rock star, equal parts celebrity survivalist and rebel, basically a working-class hero. It doesn't hurt that he shot at a couple of Yankees trespassing, or that he went to jail for it and did his time clean. Even those who don't care about the rest of it have a healthy respect for his temperament and marksmanship. Rumor has it, I'm not the only person he's shot at. Then there's the rest of it."

"What do you mean?"

Boyd opened the door. "You'll see."

Taking the lead, he guided Kirkpatrick off the road and across a spongy hollow to a ridgeline running south. In that first hour, the forest was still, but as light strengthened, a dawn chorus rose around them, a symphony of catbird and Carolina wren, of mourning dove and cardinal and the deep-throated *gunk* of green frogs in the pocosins that fingered up from the distant swamp. "Shrub bogs." Boyd gestured that way. "We could save a dozen miles cutting across, but you'd sink to the waist."

Kirkpatrick grunted, and they kept moving, staying to the ridgelines and deviating only if blowdown or deadfall blocked their way. By midmorning the temperature tipped ninety-five and kept climbing. "You good?" Kirkpatrick said he was, but sweat sheeted his face. Boyd kept the pace, and the route drifted east into the most inaccessible corner of state game lands. "From here on, it gets hard." They moved from damp earth onto gray stone. Except for a few trees, the ridge was barren, with views south across the softer hills and pocosins. Ahead was a series of jigsaw ridgelines with granite so rough, it looked shattered. "Halfway through those hills, we'll reach the northern edge of Merrimon's land. From there we follow the river."

Kirkpatrick shaded his eyes. "There has to be a better way."

"This is the long way in, but no one sees us and we don't get lost."

Kirkpatrick looked doubtful, but kept his mouth shut, and that suited Boyd just fine. He didn't want to speak of satellite mapping or geologists or the local guides who'd shown him how to get this far. "Come on. A few more hours and we're at the river."

As it turned out, it took another five. The climbs were steep, and the stone, in places, sharp as a blade. Kirkpatrick sliced his hand on a bad descent; gashed his knee in a second fall. The heat hurt him, too. By three o'clock, he looked like an old man, and Boyd had never seen that before. "Here, take a seat." He found a sliver of shade and got Kirkpatrick on the ground.

Kirkpatrick drank water; splashed some on his neck and face. "I don't get it." He pulled at his collar. His chest rose and fell. "It was hotter in India. The humidity. You remember?" He swallowed more water, choking. His color was bad. "I'm sorry, William. I've never held you up before. I don't understand."

The wash that sheltered them was raw stone, scrubbed by the last big rain. Boyd got the pack off Kirkpatrick's back. "Just breathe," he said.

"There's a weight . . ."

"No, my friend. There's no weight."

Kirkpatrick's hand settled on his chest. "I can't catch my breath. I don't understand."

But Boyd did. "We're on Merrimon's land," he said. "We've been on it for the last hour."

"What does that have to do with it?"

Boyd waited.

"What? Your grandfather's story?"

"Think about it."

Kirkpatrick opened his mouth, closed it. "Jesus Christ."

"It'll pass."

"You feel it, too?"

Boyd nodded, and Kirkpatrick tried to stand. "I can't do this," he said. "I can't breathe." Boyd pushed him back down, but Kirkpatrick fought. "There's something wrong. You don't understand."

"I do," Boyd said. "You want to run from this place. It's like a voice, or pressure—"

"Like someone's standing behind me. Jesus Christ. Like a cold breath and a whisper."

"It's different for everybody. Give it a minute." The minute turned into ten. Boyd thought he'd break a dozen times, but saw the moment Kirkpatrick's breathing eased. The man blinked twice. The panic passed. "You good?"

"I'm not sure."

"Just breathe. The pressure will fade."

"This happens every time?"

"It comes and goes. Sometimes it's worse."

"Goddamn." Kirkpatrick clawed to his feet, then walked down the wash and came back angry. "Why didn't you tell me? Warn me?"

"Would you have believed me?"

"No," he admitted. "Not a chance."

"Can you walk?"

"I'm not frightened."

"Come on, then. This way."

Boyd led him from the wash and pointed. "That's the last hill. Beyond it is the river, and a good place to camp. We'll catch our breath tonight, and start fresh tomorrow. Okay?"

Kirkpatrick said nothing.

"James? Okay?"

"Enough already. I can do whatever you can do."

Boyd had seen that defensiveness, too, a reaction common to strong men made unexpectedly afraid. It was a dangerous state, so Boyd watched him for the next hour, taking him up the hill in easy strides and pausing at the crest. Below them, the river shone like a seam of coal, then broke white for another mile before spreading into the fens and dells that marked the northern edge of the swamp. Kirkpatrick palmed sweat from his face. He looked across the swamp, and his voice was thin. "I had no idea it would be so large."

The wetlands stretched as far as either man could see, a great concavity of life and black water. "Twenty miles east to west. That's Hush Arbor directly below us, three thousand acres of it."

Boyd indicated the area he meant, and Kirkpatrick studied it in grave silence, turning at times to consider the greater swamp beyond. "It looks greener somehow."

"Greener. Denser."

"I don't understand."

"You will."

Boyd moved them back into the trees, where they made camp and ate dinner cold. Afterwards, with the sun dim behind the western trees, he asked Kirkpatrick the same question. "You okay?"

Kirkpatrick waved off the worry, but in Boyd it settled deeper. Kirkpatrick looked paler, and the lines of his face were more profound, making him appear haggard and spent. "Can we have a fire?" he asked.

"Not tonight. Too visible."

"Just a small one."

"James, look at me." Kirkpatrick's eyes darted left and right, but never met Boyd's. "Do you still feel it?"

"No. Yes."

"Is it worse?"

Kirkpatrick pressed his palms against his temples, rocking. "I'm fine," he said, but his hands were white.

At dawn, he seemed worse. Boyd handed over a protein bar and a bottle of water, but Kirkpatrick dropped them in the dirt and went to stare out at the swamp. Boyd joined him, and for long moments they stood side by side as an edge of sun put yellow on the hills and left the swamp in darkness. Kirkpatrick broke the silence, his eyes sunken and shot with blood.

"How many times have you been here?"

He was staring at the carpet of trees, the glint of black water. "Three by myself," Boyd said. "Twice more with clients."

Kirkpatrick wrapped his chest and rolled his shoulders inward. "Has anyone ever turned back?"

"From here? No."

He nodded, but it was vague. "I had nightmares last night."

"What about?"

"I don't remember."

Boyd thought that was a lie. Something about the way he stood, the weakness in his jaw. "Come on, my friend." He put his hands on Kirkpatrick's shoulders. "Breakfast will make everything better."

It didn't.

By the time they reached still waters, Kirkpatrick was mumbling under his breath, his back bent under a weight far greater than his pack. Boyd considered turning back, but every time he stopped, his friend grew angry. "Don't stop for me, damn it. I can do this. I'm fine."

For half a day they pushed into the swamp, and every hour Kirkpatrick weakened. He fell often, and Boyd found him unmoving once, a cloud of insects on his face, and his boots held fast in twelve inches of mud. Boyd got him onto dry ground, got him walking. "We'll stop soon," Boyd said. "There's a special place—"

"I said I'm fine."

But he wasn't. He wouldn't drink. The eyes were glassy.

Two hours later, Boyd parted a curtain of vine and pulled his friend onto a spit of land the size of a city block. "This is base camp. This is where we start." Boyd removed his pack, helped Kirkpatrick off with his. "Sit down before you fall down."

"It's worse here."

"Just sit."

Kirkpatrick stood, unmoving, as Boyd pitched the tent and gathered wood. When it was done, Boyd took him by the arm and forced him to sit. "Listen." Boyd looked up, gauging daylight. "We need to scout for a sign, set up the blinds. Do you feel up for that?" No response. Boyd sighed. "Okay, listen. Two game trails lead deeper into the swamp, one running south, and the other west. I'll go south. The track is just there, beyond the sycamore."

"I don't want to do this anymore."

"For God's sake . . ."

"Whatever it is, it's getting worse."

Boyd shook his head.

"Don't bullshit me, William. I know you feel it. I see it in your face."

"Yeah, I feel it. But so what? It's just the air or some shit. It isn't real."

"It's cold. Are you cold?"

"For God's sake." Boyd snatched up a tree-climber and a pop-up blind. "If you pull yourself together, I'll be that way." He shouldered the rifle, started walking. "Otherwise, I'll see you tonight."

Kirkpatrick watched him go, and felt his courage, like a dying match. Everything was weight and ice and hollowness. He stared at gray places between the trees.

Nothing . . .

But the *nothing* weighed a million pounds, and pinned him where he sat. In five decades of living, Kirkpatrick had known such helplessness only once, and that was the day he'd drawn his first breath between the legs of an alcoholic shut-in who'd dropped him like an afterthought on the sheets of a dead man's trailer in the dimmest hollow of West Virginia. He'd come into the world without a father, discipline, or love and never let it slow him down. He'd quit school in the third grade; become a coal miner at twelve, and a car thief six months later. He'd stolen, lied and schemed, and won his first bar fight five years before he was old enough to drink. When his mother died the next week, he buried her in the backyard, then took a twelve-hundred-dollar purse in a bare-knuckle brawl run out of a gravel pit by a sheriff's deputy named Jo-Jo. Those were the years that made James Kirkpatrick, and in the years since, he'd crossed jungles, toppled companies, beaten other men bloody. If he wanted something, he took it. If it bled, he could kill it. In Kirkpatrick's world, there was no mountain he couldn't go over, under, or through. Even now, he thought there was a way out.

Then the *nothing* moved.

Kirkpatrick laughed, but it was more like choking.

It was a trick of light, a shadow.

Then it moved again, a ripple of gray where the light was grayest. It flowed between the trees, and when it stopped ten feet away, Kirkpatrick closed his eyes and remembered what it was to be three years old and frozen in the shell of a lightless trailer.

Something rustled.

The sound of a breath.

Kirkpatrick turned his head, but felt a charge on the skin of his face. He smelled something musty and old. "Please," he said. "I'm sorry."

The world fell utterly still, and Kirkpatrick knew a thousand places he could be touched: the eyes, the heart, the pulse at his throat. He'd read of people awake for surgery, and knew it would be like this: the paralysis and soft places, the feel of fingers inside.

The gunshot saved his life.

It crashed through the trees, echoed off the hills; and in the throes of his fear, Kirkpatrick knew the sound—.308 Winchester, half mile away. In that moment he felt the *nothing's* rage as something touched his face, and his face burned. He screamed for long seconds, and was left suddenly alone.

An empty clearing.

No cold.

But he knew where the *nothing* had gone, and it was to the trail that led south.

Boyd was on the trail south.

His friend.

Pulling himself up, Kirkpatrick felt the battle inside, a great war between the man he'd been and the one he'd just become. He wanted to warn his friend, and wanted to run away. So great was the conflict, he actually whimpered, and that was the sound that decided him. He staggered to the southern trail, and onto it. Right foot. *He would break.* Left foot. *He would fail.*

He ran when Boyd started screaming.

The run took him along the trail, and the weakness disappeared. He was James Kirkpatrick, who'd never backed down or quit or lost a fight. So joyful was he in the rediscovery of self that he didn't feel the trail under his feet or the air that tore down his throat. He was a man, goddamn it, and his friend was afraid or hurt or dying. So he ran harder, faster. He covered the half mile in minutes, then rounded a bend in the trail and felt it break against him—everything he knew, everything he'd dreamed himself to be.

The clearing was a slash of switchgrass and mud, and water so burnished and black, it was metal. In the air above that water, the *nothing* had nailed his friend to an invisible cross. He hung in the air, arms out and stretched tight, his legs equally bound. And though no thing touched Boyd—no nails or wood or wire—Kirkpatrick would swear until death that his friend was crucified. Blood welled from his palms and feet. His eyes wept the same red tears. He hung ten feet above the water, screaming beneath whatever pressure unhinged his sockets and twisted his bones. Kirkpatrick looked for the *nothing;* couldn't find it. He saw mud, a rifle, the corpse of a gut-shot boar.

"William."

His hands opened and closed.

"William, my God."

Boyd heard him the second time. The screaming stopped; the jaw worked. "Kill it. . . ."

Blood ran from his eyes and dripped off his chin.

"James, kill it."

Kirkpatrick stooped for the rifle, and in the weight of it found the will to work the bolt and feed a cartridge into the chamber. He looked for the *nothing,* but the *nothing* found him first. Water rippled, and a shimmer parted the grass. Cold came with it, and with the cold, a face. A stroke of nothing made the smile. Gray holes were the eyes, and in the eyes was a darkness that moved and mocked and *knew.* It knew the child he'd been, all the regrets and fears and hidden failures. It dredged out the truth of his mother's death, that it wasn't the cancer that killed her, but a vomit-stained pillow and the strong hands of her only son. It knew how he'd wanted her to die, and dreaded it, how she'd begged and soiled herself, and how the bare-knuckle fight that followed was not about respect or money, but the horror of killing his mother, and of being alone in such a dim and shabby world.

"No."

The rifle slipped from nerveless fingers. He'd hated her, and loved her. She'd asked him to do it.

But you wanted to—

"Stop it!"

Kirkpatrick covered his ears, but the voice was inside and sounded like the boy he'd been.

You hated the smell of her and the sound of her and the way she touched herself when she drank—

"Stop it! Stop it!"

But the voice didn't stop. It rolled through him and deepened, and there was laughter when it said, *Run little boy, run.*

And that's what James Kirkpatrick did. He ran away from his friend and his past; he ran until Boyd screamed again, and even the screams were lost; then it was his breath and his sobbing, and a voice in his head that was his alone. *You're no son,* it said. *You're no kind of man, and no fucking friend, either.*

CHAPTER TWELVE

Johnny knew someone was in the Hush long before he heard the shot. He felt it like a touch, and that's how it happened sometimes: a sense of intrusion. The gunshot changed that. It gave direction, distance, certainty.

Three miles, he thought.

West and north.

Bottom of the hills.

Snatching a rifle off the wall, Johnny took off at a sprint. Barefoot in cutoff jeans, he was light and quick and, when he found the body, unwinded. Slowing when he saw it, Johnny dropped into a crouch and studied the clearing. He saw much, but *felt* little: heat in the blood, a gathering of flies. The body lay twisted in the shallows, part of it in the water, most of it on bruised grass. It looked wrong, he thought. How the arms bent. Looseness in the shoulders and hips. Blood made a mask of the dead man's face, but Johnny knew him.

William Boyd.

He stood above the body and understood all the *wrong* inside: the spiral fractures and crushed organs, how he'd chewed his own tongue bloody. Johnny turned away, and was nearly sick. He'd known violence and death, but never like this; he'd never *felt* it like this. The man's eyes were pulped, and his bones, in places, twisted to fragments.

Fighting the nausea, Johnny studied the dead boar, the clearing, the prints in the dirt. Most matched the boots on Boyd's feet, but others belonged to a heavy man with a long stride and a high arch. He'd come and gone on a game trail. *Running,* Johnny thought. *Sprinting.*

Touching the tracks, he wondered if he should follow them or stay with the body. It was a tough question. Coyote were denned up a quarter mile east, but the wind was moving that way, and the smell of blood with it. Other carrion eaters were close, too: buzzard and possum, hawk and crow and skunk. Even in the waters, the eel were stirring. Leave Boyd too long, and he'd be as picked over and flyblown as the boar, dead beside him.

"Shit."

The bigger issue landed on Johnny like a rock. William Boyd was dead on his land. That was a problem, and it left no choice. He had to follow the runner.

Pulling Boyd from the water first, Johnny covered the man's face and arranged the body as best he could. It would make no difference to the coyotes, but there it was.

After that he focused on the tracks.

They led north toward the river and were easy to follow, so that's how Johnny moved, fluid and smooth and easy. He discovered the camp first and took the time to search it, finding ammunition and gear, but no second rifle. That meant the runner was armed, so Johnny moved with greater care. He didn't need to catch anyone, but wanted to see the man's face, at least.

That was about the sheriff.

About what would come next.

A mile into the hills, the tracks joined the river and followed it upstream. When the water bent, Johnny cut the corner and looked down from a stone bald three hundred feet above the valley floor. He saw the man below, how he ran and fell, then dropped the rifle, snatched it up, and fell again. The next time he rose, he moved slowly and unsure, and even from the bald, Johnny saw blood on his face. He was talking to himself, or yelling. Johnny watched him follow the river until another hillside stole the view away.

After that Johnny took his time.

He knew where the guy was going.

Leon was behind the bar when he saw the white man stumble out of the brush. He was dressed to hunt, but dragged his rifle by the barrel, the stock of it hopping and skipping across the ground behind him. He appeared first from a band of river birch and wild cherry, then dropped into a gully and clambered up the other side. From a distance, he looked all kinds of wrong: the limp, the filth, the bloody skin. Leon had been drinking, so he blinked a few times to make sure of what he saw.

Still there. Still white and walking . . .

Nope.

He fell. Got back up.

Leon took quick stock of the bar. He had a few drinkers at the tables outside, some old-timers in the horseshoe pit. "Alvin." He shrugged off his apron and gestured to the only person inside. "Watch the bar."

"What's in it for me?"

"Have a drink." Leon's eyes were on the white man as he pulled a bottle of his cheapest bourbon and put it on the bar. "Have two."

Leon dropped his apron on a counter, then cleared the bar and went outside. The sun was only a hand above the trees, but the force of it was like a hammer. Leon shaded his eyes and looked across a hundred yards of scrub.

The man went down; stayed down. Leon sighed, then stepped out onto stony soil, checking the tree line, the river. Closer to the fallen man, he slowed, not much liking white folks or guns or trespassers. When he got close enough, he stopped. The man was facedown, barely conscious. Stooping until his knees popped, Leon pried the gun away and moved it to a safe place. When nothing happened, he rolled the man over, twitching once as the man cried out and what looked like a broken arm shifted.

Leon said, "Hey, man. You okay?"

He wasn't. Cuts and scratches covered his skin; his eyes showed half-white. To Leon, he looked like a man who'd run hard through miles of rough country. His clothes were torn, his lip split. Leon put him in his fifties. Expensive watch. Expensive rifle.

"Can you hear me? Do you have a name?" The man's mouth moved, but the sound was thin. Leon leaned in. "Say again."

"Crucifixion. Crucified."

"You're not making sense."

"He was crucified. Jesus Christ."

"Yeah, man, okay. Jesus was crucified."

Leon rocked onto his heels, thinking of problems he didn't need.

"Want me to call the cops?"

That was Alvin, who'd appeared unexpectedly. Leon couldn't hide his annoyance. "I told you to watch the bar."

"Yeah, but it was just two drinks."

Leon stood. He didn't want cops in his place, didn't want the questions.

"Where'd he come from anyway?"

"I have no idea." Leon looked at the trees and saw movement. "Well, shit."

It took Johnny Merrimon three minutes to cross the same broken ground. Barefoot and shirtless, he carried a rifle, a neutral expression. "Hello, Leon."

Leon nodded. "I suppose you know something about this?"

"Yeah. Maybe."

"Where are your clothes?"

"I wasn't planning to see people."

"Were you planning to shoot them?"

Johnny ignored the sarcasm, stooping beside the fallen man to check his eyes, the pulse at his throat.

Leon pointed. "Looks like he broke his arm."

"He took some hard falls. Has he said anything?"

"Yeah, Jesus died on a cross. Do you know who he is?"

"No idea."

"Then why were you following him?"

Johnny straightened. "It's complicated."

"A little or a lot?"

"We've got this one down, and another one dead in the swamp."

Johnny hooked a thumb in that direction, and Leon felt the sweat go cold on his neck. He thought of history and his grandfather, how even old and half-blind he clutched his fingers on Leon's wrist hard enough to make the boy cry. *You stay out of that swamp, boy. You stay out or I'll give you something real to cry about.*

"You okay?" Johnny asked.

"Bad juju."

"Bad something." Johnny put a hand on Leon's shoulder. "I'll need to use your phone."

An hour later, they were gathered beneath a purple sky: the sheriff and three deputies, two paramedics, Leon, Johnny, and Clyde Hunt. Hunt's badge meant little this far out in the county, but he and the sheriff went way back. They'd hated each other for a lot of years, then found their way to grudging respect. None of it would help Johnny when Boyd's name came out.

"I need to know why he was out there, tracking the victim and carrying a gun."

The sheriff's voice carried to where Johnny and Leon stood. So did Clyde's. "Listen, Willard—"

"Don't *Willard* me, Clyde. I know he's your boy and all, but I'm not leading my men into that swamp in the dead of night based on his word alone, not without knowing more. He says a man's dead. I've got no corroboration." The sheriff gestured at the ambulance, where paramedics worked over the injured man. "He's incoherent. We don't even know who he is."

"Just hang on a second, all right." Clyde waved over one of the paramedics. "What do we know about this guy?"

"He's midfifties, and fit. Most of his injuries are superficial lacerations and contusions. The arm is broken. Could have been a fall. Could have been defensive—"

"Defensive?" the sheriff interrupted.

"He could have fallen on a rock. Someone could have hit him. Until he talks, it's a guessing game."

"Has he said anything else?"

"Still talking about crucifixion and cold; and that's the funny thing. He has a lesion on his face." The paramedic touched a cheek and looked apologetic. "It sounds crazy, I know, but I think it's frostbite."

"In a swamp in this heat?"

"I've been doing this a long time, Sheriff. I'm pretty sure it's frostbite."

The paramedic went back to the injured man. The sheriff lifted a cap, scratched his head, and looked at Johnny. "Listen, Clyde. Let's forget my history with your stepson, okay. Even if I'd not arrested him once already, it's hard to live in this county and not worry about his mental state. People wonder what it did to him, losing his twin sister like that, losing his dad." He gestured at Johnny and squeezed his cap between two hands. "He lives out here alone; he's done time. Part of me thinks he's dangerous, and the other that he's batshit crazy. That being said, this is where we are. So I'm asking you cop-to-cop. Can I believe what he's telling me?"

"If he says there's a dead man out there, that's what you'll find."

"You're certain?"

"Johnny wouldn't lie about something like that."

"Yeah, shit. That's kind of what I figured. Mr. Merrimon." He raised his voice and called Johnny over. He'd already questioned him about the body, and the answers had been typically brusque. Part of that stemmed from the bad blood between them, and part from the kid's nature. He was unpredictable, untrusting, and he had a real hard-on about trespassers. None of that made the sheriff feel good about what had to happen next, not at the end of the day and the edge of so much blackness. "Johnny."

"Sheriff."

"Word around town is that you know the swamp like I know my own face. Is that true?"

"It is."

"Could you lead me to the body?"

"Yes."

"Even in the dark?"

"In the dark with my eyes closed."

"Any chance a helicopter might get in there."

"Not if you want it to land."

"So you're my only choice."

"If you want the body out before scavengers pick it to the bone."

"Christ, this just gets better and better."

"Actually," Johnny said. "I think it's about to get worse."

"Son." The sheriff got angry. "If there's something you're not telling me, now's the *fucking* time."

Johnny looked at his stepfather; kept his eyes there. "Can I talk to you?"

"Clyde—"

"Willard, give us a minute." Clyde led Johnny away from the sheriff, the deputies. When they were alone, Johnny told him the rest.

"It's William Boyd," he said. "The dead man."

"What?"

"It looks bad, I know."

"'Bad' doesn't touch it, son. You have a history. You fired on him eleven times—"

"That's why I didn't tell the sheriff. I wanted you here—"

"Jesus, Johnny."

"How bad is it?"

Clyde ran a hand through his hair. In the gloom, the sheriff was watching them. "You're positive it's Boyd?"

"Yes. I'm sorry."

"Tell me exactly what happened." Johnny repeated the story. The gunshot. How he found the body and followed the tracks. "That's it?" Clyde said. "That's everything?"

"Just like I told the sheriff."

Clyde walked away; came back. "He won't overlook your history with Boyd. He can't."

"I knew as much when I called him. Look, I did nothing wrong—"

"You should have a lawyer."

"I did nothing wrong."

"Damn it, son. That's not the point." Clyde paced, thinking of his wife, another arrest, the boy he loved like a son.

"We need to go," Johnny said. "If we don't, there'll be nothing left."

Two hours into the hike, the sheriff still carried tension in his shoulders. "He didn't have to call us, Willard. He could have left the body out there."

"I'm too tired for this conversation, Clyde."

Everyone was tired. After Johnny dropped his bomb on the sheriff, they'd waited another hour for more men, and the sheriff had made his reasons plain. "If I'm going into the woods with him, I want more men. End of discussion."

That was the attitude, and it infected every one of the sheriff's men. Even the medical examiner looked sideways at Johnny.

"Willard—"

"I said shut the hell up."

And that's how it went. Johnny was the enemy, and Clyde was, too. The hike made it no easier. The terrain was broken stone, and then mud. The bugs tormented everyone but Johnny.

"The camp is just ahead." Johnny parted the vines, and men filed onto dry ground. "I searched it earlier. There's not much to see."

"You tampered with my scene?"

Johnny put his light on the sheriff's face. "I didn't *tamper* with anything."

"Son, you'd best take that light out of my eyes."

Johnny gave it a beat, then lowered the light. "Another half mile," he said. "Then you'll have your body."

The sheriff left two men at the camp and followed Johnny deeper into the swamp. Johnny hated all of it: the noise and dislike, the strange men and their ignorance. He heard them even when they whispered.

What a shithole.

Who would live out here?

"Are you okay?"

Johnny ignored his stepfather's question. "Are *you*?" he asked, and it wasn't rhetorical. He felt Clyde's revulsion, too, and the unasked questions that followed.

Why would a young man choose this?

How normal could he possibly be?

"There's your body."

Johnny stopped at the edge of the glade and put a spear of light on the remains of William Boyd. Black wings rustled above the shape. Yellow eyes winked in the light.

"Dear God."

A deputy crossed himself as more lights found the body and those things that fed on it. The sheriff called out: "Go on! Get!" He waved his arms, and though a few birds took flight, none of the coyote moved away. They showed yellow teeth, bloody snouts. One of them kept eating. The sheriff drew his revolver and put three rounds into a mud bank twenty feet away. The coyote broke for cover, and the sheriff sighed deeply. "Okay, gentlemen. Let's see just how ruined this poor bastard really is."

Turns out he was pretty ruined. Two of the deputies got sick. Even the medical examiner covered his mouth. "Everybody settle down," the sheriff said. "Let's get some more lights over here, and do our jobs. Hankins. Martinez. Come on, boys." They got more lights on the body, and the sheriff squatted beside it. Some of the face was gone, but not all of it. "It's Boyd, all right. Mr. Merrimon, is this how you found him? Forget the scavengers. I'm talking about location, clothing, position. Is there anything different?"

"I moved him," Johnny said.

"You what?"

"His legs were in the water when I found him. The blood would have drawn more scavengers. Moving him seemed like the decent thing to do."

"That's twice you've disturbed my crime scene."

"It's twice I've done the right thing. Three times if you count calling you in the first place."

"I tell you what." The sheriff stood, trying to use weight and height to intimidate. "Why don't you stand over there, and stay out of my way."

"Are you finished with me?"

"Son, I'm not even close."

"You have the body. You can find your way out."

"I still have questions."

"I don't have answers."

"Stand over there and wait."

"Am I under arrest?"

"There! Now!"

Everyone was watching, so Johnny kept the anger off his face. He walked to the edge of the scene, and when Clyde joined him, he asked the only question that mattered. "Am I under arrest or not?"

"No, Johnny, you're not, but don't antagonize him. I'll do what I can to make this easy."

He meant well, but Johnny knew what would make things easy. That was peace and silence, his thumb on the pulse of the Hush. He gave it a moment for Clyde's sake, then slipped like a ghost into the night.

He was a mile away before anyone noticed.

CHAPTER THIRTEEN

In a tall building in a large city, Cree dreamed of the swamp. There was no bed or bedroom or plywood door, no lights from a city beyond the glass. She was in the dark in a small space, unmoving in air that smelled of earth and death and rotting wood. If she moved, the space constricted. Open her mouth, and earth filled it. She cried out in her sleep, but it was not in the nature of a dream to hold its shape. She heard rain from a distant place; felt heat rise and fall as seasons blurred and the world turned. She was in the earth, and of it; and in the dream, she rose above.

From a height, she looked down and saw the swamp, but not just as it was. She saw it before the slaves were hanged, and after the fires were lit. She saw the people who'd lived and died and been buried there, the men with broad backs, the wide-hipped women and their strong, yowling babies. She saw the hardships and the joys, the gardens and the hunts, the fears and failures and the old women who kept the secret ways. Cree saw it all, but it was like a taste that burst bright, then faded to leave her alone and empty and wanting more. But the dream was no kind of giver. It swept her through the trees and over black water; and as she drifted, the fear welled up to move inside her, penetrant and physical and vile. She cried out again and, in the horror of that moment, heard words in the darkness beyond.

Pain has always been the price. . . .

"Grandmother."

She opened her mouth, and tasted earth.

This is history. This is life.

"Not this," she said. "Never this."

But she'd experienced it before, a thousand dreams on a thousand nights. Then, as now, the fear moved deeper and Cree, again, cried out in her sleep. She heard it in the dream, and such was her life, asleep: the present and the past, things imagined and unseen. Choking on the fear, she looked down to see men in the swamp. It was dark, but she knew police by the way they stood; knew the body by its stillness. A man was dead, and he'd not died easily. She dreamed of twisted bones and screams, but not all the dream was bad. She saw a man, separate from the others, and knew the man was Johnny Merrimon. A mile away and moving east, he hummed quietly as he walked, and a soft light walked with him.

The image stayed with Cree as her eyes opened and she blinked against the sunlight. She was in her room, and the world smelled of traffic. She heard the engines, the horns. Her head ached, but it always hurt after dreams of the swamp.

"Mom," she called out, but not eagerly. The dream was already receding, and the fear with it. Soon, the images would fade like old print, another page in the scrapbook of messed-up dreams. That's how she thought of it. She didn't want the dreams. Didn't ask to be buried alive, terrified, stripped bare. The only good to come from dreams were those rare times she heard her grandmother's voice. So many years had passed since they'd spoken or touched or shared the simplest joys. Cree feared she might forget the look of her and the feel, the smell of dry skin, like cinnamon and bark and sunbaked grass.

Swinging her legs from under the sheets, Cree pulled on jeans and a shirt, and used a metal pin to pull back her hair. In the mirror, her face looked odd, the nose flatter, the eyes darker and harder and more deeply set. For that moment, she had two faces, one atop the other; but the sensation passed. Too much of the dream, she thought. Too much strangeness.

Moving into the hall, Cree heard a television in the kitchen. The volume was low, the picture grainy. Her mother sat unmoving at a small table covered with chipped Formica. She wore old slippers and a housecoat, worn thin. The cigarette in her hand carried two inches of ash. A bottle of vodka sat half-empty beside her.

"It's over." She spoke softly when she saw her daughter, flicking the ash at last, and taking a drag on the cigarette. "He's dead. It's over."

"What are you talking about?"

Cree sat, and her mother pointed at the television. "William Boyd is dead. It's been on the news all morning."

Cree looked at the television, saw a commercial about waffles. "How much have you had to drink?"

"Not much. What's the point?"

"There are other ways—"

"What other ways?" her mother snapped. "Our appeal is based on *policy*! No lawyer will take that on contingency. You know that. We've tried every firm in the city. They laughed at us. You were there. You remember."

"We can raise the money ourselves."

"For lawyers at five hundred dollars an hour. No." She laughed sadly. "It's over. We lost."

"Are you okay?"

"We were this close."

She held up a thumb and forefinger, a half inch apart. Had they won the case, Boyd would have paid millions for the land. Many millions. Cree's mother had dreamed of that money. She wanted to leave this thin-walled apartment in a dirty needle of a building. She wanted a house with a yard, and for her daughter to go to college. They were normal dreams, free of avarice, and Cree had wanted her to have those things, but only later. She wanted time in the Hush first, years if that's what it took. She had questions from childhood, the memories of lessons painfully taught. Such things should make sense. Why else the dreams, the visions of old women that haunted, still?

"Will you talk about it now?"

"That place?" The mother showed a bloodshot eye. "Those crazy old women? No. I'm not going to talk about it."

"It's my history, too. I have a right to know."

"About what? Life in the mud? Why I left? Haven't I apologized enough for sending you there? Best thing you can do now is move on."

"To where? A bottle? Four different husbands?"

"I've said all along that place is money for us, and nothing else. You're too young to judge."

"But there's something special there. I feel it."

"No, child." The mother stubbed out the cigarette, and a hundred pale scars showed on the skin of her arms. "There's not a thing that's special."

When Johnny woke, he felt the search: a dozen men and even more resentment. They were angry about the mud, the heat, the biting flies. Mostly they were upset about the night before. They'd had Johnny and let him walk away. Now they had an angry sheriff, a hundred questions, and a billionaire, still dead.

None of it bothered Johnny.

He made a smokeless fire and cooked breakfast. When he was finished, he doused the coals and focused on the search.

They were lost.

Four men had blundered two miles east, following a track that filtered into a peat bog and left them there, thigh-deep. Another three had been walking a circle since dawn. The sheriff and four others were closest, but even they were bogged down and pointed in the wrong direction.

The helicopter appeared midmorning. It worked a grid east to west, but Johnny had built his cabin under the trees and kept his footprint small. Maybe they'd spot a woodpile or an edge of a skiff, but Johnny doubted it. What wasn't water was forest, and the forest hid its secrets well.

Of course, Johnny wasn't fooled about the outcome. Boyd was rich and powerful, and people like that didn't die without ripples. Johnny would have to talk to the sheriff sooner or later; it wouldn't be fun.

But this was.

Johnny tracked the sheriff's group for three hours. He watched them struggle and sweat, and if they turned his way, Johnny ghosted. He was in the trees, a flicker. They never saw him.

Jack arrived at noon, and Johnny felt it ten seconds before the sheriff's radio squawked. "Sheriff, it's Clark. We got Jack Cross here, like you asked."

The sheriff palmed sweat, muttered a quiet *about damn time,* then keyed the radio. "Hold him there. We're coming to you."

For Jack, it was a nightmare: the newspaper and the cops, the worry as they'd walked him to a car, then dumped him beside the old church and told him to wait.

"For what?" Jack asked.

They didn't answer, so he swatted mosquitoes and watched cops circle a table covered with maps and radios. It took the sheriff another hour to get there, and he looked like a bite of food the swamp had found distasteful enough to spit out. Black mud stained the uniform and caked his shoes. His face was swollen from bug bites and brambles and heat. "Show me where to find him." He took Jack by the arm and propelled him toward the map-strewn table. "I know you come here. I know you know."

Jack caught his balance, unsurprised at the level of hostility. He was a lawyer and Johnny's friend, the son of a dirty cop. "What, exactly, is happening here, Sheriff?"

"You know about William Boyd, dead on your friend's land?"

"Yes."

"Well, Johnny's the one who found him."

"And you want him for questioning?"

"I *had him* for questioning last night. He ran before I could finish."

Jack studied the men in the clearing. They were angry. The anger landed on Jack. "Is Johnny a suspect?"

"He and Boyd had a violent history."

"That seems circumstantial, at best."

"Will you help me or not?"

Jack thought about it and took his time. He was new in the law, but had been a son of law enforcement for a long time, and knew how sideways things could get when cops took things personally.

This looked personal.

All of it.

"Where's Johnny's stepfather?"

"This is a county matter. Clyde Hunt is neither welcome nor invited."

"Is he aware of the search?"

"I'll ask you one last time, Mr. Cross, and then I'm going to get truly, biblically angry."

"If you want my help, there are things I need."

The sheriff turned so red, he was purple. "What?"

"First of all, I go in alone."

"No."

"Second of all . . ."

The negotiation took ten minutes, and in the end, Jack went after Johnny alone. At the edge of the clearing, he faced the sheriff and hammered the high points one more time. "If he says no, I won't force him."

"Then I'll find him myself, and drag him out by the feet. His choice."

"If you follow me, I walk out."

"You have two hours. No one will follow you."

"If I bring him out, you're gentle—"

"Jesus Christ."

"No force, no cuffs. He's a cooperating witness."

"Fine. Yes."

Jack turned for the swamp, but stopped. "One last thing," he said. "I'm going in there as his lawyer, not his friend. Anything he tells me is privileged."

"Goddamn lawyers . . ."

"So long as we understand each other."

"Just go," the sheriff said again. "Get out of here before I change my mind."

Jack gave it a beat, not for the sheriff's sake but for his own. Even as a trained attorney, he disliked confrontation. More than that, he hated the swamp. The feeling was new, but even here, on the soft edge of it, the wilderness felt hostile. Jack peered beneath the trees, trying to pinpoint why it felt so different than it ever had. The colors were just as vivid, the shadows equally deep. It was *knowledge,* Jack decided, the awareness of Johnny's behavior and strange healing, of dream walks and terrors and midnight cold. On the brightest day, that would be enough, but there was death in the Hush, too, and not just any death. The newspapers were vague about what, exactly, killed William Boyd; but Jack knew damn well it wasn't Johnny.

What did that leave?

The question followed him under the trees and away from the ruins of the old settlement. So dense was the forest that he lost all sight of people after two minutes' walk. Ten minutes in, things looked wrong. The trail bent when it should have run straight; water flickered where none had been before. After twenty minutes, Jack stopped, and turned a circle. He'd been to Johnny's cabin a hundred times, at least. He'd walked the same trail, touched the same trees. Everything, now, was different.

"I've never seen this place."

He turned another circle, but the disorientation was so strong, it made breathing difficult. There was too much water in the air, too much weight. Digging deep, he picked a direction that felt almost right, and kept walking. Four minutes became another ten. There was no trail left, and a voice inside spoke bitter truth: *This is wrong, so wrong.* But Johnny was still out there, as was the pressure, the weight, whatever killed William Boyd. Jack scrubbed at his face, ducked beneath another branch. When something small and hard struck him in the back, he flinched, and almost screamed. Then he saw a pebble, lying pale on the damp earth.

"Goddamn."

Jack slumped to the ground and buried his face in his hands. He could be weeping; he wasn't sure. There was so much relief, so much sudden anger.

"You scared me, Johnny. Jesus."

Johnny stepped from the trees, bouncing a second pebble on his palm. "Ah, don't be dramatic."

"Really, man. Something's wrong."

"What do you mean?"

"Look around, dude. I'm lost."

"Don't be stupid."

Jack kept his eyes down and shook his head. He was embarrassed by the fear, the dampness on his cheeks.

"Jack, come on. Look at me." Johnny knelt at Jack's side. He pulled leaves from his friend's hair, brushed dirt from his clothes. "I'm sorry if I scared you. I didn't mean to. You're okay, man. I promise. Just look at me."

Jack didn't want to, but it was the same Johnny, the J-man, the same friend.

"It's easy to get turned around in here. It can happen to anyone." Johnny took Jack's hand and pulled him up. "See. No problems. You've been here a million times."

"You're not listening."

"Same trail, same view."

Johnny gestured across an expanse of water, and in the distance was a hillside, a hint of stone. Jack's stomach sank; he felt sick. "That's not possible."

"You're not lost."

"It wasn't like this . . ."

"Mm-hmm."

"Don't judge me, man. You have no idea!"

More frightened than ever, Jack stalked away and sat against a birch whose bark was loose and peeling and dusty red.

What the hell is happening?

Jack knew where the cabin was. He could almost see it.

"I swear I was lost."

"You were on the trail the whole time."

"How can you know that?"

"You're here, aren't you? Can't get here unless the trail brings you."

Jack opened his mouth, but Johnny was right. He was here. He knew the place.

"Tell me about the cops," Johnny said.

"What?"

"The cops." Johnny leaned against a second tree. "Are they pissed off? What about the sheriff? Did you see all that sweat? Priceless."

"How do you know about the sheriff's sweat?"

"I've been watching him all morning. You should have seen him, Jack. Hip deep in mud. Poking at sticks he thought were snakes."

"You followed him?"

"It was hilarious."

"Do you think this is some kind of game?" For a moment, Jack forgot his fears. He came off the tree, furious. "William Boyd is dead. The sheriff is fifty–fifty you did it. Why make him angry?"

"Because screw him, that's why!"

The sound of Johnny's voice, raised in anger, pushed Jack back a step. Johnny never yelled. It didn't happen. "He has twenty people out looking for you."

"A dozen," Johnny said. "Unless you count the ones by the church."

"Dear God. You *do* think this is a game."

"Of course it's a game, and I'm winning."

Jack studied his friend more closely. He was worked up. The dark eyes glinted. "Why do you hate him so much?"

"I just do, is all."

"Because he locked you up?"

"Have you ever been in jail, Jackie-boy?" Johnny lobbed a final pebble; it bounced off Jack's chest and landed at his feet. "I'll talk to that old bastard when I'm good and ready."

Eventually, Jack convinced Johnny to leave the swamp. He asked a lot of questions, and got the full story: the body and Johnny's walk out, how he brought the sheriff back in, and what they found. It took some time, and in the end, he gave Johnny the best advice he could.

"Keep your mouth shut until I find you a criminal lawyer."

"That's all you've got?"

"Yeah, that's it. You need a no-bullshit, thirty-years-in-court, criminal attorney."

Johnny shook his head. "They'll never hold me."

"Don't be so sure."

Johnny grinned the same grin, and that's how it had always been: the certainty and the reckless smile, the confidence that was as alien to Jack as life on Mars.

"You coming?" Johnny asked.

He was twenty feet away, and Jack was already lost in thoughts of consequence and worry. Where Johnny was good on instinct, Jack's strength had always been in gauging risk. That was about deeper understandings, patience, the careful path. Jack knew what the sheriff wanted. That worried him, but the Hush was here and now. So, on the way out, Jack walked behind his friend, and as he did, he watched the trail. Where were the dim places, the odd turnings? None of it made sense.

"Watch your step."

Johnny pointed at a coral snake, and even that seemed harmless compared to the walk in, alone.

"Does it ever worry you, J-man? You know. Being here by yourself?"

"That's a silly question."

A week ago, Jack would have agreed. "What do you think killed Boyd?"

Johnny stopped, and turned. "Say that again."

"Huh?"

"You asked *what* killed Boyd, not *who*. Why'd you phrase it like that?"

Jack tilted his head, thinking about it. "I honestly don't know."

"You sure?"

"I said, I don't know."

And he didn't.

But he thought about it as the walk resumed.

What killed William Boyd?

What?

The question felt right.

When they reached firm ground, Johnny paused beneath the final trees, looking out. "A lot of people."

Jack peered past his friend and saw fifteen cops, at least. Groups of them stood and smoked and looked tense. The sheriff was bent over the maps, his big hands on the edge of the table. "Just remember what I said."

"Wait for the lawyer. Got it."

"Let me go first."

Jack took the lead, and it felt strange, the leading of Johnny Merrimon. When they were halfway to the church, the sheriff spotted them.

"You cut it close, Counselor. Two more minutes, and I was coming in after you."

"I said I'd find him, and I have." Jack stopped a few feet from the sheriff and the men who gathered behind him. "I expect you to honor your side of this, too."

The sheriff brushed past Jack. His eyes were heavy on Johnny's, and Jack wondered if he'd ever seen such animosity. "You gave us a pretty run of it this morning."

Johnny shrugged, and the sheriff's eyes narrowed. The mud on his uniform was partially dry. His hands and face were smeared with it. Beside him, Johnny looked fresh as a daisy. He was almost smiling.

Shit . . .

"Why did you run off last night?"

Johnny said, "You were being an asshole."

"I had a dead billionaire on my hands. Such a thing can make a man tense."

"It felt like more than that."

"I won't lie to you, son. I don't understand you, and won't pretend to like you. That's nothing new and no surprise, either. But as long as you answer my questions, and do it in a respectful manner, I'll keep this professional and quick and clean." The sheriff turned sideways and raised an arm. "If you'll come with us to the station—"

"No."

"I'm sorry."

The sheriff blinked twice, mouth open. It didn't bother Johnny at all. "Nobody said anything about the station. We can talk here."

"I'm sure you'd like that, but I can speak for the rest of us when I say we'd like air-conditioning and a change of clothes."

"Tough day in the swamp?"

The sheriff's eyes hardened further as, behind him, two deputies showed faces just as bitter and bug-bitten and angry. "I should take you down for that."

Johnny pointed. "You have a leech."

The sheriff touched his neck, found the leech, and pulled it off, bloody. "Son of a bitch."

A smile slid onto Johnny's face.

The sheriff took him down.

At the station, it was chaos in the parking lot, chaos in the halls. A deputy had each arm. Two more moved in front, and in back. Johnny fought them for most of it. He knew what was coming.

"Don't say anything, Johnny!" That was Jack, yelling through the crowd. "Sheriff, this is unacceptable. Is my client even under arrest?"

The sheriff turned, still angry. "Your moment will come, Counselor." A buzzer sounded, and the crowd of cops squeezed Johnny through a doorway. "But it's not now."

A metal door clanged, and Johnny was alone with men in uniform, in a hall he remembered. He knew Jack was upset; but the sheriff had never questioned Jack, never leaned on him, breathed in his face, locked him up. Jack could not know how personal that felt. Nor could he fathom the hell an isolated box could be for a man like Johnny. The sheriff, though, had seen it. He knew Johnny paced like a caged animal, that he couldn't eat, couldn't sleep, that collapse alone had broken the cycle. A full week had passed in isolation before Johnny woke with a drip in his arm and a nurse peeling back an eyelid.

Can you hear me?

Do you know where you are?

The sheriff had been there, too, not smiling but satisfied. When he'd leaned above Johnny, he'd smelled of toothpaste and hair tonic. "There are no hunger strikes in this jail."

"I wasn't striking."

"I need to hear you say it."

"I'll eat," Johnny said; and when he'd swallowed enough to convince them, they returned him to the concrete box where he couldn't run or see the stars or *feel* anything.

"Interview three."

The sheriff directed the deputies, and they got him into the third interview room, though Johnny didn't make it easy. With his cuffs bolted to the table, the deputies stepped away, making room for the sheriff, who pointed at Johnny's scrapes, the split lip. "It didn't have to be like this."

"We both know you wanted me here."

"Yeah, well. You're the only one in the county who's tried, once already, to kill my victim."

"I didn't kill him."

"Maybe and maybe not. We'll talk about that once I wash the swamp off my face."

The sheriff turned for the door, and Johnny smiled the dangerous smile. "There's rarely the one leech, you know." He licked blood from his teeth and spit it, pink, on the floor. "You might want to check your pants."

The sheriff did exactly that. He showered in the locker room and changed clothes.

No leeches.

In the hall, one of his deputies stopped him. "Clyde Hunt is in your office."

"Tell him I don't have time right now."

"He's a city captain. You can't blow him off."

"Shit."

"You knew this was coming."

"Thought I'd have more time."

"You can blame the lawyer for that."

"Okay, yeah. I'll deal with it."

Sheriff Willard Cline was not a bad man—he'd say as much to anybody. He didn't take payoffs, or drink to excess or favor the powerful. He did the job as clean as any lawman could, and for the trouble, he'd been reelected for forty years straight. Even at seventy-one, he was trusted by the people of Raven County. They thought he had a good head. He thought so, too; but the Merrimon kid bothered him.

"Clyde." The sheriff entered his office with both palms up. "You don't have to say it. I know you're upset."

"Is he under arrest?"

"Not yet, no."

"Then I want him released."

The sheriff circled his desk and sighed inwardly. Clyde was a good man, and he was right about most of it. "Just sit down, okay. I know you're angry. I understand it. Please." The sheriff gestured to a chair and waited. Clyde was agitated, but eventually sat.

"Why is my stepson in custody?"

"It's complicated."

"Short version."

"History." The sheriff rolled his shoulders. "Means and opportunity."

"No motive."

"I just want to talk to him, Clyde. You'd feel the same way."

"Jack Cross tells me the arrest got violent."

"Yeah." Another sigh. "There's that."

The sheriff looked at everything but Clyde. The shower had offered time to calm down, and he was not proud of how he'd behaved. It was the swamp, the sleeplessness, and that kid, that . . . damn kid. "He bothers me, Clyde. All right. I admit it."

"Bothers you, why?"

How could Willard explain that something untouchable lived in Johnny Merrimon? He asked for nothing, took nothing, gave nothing. Even as a child, he'd maintained a deep-eyed implacability that would be unnatural in a grown man.

Could it be resentment?

"He rubs me the wrong way, Clyde. I can't explain it."

"He's my wife's son. I've raised him since he was thirteen."

"I just want to talk to him."

"Then talk to him, damn it. Don't pile on three deep and haul him in, cuffed. You wouldn't even know Boyd was dead if Johnny hadn't called."

"And that doesn't bother you? That he just happened to find a body in all that wilderness? We're talking countryside dense as a thicket. You honestly think your boy just stumbled on a dead man he'd already shot at once? You're a cop, for God's sake. You know better."

"You brought my son in bloody. That's all I know for sure."

The sheriff scrubbed his hands across his face. He'd been up for thirty-six hours, and in the swamp for most of it. It shouldn't have happened like this, but he'd known Johnny when he was a wild-eyed boy in war paint and eagle feathers, a heartsick, screwed-up kid with a stolen pistol in one pocket and the keys to a stolen truck in the other. The papers called him a hero, but he'd been a trespasser, a truant, and a thief; and that was just in childhood. As a man, he'd quit everything wholesome and good. Now Boyd was dead, and it was impossible—here, of all places—for the sheriff to discount the behavior he'd seen Merrimon exhibit in jail. He'd almost died, alone in a cell. He'd gone damn near catatonic, and that was in isolation, the first week. No one fell that hard in a room alone, not unless they were already broken.

"I want him released, Willard. I'm asking as a friend."

The sheriff shook his head, and was genuinely sad for the cop across his desk. "He'll disappear if I let him go, and I don't much care to go in that swamp again."

"You can't arrest him without cause. I'll call a judge if I have to. I'll call the goddamn DA."

"I've already called her, Clyde." The sheriff leaned away, and took no pleasure in what came next. "I want authority to charge."

The district attorney was in court, so it didn't happen fast. *Three hours.* Word spread from the sheriff to Clyde to Jack. In three hours, the DA would come.

"I want to see him. I'm his lawyer." The sergeant at the front desk was not impressed by Jack's voice or by the card Jack smacked against the bulletproof glass. "Lawyer." Jack said it slowly, in case there was some confusion. "Lawyer."

Clyde put a hand on Jack's shoulder. "You'll have to go higher than him to get what you want."

"Who, then? Every sitting judge is on the bench, and wouldn't get involved this early, regardless. The DA will side with the sheriff—"

"Maybe, Jack. But she's answerable, too. I don't think they have enough to hold anybody."

Jack showed the desk sergeant his back. "You're talking about motive."

"Motive. Murder weapon. As far as I can tell, no one knows exactly how Boyd died or even when."

"So, why the arrest? Why now?"

Hunt sat on a plastic chair. The wall behind him was cinder block, painted green, the floors stained concrete. "He's hoping Johnny will say something stupid."

"I told him not to talk."

Clyde smiled sadly. "Does he often do what you say?"

Jack sat down, knowing the big detective was right. Johnny played by his own rules. Always had. "Can't you do something?"

"The body was found in the county. I'm city."

"What about back channels to the DA? Connections? Favors?"

Hunt shook his head. "I've called in every favor I have, but Boyd died a billionaire. People worry about blowback."

"Does Johnny's mom know?"

"She's on her way home from the coast, and, yes, she knows."

"Shit."

"Yep." Hunt scrubbed his face. "That pretty much sums it up."

After that, the minutes ticked past, and neither spoke. Pressure built until Jack stood and paced, then sat again.

"You're not making this any easier."

But Jack couldn't stop. He went from the front door to the bulletproof glass, back and forth until he turned, once, and found the sheriff behind the glass. "Cross."

The sheriff mouthed his name and pointed at the inner door. Jack crossed the room, and looked at Hunt as the door buzzed and clicked open.

"Jack . . ."

Hunt was on his feet, with something like despair on his face. Jack tried for confidence, but his voice sounded thin. "I won't let him talk."

After that, Jack was through the door and alone with the sheriff. He started to speak, but the sheriff waved him down. "Keep your shorts on, Counselor. Your client is safe and unharmed, and nobody's said nothing."

Jack followed the sheriff, and tried to appear as if keeping quiet were his choice. In the third hall, the sheriff stopped beside a metal door with a window at chin height. Jack saw wire in the glass, his friend beyond the wire. "Thank you for letting me see him."

"This is no favor, Counselor. Mr. Merrimon decided he wanted an attorney after all."

"Didn't he tell you that two hours ago?"

"Nope." The sheriff opened the door. "He did not."

Jack looked into the room and saw what he'd always imagined. Metal furniture. More concrete. Johnny's hands were cuffed to a steel ring in the table's center. He faced the two-way glass, his back to the door. "How much time do I have?"

"That'll be up to the DA." The sheriff gestured Jack inside, smiling as if he knew the young lawyer had never had a real client or seen the inside of a jail. "Make yourself at home. Microphone's off."

Inside, the room smelled of concrete, industrial-strength cleaner, and old sweat. Jack waited until the door clanked shut behind him, then moved to the table, where he saw an unsigned Miranda waiver and a felt-tip pen. His friend did not look up, so Jack sat down, shocked by the sight of Johnny's face. There was no color left; dark circles spread beneath his eyes. "Johnny?" His friend dredged up a smile, but it came from some distant, painful place. Jack had never seen anything so hollow before. "Jesus, man. What'd they do to you?"

"Not a thing." Johnny shifted, and the restraints scraped in the bolt. "Thanks for coming."

Jack looked away from Johnny's face. It was so drawn, it was gaunt. "You sure you're okay?"

"It'll get worse before it gets better."

"What does that mean?"

"Nothing, man. Just talk." Johnny's eyes tracked up the wall and settled on a point near the ceiling. "Is the sun down yet?"

"What?"

"I can't feel it."

Jack felt something like panic. He was out of his element, and there was no logic in his friend. Eager for something to do, Jack scanned the Miranda waiver. All the blanks were filled in: Johnny's name, the date.

"That was the sheriff," Johnny said. "He wanted me to sign it."

"Did he question you? Did you say anything?"

"Just that I wanted to see you." Johnny's eyes drifted to the same spot on the same wall. Jack looked there as well, but saw nothing. "That's west." Johnny's eyelids drooped, and he tilted his head, looking at Jack. "How long did you say I'd been here?"

Jack ignored the question. "I've been talking to lawyers," he said. "Big names. Heavy hitters. Clyde's paying for it, so don't worry about the cost. Just keep quiet until I get somebody lined up."

"Tell Clyde to save his money."

"Johnny—"

"I'll be out by tomorrow."

Jack leaned back and frowned. "You can't be certain of that."

"Is the sun down yet?"

"Why do you keep asking that?"

Johnny looked at the same spot on the same wall. "I can't tell if it's down or not."

CHAPTER FOURTEEN

Bonnie Busby had been the Raven County district attorney for seven years. Before that, she'd been an assistant DA for another twenty. Trim at fifty-one, she worked seventy hours a week for little money or appreciation. Still, she loved the job, and that emotion was not about politics or power or the joys of the fight. Bonnie was a law-and-order DA, plain and simple. She believed in justice and the power of the state. Satisfaction, for her, came from the efficient harnessing of that power to make the world safer for the good people of Raven County—emphasis on the word *good*. Were it up to her, every killer, rapist, drunk driver, dirty politician, crooked cop, burglar, thug, voyeur, trespasser, arsonist, jaywalker, and litterbug would be penalized to the full extent of the law. But that was not realistic. She had six ADAs, seven legal assistants, a budget.

Time was a problem, too.

She took the sheriff's call in a hallway outside Superior Court. She was one recess away from closing arguments on a child endangerment charge where the girl's mother had left her four-year-old on the side of a county road as punishment for talking back in the car. The kid had stood there—barefoot and bawling—until a bartender, on his way to work, stopped and called the cops. The kid could have died, disappeared; and Bonnie didn't stand for that shit.

Closing arguments took an hour.

The jury took half as long.

"Call the sheriff." Bonnie straightened files and watched bailiffs lead the mother away. "Tell him I'll be there in five."

Outside the courthouse, no one would look at Bonnie twice until they got close. Then it was all about the eyes and the focus. Even at one inch over five feet, she moved with more purpose than the six district attorneys who'd gone before her. People stepped from her path. Those who knew her nodded with sincere respect.

Two blocks from the courthouse, she rounded into the secure entrance of the building that housed the sheriff's department and the county jail. A key card got her through the outer door. After that, she passed through a magnetometer and signed the log. "Where's the sheriff?"

A uniformed deputy buzzed her through another door, then led her deeper into the labyrinth. She knew the gist of what was coming. She knew Clyde Hunt, too. He was one of the good ones.

Ten steps before the sheriff's office, she put on her toughest face, and that was not just for Clyde's sake. She had a dead billionaire—which was bad enough—but she had Johnny Merrimon, too, and that was a complication she didn't need. Ten years had passed since he put Raven County on the map, but for people in her jurisdiction, it felt like yesterday: *the warrior, the little chief.* Except for the dustup with William Boyd—which was unfortunate but understandable—Johnny had kept his head down, and she respected that. But he still wore the kind of dark celebrity that would draw attention from coast to coast. Bonnie didn't want to see her town in magazines or books or newspapers, didn't want it on television again, or dissected in the news. She hated that kind of attention. It complicated things.

"Willard." She entered the sheriff's office the same way she entered every room, and he came to his feet like a puppet on a string.

"Bonnie. Thanks for making the time. You know Captain Lee, my number two."

Tom Lee stood. He ran major crimes for the sheriff's department, a sharp man with a genuine smile and a hand extended. Bonnie shook, but otherwise ignored the pleasantries. She took a chair opposite the desk. "My office tells me Clyde Hunt is here as well. Will he be joining us?"

The sheriff sat; so did Captain Lee. "Detective Hunt's presence would be inappropriate."

"Okay. Fair. How about you bring me up to speed."

The sheriff did just that, keeping the story linear and simple and clean. "There's no way he *stumbled* on that body, not in thousands of acres of swamp."

"He owns the land. I assume he's familiar with it."

"If you saw the property you'd know that's irrelevant. In places, you can't see more than twenty feet."

"What about the site itself?"

"The body was in grass, waist high. All but invisible until you get close."

"Boyd was trespassing?"

"Hunting," the sheriff said. "Just like the last time."

Shit. Bonnie remembered the last time. She'd prosecuted the case. "That's your theory, then? Johnny tried once to scare Boyd off—"

"Shoots up the camp, makes his feelings plain."

"Then Boyd shows up again, and gets killed for the trouble. Decent theory. What about the witness?"

"James Kirkpatrick. He's still not talking."

"Rumor is he's catatonic."

"That's a fair statement."

"Doctors?"

"Uncertain when or if he'll come out of it. They're saying it's psychological."

"How so?"

"Emotional trauma of some sort. Whatever the hell happened out there."

Bonnie frowned again. Witnesses were like gold, but only if they could communicate. Considering the case from all angles, she shook her head. "It's not enough motive—"

"Come on, Bonnie—"

"Do you really think he'd kill a man for trespassing?"

"If the man had trespassed before," the sheriff said. "If he'd put Johnny behind bars for four months." The sheriff leaned closer, ticking off points on his fingers. "The motive may be thin, but it exists. That's one. The death happened on Merrimon's land. That's opportunity, and it makes two." He bent another finger. "Merrimon has the means—"

"Let me stop you there. Do you have cause of death?"

"The body is with the medical examiner. We should have something preliminary by tomorrow."

"Tomorrow?" The doubt weighted her voice, but she saw no reason to hide it. "This is premature. All of it."

"Bonnie, listen—"

"You want to charge Merrimon before you have cause of death. Are you kidding me? If you're even slightly wrong, it'll be a circus."

"Do you know how many calls we've received in the past two hours? Reporters. Investors. The mayor." The sheriff leaned back in his chair, agitated. "A private jet landed ten minutes ago. Apparently it's full of fund managers, estate lawyers, and relatives hoping to get lucky. There's your damn circus. Tomorrow it'll be worse."

Bonnie studied the sheriff from behind lowered lids. She'd known Willard Cline for a very long time. He was a smart man, and a fine sheriff. Right now, he was hiding something. "What am I missing?"

The sheriff glanced at Tom Lee, and Lee shrugged. "All right, Bonnie." The sheriff kept his voice level. "I believe Merrimon will talk if you let me keep him."

"Explain."

"He doesn't handle confinement well. Actually, that's an oversimplification. Johnny Merrimon handles confinement worse than any person I've ever seen. It's psychological *and* physical, like withdrawal but times a thousand. You'd have to see to understand, but it's deep and it's real. Forty-eight hours, and he'll break like a piece of glass."

"We're talking about Clyde Hunt's son."

"Stepson."

"Doesn't matter. Clyde is one of us."

"No one's forgetting that, but we're talking about a dead billionaire, too. Normal rules don't apply." He paused a beat. "People will ask why Johnny Merrimon wasn't charged with attempted murder the first time."

"Because Boyd didn't want us to bring those charges." The DA came to the edge of her seat, angry. "He refused to testify. You know that as well as I."

"Yes, I do. But the people of Raven County do not. By this time tomorrow, people will be asking if William Boyd had to die. They'll wonder if you could have stopped it."

"Damn it, Willard."

"You know it's true. When the kid shot up Boyd's camp, you made a fair call. Victim didn't want to testify; didn't want a trial. If Boyd were on a beach in Monaco, no one would question your judgment. But he's not on a beach. He's on a slab with half his face eaten off."

Bonnie settled back in the seat. The sheriff shouldn't be right, but he was. Money brought pressure, eyeballs, expectation. Bonnie took it apart, put it back together. She'd look bad, no matter what. "You really think the kid did it?"

"Pretty sure."

"Hundred percent?"

The sheriff made a steeple of his fingers. "No way he found that body by accident."

Bonnie looked at her watch. It was after five. "Can you push the medical examiner?"

"Trenton Moore has the case. He's probably the only medical examiner I can't rush."

"It's thin, Willard."

"The kid will break."

Bonnie drummed her fingers, thinking. She hated politics, but the politics were real. Johnny had shot at Boyd once, and now Boyd was dead. A confession would clean things up, shut down the circus before it got started. "It's still not enough."

"Forty-eight hours. He'll break."

She started to answer, but someone knocked on the door, interrupting her.

"Go away," the sheriff said. The knock sounded again.

"I'm sorry, Willard." Bonnie stood. "Unless you have more, you need to cut him loose."

"How much more?"

"Cause of death. A coherent witness. A better motive. One or more of those would be helpful."

"Bonnie, wait."

The sheriff stood, almost begging. When the knock came again, he lost his temper. "What, goddamn it? What?"

The door opened a crack. Bonnie saw a uniform, the face of a white-haired deputy with creased skin and pale blue eyes.

"I'm sorry, Sheriff. I don't mean to interrupt—"

"What is it?" the sheriff asked.

"I just thought, you know. With the DA here and all—"

"What is it, man? Spit it out."

"Um, there's a Luana Freemantle here." The deputy hooked a thumb down the hall and looked apologetic. "She says she knows why Johnny Merrimon killed that billionaire, William Boyd."

In a space of minutes, everything changed. Attitude. Body language. It moved like a wave, and Jack saw it first. "Something's happening." He motioned, and Clyde stood, too. Beyond the glass, people spoke in low voices and looked their way. No one smiled. No one met Jack's eyes. "Something's wrong."

Bonnie Busby carried that truth on her shoulders, and in the lines of her face. She moved like a warship into the dead space beyond the glass, where she paused for a final word with the sheriff, then made for the lobby beyond the metal door. Jack glanced at Clyde and saw his worry reflected. Clyde knew the DA. He would know the face. "What? What is it?"

"Just wait."

Jack did, but it was hard. When the DA buzzed through the door, she looked at Clyde and only Clyde. "We're charging Johnny with the murder of William Boyd."

"You can't be serious."

"The sheriff thinks he's a flight risk. I think we have enough to charge. I'm sorry."

Jack took the words like a slap in the face, and Clyde felt the same way. His mouth dropped; the light drained out of his eyes. "Bonnie, please—"

"I'm informing you as a courtesy, Clyde. I can't tell you any more."

"Can you tell me if it has something to do with the plane that just landed at Raven County Airport?" Bonnie's mouth pinched, and Clyde nodded understandingly. "Yeah, I know about that. Big money. Big pressure."

"You're wrong about me."

"Politics is a damn dirty business. Am I wrong about that?"

The DA looked away from Clyde, and saw Jack as if for the first time. "Who are you?"

"Johnny's lawyer."

"Hmmm."

She was dismissive. Jack didn't like it.

"I'm sorry, Clyde. I know he's been like a son to you."

"Not *like* a son. A son. He wouldn't do this." Her mouth pinched again. She was small in his shadow. "Help me understand."

She looked at the glass, the empty room. "How long have we known each other?"

"Twenty-five years."

"In all that time, have you seen me lie, cheat, or play dirty politics?"

"I shouldn't have said that. No."

"Then tell me this, Detective. Does Johnny love that land he owns?"

"You know he does."

"Would you say he loves it dearly?"

"More than most," Clyde said.

"And therein lies the problem." She found his eyes, and held them. "William Boyd was trying to take it away."

To Jack it made sense. Luana Freemantle was poor. Boyd was funding her appeal with plans to buy the land if she won. He could do it cheaply, too, for a lot less than thirty million. What would she take to sell? Ten million? One? Johnny was the only one stupid enough to turn down real money for six thousand acres of swamp and stony hills. All of which begged the larger question.

Why did Boyd want it in the first place?

What made the Hush so goddamn special?

The thoughts drew Jack from the hard edges of the room. He was in the Hush, at the water's edge, and something cold was moving.

"Jack, did you hear me?"

Jack blinked, and focused on Clyde. The DA was gone. They were alone. "I'm sorry. I'm tired."

"I'm going to see the medical examiner. Are you coming?"

"Do you think he can help?"

"I don't know, but I have less than two hours before Johnny's mother gets home. I'd like some answers by then."

"You go ahead. I need to see Johnny."

"Don't let him talk."

"I won't."

Clyde vacillated, big hands fisted. He wanted to see Johnny, too. Jack felt it. "Tell him I love him," Clyde said. "Tell him we'll make it right."

"I will."

"And, Jack."

"Yeah."

"You're a good friend."

Jack nodded, but Clyde was already turning. Could the ME help? Maybe. What about Johnny's mother? She'd lost a daughter already. Could she lose another child and survive?

"Sergeant." Jack rapped on the glass. "I'd like to see my client."

When they took Johnny from interview room three, he was already in the dimness. The halls were gray tunnels, the elevator down, a black shaft. That's where they took him, to the lowest floor and the deepest room, the darkness beyond the darkness.

"What's wrong with him?"

"He was like this last time. Don't sweat it."

Johnny heard the guards, but the guards were barely real. The world was concrete and weight, the faint etchings of life beyond the door. He tilted his head, but even the jail was fading. He heard the guards breathing, the jangle of his restraints, the door when it closed. He stood, but was unsteady. His hands were out like a blind man's. Closing his eyes, he felt concrete, bedrock, nothing.

"Hello."

Even his voice was gray.

I knew this was coming.

But it had seemed easier in the warm light of the Hush. He could feel movement there, the turn of the earth. He'd forgotten what it was to be buried alive.

"Just till tomorrow," he said; and it echoed in his mind.

Tomorrow . . .

Sorrow . . .

Johnny laughed, but it was broken.

Already, the seconds were hours.

Jack wasted thirty minutes with the sergeant. He raised his voice, made a scene. Eventually, the sheriff got involved. "What are you doing here, Counselor?"

He moved slowly through the metal door and wore a pained expression. Not intolerant or angry. Just worn out. Jack didn't care. "You can't question my client outside of my presence."

"No one is questioning your client. He's tucked in and safe."

That caught Jack by surprise. He'd imagined good cop–bad cop, cigarettes and bright lights and videotapes. Problem was, he knew so little about criminal law. He was a numbers guy, and the sheriff understood as much. It was in the soft eyes, the quiet voice.

"Why don't you go home, Mr. Cross? It's been a long day for all of us."

"I think I should see my client."

"I've placed him in protective isolation."

"What? Why?"

"He's not adjusting well. That makes him a danger to himself and others."

"That's absurd."

"Yet the decision is entirely at my discretion. Your friend is not my only prisoner."

"But—"

"You're new at this. Okay. I get it. This is frustrating, but it happens."

The sheriff frowned knowingly and put a hand on Jack's back, guiding him to the door. "Come back tomorrow, okay? I'm sure you'll be able to see him then."

The civility stole Jack's fire. How could he rage at a turned back, a quietly closed door? In the silence, alone, he pictured his friend. Was he really a danger to himself? Jack couldn't see it. But could he be a danger to others? Jack worried about that. Life was on the wrong side of a bad slope. Johnny's life. Jack's. There were things about his friend he didn't know. Bad things, maybe. Troubling ones.

Leaving the sheriff's department with a heavy tread, Jack stepped onto a sidewalk devoid of people. The sky was dark, but not completely. Cars moved slowly past. Crossing the street, Jack sat in his car and checked messages on the cell. Two were from lawyers who'd consider the case but wanted to talk fees. They'd call back tomorrow. Three calls were from an assistant at the firm. One was from Leslie Green. The message was simple, the voice throaty.

Call me, Jack. Call me as soon as you can.

Jack didn't call her. She'd want the story, the details. For an instant he imagined what she might offer in exchange, but that second was as filled with self-loathing as it was with the memories of pale skin and movement.

Cranking the engine, Jack turned across traffic and drove for the east side of town. He'd never been to the medical examiner's office or the morgue, but thought it was in the basement of the old hospital. He was right about that. Signs led him from the parking lot to the emergency room, then down a hall and through a small door, painted beige. An inoffensive color, Jack thought, for a wholly offensive place. The stairs beyond the door took him into the bowels of the building, to a hall with low ceilings and a brushed-concrete floor. Lighting was dim in the first hall, and dimmer in the second. Halfway down its length, a glass window broke the expanse of cinder block to reveal a wall of small metal doors beyond which the bodies were kept cold and silent. Jack felt that silence as he walked.

Eighteen small doors.

He counted them.

How many bodies?

This is why he'd steered clear of criminal law, because it was too real, and too permanent: the death and incarceration, the foundations of despair on which such things were invariably built.

Jack suppressed a small shudder, embarrassed—even alone—by the dread he felt as the refrigerators fell behind and white light spilled from a second row of windows. A sign extended above a wooden door, and announced the office of the medical examiner for Raven County. Stepping inside, Jack found an office like many others. There were closed doors and filing cabinets, as well as space for secretaries and assistants. The only real difference was the smell. Whether it was embalming fluid or exposed organs, Jack had no idea.

"Hello?"

No one answered, though lights burned brightly throughout the space. Moving past desks and a cluttered office, Jack discovered an open door that led to an antechamber and a second door, beyond which were tables and jars and focused lights, all of which were a blur to Jack.

He couldn't look past the body.

It lay on a metal slab, the skin discolored by bruising or dirt, the abdomen cracked open, with some organs out and others still inside. He saw a liver on one scale, and what looked like the heart on another. Beyond the body and the metal table, the room faded into a greenish gloom that hinted at more tables, other gear. Hunt was there, in the dimness. So was Trenton Moore, the medical examiner. They were arguing.

"You can't be here, Clyde—"

"We're talking about my son. I have a right to know—"

To Jack, the voices barely registered. His world was meat and skin, the pale gray of an open sternum. He wanted to look away, but could not. The top of the skull had been removed. One arm bent at an impossible angle. The ribs looked shattered.

Jesus . . .

He crossed himself from an almost-forgotten habit of childhood. There was no mystery of life on that table, just muscle and tendon and marbled fat. Most of the face was missing. The smell was liquid.

Stumbling back, Jack felt his way along the wall and to a table where the view was entirely hidden. He spread his hands on cool metal and worked to breathe through his mouth alone, trying to unsee the shattered bones, the places where flesh had been chewed and shorn off and ripped. Ten seconds passed. Another five.

Steady, he thought, but was not. He was on the slope, and the slope was taking him down. He felt it on the crosstown drive: a blur of lights and mirrors and shadowed buildings. Jack could not explain the cold in his heart, but thought it might be the most genuine emotion he'd ever known.

The ruined body.

The hard questions.

At his building, he took the stairs three at a time until the apartment door was locked and the world around him silent. For long seconds he stood in the darkness, then looked down on the city street. Cars moved, but normally. The night was just the night. Turning on a single lamp, Jack poured a drink that went down fast. He told himself that an explanation would come, that Trenton Moore's hard work was justified and that the reasons for Boyd's death would, in the end, make some kind of sense; but Jack didn't believe it.

Something terrible moved in the Hush.

He tried for a long time to dissuade himself of that notion, but Johnny was not right, either. He was lying, keeping secrets. Jack considered another glass, but called Leslie Green instead and asked her to come over. She'd use him and he'd use her, but that was okay. After what he'd seen at the morgue, Jack needed someone soft and human and real; he needed someone warm.

CHAPTER FIFTEEN

Hunt woke before dawn, and his first emotion was relief. In the bed beside him, Johnny's mother slept at last, and for that Hunt was thankful beyond words. His night with Katherine had been hard. Her only son faced a murder charge, and Clyde could offer no assurances. The weeping had been brutal, the anger that followed, irrational.

She wanted Clyde to fix it.

He couldn't.

Moving with exaggerated care, Clyde extricated himself from the bed, relieved to find his feet while his wife still slept. She required rest, and he needed space to think. The day would matter more than most. He had to find the best possible attorney. He needed to raise cash, try again with the medical examiner, the district attorney. He needed to see Johnny, too, but mostly he wanted to speak with James Kirkpatrick, the survivor. If quick answers were to be found, that's where Hunt would find them. Maybe Kirkpatrick knew something. Maybe he was the killer.

Slipping from the room, Hunt dressed in the hall, then made coffee and took a cup onto the front porch, where he watched the silent street, the dew on pale grass.

A newspaper waited beyond the gate.

Clyde was not eager to see it.

For the length of a cup, he stared at the blur of it, hating how it lay there, unassuming. It was paper, wrapped in plastic, a simple thing. But cops talked, and that meant Johnny was page one. Hunt knew it.

Draining the last sip, he sighed and stepped off the porch. The walkway was white gravel, the gate painted the same color. It opened silently, and Hunt bent for the paper, waiting until he was in the kitchen to break the fold. The headline was three inches tall.

"LITTLE CHIEF" ARRESTED IN DEATH OF BILLIONAIRE

They'd run two pictures of Johnny, side by side. The first was ten years old, the same iconic photo that had made Johnny famous from one side of the country to the other. He was thirteen, his face streaked with berry juice and ash, his chest covered with blood and feathers and rattlesnake rattles. He was in a car as grown men pulled him out. Beside him was the girl he'd saved.

Tiffany Shore.

Hunt remembered.

The second photograph was a booking photo taken after Johnny shot up William Boyd's camp. In it, he had the same cheekbones and black hair and impenetrable eyes. He was unsmiling, and looked dangerous.

"Damn it."

Hunt hated the pictures because they made Johnny seem damaged and capable, especially in light of the original assault against Boyd. The first two paragraphs spoke of that history and of the DA, who looked disturbingly out of touch. People wondered if warning signs had been missed or ignored, and if—had Johnny faced a harsher charge—William Boyd might still be alive. Such questions were inevitable; it was the nature of things. Beyond that, the reporter had little. But what he had, he used well.

The body on Johnny's land.

A manhunt in the swamp.

Clyde read it again, more carefully. No mention of Luana Freemantle or possible motive. That left room for doubt, and any doubt was good.

Moving quietly, Hunt checked on Katherine, then disconnected the phones and drew every curtain in the bedroom. He wanted the room dim and quiet, because he knew what was coming. Reporters would camp on the street. The phone would ring off the hook. It was only a matter of time.

Locking the front door, Hunt took the paper with him.

His first stop was the hospital, and it was close. He drove a mile down treed streets, then crossed a four-lane and turned into the medical district, passing the offices, clinics, and pharmacies that grew like mushrooms in the shade of the tall building. After parking in the deck, Hunt crossed a sky bridge that took him into the hospital one floor above Reception. Stairs took him down, where he flashed the badge and put his questions to a round-faced woman behind a cherrywood desk. "James Kirkpatrick," he said. "What doctor and what room?"

Keys rattled, and the woman said, "Ah. Seventh floor."

Clyde disliked the answer enough to frown. "Seven? You're certain?"

"Psychiatric, secure. Dr. Patel."

Hunt thanked the receptionist, then went for the elevator.

Psychiatric, secure . . .

Kirkpatrick was on suicide watch.

Finding Dr. Patel took Hunt thirty seconds in the elevator and five minutes outside a locked door. "I'm sorry, I'm sorry." The doctor came from behind, coffee in one hand and a bagel in the other. "They told me you were here. It's just that cafeteria." He juggled his coffee, bagel, and key card, pushing his right hand out at Hunt. "Vijay Patel. Nice to meet you."

Hunt took the offered hand. "We've met before. The jumper."

"Right, right. Sure. Four years ago. The teenager. You're here about James Kirkpatrick?" He waved the card at a black box by the door. When the door clicked open, he tipped his head left and held the door with a foot. "We can talk in my office. Mind if I eat while we do it?"

In the office, Dr. Patel sat on the business side of an overflowing desk. He made room for the coffee, the bagel; and Hunt tried to gauge the man. Early forties, he had light brown skin and a touch of gray at the temples. Heavy glasses rode an average nose. The forehead was narrow, the chin soft. The overall effect was one of pleasantness. The slight bemusement. The easy smile. It seemed to fit what Hunt already knew of the man. He worked for the county and made county wages, but the diplomas were from Davidson and Duke and Harvard. He was either a giver or a classic underachiever. Hunt was thinking *giver.*

"I'm sorry about the mess. My daughter plays summer league hockey. I'm the assistant coach."

He said it off the cuff, but it confirmed Hunt's theory. "I need to know about James Kirkpatrick. Anything you can tell me."

The doctor leaned back and put a foot on an open drawer. "I thought Kirkpatrick was related to a county matter."

Hunt adjusted his assessment. A giver, yes. Stupid, no. "You've read the paper?" Patel lifted a newspaper from the desk. Johnny's face. Page one. "Then you know why I'm here."

"The sheriff told me you might come by. I'm sorry for your family. I wasn't here when Johnny's sister turned up dead, but I know of your involvement, and that you married the boy's mother. I've always thought it was a good thing. Hope from the ruins. A fresh start."

"It was a good thing. It still is." Hunt paused, measuring the mood of the man across the desk. "Did the sheriff tell you not to talk to me?"

"He suggested it might be in my best interest to simply avoid you."

"Yet here we are."

Patel smiled. "Family comes first for me, whether it's mine or someone else's. Were my daughter locked away, I'd move heaven and earth to get her out. So, Detective." Patel sipped his coffee. "What can I tell you?"

"Thank you, Doctor. I appreciate that attitude. Is Mr. Kirkpatrick on suicide watch?"

"He is."

"Can you tell me why?"

"Mr. Kirkpatrick tried to kill himself in the emergency room."

"How?"

"Scalpel," Patel said. "A deputy managed to restrain him in time."

"Is he sedated?"

"He's conscious, if that's your question."

"May I see him?"

"From a distance, if you like. I don't want him agitated."

Hunt followed Patel to a second secure door, then down a scrubbed hall. It was quieter than Hunt imagined. He knew the secure ward could, at times, be chaotic. "We'll remain in the hall." Patel stopped at a closed door. Through a small window, Hunt saw a bed, a glimpse of restraints. "Agreed?"

Hunt nodded, and the doctor opened the door. Inside, Kirkpatrick lay on his back, restrained at the ankles and one wrist, and by heavy bandages that secured his broken arm. His eyes were open, and his mouth moved. Every few seconds, he twitched. "Is he talking?" Hunt asked.

"About the death of his friend, no."

Hunt watched for long seconds. Kirkpatrick didn't blink. His eyes were bloody red, and wet. The cracked lips kept moving. "Has he been like this for long?"

"All night."

"What's he saying?"

"It's an apology of sorts, and one of the most desperate things I've ever seen, the same words over and over, the only thing he's said since the sheriff brought him in."

"Nothing about the swamp?"

"No."

Hunt leaned far enough to break the plane of the door. Kirkpatrick's movements were spasmodic and irregular. His head jerked side to side. The scrapes on his face glistened with ointment. "What exactly is he saying?"

"It's heartbreaking, really." Dr. Patel crossed his arms and leaned against the frame of the door. "The poor man thinks he killed his mother."

Hunt stayed for another ten minutes, asking the same questions and getting the same answers.

No, the patient had not spoken of the swamp.

And no, Dr. Patel had no idea if he would recover enough to do so in the near future.

"Imagine a crystal vase, Detective. Now imagine it dropped from a great height. Perhaps it can be reassembled, and perhaps not. Only time and effort will tell."

Hunt tried twice more, but the doctor knew nothing of Boyd's death or Johnny or the cause of Kirkpatrick's fractured mind.

"Physically, he's in acceptable condition. The rest . . ."

Patel showed his palms, and Hunt swallowed the disappointment. "Thank you, Dr. Patel." He handed over a card. "My cell number is on the back. Call me if anything changes. Anything at all."

From the seventh floor, Hunt took the elevator to the basement level and followed familiar halls to the medical examiner's office. The door was locked, the space behind it lightless.

"Damn it."

Hunt rattled the knob, then checked the time. Seven o'clock. Too early. Taking out his cell, he called Trenton Moore at home. No answer. Same with his cell. "Trenton. Clyde Hunt. It's early. I'm sorry. Please call me as soon as you can."

Hunt wanted inside information, but knew from long experience that Trenton Moore responded poorly to both threats and entreaties. He would help or not, according to his conscience. This was the first time Clyde had ever disliked that quality in a man. He wanted to shake trees, break down walls.

His next call went to Jack Cross, who answered on the second ring. He sounded alert and ready. "Jack, it's Clyde. Can you meet?"

"Absolutely. When and where?"

"Sheriff's department. Twenty minutes. It's time we speak to Johnny."

Jack replaced the phone on its cradle and slipped on his coat. He'd been planning to leave early, anyway. There was only one complication.

"Leslie?"

Jack knocked on the bathroom door, which stood partly open. Pushing it wide, he shoved hands deep in his pockets and stopped by the sink. Leslie was in the shower. She smiled through the glass. "Get in."

Jack shook his head. "I need to go."

"Ten minutes."

Jack was tempted. When she'd come over the night before, there'd been none of the awkwardness or quid pro quo he'd expected. She'd been in jeans and boots; and her face, in the dim light, had softened almost the second she'd seen his. He'd like to think it was affection that led her to kiss him the way she had, but deep down he knew better. He'd been distraught and shaken, and no kind of man.

What he'd seen on her face was pity.

Even now he saw hints of it.

"Listen, Jack." She wrapped herself in a towel. "Boyd's dead, so the partners don't need you anymore. That makes your position a little fragile. Do you understand?" Jack nodded, and she stepped closer. "Are you going to the jail?"

"I'm meeting Detective Hunt."

She looked down, then showed the blue eyes. "Will you call me later?"

He nodded. "About last night—"

"We don't need to talk about it."

"It's just that you were . . . I don't know. You were nice when you didn't have to be."

"Did that surprise you?"

"Yes."

"Women can do that, you know. Surprise a man."

She straightened his tie, smoothed his lapels. Jack looked for the pity, but it was gone. "You never asked about Johnny."

"The timing was wrong."

"So why did you spend the night?"

She leaned against him, kissed his cheek. "Give yourself a little credit."

A little credit. It was a nice thought that made the day less grim. Would he trust Leslie with his life? No. But it felt promising, the unexpected gentleness. Maybe the day would surprise. Maybe the sheriff would, too.

Skipping the car, Jack walked four blocks to the jail. The morning was strangely cool, the sky above heavy with gray clouds. Around him, the sidewalks were empty. Window glass reflected the stillness, the same low sky. A block from the jail, traffic began to thicken. The courthouse was on the same block. So was the sheriff's department, the offices of a dozen different law firms. Jack saw squad cars and cops and men with briefcases. He was too new in the law for any of it to feel familiar, but the movement felt right: the courthouse and jail, the early churn of men and women who served them both.

Clyde Hunt was at the curb, pacing the sidewalk beside an unmarked cruiser. When Jack got close, Hunt handed him a coffee and said a terse good morning. He looked tired to Jack, fresh-shaven but with pale skin and glassy eyes that spoke of a wakeful night. "Any news?" Jack asked.

"It's too early for the medical examiner, and the witness is . . . broken. I've called three different friends inside the sheriff's department, but word's come down to stay quiet. No one will cross the sheriff."

Jack stripped the lid from his coffee. "When you say 'broken' . . ."

He trailed off, but Hunt understood. "Kirkpatrick comes from West Virginia coal country, a wealthy man, self-made. It's a brutal life, mining; and some deep, damn hollows in that part of the world. Most of those mines will ruin a man by the time he's thirty. Coming from nothing. Getting rich." Hunt's eyes glittered. "Maybe one in a million can make that happen." He put his coffee on the car, untouched. "Something happened out there, Jack. Something went down in that swamp, and it was bad enough to break a strong man's mind."

"Maybe it was already cracked."

Hunt squinted at the jail. "Maybe."

"Maybe Kirkpatrick's the killer."

"I've considered that. The sheriff won't."

"Because he has his man."

"Something like that, yeah."

Jack followed Hunt's gaze. The jail was six stories of concrete with hardened doors and slits for windows. Beside it, even the courthouse looked small. "Visiting hours aren't till one."

"I'm a cop. You're his lawyer."

Jack nodded, glad that Hunt was there. "All right. Let's do it."

Inside the foyer, Hunt locked his weapon in a steel box and informed the officer behind the glass that he wanted to see Johnny Merrimon.

"Name, please."

Hunt gave both names.

"Reason for visit."

"Attorney–client conference."

Hunt used specific language, and to Jack it looked like a dance. Hunt knew the guard; the guard knew Hunt. Yet both men acted the part of a stranger. Body language was stiff, the words clipped. It ended unexpectedly, and badly. "I'm sorry, sir. No visitors are allowed this morning."

"What? Why?"

"We're on lockdown. Sheriff's orders."

Hunt looked beyond the guard, then through barred doors, down still corridors. It was quiet, the guards relaxed. "I don't believe you."

"There was a disturbance last night."

"What kind of disturbance?"

"I'm sorry, sir. No one goes in. No one goes out. That's all I can tell you. You're welcome to wait."

He gestured at a row of plastic seats, and Hunt seethed. "For how damn long?"

"Until the sheriff says."

Hunt choked down angry words, but his hands were shaking. Retrieving his weapon, he stopped at the exit and looked back. "You know this is bullshit, right?"

Jack had no idea what he meant. "If there's a lockdown—"

"There is no lockdown. That's the sheriff, keeping us out. It's an old trick."

"Why would he do that?"

"Time," Hunt said. "He wants time with Johnny alone."

Two stories down, time did not exist. Lights went on and off. It didn't matter. Johnny stared at the wall, but barely saw it. He touched the floor; felt nothing. Under the weight of that isolation, the anxiety grew worse, as did the headaches, the restlessness, the tension in his chest. Johnny pulled himself up, his palms slick on the walls, his heartbeat uneven. He tried to swallow. He couldn't breathe.

You've done this before.

You can do this.

The words were in his head, an echo. He felt his way from one corner to the next.

The room was a box devoid of life, a hole that robbed him of the things he loved.

Nothing is forever.

Nothing lasts.

He thought that was a lie, but footsteps sounded in the gray. Metal scraped. "Are you ready to talk yet?"

Johnny told himself it was the sheriff's voice. It came and went. Distant surf. Johnny turned another corner; saw grim eyes, an old man's face.

"Nothing . . ." He coughed, and tasted vomit. "I have nothing to say."

"You won't leave this room until you talk to me." Johnny swayed where he stood. "Speak up, son. I can't hear you."

Johnny looked for the face, and started laughing.

Speak up, he thought.

He was already screaming.

When the sheriff came again, Johnny had walked the cell 967 times. He'd counted. Six steps, then four. Six and four.

The emptiness.

The coffin.

When metal scraped again, he felt air move, and with it came the smell of sweat and skin and coffee. Johnny swayed where he stood. Nothing had ever smelled so good, and for that moment it was real—the realest thing he'd ever known—then metal scraped again, and Johnny was alone in the empty. He bit his tongue and pinched himself. He shuddered until his muscles hurt, then closed his eyes and paced the shape of his cell.

Eleven hundred times.

Two thousand.

At some point, he drifted to a stop without knowing. When he woke, he was still on his feet. What was the count? He didn't know, and that was another loss.

He paced the room again, and mumbled in the quiet.

One . . .

Hunt and Jack were on the sidewalk when the medical examiner called.

"Clyde, it's Trenton Moore. I got your message."

"Trenton, thank God." Clyde nodded at Jack, who stood beside the unmarked cruiser. "I appreciate this."

"Don't thank me yet. This is not your case. I can't discuss specifics."

Clyde's hand tightened on the phone. "Then why are you calling?"

"Because I've known you for fifteen years. Because you asked me to."

Hunt closed his eyes and pinched the bridge of his nose. He told himself that Trenton was his friend, and that there were, in fact, rules about this kind of thing. It didn't matter. "I need more than that."

"I know you do."

"Then talk to me."

A pause traveled down the line. Traffic noises. Faint music. "I'm meeting Bonnie and the sheriff at two o'clock at the DA's office. It would be in your interest to attend."

"Bonnie will never allow it."

"Then be there when it's over."

"Two o'clock. Jesus, Trenton. That's half a day."

"I'm teaching a seminar in Chapel Hill. It's the soonest I can get back."

Hunt looked at the jail, thinking of the sheriff and long hours, of the boy who was damn near his son. "Is it good news or bad?" The pause came again. "Fifteen years, Trenton. You said it yourself."

A sigh carried over the line. "If this gets out, I'll deny this phone call ever happened."

"All I need is the bottom line."

"I have your word?"

"Yes, Trenton. Please."

A final, horrible pause. "No way in hell your boy killed that man."

When the connection broke, Trenton Moore put the phone on the seat beside him and wondered, seriously, if he'd be fired over the phone call. The sheriff was a narrow-minded man, the DA serious about rules. Either one could call down the thunder if word escaped of what was, in fact, a serious breach of protocol. Chain of communication. Chain of custody. The concepts were not dissimilar.

The case came first: its sanctity, its cohesion.

But Clyde Hunt was more than a friend. He was an iconic lawman, a straight shooter, and a man to admire. When Trenton had first arrived in Raven County—a slight, myopic man fresh from his residency—Hunt was one of the few who'd not laughed at his lisp, his effeminate manner, or his very particular sense of humor. Other cops had been crude and cruel, but not Clyde. Fifteen years later, they were friends. They had dinner once a month, coffee on the odd morning.

Trenton turned up the radio, merged onto a state highway, and followed it north.

He'd sacrifice a lot for Clyde.

Thought maybe he just had.

It took Trenton another hour to reach Chapel Hill and find the right building in the sprawl of the UNC Medical Center. The class was like many others he'd taught, but his mind wandered; he repeated himself. On the ride back, he was still thinking of Boyd's autopsy and of the sleepless night it caused. He ran through the findings as he drove: the bones and organs, the chill he'd felt as the clock ran from eleven to midnight and he'd sat, unmoving, and sought to distill his findings. How many times had an autopsy made him question the science he revered? How many times the superstitious chill? The answer was unsettling in its simplicity. *Twice.* That's how often he'd been made to doubt the boundaries of rational thought. *Twice in ten years.*

Both times involved Johnny Merrimon.

And both times, the swamp.

Arriving back in town three minutes before the hour, Trenton bypassed the hospital and went straight for the suite of offices occupied by the district attorney and her staff. That meant the rear entrance to the Courthouse Annex, the secure elevator to the third floor. In the hall, he pressed an intercom, announced himself, and was buzzed into a waiting area with four chairs and a sofa. Clyde sat on one of the chairs. Johnny's friend Jack sat beside him.

"Clyde."

Hunt nodded once, but said nothing, and kept his gaze level. Behind him, a secretary of some sort was watching through the glass. Trenton took the cue from Clyde, and walked past without another word. Resting his briefcase on a narrow ledge, he spoke through holes in the bulletproof divider. "Trenton Moore. Here to see Bonnie."

"She's expecting you." A second buzzer sounded, and Trenton walked through a metal door that opened into the secure offices of the Raven County district attorney. "This way." The secretary led Trenton past filing cabinets and small offices. People kept their heads down, working. At the end of the hall, she knocked on double doors, opening the right side without waiting for a reply. "Trenton Moore."

The DA's office reflected the woman who'd held it for so many years. Heavy furniture. Muted art. Behind the desk, Bonnie Busby almost disappeared into the dark colors. She wore a black watch, a black suit. Her mood was the same color. "Can you tell me why Clyde Hunt is waiting beyond that door?"

Trenton stepped into the office. "Nice to see you as well. Sheriff. Captain Lee."

He nodded at the sheriff and his number two. No one smiled.

"Did you tell him about this meeting or not?"

Trenton sat. "Did he know of the meeting?"

"He wanted to be part of it."

"It's his son. That's understandable." The DA tried to intimidate with a stare, but the North Georgia childhood of a lisping boy had ingrained in Trenton a certain calm. He smiled easily, crossed his narrow legs. "Yours is not my only meeting of the day. Perhaps we can begin."

"Very well, Trenton. As you are the man of the hour . . ."

She gestured graciously, but no one was fooled, the ME least of all.

He opened the briefcase, passed out copies of the autopsy report. "The tox screen will take time, as you know, but my findings suggest its irrelevance."

All three scanned the report. The sheriff was the first to reach Trenton's official summation. "Well, shit. Are you kidding me?" He scanned for two more minutes, then tossed the report on the floor. "That's bullshit."

Trenton had seen similar reactions when a case went suddenly sideways. "Any other medical examiner will draw the same conclusions."

The DA closed her copy of the file. Her eyes narrowed, but her voice was even. "Walk me through it."

Trenton did just that. Every page. Every finding. It took half an hour, and it got technical. By the time he was done, even the sheriff was pale. "That doesn't make sense."

Trenton shrugged. "The body doesn't lie."

"And you're certain no single man could inflict this kind of damage?"

"Sheriff, I doubt a dozen men could cause this damage, not with their bare hands."

"Explain."

"William Boyd's limbs were bilaterally dislocated at both the glenohumeral and acetabulofemoral joints, the hips and shoulders. The tendons were not just stretched, but ripped. That requires tremendous force, remarkable force." Trenton lifted the report to accentuate his words. "There's spiral fracturing in the humerus and femur, again bilaterally. In places the bones are bare fragments. The decedent has seven crushed organs, torn ligaments, intracranial hemorrhaging. Both eyes were crushed in their sockets, and that includes the optic nerve, which, as you know, lies deep in the skull. Injuries such as these require pulling force, twisting force, compressive force, perhaps at the same time. The report is incontrovertible. Johnny Merrimon could not have inflicted this damage. No single man could."

"Then what?" The sheriff leaned back, heavy on sarcasm and drawl. "How do you explain it?"

"I'm sorry, Sheriff." Trenton looked from one person to the next, then lifted his palms in the kind of transcendental awe he'd known only once before. "I'm not sure anyone can."

CHAPTER SIXTEEN

Johnny's torment began with the sound of a metal door, and though the same door eventually swung wide, the suffering did not end so quickly or cleanly. He saw rust and flaking paint, but it remained at the end of a long, dim hall. Sound traveled even farther. Lips moved, but the words came later, echoes in the tunnel. "On your feet. Let's go."

Guards fastened waist restraints and cuffs, then took his arms and lifted. Beyond the door were stairs that led up. His feet couldn't feel them. "How long?"

"What?"

He tripped, but the guards held him up. He tried again, thinking the answer would be *weeks*. "How long was I in there?"

"Twenty-seven hours."

Twenty-seven . . . ?

That wasn't right. Days had passed. Many days. Johnny tried to feel his cheeks, but the guards wouldn't have it. "Quit screwing around. Move your feet." Johnny stumbled up the stairs, and from the subbasement took an elevator up an additional floor. In processing, they removed the restraints and gave him his clothes. "Get dressed. You're being released."

Johnny slipped into his clothes like a second skin. They smelled of mud and black water, and that smell was the beginning. Two halls later there was light—real light—and a waft of air that tasted of exhaust and hot pavement. It was a start, but only that. Johnny knew what he needed. Another door. Blue sky. Home.

The sheriff blocked the end of the final hall. He looked down with distaste, and Johnny straightened under the stare. Half blind, half deaf—it didn't matter. This was animal.

"Sheriff."

The sheriff was rawboned and lean, 90 percent hard eyes and bitter smile. "Give us a minute, will you." He dipped a head at the guards, and they disappeared. He studied Johnny with a critical eye, took in the tremors, the cold sweat. "I'd like to understand you," he said. "Can you help me with that?"

"I thought I was being released."

"Oh, you are. But I like to take this moment sometimes, these last few seconds."

"Arrest me again or stand aside."

The sheriff narrowed his eyes. "You're lying to me about something."

"About what?"

"I don't know."

Johnny saw a waiting room through a square of glass and, beyond that, a hint of open air.

"What aren't you telling me?"

"I didn't see Boyd die. I don't know what killed him."

"How did you find the body?"

"I told you—"

"Yeah, yeah. You heard a shot and went walking. We both know that's bullshit."

"I'm going to leave now."

"Don't pretend this is over." The sheriff gestured at someone unseen, and the steel door clicked open. "This is my card." He actually handed one over. "Call me if you grow enough spine to do the right thing."

Johnny pocketed the card; blinked at the light beyond the door. He saw glass windows, a hint of green. Clyde and Jack were waiting. "Goodbye, Sheriff."

"Don't kid yourself, Mr. Merrimon. I'm not going anywhere."

After that came another blur. Clyde's arms went around him; Jack's hand fell on his shoulder. Words came, too, but Johnny was starving. "Home," he said. "I want to go home."

"That's good," Clyde said. "Your mother's waiting. She's been worried, desperately, so . . ."

He kept talking, but Johnny shook his head. "My home. The Hush."

"Don't be silly—"

"Jack, please. Will you take me?"

"Come on, son . . ." But Johnny saw Jack's car, and stumbled toward it. "Damn it, son. What about your mother?"

"Tomorrow," Johnny said.

"She's worried."

"Dinner, then. I promise. Jack. The door."

Clyde said, "Don't do it, Jack."

"Jack, the door."

"I'm sorry, Clyde." Jack keyed the locks. Johnny fell into the car. "He gets like this sometimes. I'll talk to him about tomorrow."

"What am I supposed to tell Katherine?"

"I'm sorry." Jack spoke as he circled the hood. "Really, Clyde. I'm very sorry."

The car rocked as Jack got in. Johnny put his hand on the glass, and Clyde faded away. The car moved faster, and the world blurred. The city. The city's people. "He deserved better than that," Jack said.

"Just drive."

Johnny's forehead touched the glass.

"What the hell's wrong with you?"

"Not now," Johnny said.

"Are you serious?"

"Tomorrow, Jack. You, too."

Jack had other words, but Johnny didn't hear them. Buildings fell away, and he watched them fall. A mile from the Hush, he felt the first stirring, like a fire in the cold. "Slow down," he said.

"We're not there yet."

"Stop the car."

Jack rolled onto the verge and parked in the stillness. "Now what?"

Johnny opened the door.

"You're getting out?" Jack asked. "Here?"

Johnny looked back toward town, then in the opposite direction. A half mile farther, the road bent. Beyond that it turned again, then ran off from a dirt road that smelled of loam and grass and distant water. Johnny couldn't smell it yet, but he would. "I'll walk from here," he said. "Thanks for the ride."

"That's it?"

"For now."

"Well, that's just fucking fine."

"Tomorrow," Johnny said. "Five o'clock. I'll come to your apartment."

"And your parents?"

"Right after. We'll have that dinner. The four of us." It was a difficult moment because Jack wanted his friend, and Johnny wanted the walk, to feel it build. "Are we square?"

Jack nodded slowly, and to Johnny it was an ending. He stepped back, and waited as Jack turned across the empty pavement. When he was gone, Johnny walked the bent road and the long, sweet dirt. He climbed a buckled gate, and then another, until home was a line through the forest, a shimmer he could actually see. Maybe that was wishful thinking, or delirium. It didn't matter. He stepped over the line, and felt the place flood into him. It was a weight, a warmth; and with all that heat inside, Johnny folded into the earth as if he were an orphan child and the Hush his mother, resurrected.

When Jack returned to town, he went to the office. His billable hours were way down, and he was most likely on a blacklist over Johnny's apparent involvement with Boyd's death, and the sudden loss of that potential revenue. Some partners were reasonable; others lived on ego, spite, and power. That was the nature of the business, and something Jack understood by the second year of law school. It still mattered to him, though: the diplomas, the nameplate on the door. That was about growing up voiceless and small and crippled. Jack loved his career for the same reason he loved Johnny—because they were the only things of worth to survive that childhood.

"Susan." He spoke to an assistant; nodded at an associate beyond an open door. He kept a smile on his face, but it was all an act. A paralegal brushed his shoulder, and he flinched. Cold eyes watched from a corner office. Safe in his own space, Jack closed his door against the firm, trying to understand why it felt so pointless and shallow and false.

Because it is.

The smiles. The brief nods. Had Johnny killed William Boyd, it would have gone away, all of it. And people expected it to. That's what he'd seen on the way in. Surprise and pity and dislike. Jack's suspicion was confirmed when he turned for the desk and saw the daily paper with a photo of Johnny and of a private jet beneath bold print reading, BILLIONAIRE'S FAMILY ARRIVES AT LOCAL AIRPORT, NOTORIOUS LOCAL STILL IN CUSTODY. Beside the paper was a battered copy of the book about Alyssa's death and Johnny's childhood. Jack's picture was in there somewhere. The sunburned face. The gimp arm.

People don't know . . .

They thought Johnny was still in jail, thought Jack's best friend was a killer. The firm would never fire him for that—it would be impolitic—but Jack had been found guilty by association. For a moment, Jack was frozen; then the anger came, a coal of it down low.

"Who put this in my office?"

He was in the doorway, and people were staring.

"Susan? Mark?"

A dozen people were close enough to hear, but no one met his gaze.

"Is there a problem?" A senior associate stepped from the adjacent office and looked pointedly at his watch. "Nice of you to join us today."

Jack raised the paper. "Did you put this on my desk?"

"It's a newspaper, Mr. Cross. I'm sure there's one on most desks in the building."

"He's no killer," Jack said. "They let him go this afternoon."

"I'm sure we don't care."

He turned away and left Jack in a bubble of quiet rage. Heads were still down, no one looking. Back in his office, Jack tossed the paper, tossed the book. His anger felt foreign and strange. He'd known so much of it during childhood that he'd trained himself to go cold rather than hot, to think before reacting. It's why the law appealed, because it was cerebral and offered control.

But Jack had no control.

Emotion moved him from the door to the window and back, then awareness settled like a cool fog. It wasn't anger, but fear.

Jack was frightened of losing his friend.

Choosing files at random, Jack stepped from the office and stopped at an assistant's desk. "I'm working at home this afternoon. Call me there if anyone needs me."

"Yes, sir." The young woman nodded, and Jack turned. "Oh, sir. Excuse me. Messages."

She held out a sheaf of messages, and Jack took them without a word. From the downstairs lobby, he pushed onto the sidewalk and turned for the apartment. It was hot, traffic moving. Three cars down, he saw two men in an Escalade, but paid no attention. They were watching, but he didn't care. Maybe it was the bad arm, the fast walk. A right turn took him past condos and the local bank. Two blocks after taking a left, he slipped into a door beside the bakery and pounded narrow stairs to his apartment on the third floor. Behind the heavy door, he put down his things, splashed water on his face, and sat in the gloom beside drawn curtains.

Am I really losing my friend?

Johnny liked his secrets—that was true. He'd always been quieter than most. But the secrets had been smaller, too. What he felt. What he wanted. Even as a boy, he'd rarely looked for permission or understanding. To Jack that quality had made Johnny dangerous, and he'd liked being part of it: them against the world. But the secrets now were darker.

Jack sat at the desk and flipped through the stack of messages he'd brought from the office; saw numbers for other lawyers, the clerk of court, Leslie. A name he didn't recognize appeared two different times, along with a note from the assistant: *In re: Johnny Merrimon.* Jack considered for a moment, then threw the messages away. The ten-year anniversary of Alyssa's discovery was approaching, and anniversaries brought out the crazies, the journalists, the twisted fans. The ten-year mark would be even bigger. A new edition of the book was planned. The documentary would air another dozen times.

Jack wanted nothing to do with any of it.

Determined to salvage something of the day, he opened the first file and got to work, summarizing financial statements, loan histories, and debt service. The client was a complicated entity, with multiple subsidiaries and dozens of accounts at nine different institutions. The work took time, but Jack found comfort in the flow of numbers, the rattle of keys. He drew order from the chaos, took notes, charted a path. His preliminary thoughts filled a four-page summary for the client CEO; then he opened the next file.

When Jack finally stood, hours had passed. Checking his time sheet, he did the math: 5.2 hours. He was hungry.

Stretching, he pulled a beer from the refrigerator and opened the curtains to see what remained of the day. It was after eight. Dusk. He watched the restaurant across the street and sipped slowly as light faded and the sky turned the kind of purple Jack had always loved: too dark for true day, too warm to be night. A headlight came on, and then another. Jack watched cars move, then saw the Escalade at the curb across the street. For a moment he thought it was the same one he'd seen earlier in the day, but that made little sense. Why park at the firm and then again four blocks away? Jack sipped the beer and wondered if anyone sat inside. He watched for a minute, but that was the thing about purple light. Pretty soon it turned black.

The next day was Saturday, but Jack went to the office anyway: 6:00 A.M., a normal day. He carried a briefcase in his right hand, and the morning paper folded under his bad arm. The morning was gray and cool, his step light.

At the office, he keyed the door and took the elevator up. Another message slip lay on his desk, and it showed the same number, the same message about Johnny. The caller was a man named Peter Drexel, the callback a New York number. The name still meant nothing, so Jack did an online search and found an editor in New York with the same name. To Jack, editors were right up there with reporters and TV producers, so he ignored the message, closed his door, and worked straight through until two thirty.

Order, effort, billable hours.

He took comfort from the work, but caught himself whistling on two different occasions. Did that make him spiteful? He wasn't sure, but when the last file was put away, he kicked his feet onto the desk and read the front-page article a second time.

MERRIMON RELEASED WITHOUT CHARGE

It was not a ringing endorsement of Johnny's character—the reporter cherished nuanced phrases like *still-notorious landowner* and *hermitlike privacy*—but the district attorney had offered expansive, if political, apologies. Bottom line: Johnny was a free man and everyone knew it.

Turning off his lights, Jack studied the empty desks and silent offices. A few people were on the floor, but he didn't care at all. Still whistling, he entered the adjacent office and placed the newspaper on the senior associate's desk. He almost left, but went back to square the edges. Then he turned on the lamp.

After that, the day was his. He called Clyde to confirm that Johnny was coming to town. "He'll be at my apartment at five o'clock. I'll have him there by six."

"Do you think he'll actually come?"

"I'll make sure of it," Jack said. "Tell Katherine I'll bring wine."

Jack was outside by then, and a block away from his favorite deli. A late lunch was tempting, but dinner would be soon, and his time with Leslie had made him painfully aware of the extra notch on his belt. He decided on a walk instead. The wine shop was up the hill and six blocks east.

Jack was home by four, slightly flushed. After showering, he put on a seersucker suit and pink bow tie. Johnny would be casual, but Catherine Merrimon held a special place in Jack's heart. When he'd lost his own mother to vindictiveness, bile, and a snake handler's religious zeal, Katherine had put her own loss aside to seamlessly fill the void. She'd held his hand on the difficult nights, convinced him of college, law school, the chance of a future. Pink was her favorite color.

For the next half hour, Jack fussed over the apartment, the gift bag and the tissue paper he'd used to wrap the wine. Katherine preferred red, but he'd bought white as well. At 4:59 he poured an iced tea. Johnny knocked a minute later. When Jack opened the door, he stepped back, stunned. "Johnny. Jesus. You look . . . shit."

Jack wasn't sure what he'd expected. Yellowed eyes. Dark circles. The last time he'd seen Johnny, he looked anemic, as if from a long illness. But not now. Right now he glowed.

"Woodford Reserve. For you."

Johnny lifted a bottle and stepped inside. Jack took the bourbon, unfeeling. "What the hell, man?"

"What?"

Jack put the bottle down. "You look like you just stepped off a two-month cruise."

"A bath, I guess. A day away from jail." He pointed at the bottle. "You going to open that?"

"Yeah, yeah. Sure."

Jack agreed because he wanted time. In the kitchen, he rattled ice, poured the bourbon. When he returned, Johnny was on his feet. "How about the roof?"

"It's kind of hot."

"Nah, there's shade."

Johnny led, and Jack followed. In the shade of an adjacent building, they took a spot against the parapet wall. Johnny clinked Jack's glass, and proposed a toast. "The medical examiner of Raven County."

He drank, but Jack didn't. He was unhappy. "How did you know?"

Johnny sipped, and offered up the grin. "It's like I told the sheriff. I heard a shot, found the body." Jack shook his head, but Johnny spoke over him. "I know it's hard to track a single shot from three miles—"

"It's impossible."

Johnny's eyes glinted over the rim of his glass. "Not if you know the land."

"That wasn't even my question."

"What, then?"

"When I came for you in the swamp, you weren't worried about being held or charged. You said you'd be out the next day. How did you know the sheriff would be forced to release you?"

"I looked at the body. . . ."

"And what? You just knew?" Jack's voice climbed more than he wished. "You knew from looking at a corpse that no one could possibly find you capable of the murder?"

"Something like that, yeah."

"How did you know?"

"I just did. It was too *wrong*. The bones. The injuries. More hurt was done to that man than I could have ever managed."

Jack looked away from his friend. He watched light stretch out, yellow on the roof across the street. "It doesn't bother you? All that hurt?"

"It's the wilderness. People die in the wild."

"Yeah, they do. From accident or gunshot or sickness. William Boyd didn't starve to death, Johnny. It wasn't an animal attack. He didn't fall down some goddamn hole."

"We don't really know what happened. Do we?"

"Have you seen the autopsy report?"

"Have you?"

Jack put his glass on the wall and gripped warm concrete with both hands. Beside him, Johnny was relaxed. It was infuriating. "There's something wrong with that place. I'm telling you, man. I have a bad feeling."

"Well, I don't."

"You love it too much."

"That's ridiculous."

"Then explain it to me as if I were a child. Tell me how you found the body. Really. Tell me why you need it so much. Tell me how you *knew*."

The moment stretched in a way Jack thought his own soul might never stretch again. The breeze was languid, the evening impossibly soft. When Johnny spoke, his voice was too quiet for the wariness in his eyes. "I think it's time to go."

"It's early."

"Then we go early." Johnny flicked his wrist and dumped ice into the alley below.

"Seriously? It's like that?"

For a moment the chill between them held; then Johnny hooked an arm around Jack's neck and pulled him close. "You can be a real pain. You know that?" Jack had nothing to say, and Johnny seemed to understand, nodding once and flashing the old grin. "Have I ever let you down?" he asked.

"No . . ."

"Broken a promise?"

"We both know you haven't."

"Then come on." Johnny squeezed him a final time, and laughed. "Lighten up. I know what I'm doing."

A day ago, Jack would have reveled in all of it, in the strong arm and laughter, in the hot roof and the memory of all they'd been. He'd have laughed, too, and said: *We have time; let's have another drink.* They'd have poured heavy and savored every sip, then gone to dinner free of doubt, young men afoot in the world. It's what Jack had known and wanted and what, even now, he valued more than anything but the air in his lungs. They'd been best friends as long as he could remember, closer even than brothers. The thought propped him up as they passed through the apartment and down to the street. Johnny was forever, and *forever* never changed. The boy in him wanted to believe as much, but the man he'd become knew better. The laughter rang false; the evening would be false, too.

Neither one saw the Escalade across the street.

CHAPTER SEVENTEEN

On the surface, dinner was a delight. The evening cooled, and they ate in the garden, surrounded by hydrangea, periwinkle, and climbing rose. It was a familiar, private space, and everyone there loved everyone else. Stepfather, mother, friend—the distinctions meant so little. Only Jack was truly quiet, so Johnny watched him when he could. He knew his friend's face the way he knew his own: the insecure smile, the adoration in his eyes each time he looked at Johnny's mother. They'd been a family for so long that glances were like language, and silences rarely awkward. Jack's quietness was different because it focused entirely on Johnny. He studied the trees when Johnny spoke, and excused himself when conversation turned to the Hush. His only true animation occurred when Katherine asked about Johnny's time in jail.

"Was it horrible?"

Johnny squeezed her hand. "A walk in the park."

"Bullshit." Jack coughed the word into his napkin, but everyone heard it.

"Excuse me?" Katherine said.

"No. Excuse me."

Jack left the table for the second time, and Johnny shrugged under the weight of another expectant silence. "He's upset with me. I'm sorry."

Katherine looked worriedly after Jack. "You two are fighting?"

"That's too strong a word."

"Well, you're here." She touched his arm, and was beautiful in the light of a garden at sunset. "That's all that matters to me."

"Cheers, then." Johnny raised his glass, but the mood had turned somber. They spoke of William Boyd, and what Katherine called *that poor man in the hospital.* "I feel for his family," she said. "They must be worried to death."

Johnny absorbed the seconds that followed: how Clyde's fingers brushed the back of her neck, the way he leaned close as if warmth alone could salvage the smile she'd lost. It was love—the purest kind—and Johnny understood that power.

"I should get home."

"I'd hoped you'd spend the night."

Johnny rose, and kissed her cheek. She had her love. He had his. "Will you tell Jack I said goodbye?"

"Of course."

"Thanks for the dinner."

He nodded at the big man beside his mother, then left through the garden gate and followed a side street to where he'd parked his truck. For a moment he paused to watch a flock of smudge-gray chimney swifts bank and whirl above the treetops and rooflines. It was all so familiar: the stiff wing beats, the chattering call. Any moment now, they'd drop as a flock into one of the old chimneys that rose against the sky, and Johnny wondered which one it might be. Were it a hollow tree in the Hush, he'd know exactly where it stood, but in the city was unaware. So he waited and watched; and when the light was perfect, the flock whirled and dived and, like that, was gone.

Third chimney to the left.

The old Victorian.

After cranking the engine, Johnny rolled down both windows and drove for home. The route was familiar, and the steering wheel spun beneath his hand as if it had a mind of its own. The historic district. The courthouse. The old, bricked street that led across the tracks. Johnny was content at first, but thoughts of Jack and his anger drained that contentment away. There was no joy in the faded city, or in the first bright star.

Jack wanted answers.

Johnny wanted nothing to change.

Did that mean he lacked questions of his own? Hell no. Johnny had questions. Hundreds. Would he risk the life he'd made in order to find the answers? That was the simplest question of all, and the answer simpler still.

No way.

Not a chance in hell.

He recognized the denial, but didn't care. Whatever he had was faultless and perfect and pure. He came back to those words again and again. *Purity. Perfection. Faultlessness.* They meant the same thing, but rolled off the tongue in threes.

His life was magic.

Magic was good.

Johnny tapped a rhythm on the wheel as the city sank behind him. Jack was overworried. That was his nature.

Nothing had to change.

Johnny turned that thought in his mind, and the anger faded as he pushed farther into the northern parts of the county. He passed an abandoned farm, an overgrown drive.

The Hush loomed in the distance.

He could feel it.

Three miles later, Johnny saw the headlights far behind, a small glow that exploded as the car raced up at terrific speed. Johnny used a hand to shade his eyes.

"What the hell?"

It was ten feet off the rear bumper. High beams. A flash of chrome. Something big. Johnny risked a glance at the speedometer—62 mph, which was about all the old truck could handle. He motioned with his arm through the window, but the driver had no plans to pass. The vehicle fell back and accelerated, twenty feet off the bumper, then five.

Johnny pushed it to 68, then 70.

"Son of a—"

A tire slipped off the road, and the wheel kicked in Johnny's hands. His next turn was a half mile up, a final stretch of tarmac before the dirt road that would take him home. Johnny held the truck straight, kept his eyes down. Twisting away at the mirror, he watched for the turn, and felt the truck complain at the speed he took it. The back end shuddered left. Smoke rose off the pads. On the straight he gunned it, but the lights stayed with him. Five feet. Less. Johnny's mind filled with cold, clear anger. His foot moved for the brake, but the impact came first, a crash that slammed the truck forward and knocked the back end loose. Tires screamed as Johnny fought, but the big vehicle hit him again, and that was all it took. The bed skewed right and left, and then the truck was sideways and rolling. Johnny's head struck the dash, the glass behind. The noise was an avalanche. He saw slashing light, then gravel and grass and black trees. When the truck stopped, he was right side up, the roof crushed, glass shattered. Something ticked in the sudden stillness. A single headlight flickered and died.

"Ow. Jesus."

Johnny touched his face, and the fingers came back red. He checked again; found a gash in his scalp, a slick of blood on the right side of his face.

"Where . . . ?"

He looked for the car that had wrecked him, found an SUV, black and broad and still. It idled in the road, the lights cutting twin grooves above an empty field. Johnny watched, trying to get his head straight. Failing.

Why?

The car didn't move until Johnny released the belt and fell from the open door. Something was wrong with his leg, his balance. He heard tires on crushed glass, and dragged himself up by the door, the steering wheel. The SUV dropped two tires onto the verge and stopped ten feet away. Johnny thought *accident, apologies, idiots out drinking.* That illusion died when the doors opened and figures emerged behind the lights. For an instant more, Johnny believed. Then they stepped his way and he saw the ax handles. The driver carried his low against the leg; the other man gripped his two-handed.

"Fellas."

Johnny tried for normal, but his voice sounded thin. He blinked blood from his eyes; looked for some kind of weapon but had nothing.

"Your name is Johnny Merrimon."

That was the driver. His body blocked one of the lights, and Johnny saw an Escalade with West Virginia plates. The passenger moved into the light, too. Young men, Johnny thought, late twenties and rawboned and serious.

Johnny limped to the truck's crumpled hood. "Maybe it is."

"It wasn't a question. Your name is Johnny Merrimon. Yesterday, you were in jail for the murder of William Boyd."

"What do you want?"

They moved closer. "For starters," the driver said, "I want your undivided attention."

Johnny saw the backswing. The rest was a blur. When his vision cleared, he was on the ground with another gash in his head. He rolled for his side, but a boot swung in and broke a rib. Johnny felt it go. He spread his fingers on the dirt; tried to rise.

"Not yet."

The voice came first, then the hickory. One blow shattered Johnny's wrist. Six more found his kidneys, his shoulders, the back of his head. The world went black another time, and when he came back, the pain traveled with him. It was agony. His head. The world. The driver was squatting beside him. "Are we clear on this question of attention?"

Johnny spit blood in the dust, choking. The man had bristled hair, a broad nose, and wide-set eyes. The boots were steel-toed under faded jeans, the watch a gold Rolex. "Who the hell are you?"

"My name is James Kirkpatrick Jr. You put my father in the hospital. I want to know what you did to him."

"Your father." Johnny choked again. "I don't know your father."

"The rules here are very simple. You lie to me, you hurt."

He nodded at his friend. An ax handle whistled in, and Johnny's kneecap split like a melon. He screamed for a long time after that; couldn't help it.

"What'd you do to him?" The driver was intent, but patient when the silence came. "He's the strongest man I've ever known, now he's shitting the bed and scared of shadows. What'd you do?"

"Nothing." Johnny's face was in the dirt. "I didn't do anything."

Kirkpatrick nodded again, and his friend went to work. He shattered Johnny's hand; beat his legs and back so hard and so many times that Johnny went black again.

"Jesus . . ." He woke, curled around the broken hand.

"What'd you do to my father?"

"The sheriff . . ."

"What?" Closer.

"The sheriff let me go." Johnny heard the slur in his words. He dug deep. "I didn't do anything. He let me go."

"You think I don't know about corrupt sheriffs? We own coal mines. That means we own sheriffs, too." He took a fistful of Johnny's hair. "Perhaps you don't understand the kind of man my father raised. I've broken unions, and beaten miners bloody just to make a point. I'm talking about West Virginia coal miners, hard men. I've threatened reporters and politicians, and walked away untouched. I killed a blackmailer once, and no one even knows he's missing. You don't think I'll kill you, too? Now, I'll ask one more time. The hell did you do to my father?"

Johnny saw the hate; felt the breath. He wanted a way out, but truth was all he had. "I don't know your father."

"Don't say it."

He slammed Johnny's skull against the dirt, but Johnny's course was set. "I don't know him. I don't know you. . . ."

"Is that right?"

Johnny showed red teeth, and spit blood on Kirkpatrick's boots. After that it got ugly. Two ax handles. Two angry men. Johnny curled as best he could, but they beat him loose and limp, then rolled his truck into the brush and came back to the place he lay dying.

"He dead yet?"

A foot settled on Johnny's chest, and blood bubbled past his teeth. "I don't know. Maybe."

"Let's get him off the street."

"Put him with the truck?"

"No. Further down." In Johnny's mind, he screamed as they dragged him over the ditch. "Come on. Just haul his ass over." Rocks tore skin, and forest closed like a black glove. They dragged him a long way. "This is good. Right here."

"It's not too close?"

"To the truck? Maybe. Grab that."

They drew rotted logs over Johnny's body, then piled on brush and rocks and loose soil. It took time.

"Good enough?"

"We'll be long gone before anybody finds this son of a bitch."

Other words followed, but Johnny missed them. He heard the engine; had a sense of slashing lights and then nothing. Maybe they thought he was dead. Maybe he was close. Breath ran shallow behind his teeth. He tasted blood and rot, but the road was near and so was the Hush.

Johnny tried to crawl from the shallow grave.

His smallest finger moved.

Cree woke twice from dreams of Johnny Merrimon. She saw fire and faces and flickers of bright metal. In the third, she was buried alive and Johnny was in the dirt with her. Swelling blacked his eyes, but the bloody mouth moved.

I see you.

Cree moaned in her sleep, aware of the dream but held in that dark place by an unseen force that pressed her against the white man's broken bones, the beetles that moved on his skin. She wanted to scream and run, but knew from childhood that there was power in dreams, and vision for those not frightened of deeper truths. So even as she moaned in her narrow bed, she felt the shattered legs and the broken arm, the soft spots in his skull that felt like cornmeal when she pushed. Moving dirt from his face, she spoke the bitter truth.

"You're dying," she said; and his eyelids fluttered. "Can you hear me?"

She pressed closer in the blackness, felt the length of him, the warm center that was his beating heart. It fluttered, too, and she closed her eyes so she wouldn't see him die. Somehow, though, his hand found hers, and squeezed. She opened her eyes to see him watching. His mouth moved, but the voice was someone else's.

Help him, it said.

And Cree bolted up a final time, frozen and afraid and sheeted in sweat.

It took her thirty minutes to find the courage to do what needed doing. She climbed from bed and dressed without lights. The clock read 2:19. Across the hall, her mother tossed under light sheets. It was hot in the apartment, but Cree put on thick socks and tall boots and heavy, denim pants. She was frightened of the dream and of what she might find, but what drove her was profounder and older and part of a near-forgotten life. Was it really her grandmother's face she remembered? Her great-grandmother's? There were no photographs by which to judge, and her mother would not discuss the subject other than to apologize for sending her to the swamp in the first place. But Cree was a child of old women and still waters. Part of that childhood involved pain and fear, but part, too, was warmth and love and mystery. Time had blurred the old faces, yes, but not the eyes or the voices.

There is such magic in the world. . . .

How many times had those words found her, either warm beneath the covers or seated barefoot on black earth?

There is such magic in the world, and such strong hearts to hold it.

It was a favorite memory and a favorite voice, her grandmother's voice, same as in the dream of Johnny.

Pulling on a dark shirt, Cree cinched up her belt and eased past her mother's door, moving with familiar care. In the kitchen, she filled a bag with apples, bottled water, and two slices of pizza, cold from the fridge. The last thing she took was a flashlight, then she was in the outside stairwell that smelled of urine, and in the courtyard formed, it seemed, of cracked concrete and condoms and empty bottles. She hated life in the city. The smells were caustic, the violence random and needless and unremitting. She kept the light off and stayed near the walls, swinging wide at blind corners. Experience had taught her that this was the sweet spot of the night, the slow time and the safest; but she hid when cars passed, music thumping, or if other people drew too close. It took an hour to find a better part of the city, and on that downtown street, with lights and cars and occasional cops, she put out her thumb and walked north. She got lucky with an old man in a Pontiac wagon. He was white-haired and withered and driving early to beat the heat. "A granddaughter up north," he said. "About the same age as you." He thumped the dash. "Air-conditioning went out four years back, so I make the drive at night. It's prettier that way, too. Stars remind me of my wife."

His wife had died fifteen years ago. *Taken,* he said, *by the cancer.* He was nice and soft-spoken and as safe as any ride she'd ever had. *Up north* meant Raleigh, but he went twenty miles east because he was worried about a young girl, pretty and alone in times such as these. The truck stop where they said goodbye was well lit and on the main road to Raven County.

"Sun's up in a few hours." He leaned across the seat, peering up as she stood beneath red neon. "You have people waiting where you're going?"

"Yes, sir," she lied.

"You have money?"

"I'll be okay."

"Here, take this." He held out a ten-dollar bill, and refused to leave until she accepted it. "You wait on the sun, okay." He peered down the empty road. "It's a dangerous world for young ones alone. You hear me? Not everyone's an old man at the tail end of a good life."

"Yes, sir."

"You wait on that sunrise."

She thanked him for the ride, the advice, and money, and waited until he was gone before approaching the first trucker she saw and asking the same question she'd asked a hundred times in her life.

You going east?

Like most times, the ride ended at the crossroads, and after that she walked. It was dark enough to use the flashlight. Otherwise, she wandered off the tarmac and into wet grass. Two miles took her to a smaller road, and more walking to another road after that. By the time she hit rutted dirt, the sky was pale in the east, and the low places filled with mist. It gathered in the ditch lines and hollows, and on black water when it showed through the trees. Cree watched her feet when light found them, and saw the first blood two minutes after that. It was so shiny-wet, she thought it was oil; then she saw the drag marks. They were plain in the dusty road—scraped earth and blood—and Cree stopped, as suddenly cold and afraid as she'd ever been this close to the swamp.

The trees were mist and darkness.

A night heron called, unseen.

Clicking on the light, she flashed it in a circle, then put it on the drag marks, and bent low enough to touch the damp spots, which were fresh and dust-choked and sticky. She tracked them with the light, but the mist swallowed them after fifty feet. That left two choices: forward or back. Cree thought for a second, but had never been a going-back kind of girl. Besides, the dream had been bloody, too, and the dream was why she'd come.

Moving slowly, she followed the drag marks as the roadway filled up with false dawn's ashen light. She kept her footsteps quiet, which wasn't hard in air so damp and heavy, it felt to Cree that even a scream might be swallowed up. She'd known a childhood of similar mornings, but this one was colder and quieter, as if the sun might never rise. She thought of the times her grandmother had squeezed her tight and said, *Don't go into the forest just yet.* It was easy to forget that the old women had feared at times, and that they'd warned her to stay inside if mist came off the river or the skies filled up with strange light. Cree had never thought the worries justified. She'd believed them to be the fears of old women, but not now.

The drag marks went a hundred yards, then farther.

The dawn was a shuttered breath.

She saw Johnny at the same time she saw the gate, both of them dark and unmoving. He lay between the ruts, and even at a distance she saw the twisted arm, the shattered legs. Closer, his head was a mask of earth and blood so profuse and viscous, he had to be dead.

Then he moved.

The good arm stretched out, and the body followed. One drag. Another. His right foot hung up on a root, and the leg twisted the way no leg ever should. She heard a sob, but it was hers.

How far had he crawled?

Cree dropped her things, then stumbled up the dirt road and fell to her knees at his side. He kept crawling.

"Johnny." It was the first time she'd said his name, and it hung in her throat. She could barely look at him. "Mr. Merrimon. Stop. Please. I'll get help. Just stop moving." She couldn't bear the sound of it: the rasp of bone, the wet breath. He reached out; dragged himself. "Oh God."

"Help me."

Sound slipped past his lips, but the words were barely words. Cree looked around; saw nothing but mist and the gate. It was getting colder.

"What should I do? I don't have a car." Another sound escaped his throat. "What? I don't understand."

"Gate . . ."

He pointed at twisted steel, loose on a cedar post. Beyond it was his land, her childhood. "You need an ambulance." She dug out the cell phone, but it had no signal. "Shit." She could barely look at him: the dirt-packed cuts and shattered nose, the shredded trousers and shards of bone. He tried to crawl again. "Stop." She was still sobbing. "Please."

"Home . . ."

He slid another foot, and mist curled beyond the gate. It gathered and thickened, a shape, like a man, but not.

"Oh my God."

Cree's phone fell from dead fingers. The mist was more than mist. She saw gray holes and limbs and swirls of movement. She wanted to run but could barely breathe. Johnny scraped out a foot, another two.

"Johnny, please . . ."

"Go away," he managed.

Then something opened the gate.

And something dragged him through.

CHAPTER EIGHTEEN

Jack fumbled out of damp sheets, wondering if he'd ever know another good night's sleep. The bed was too hard or too soft. Light shone in from the street, but closed curtains made it too dark, and things got worse in the dark: worry for his friend, his fear of the Hush. Dressing in silence, Jack drew back the curtains and was too ashamed to find comfort in familiar sights. He'd behaved dreadfully in front of Katherine, and that was bad enough. He should have kept the smile on his face or summoned the will to speak plainly, to stop Johnny from leaving. It was the blindness that tortured Jack: his friend's reluctance to see the aberrant nature of his need for the Hush. Or was that explanation too simple? Maybe Johnny did see. Maybe he saw entirely too well.

What can I do to help my friend?

It was not a rhetorical question. Turning to the mirror, Jack studied the Windsor knot, the fine suit. He looked exactly like the lawyer he'd worked so hard to become, an academic, a researcher, a seeker of fact.

"All right, then."

He buttoned the coat.

"That's how we'll work it."

He was in his car by seven and at the offices of the local paper six minutes after that. That early, the newspaper was closed to the public, but the features editor had known Jack's brother in high school. She wasn't really a friend, but then again, Jack wasn't asking for a kidney. "A few hours," he said. "In and out."

She led him to the archives and explained how to run the microfiche machine. "Storage cabinets are here. Issues run from newest to oldest."

Jack took in the rowed cabinets. "How far back does this go?"

"Eighteen ninety-one."

"Well, damn," Jack said; but the attitude didn't last. Research had a rhythm, and he was a master. He started with headlines, but struck gold in the obituaries. Deaths led to places, and places to larger stories. The first was about a lost trapper, found dead on the banks of a creek deep in the Hush. That was in 1897. Three years later, a prospector went missing in the same area. After that, Jack dug out the obituary of a dead logger, and stories of lost boys, finally found. He read a ninety-year-old opinion insisting the swamp be drained for the greater good, then found the deathbed confession of a priest gone mad trying to convert those lost souls who dwelled deep in its interior. The stories were small, but part of a larger tapestry: hunting accidents, suicides, a road-building project abandoned after its foreman—like the preacher—had gone stark raving insane.

In the parking lot, Jack leaned against the car, feeling sick. The problem was real.

Others had died.

Many others.

Rolling down the windows, he reread an article published in the winter of 1931: LOST BOY RETURNED TO MOTHER. Beneath the headline was a picture of a tumbledown house behind a starved-looking woman and a blank-eyed boy. Jack peered into those eyes, trying to imagine what Randolph Boyd had felt on the day he'd been found and brought back to his mother.

At home that evening, Jack went through the articles again. Four others discussed the boys, lost in the Hush. Most reporters labeled Boyd a stoic, with one saying he possessed the kind of rawboned courage certain to stand him in good stead later in life. His friends were less reticent about their ordeal, telling such outrageous stories that one reporter wrote that, "Randolph Boyd stands in stark contrast to his more fanciful friends, determined, it seems, to mine fame and glory from the unadorned tragedy of Boyd's near death." Other accounts were equally dismissive of Charlie and Herbert, yet Jack paid close attention when either boy was quoted, using a red pen to circle words like *chased* and *terrified* and *laughter.*

The final article spoke less of the boys and more of the search. It included photos of the swamp, which appeared forbidding and raw. Most interestingly, it included the names of the volunteers who'd searched it—a two-column list with print so small, it was difficult to read. The local VFW had turned out in full, as had three volunteer fire departments and sixteen members of the national guard. Other volunteers were listed by church affiliation or school. The last seven were labeled *miscellaneous.* For an hour, Jack plugged names into a white pages search and then into Google. Most would be dead and gone, but nineteen high school students had taken part in the search. Jack thought some might be alive, and he might yet get lucky.

He didn't.

Not just then.

When he crawled into bed, it was two in the morning, and he was wide awake. For long hours he stared at the ceiling, then left a message on Johnny's cell and tried, at last, to sleep. The message was brief and simple.

Call me, you bastard.

In spite of a sleepless night, Jack made it to work early. He pushed files around the desk for a few hours, but his thoughts were on darker things.

"Tell me I'm awesome."

Jack looked up to see Leslie in the door. "You're awesome."

She sat and crossed her legs, looking beautiful. "I talked to Reamer." She flashed the smile, the bright eyes. "You're on the Tech-Stone bankruptcy trial. You'll be carrying his briefcase, but still—"

"Wait a minute. What?"

"You can thank me later."

Jack's head spun at the news. Tech-Stone was the state's largest bankruptcy in thirty years. Billions of dollars. Three thousand employees. "How did you do it?"

"Jump-start your career? Change your life? What can I say? You're not the only lawyer who finds me irresistible."

"Leslie, my God. Thank you."

"Don't thank me yet. I want something in return."

"What?"

"I'll tell you later." She stood. "The team is meeting at three in Reamer's office. Four other lawyers, seven assistants. Don't be late."

She left with a flourish, and Jack thought about what it would mean to impress Randy Reamer. If a large firm from a major city took a bankruptcy trial in the South, they invariably partnered with Reamer. Same thing with corporate malfeasance, mergers, leveraged buyouts. He was as close to a celebrity as an attorney could get, and juries loved him. When asked once why he chose to live in a place as small as Raven County, he said it was for the golf, and because he'd met the snakes who live in big cities. In spite of that, CEOs revered him. So did other attorneys, business reporters, all the big-city players he pretended to scorn. The associates' mantra was that law school teaches law, and Reamer, all the rest.

If you're lucky, Jack reminded himself.

If you have a friend like Leslie Green.

There were a hundred things Jack should do before the meeting at three. To impress Reamer, he needed to research Tech-Stone. That meant its history, its public face, its financials. Jack had the time and the desire, but opened Johnny's file instead. Last night's internet search had found no matches for people who'd searched for Randolph Boyd on that frozen day, but a near miss involved a student named Bert Showalter. As far as Jack could tell, a single Showalter remained in Raven County. It wasn't Bert, but how many families named Showalter could there be? Jack picked up the phone, dialing.

"Five minutes," he told himself.

It took less than two.

Tyson Showalter lived on a shaded lane four blocks from the local college. He was a political science professor, so the location made sense. Jack's call had found him at home between classes, and he'd agreed to meet. A cool shade filled the porch as Jack stepped onto it. Windows stood open. The paint was white and fresh. Knocking on the screen door, Jack saw antiques, a shotgun hall, and hints of a kitchen in the back. The air smelled of fried chicken and coffee and hot butter. Jack knocked a second time.

"Just a minute. I'm coming." An older man appeared from the kitchen. He wore an apron, spectacles, and loafers with no socks. His hands were busy in a small towel. "Sorry, sorry. I was trying to get a head start on the dishes. You must be Mr. Cross."

"Jack, please."

"Fair enough. Call me Ty. Everyone does." Ty pushed open the screen, and shook hands. "Do you mind if we talk in the kitchen?"

"Of course not."

Ty led Jack down the hall and into a small, neat kitchen where chicken cooled on a tray and beans simmered in a pot. The rear yard showed through equally spotless glass, and Jack saw the nose of an old Triumph through the open door of a detached garage.

"You like antiques?"

"Absolutely. All kinds. The older, the better." Ty used a hot pad to pull biscuits from the oven. "You were a little mysterious on the phone. You wanted to talk about my mother?"

"Um, no. I'm sorry. I was hoping to discuss Bert Showalter. I thought maybe you were related."

"Not Bert, no. I'm afraid there is no Bert." Ty laughed an easy laugh. "Bertie is my mother. Her real name is Beatrice, but she's been 'Bertie' for a hundred years."

"Bertie? No." Jack's head tilted. "The newspaper said Bert."

"What newspaper?"

The article was folded into Jack's suit coat pocket. He removed it, handed it over. Ty recognized it, and a frown appeared. "Oh," he said. "That."

"You've seen it?"

"Yes."

Jack looked for the right response, but Ty's mood had changed. The affable gentleman of seventy or so was gone.

"I'm not sure we should be talking."

"Mr. Showalter. If I've upset you somehow . . ."

Jack trailed off as the older man pinched the bridge of his nose and shook his head. "No. I'm sorry. Look, I don't mean to appear rude, but it's a lesson we learned young: Don't talk about Randolph Boyd or the winter of '31 or what happened in that godforsaken swamp."

"Forgive me, but I'm confused."

Ty slumped a little, and the soft smile came back. "Would you like some coffee? I seem to have misplaced my manners." Jack watched him pour coffee, then nodded his thanks. "Come with me, Mr. Cross. I'll show you something, then try to explain." Ty led the way to a small bedroom, where an old woman lay in a hospital bed. An IV fed the right arm. A tracheotomy tube was centered at the throat, a machine helping her breathe. "This is my mother, Bertie. I take a long lunch every day to watch her for a few hours. It gives the nurse a break, helps with the costs. It's good time for me, too. She was lively once. We were close."

The machine hissed, and monitors blinked, green. Jack didn't know what to say. "How old is she?"

"A hundred and one."

"Can she . . . ?"

Jack motioned with a hand, and Ty understood. "Speak? No. She's not opened her eyes or spoken for almost three years. Come on. Let's go outside."

They moved to the front porch and sat on iron chairs as old as everything else in the house. Beyond a picket fence, the lane was quiet. Traffic sounds were distant. Jack gestured at the article, still in Ty's hand. "Can we talk about that?"

"Randolph Boyd, yes." Ty unfolded the photocopy and smiled wistfully, looking at it. "They would allow only young men to join the search. My mother told them she was a boy. With covered hair and bulky clothing, no one knew the difference or cared enough to call her out on the lie."

"Why lie in the first place? The article says it was ten below zero that day. Why go at all?"

"My understanding is that Randolph Boyd was a gangly young man, but not entirely unattractive."

"Your mother was involved with Boyd?"

"Not involved, no." Ty laughed a bit. "What my mother had was a crush, though time has led me to believe it was a ferocious one. What's your interest in all this?"

"You heard of the billionaire, found dead in the swamp."

"You're not implying that William and Randolph Boyd are related?"

"Actually, I'm stating it as fact." Jack explained Boyd's hunting lodge, his vast holdings of local real estate. "Can you tell me about the winter of '31?"

"It's been so long. . . ."

"Please."

The older man looked at the street, but didn't seem to see it. "She used to wake screaming, my mother. For years, it was like that. She'd scream so loud and long, we slept with the windows closed so as not to concern the neighbors. They knew, of course. Even as a boy, I could see how people looked at her on the street, how the church ladies and schoolteachers would touch her arm gently, and ask, 'How you holding up, dear?' The nightmares ate us all down. The screaming. The long silences. She got a little better with time. The screams died to whimpers. The nightmares came less often. By the time I was grown, most people couldn't tell that she was haunted, still. Those of us who knew her best were denied that gift."

"What do you mean?"

"Do you believe in higher powers?"

"I believe in friendship."

"I never knew my father, Mr. Cross. I never knew what to trust, growing up, so I put my faith in systems: the systems of government and education, those inspired by decency and faith in people. Are you an understanding person?"

"I believe so."

"May I show you something?"

Jack nodded, and Ty led him back into the house, taking the stairs that led up. "This was my mother's room for thirty years. She has no use for it, of course, but I've left it unchanged." Opening a door, he gestured for Jack to enter, then followed behind. The room was on the front corner of the house, with views into the tree canopy and down onto the street. A large, airy space, it felt like the room of an older woman. A clock ticked from the mantel. Motes hung in beams of yellow light. "I imagine you see the reasons I brought you here."

The walls were covered with drawings. Every inch. Every bit of surface. "May I?" Without waiting, Jack approached the nearest wall. The sketches were done in charcoal or pencil, and showed finely rendered scenes of winter forest and frozen water, of bare rock and tangled vine. "This is . . . ?"

"Hush Arbor," Ty said. "The winter of '31."

Jack moved along the wall, marveling at the delicacy of the sketches, the perfection of the tree bark and drifts, the branches and emptiness. Jack stopped when he reached the drawings of the great deer. Partially butchered, it lay on snow stained black. Its eyes were closed, the antlers enormous and smooth. Beside the dead animal, a young man clutched his knees for warmth, his features perfectly captured to show the cold and lonesomeness and fear.

"Haunting, isn't it?"

Jack felt the old professor behind him, but couldn't look away. A dozen drawings showed different angles of the same scene. The boy was frostbitten and gaunt, his skin and hands black with the same blood that stained the snow. Jack felt a horrible dread, looking at it. "What is this place?"

"It's where they found him."

Behind the boy, a frozen waterfall descended from a stone face marred by scrub and snow. Atop the knoll a stunted tree rose ten feet before splitting to form the shape of a perfect V.

"Your mother drew these?"

"They offered some comfort, I believe. These were the only ones I'd allow her to display."

"There are others?"

Tyson nodded and spoke softly. "She was a girl when she lied her way onto that search, just a child, really. She told me once that something drove her from the others. She said it was like a hand on her back, the way she drifted left."

"I don't understand."

"All I know is she was with the group and then, suddenly, quite alone."

Jack studied the sketches of Randolph Boyd. They were the most delicate, the most *personal.* "She found him, didn't she?"

"Yes."

Jack felt a chill, as if he'd been there. "May I see the other drawings?"

"Actually, Mr. Cross." Ty opened a closet door, revealing large boxes, stacked one atop the other. "I'd consider it a kindness if you'd *take* them."

The boxes filled Jack's car. The trunk. The backseat. At the bakery, he parked and carried them up the narrow stairs. It took four trips. Rowing them beside the dining room table, he opened one box and then another, lifting the drawings out in dusty sheaves and piling them on the table. The oldest were yellow and brittle. Others seemed newer. Few were as finely rendered as the ones he'd seen, but all were more disturbing, the strokes of charcoal heavy and broad and *angry.* Most involved the landscapes of Hush Arbor, but were drawn in a way that made implicit the sense of malice. Dense forest. Jagged rock. Branches swept the ground to hold shadows that hinted at wicked things; fingers curled over broken stone; eyes peered from the gloom behind, but were hints of eyes, slits in the blackness.

Jack's worst moment came when he reached a stack of sketches bound with twine and folded into the bottom of the last box. Spread across the bed, they showed a cavern full of mounded remains, a great sprawl of pelvis bones and skulls and long ones he thought were femurs. They filled the hollow places and spilled over stone, a world of bone and rotted cloth and tufted hair.

Disturbed, Jack left the drawings on the bed, fixed a drink, and drained it dry. Whatever happened to Bertie Showalter, it had clearly haunted her for years. There were hundreds of drawings, maybe thousands. Jack went through them again, culling out the ones that were darker, more erratic. He missed the meeting with Reamer's team, but didn't think about it. He was lost in sketches of eyes and falling snow and hints of movement. At the end, he returned to the dead deer and the frozen waterfall behind it. Jack's gaze moved up the face of rock and settled on the V-shaped tree that crowned the knoll. He touched it with a finger and faced, at last, the cold place in his troubled heart.

Jack knew the tree.

He'd seen it before.

CHAPTER NINETEEN

It was night when Cree returned, limping, to the city. She was exhausted, afraid; and though most of a day had passed, the same question rang in her head.

What the hell did I just see?

All she knew for sure was the run from the gate: the blur of mist and ditches and sudden falls. Now she was in the city with no real sense of getting there. Even the cars in which she'd ridden seemed somehow less than real. Questions. Conversations. Forgotten faces.

A block from home, she saw her building, like a middle finger to the city that tolerated it. She'd hated it every day of her life but this one. Now she wanted its walls and doors and concrete.

Crossing the filthy courtyard, Cree leaned into the glass doors and almost fell into the elevator, breathing shallowly as it creaked up to the twenty-third floor. Pulling out her phone, she thought again about calling the cops. She had no feelings for Johnny Merrimon one way or another, but he was dead or dying.

"Damn it."

She shoved the phone in her pocket for the eighth time. What could she say? *He was already half-dead when I found him, then something terrible dragged him into the woods.* They'd think her insane or on drugs, or maybe that she'd killed him herself. There must be smart cops somewhere. One of them would figure out the lawsuit and see it the wrong way.

Uh-uh.

Not happening.

In the kitchen, Cree's mother sat at the table, a glass in her hand. She was drunker than normal, a tiny thing in the small, hard chair. "What happened to you?" she asked.

"I fell. It doesn't matter."

"You look like you've been dragged behind a mule."

Cree dropped the backpack, and the day rolled over her like a wave: the blood and twisted bones, the long trip out and the dream that sent her in the first place. She was frightened—utterly terrified—and this was what she had in life: a rented box in a rotting building, a mother too thoughtless or drunk to know her daughter's world had come undone.

"Get me some ice, will you?" Her mother held up a glass and rattled the melted cubes. "Go on, then." She shook it again, and Cree blinked in the stillness that followed. She saw her grandmother and her childhood, and was suddenly crying. She pictured her great-grandmother, too: the ruined eyes and scarred hands, the way she liked to smile and nod, and how she felt at night, as dry as a leaf and warm in the big bed. "Why did you send me there? I was only four years old."

"Are you crying?"

"Tell me why."

"It's no secret." Her mother lowered the glass, and lit a cigarette. "They wanted you, those old women. They thought you'd be special."

"What does that mean?"

"You'd have to ask them, wouldn't you?"

"Let's talk about you, then." Cree sat, but was unforgiving. "Why did you run away?"

"What?"

"You left the swamp when you were nineteen. We've never discussed it."

"Because it's none of your business."

"Grandmother said you were afraid."

"Is that right?" Cree's mother frowned and poured vodka over melted ice. "Has it occurred to you that I wanted something bigger than life in the swamp, something better than mud and chiggers and men of low ambition?"

Her mother looked away, and Cree saw the old stubbornness in her face. It made her angry and bitter. "You know, I make this very easy for you: the bad men and laziness, this." Cree nudged the bottle, her gaze remorseless. "I shop. I clean. Now I want something in return."

"What?"

"I have dreams."

The words fell into a vacuum of sudden silence. Her mother's shoulders rolled inward. Her chin settled low, and the response, when it came, was very quiet. "What kind of dreams?"

"Terrible ones," Cree said. "The hanging tree and slaves and murdered men. I see it like I was there."

"Stories," her mother said. "Everybody knows about the hanging tree. We've all heard the stories."

"It's too real," Cree said. "I know what they looked like and smelled like and how they screamed. I'm holding the knife. I know their names."

"No, you don't."

"Two are slaves. One's a foreman—"

"I said no, damn it. Dreams are just dreams."

Her voice broke, and Cree saw the lie in her mother's face, the shiftiness and fear, the thirsty swallow. Her eyes were on the bottle; Cree beat her to it. "What's in the swamp?"

"You should have asked my mother, you loved her so goddamn much."

"I was just a kid."

"You think age matters, you stupid girl? You think it mattered for me?"

"Why did you leave?"

"I told you once—"

"I dream of Johnny Merrimon, and the dreams are true."

Her mother rocked back in the seat, her mouth open as if slapped. "Don't you say that. Don't you dare."

"It happened last night."

"Not this far from the swamp, it can't. Not this far away."

"Wait. What?"

"I'm sorry, no." The older woman stood, and the chair fell over as she shoved it left and stumbled from the room. Cree heard a door slam, and knew the lock had dropped, too. In a still-dazed state, she straightened the chair, then ran water in the sink, washing dirt from her palms and scrubbing gently at dried blood from one of her falls. Cree had seen her mother drunk, angry, and bored, but never like this, not panicked and afraid.

Trailing down the same hall, she knocked at her mother's room, and heard rustling beyond the door.

"Go away."

Her mother was crying, too: a dreadful sound. "I'm afraid of the dreams," Cree said.

"You should be."

"Is that why you left?" Nothing. Silence. "Are you still there?"

Cree heard a long sigh, then another silence. "Few have the dreams. Most don't. No one's ever had them outside the swamp."

"But you had them?"

"The hanging tree, yes. So did your grandmother, your great-grandmother. It finds the women in our family. The girl with the knife. What happened at the tree. I've tried to leave that behind. Don't you see? There are other dreams, worse dreams. You're too young to know."

"I'm the age you were when you ran away."

"Sweet Lord . . ."

"Tell me what to do."

"I can't. I'm sorry."

"Why not?"

"Talking about it makes it worse, like opening a door. They come darker then, and faster. It's like drowning."

"I don't understand."

"Of course you don't, you stupid child, you stupid, foolish girl."

"What do I do? Mom . . ."

Cree's voice trailed off, and she pressed a cheek against the door. The old women had told Cree she was special, and that she'd come to them for a reason.

"Please . . ." She said it again, her fingers on the door. "I don't want to dream."

There was no response, and she didn't expect one. Her mother was a coward; she'd always been one. Turning away, Cree returned to her room, and on the bed, she hugged herself. When she began to nod, she crept onto the roof of the building and sat in an old chair she'd found there years ago. Traffic sounds rose up the walls, and city lights burned in other towers. Cree watched the moon rise, and by midnight sleep was circling.

What if she dreamed again?

What if she saw things?

Settling deeper, she watched clouds roll across the moon. Exhaustion pressed down, and she drifted twice. There was no wind. The world was heavy. Cree struggled for hours, then blinked a final time as darkness pooled at her feet, and she fell through.

She was choking in the black.

Buried alive.

The shock of it was like an electric current. She couldn't breathe or see. Damp earth crushed her.

She was Cree.

And someone else.

A scream forced her lips, but dirt fingers snaked inside.

She was choking . . .

Dying . . .

Cree woke, screaming so loudly that birds erupted from the parapet across the roof. Cree barely noticed. They were black; everything was black.

She fell from the chair, retching; tasted dirt but there was only bile.

"Sweet Jesus."

On her hands and knees, Cree thought of God, as she'd not since early childhood.

It was real.

So damn real.

Finding her feet, she stumbled into the building and down to her room, where she locked the door and swore to God she'd never sleep again. When the sun rose, she was hanging by a thread. She stayed in the room, didn't eat or drink or risk the bed. At sunset, her mother turned on the TV, so Cree went back to the roof to be alone in the open air.

She knew things from the dream.

Terrible things.

She watched stars come out as if she'd never seen them before, and at times she touched her face, expecting a broader nose, smaller eyes. When the moon rose, she was in the same chair, and when it set, she was still there, wrapped in a blanket and fighting sleep as if her life depended on staying awake. Three hours past midnight, clouds rose in the west, and Cree's head dipped as thunder rumbled and wind on the rooftop made a lullaby of lost words. In time a raindrop fell, but Cree didn't feel it.

She was buried alive.

Screaming in the earth.

CHAPTER TWENTY

Bonnie Busby had been the district attorney long enough to recognize the sheriff's mood, and unpleasant words rose in her mind as she watched him across the desk.

Dogged.

Unreasonable.

Blind.

"I hear what you're saying, Sheriff Cline, but Trenton Moore has ruled out Johnny Merrimon as a possible killer. The trauma's too extreme and random and . . . inexplicable."

"Inexplicable?"

"Come on. You were in the same meeting. You heard him."

"Well, I don't care what that little man says. Just because he can't figure out how Merrimon did it doesn't mean the kid's not responsible. Who knows what he has out in that swamp. Conspirators. Contraptions—"

"I'm sorry," the DA interrupted, holding out a hand. "Did you just say 'contraptions'?"

"The point, Bonnie, is that it's premature to rule out anyone. We have an exceptional death, so exceptional measures must be taken. I've found his cabin." The sheriff spread an aerial photograph across the desk. "You can see hints of roofline here and here." He pointed. "This looks like a garden, these rows." He met her eyes, frowning. "You're not even looking."

"Because you need probable cause for a warrant, and you have none."

"The kid's not right."

"It doesn't make him a killer."

The sheriff rolled up the printout, snapped a rubber band around it. This was his third visit in two days.

Disdain.

That's what Bonnie saw in his eyes. He thought her weak and easy and simple. "I'm not your enemy, Willard."

"You're Clyde Hunt's friend, and in this case, that's the same thing."

"Tread carefully, now."

"Or what?"

"Bring me probable cause, and I'll take it to the judge. It's as simple as that." He stared across the desk, eyes blazing. She'd seen him like this before. Not often, but it happened. "Is there anything else?"

"You weren't here ten years ago. You didn't see what the boy was like. He walked a terrible road, Bonnie, and it broke something deep. That means people are going to get hurt. They already are. Now, you can sit there smug and prim, looking down on me like I'm some dumb-ass redneck too far down a forty-year stretch, but you weren't here. You're making a mistake."

"Perhaps, but it's mine alone to make."

"He's dangerous, damn it."

"That's your opinion."

The sheriff straightened and stared down.

"Probable cause," she said. "You do your job and I'll do mine."

Sheriff Cline trusted two men in the deep woods. They were hunters and trappers, rawboned woodsmen who believed that if an animal walked or flew, it was there to be killed. And they'd go anywhere to do it. Private property. Parklands. They didn't care, and they didn't get lost. That's what mattered to Sheriff Cline.

He met them in a vacant field two miles from the edge of town, both men geared up with cartridge belts and snake boots and thorn-proof pants. Behind them, stubbled hills rolled into the distance, a speck of combine trundling across the last hill before the forest rose. "Jimmy Ray. Waylon. Thanks for coming on short notice. This is what I'm talking about." The sheriff spread the aerial photograph across the hood of his cruiser. "Northern edge of the county, the swamp here, then up into the base of these hills."

Jimmy Ray pressed close, putting a broad palm on the corner of the printout to hold it down. His eyes were faded blue under white hair. Waylon—balding and heavier—crowded in as well. "What about your deputies?" he asked.

"This is unsanctioned."

"Illegal?"

"I just want a look around. The last time I took in uniformed officers, half of them got lost and the others wouldn't stop bitching. The place is a maze."

"How large?"

"Six thousand acres. Half is swamp, here. The rest is this stretch of hills running north."

Jimmy Ray leaned closer, studying the photograph, the red-ink circles indicating the garden, what looked like a roofline under hardwood trees. "You say this is Johnny Merrimon's land?"

"Do you know him?"

"Heard of him."

"What have you heard?"

"That he's a ghost. That he's one of us."

Sheriff Cline had worried about that reaction. To people like Jimmy Ray Hill and Waylon Carter, Johnny Merrimon had become something of a hero. It was the independence and grit, the way he'd shot up a billionaire's camp and done his time clean. "He's nothing special," the sheriff said. "I've known him a long time. Trust me."

"You really think he's a killer?"

"He either killed William Boyd or knows who did."

Everyone chewed on that for a bit; then Waylon tapped the map. "How long would you need me? Merrimon may own six thousand acres, but that swamp is fifty square miles. We can't search all of it."

"I don't plan to linger. Two days, maybe three. We'll hit the cabin first, then make a plan if he's not there. You boys in or not?" It took a moment, but Jimmy Ray nodded, and that was no surprise. "What about you, Waylon?"

"I don't know, Sheriff." Waylon scratched his cheek, the top of his head. "I was thinking we'd be in and out. Tomorrow's Danielle's birthday. I said I'd take her to Myrtle Beach. It's Bike Week."

"You're shitting me."

"I'm lucky to have a girl like Danielle." The sheriff rolled his eyes, but Jimmy Ray nodded in agreement. Danielle had a job and her own place and a gentle disposition. "I'm really sorry, Sheriff. Any other time . . ."

"All right. Fine. Jimmy Ray, it looks like it's you and me." The sheriff rolled up the topographical map and the aerial photograph. "You have everything you need?"

"Gear's in the truck."

"Waylon, last chance." The big man showed his palms, and the sheriff dropped into the cruiser. "Myrtle Beach." He shook his head and frowned. "Goddamn Bike Week."

The sheriff led Jimmy Ray to his house, where he transferred gear and dropped his car. In Jimmy Ray's truck they spoke little, but that was how it had always been. Hunting buddies. Old friends. At Hush Arbor, they drove a half mile past the gate, parked the truck, and hiked into the original settlement. Jimmy Ray had never been there, so he studied the rotted buildings, the wall of trees. "This place is old."

"Yeah, no shit."

But Jimmy Ray wasn't thinking of the buildings. The trees were tall and twisted, with a thickness of limb he'd rarely seen. "We're on Merrimon's land?"

"The edge of it."

"Show me."

They met over the map, and Willard showed him where they were: the swamp, the river, the hills. "His cabin is that way. It gets wet."

They leaned closer to the map and aerial photographs. Beyond the church, black water moved with sluggish determination, and Jimmy Ray knew without thought that it was deep and certain, one of the main bodies draining into the river south of where they stood. He'd hunted up and down that river, but never this far north. "It's a good location." He tapped the area where a hint of cabin showed. "Center of the property with a southern exposure and westerly breeze. Good water and hills at his back. Largely inaccessible."

"You can get us there?"

"Of course."

"Gear up, then."

The sheriff slung a rifle and pack, but Jimmy Ray kept his eyes on the woods around them. Something was off, and it took a moment for small hairs to rise on the backs of his arms. "There's no sound in that direction." He pointed at the nearest woods.

"Don't spook on me, now."

Jimmy Ray put his gaze on the sky, the tree line. A woodpecker rose in a flash of red, the silence behind it still unbroken.

"Which way?" the sheriff asked.

Jimmy Ray nodded at the unmoving woods. "East," he said. "Then north."

"All right, then. Smooth and easy."

They set off single file, Jimmy Ray in the lead. He'd known a few hunts as quiet as this, but only at dawn on new snow. Such mornings brought a hush that was lovely for the promise of daybreak.

This was nothing like that.

Stepping with the care born of long habit, Jimmy Ray moved them along dry ground, then north when the water spread. After that, the silence was behind them, too.

"Do you feel that?" the sheriff asked.

Jimmy Ray was unsure what he felt, but thought it was the same sense of wrongness any hunted animal might feel at the first, far cry of dogs. He pointed fingers at his eyes, then down the trail behind them.

Watch your six.

The sheriff nodded, looking pale. They pushed on, and mud pulled at their shoes. Jimmy Ray leaned close, whispering. "We're moving too far east. The topo showed dry ground at least this far in. I don't understand it."

"Maybe the map's old."

"I'm going to take us across."

Holding his rifle high, he took them across a hundred yards of mud and water. Jimmy Ray made it first, then hauled the sheriff out, and led him along a narrow spit that took them farther in the wrong direction. "We have to cross again."

The second crossing was brutal in that it was no crossing at all. Water rose to their chests, and every promise of dry land became a broken promise. They found stumps and grass and clusters of root. Birds flitted in the distance, and for long hours, nothing changed. Shin deep. Waist deep. Nothing but water.

"I don't understand it." Jimmy Ray staggered to a halt. The sun was on the wrong shoulder; shadows made no sense. "This is not where we're supposed to be." He shook the compass. "Was it like this before?"

"No."

"We should be there by now."

"I need to rest." The sheriff bent at the waist. His color was bad.

"We have ninety minutes of daylight."

"God . . ."

"I'll find something. We'll make camp."

"Thank you, Jimmy Ray. Thank you."

"Hold on to my pack. Lean on it if you need to."

The sheriff did as he was told, and Jimmy Ray pushed on in the black water, the failing light. The water passed his belt, his stomach; and he had most of the sheriff's weight. Stumbling once, he caught himself, then staggered again and they went down together. Jimmy Ray dragged the sheriff up, water streaming from his hair. He pushed on, but the light went out, and when it did, the mosquitoes descended in a solemn cloud. They fed on his eyes and ears and lips. Jimmy Ray sprayed repellent and smeared mud on his face, but it made no difference. They got under his collar, into his sleeves. An hour later it was full dark, and Jimmy Ray drifted to a stop. There was no sound beyond mosquitoes and breath and dripping water.

The men stood chest deep.

The sheriff was weeping.

That night in the swamp was the worst Jimmy Ray Hill had ever known, worse even than Vietnam. The mosquitoes swarmed with a density and determination that felt purposeful. The air was heavy with them. Thousands. Millions. They matted in Jimmy Ray's hair, plugged his ears and nostrils; filled his mouth if he opened it. The only true relief was to submerge, and that was heaven, sweet bliss. But they waited an inch off the surface, and spun in from the blackness when he rose. Jimmy Ray was not a churchgoing man, but by midnight knew one thing for sure: God hated him.

"Willard? You okay?"

The sheriff hung on Jimmy Ray's shoulder, and hours had passed since he'd spoken. He didn't go underwater; didn't even try. Jimmy Ray smeared more mud on the sheriff's face and neck.

"Just hold tight, all right. Daylight in five hours."

They were the longest hours of Jimmy Ray's life. When first light finally came, he almost missed it. Mosquitoes were a cloud, a gathering. He watched the daylight swell through swollen eyes, and when it touched water, the swarm broke apart like tissue in the rain.

"Willard, it's done. Are you still with me?"

The sheriff's head hung loosely, his chin on his chest. Jimmy Ray turned him to the light.

"Dear God." Under the mud, the sheriff's eyes were swollen shut. The nose was grotesque, his whole face inflamed, the tongue protruding. "Willard? Can you walk?" The sheriff groaned, and tried to move. He went down like a puppet with its strings cut. Jimmy Ray pulled him to his feet, then took his arm and felt the leeches. They were on both hands, under the sleeves. He scraped them off, then took a firmer grip. "Come on. We're getting out of here."

Taking the sheriff's weight, Jimmy Ray dragged him through the water, muttering, "Old man, stupid old man." He was talking to the sheriff, and to himself. They had no business in this swamp—no one did—and leaving it should have been simple. Sunrise was as *east* as it gets. That made south and west an easy target, but six hours later, nothing had changed: shallow water, deep water, the clinging, black mud. By two o'clock, Jimmy Ray thought he was losing his mind. Trees looked like ones he'd seen before: the cypress with a broken top; the birch, half-dead on one side. By dusk, even Jimmy Ray's strength had failed. The sun was on one shoulder and then the other. He had the sheriff's full weight, and light, again, was dying. Hauling the sheriff up, Jimmy Ray dragged him through deep water, and felt the bottom shelve. To his right was a cypress with a broken top. Beside it was a birch, half-dead on one side. Jimmy Ray stopped where he stood, and felt his spirit break at last.

The cypress.

The birch.

He was walking in circles.

When night fell, the mosquitoes came again and were terrible in the blackness. The assault lasted for hours, and at some point Jimmy Ray's mind broke. The air felt freezing cold; so did the water. The delirium grew worse because he saw blue light through the cloud, a sense of shadow and movement, of something else in the water with them. Jimmy Ray held very still, for nothing in life had prepared him for the sudden sense of expectance. The silence crackled; the air felt *electric*. He pulled the sheriff closer, and the light moved left, circling. Jimmy Ray felt pressure on his skin, and in his mind a touch.

Shhhh . . .

Jimmy Ray stopped breathing, not knowing if he'd heard the sound or felt it, or if his mind had truly snapped. He couldn't move or think. The mosquitoes lifted and only the terror was real, the bang in his chest. Something was close. It tugged at the sheriff, but Jimmy Ray held on.

Will you die for this man?

He heard the words in his mind, or perhaps it was the delirium. All Jimmy Ray knew for sure was the steady pull, the hammer behind his ribs. "He's my friend."

Your friend is a danger to me and mine.

Jimmy Ray tried to see beyond the glow, but his eyes were swollen to slits. He saw the pale light floating, and felt it out there, its will and anger.

They weren't supposed to be there.

They were unwanted.

Let him go or die with him.

Jimmy Ray almost broke, but did not. "I can't," he said. "He's my friend."

Very well.

Something ripped the sheriff from his grip and dragged him through the water. Jimmy Ray staggered behind in grim silence, then something took him by the neck and dragged him, too.

CHAPTER TWENTY-ONE

Johnny drifted in a lake of pain. It was acid, fire, lightning in the dark. There was no time, but time was all he had. Just pain and time.

Days of it.

Years.

"What's happening to me?"

Don't talk, a voice said. *You're dying.*

Or dreaming, Johnny thought. His limbs were twisted and bent. The left eye was full of splintered bone. He forced the good eye open, and saw haze and blue light and something shapeless.

This will hurt, he heard.

Then Johnny's world was pain and fire and screaming.

Hours of it.

A lifetime.

When the nightmare broke, Johnny touched his left eye and felt heat. His lips were cracked. In the darkness, a fire burned. "Thirsty," he said. And something gave him water.

Sleep, it told him. *Forget.*

The next time Johnny woke, he stood by a stream with no memory of arriving there, though he knew the stream well. It spilled from northern hills then slowed to meet other waters. Sunlight seeped in from the east. It was morning. He was home. Touching his face, Johnny expected pain.

He remembered flashing lights and violence, but the rest was vague. There'd been a gate, the feel of dirt under his fingers. Looking down, he saw dried blood on his clothes and shoes, but there was no sign of injury.

Nothing.

Not a mark.

At the cabin, he scrubbed blood from his hair and fingers and from the crevices beneath his nails. He put on clean shorts, and as he did, an image rose of cedar posts and rust, old steel in the mist. There'd been an accident, black trees, the gate.

Was there something else?

Pulling on a shirt, Johnny ran the swamp as only he could run it. When he reached the shed, he stripped the chain from the door, but the truck was gone. He found it a half mile past the gate and wedged into the understory. Johnny saw the broken glass first, then a rip in the ditch line. He touched bare metal and remembered the crash, but like the dream of a dream, a ghost of lights and noise and shattered glass. On the verge again, he looked up and down the road, trying to remember. There'd been men and violence. He tried to hold the image, but couldn't.

Back at the cabin, he tore open boxes and drawers until he found the cell phone in a coffee can full of screwdrivers and drill bits and chisels. Taking it to a hill where he had reception, Johnny powered it up and stared for long seconds at the date on the home screen.

It was the ninth of September.

He'd lost five days.

Johnny sat on that hilltop for a long time. Eventually, he arranged a flatbed, then hiked out to meet the driver, who hitched the truck to a cable and winched it out of the woods. "That's not what you want to see." He slouched under an old cap, a young man in stained denim with a patch on the chest that said DAVE. "Truck's what, a 'sixty-two?"

"'Sixty-three."

"You the one who rolled it?"

"It's kind of a blur."

"I can take it in for you, put it on the lift, and see if the frame bent. Not much we can do if it is."

"How much for the tow?"

"Hundred bucks?"

"How about fifty?"

They split the difference, and Johnny rode with him to a two-bay garage, where they slipped out of traffic and into a gravel lot. "Second lift is broken," Dave said. "But we can get it on that one as soon as it's free. You can wait if you want."

An old Datsun was already on the lift, and didn't look like it was going anywhere soon. All four tires were off. So was the exhaust manifold, the rear bearings. "There's no rush," Johnny said. "You can call me. I probably won't answer. You can leave a message."

"Suit yourself."

They got out of the truck, and an eighteen-wheeler rumbled past on the two-lane. Johnny pulled the sheaf of bills from his pocket, and counted off seventy-five dollars. "I need something to drive."

Dave pointed at a rusted convertible. "I'll rent you that old beater for eighty bucks."

"For how long?"

"Week."

"What about that?" Johnny pointed at a moped with bald tires and foam stuffing sprung from the seat.

"I can't even say she runs."

"If she does, how about fifty bucks for a month?"

"I'll tell you what." Dave gave the same appraising stare, one eyebrow up. "Make it a hundred, and she's yours to keep."

Back at the Hush, Johnny sat beneath a tree and tried not to panic over the days he'd lost. He focused first on the heat, then on his heart, the blood in his veins. From that place, he turned outward to the bark against his back, sinking through it to the sapwood, then through the roots and into the stone that reached deep and cool, and was the floor of the world.

"Five days."

He flexed his hand and felt the tendons shift. The truck was not just damaged; it was destroyed. That was real. What about the slashes of color that came and went? The gunfire flashes of sound and blood and violence, the impossible visions that left Johnny wondering if life in the Hush came with a price he could not afford to pay so blindly? For a moment he considered calling Jack, but Jack would worry, and Johnny wasn't ready for that argument.

What did that leave?

Getting back on the moped, he left the Hush and circled north to Leon's, where he found the big man behind the bar.

"A little early for you, isn't it?"

"I'm not drinking," Johnny said.

"Food?"

"That's not why I came, either." The big bartender took the comments in stride, his hands on one glass then another, an old rag rubbing the insides and out. On the ride in, Johnny had thought hard about how to approach his question, but in the end, there was no clever way to do it. "You told me once you grew up hunting."

"That's right."

"That you could track anything that walked or crawled. You said it was the best thing you do."

"It is."

"Why don't you go into the swamp?"

"Who says I don't?"

"You."

He shook his head. "I don't remember saying that."

"The first time I came here. You said walking into that swamp was an act of surrender you were unwilling to make. You called me a dumbass kid without the sense God gave rocks."

Leon smiled that time. "Yeah, okay. I remember."

"So, what are you afraid of?"

"You want to talk about the swamp? Now? After all these years?"

"Yeah, I do."

Leon put down the glass and the rag. He spread his hands on the bar and leaned into it. "Why the sudden interest in something I said six years ago?"

"Maybe something scares me, too."

"What?"

"I'm not sure."

Tipping coffee into a mug, Leon slid it across the bar. "Drink that," he said.

"Why?"

"Because I need time to think."

For the next hour, Leon polished glasses and swept the floor. Once, Johnny caught him watching, the broom very still, the big head tilted. At noon the lunch crowd came, and Leon gave Johnny a sandwich. Two hours later, Leon went to the horseshoe pits and led one of the old men back, handing him the apron and putting him behind the bar. "Don't burn the place down. You. Come."

He picked up a paper sack, then led Johnny to an old truck that spit blue smoke when he turned the key. Leon kept his hands on the wheel, the engine idle. "I've been more than fifty years on this earth," he said. "And this is my place in the world: this truck and those people, twenty square miles, and maybe less." He turned to face Johnny straight on. "Whatever brought you out of that swamp today, I don't care to know it—not if you saw something or heard something or if God himself reached down to feed you breakfast. Understand?"

Johnny nodded.

"I'll help you this once," Leon said. "And after that, we'll never discuss it. You can come back anytime. You can eat my ribs and drink my whiskey. We'll talk about the weather or problems at the sawmill or about any of the soft, round ladies in their cutoff jeans and too-tight shirts. You tell anyone where I'm about to take you, and it's over, this thing we have."

"I understand."

Leon studied Johnny's face, then put the truck in gear. "Don't make me regret this."

They jolted through the dirt lot, and Leon drove them across the river, then along the edge of planted fields. Phone poles ran beside the road, and when the poles bent east, he kept north on a dirt track. The world around them was green and brown and September shimmer. Two miles later, Leon turned them into the trees and across a stream, engine gunning when the tires slipped. In the clearing, he stopped where a shack leaned between tulip poplars and a black oak. The shack had a cinder block chimney and a stained, metal roof. Skinned rabbits hung from rafters on the left side, and potted plants splashed color on the steps.

"Wait here."

Leon crossed the yard, and dust rose at his feet. The porch took his weight, and the door opened before he could knock. An old woman glanced at Johnny, then closed the door between them. Four minutes later, Leon came out alone. He spoke as he neared. "She doesn't like visitors, but she'll see you."

"Who?"

Leon settled into the truck. "You can call her Verdine. She's old as sin and doesn't care for visitors, which means I'm in a box if you treat her poorly. You'll need this." He handed Johnny a paper sack. "Sugar," he said. "Little gifts. She values them."

"Anything else?"

"The left eye is weak, so look her in the right. Don't raise your voice or be impertinent. She likes a pretty face, so you should do okay."

Johnny looked at the shack. The door hung ajar, and beyond it stood a tiny figure in a washed-out dress. "She knows the swamp?" Johnny asked.

"Better than you."

"How?"

"She lived there half her life."

Johnny felt a tug of connection. "Anything else I should know?"

"One last thing, I guess." Leon leaned forward, and watched the old woman, too. "She's pretty much my grandmother."

Johnny waited for something more, but left the truck without it. At the porch, he saw flies on the rabbits, a rifle by the door. The old woman was waiting. "Come closer," she said. "So I can get a look at you."

Johnny broke the plane of the door, and she met him where the light spilled in. She was very small, her hands light and steady as they touched his face and turned it toward the sun. "Leon says your name is Johnny Merrimon."

"Yes."

"Hmm. You look it." She turned for the dim interior and settled into a rocking chair by the cold fireplace. The cabin was a single room: stove to the right, a bed in the corner. "Well, come on in," she said. "I told Leon I'd talk to you. I didn't say I'd spend all day."

Johnny took a second chair across the hearth, and Verdine watched him settle. "Leon says he's your grandson," Johnny said.

"His momma had the roundest heels in the county, so maybe he is and maybe not. Is that for me?"

Johnny offered the sugar, and the old woman stuck a finger in the bag and sucked the sugar off. "All right." She tucked the bag in the crook of her lap. "Tell me what you want to know."

"You said I look like a Merrimon. What did you mean?"

"That you favor the men in your family."

"How do you know that?"

She made a scoffing sound in her throat. "Your family owned mine for a lot of years. Or had that fact slipped your mind?"

Embarrassment made Johnny blush. He'd never thought it through. Had Leon?

"You smoke?" she asked.

"No."

A hand-rolled cigarette appeared from one of her pockets. She struck a match, and smoke rolled out. It wasn't tobacco smoke. "Leon says you own Hush Arbor."

"Yes, ma'am."

"The buildings? The land?"

"All of it, yes."

She pulled in more smoke, then let it out and picked a piece of stem from her tongue. "He also says something scared you. What was it?"

"I'm not sure."

"You're not sure or you won't tell?" Johnny didn't answer, and she nodded, watching him. "Smoke this," she said.

"I don't smoke."

"You can smoke or you can leave."

Johnny watched it burn in her hand. "What is it?"

"Marijuana. Mushrooms. Nothing that doesn't grow from God's green earth." She held it out, waiting. One end was damp, the other an orange coal. After a moment Johnny took it and smoked. "Deeper." He pulled in more smoke, choking. She took the cigarette back, satisfied. "What did you see that scared you?"

"Nothing. I lost days. That's it. I lost five days."

"You remember none of it?"

"Flickers," he said. "A few images. I think I was hurt, and then I wasn't. None of it makes sense."

"Do you dream?" He hesitated, and she blew smoke in his face. "In the swamp? Do you dream?"

"Yes. I suppose."

"Of what? Don't lie."

Johnny swallowed. It was hot in the shack, no breeze. The smoke was making him dizzy. "I see people hanged," he said.

"What people?"

"A white man. Two slaves."

"What else?"

"What do you mean?"

"Smoke." She passed the cigarette again, then leaned close as he smoked. "You're at the tree. Men are screaming."

"How do you know that?"

"Men are screaming. What else do you see?"

"There's a girl with a knife. The men have been mutilated."

The old woman drew back, and Johnny choked on smoke. He tried to breathe; couldn't. "Tell me what you hear."

"I don't like this—"

"Tell me."

"Screaming. Jesus Christ. I hear the men screaming." Verdine leaned away, and for that instant Johnny was in the dream. He saw firelight, the twitching legs. Then he blinked and it faded. He started coughing; cleared his throat. "How do you know my dream?"

"Because dreams of the swamp are rarely dreams. Do you have others?"

"Maybe. I'm not sure."

"Take this." She handed him a second cigarette. "Smoke it tonight, then come back and see me."

"I told you, I don't smoke."

"Then make tea with it. I don't care. The point is it will help you dream."

"All I want is the truth."

"Of course you do, but I told you once already: nightmare or vision, dreams of the swamp are rarely dreams."

Johnny spent that night in the cabin, and it was late before he tried to dream. He didn't trust the old woman or what was in the cigarette, but he sat on the bed with a mug in his hand whose contents smelled like boiled dirt and tasted about the same. That's how desperate he was, and how afraid of lost days. When the last of the tea was gone, he stretched out and tried to find the peace that would lead him down and dark. Most nights it was simple: a few breaths, a gentle slope. Tonight he was nervous, and wanted it too much. He tossed and turned, then walked beneath the stars and lay down on the mosses and ferns. It was warm and still, and he imagined the sky as a great weight. He pictured himself as if seen from above. The earth turned and he was a heartbeat, another breath, a smudge on the green. The moss beneath him took his shape and held it. Stars faded, and Johnny drifted down. He was a man and a boy, then a flicker of thought in the moment before his birth. He glimpsed his father's eyes, and his grandfather's in the dimness beyond. He was Johnny Merrimon—named for John—and this was the line of men who'd made him. Johnny sank past one face and then another.

He was falling in the black.

He was dreaming.

When his eyes opened, the fear crushed him. She was dying, his lovely wife. The heat burned his skin where he touched her. No one had ever seen such a fever: none of the family and none of the slaves, not the doctor from across the river who'd told him the best he could do now was pray.

Leaning close, he pressed his cheek against hers, and felt more of the heat that was burning her alive. She moaned at the touch, but he kept his cheek against hers and placed a hand on the swollen belly that held their child. "Bring more ice," he said.

"The icehouse is empty."

He looked up, and the slaves were weeping, too. They loved Marion as well as he. Everyone did. She was nineteen and beautiful and kind.

"Towels," he said. "Bring wet towels."

Two of the women hurried off, and John took his wife's hand. He owned forty thousand acres and would trade it all to have her back and well. They'd played together as children, and he'd loved her since she was thirteen. He was two years older, but it was she who'd touched his hand, that day in the shade. She'd said, "We'll marry one day," and he remembered how her eyes had gone from playful to sincere, his first look at the woman she'd become. She'd always been the wisest, the strongest.

"John . . ."

It was a gasp, a wretched sound.

"I'm here, Marion, beside you."

"Water . . ."

He tilted her head, and raised a cup to her lips. She managed a sip, choking. John dabbed at the cracked lips, smoothed hair from her face. She was wasted and pale. Only the heat gave her color, only the fever. He wanted to squeeze her hand, but feared the skin might tear, the bones break. For three weeks, she'd spiraled into fire and delirium. How many days since she'd spoken? How many terrible nights?

"The baby . . ."

"Yes," he said. "We'll have a beautiful child, you'll see. You'll get better. The child will be fine."

She moved his hand to her stomach. "Take it. . . ."

"The doctor is coming—"

"No time."

"Marion—"

"Only the baby matters." She blinked, and was dying. "Only the child . . ."

He kissed her forehead and burned from the heat.

"John . . ."

"I'm here."

"If it's a boy . . ." Her lips moved, but she had nothing left. "Do it now," she said. "While I have the courage."

"I can't."

"Yes."

"My love . . ."

She begged with her eyes, and John's hands shook, pale and empty. He kissed her once again; then someone pressed a knife against his palm. . . .

Johnny woke in starlight, and felt emotion like he'd never known.

He was two men.

Two lives.

An hour later he was still weeping.

CHAPTER TWENTY-TWO

Jimmy Ray Hill woke in darkness with no knowledge of where he was or how badly he was hurt, though he thought it was bad. He smelled dampness and blood. One of his hands was broken. He tried to move, but nothing happened from the waist down, and when he touched his legs, he couldn't feel them.

"Sweet Jesus . . ."

He lay back on the rough stone, and something in his back ground where it should not.

"Ah . . . shit."

Touching his face, he found blood and torn skin. He felt his eyes to make sure they were open. That's how black it was, like the bottom of the world.

"Willard?"

The name went out and died in the void. He said it again, then cradled the broken hand against his chest, and checked himself with the other. He found scrapes and mud and more blood. His back was broken.

"Ah, Christ."

Jimmy Ray shifted, and stone and sticks moved beneath him. He risked a hand on his spine, felt the bone, like cornmeal. He was in the dark and broken and alone.

"Just breathe, old man."

But his breath came short and fast.

"Willard!"

The sheriff didn't answer. He was unconscious or somewhere else or dead. Jimmy Ray dug deep for the courage he'd known as a young man in Vietnam. He'd been shot twice, left on a battlefield. He remembered the long night, and high, pale stars, the sound of footsteps as he'd closed his eyes and prayed. The memory was a start. He focused on his breathing.

Slow and deep.

You're still alive. . . .

Deep and slow.

Don't you panic. . . .

It was hard with the pain. It spiked up from the shattered spine, throbbed in his hand. Through it all, he remembered the swamp and the light and bits of what followed. He'd been dragged, and then carried and dropped.

Dropped . . .

It was more like being tossed, as if he'd weighed nothing at first and then a thousand pounds as the earth fell away, and he hit the stony slope, the sheer drop that followed. Jimmy Ray remembered the fall, the rocks at the bottom, his back.

He was in a cave.

He heard water drip.

"Hello! Anybody!"

There was no one, and it took a long time to accept the fact that if he wanted to live, he'd have to do it on his own. Working carefully, he used his good hand to explore the area around him. He found a boulder behind his head; thought it was the one that'd broken his back. The other stones were smaller, like softballs and grapefruit, but jagged. His fingers touched a few old sticks, then moved on to smooth stone and sticky bits he thought might be his own blood. He needed his pack, some kind of light.

He found the sheriff instead.

"Willard, thank God." He touched the sheriff's boot first, then dragged himself closer, even though it hurt like hell and twisted the ruined spine. He couldn't think about that, though. The damage was done; he was ruined. All that mattered now was his friend and getting out and living. He found the sheriff's belt, his chest. He wasn't breathing. He was cold. A final heave brought him even with the sheriff's face, and Jimmy Ray felt for it, finding the nose, the swollen lips. He checked the throat for a pulse, but knew it was too late.

The sheriff was dead.

He'd been dead for a long time.

"Anybody!"

Jimmy called out, afraid, and the shame of that capitulation was almost as bad as the broken spine. Since that terrible night in Vietnam, he'd never needed anyone. He lived alone, worked alone. There was not a fight he couldn't win, a horse he couldn't break, or a machine he couldn't fix. Now he was shaking beneath the earth, as lost and alone as he'd ever been.

Rolling the sheriff, Jimmy Ray checked his pockets, looking for matches, a flashlight. He felt behind him, but the rock rose up where he'd been dropped. Moving deeper, Jimmy Ray dragged himself past the body, finding smooth stone and a slope that angled him down. For an instant he was poised; then he slipped and tumbled. He bounced off another stone, and collapsed into some kind of deadfall, the old branches shifting. Reaching out, he touched nylon, and knew it was a pack, either his or Willard's. Praying as he had on that distant battlefield, Jimmy Ray dragged out the heavy flashlight he'd bought ten years ago on a cold winter's day. In its light, he saw damp stone, a hint of his friend and a stark, damn truth he'd never thought to see. The branches weren't branches at all.

He was in a mass grave.

He was in a tomb.

CHAPTER TWENTY-THREE

When the sun broke, it was watery pale, and Johnny remembered little of the drive to Verdine's. There was blacktop and dirt, then weeds and trees, a covered porch and clapboards baked the color of old bone. She was on the porch beside the ancient rifle, a smile on her face as Johnny took the dust yard like a breaking storm. He couldn't help it. The darker emotions ran loose. "What the hell did you do to me?"

"Nothing."

"That's a damn lie and you know it. Whatever that was, it was no dream."

"Anything you saw was between you and your people. The connections have always been there. I just opened the window."

"What connections?"

"Hush Arbor, of course, your family and mine, those of us who lived there and died. Time is truly the thinnest of things."

Johnny tried to settle. There was steadiness in her voice, and in the rhythm of the chair. "What was in that cigarette?"

"The cigarette's not your problem."

"Yesterday, you said 'vision.'"

"Yes."

"Last night, then." He clenched his fists and fought for calm. "Was it a dream or drugs or something else?"

"Saw him, did you? John Merrimon."

"No." Johnny spoke from a still-troubled place. "I *was* him."

"Tell me."

"I saw a woman, dying. She was pregnant."

"Marion Merrimon, your great-great-grandmother."

"So, it's real."

"Summer of 1853, a mighty fever."

Johnny sat on the top step and put his face in his hands. He knew their first kiss and their secrets, the touch of skin and the words they whispered. The love they shared was greater than anything Johnny had ever known. Even now it closed his throat. He'd never felt that kind of emotion. "I was there," he finally said. "I held her hand. I felt the baby move."

He broke off because it was too much. This other life. These feelings.

Verdine drew smoke and let it linger. "Your people and mine," she said. "The visions find us, time to time."

"How?"

"That truth is for later."

"I need to understand."

"What you *need* is to listen to me and be careful. Hush Arbor is a dangerous place for those who don't respect its secrets. Dream enough, and you'll find most every truth you need. Dream too much and this life pales. Understand? This life. Yours. Don't get lost in the past. I've seen it happen."

"So last night's dream?"

"Is only the beginning." She tried to smile, but Johnny saw sadness and hurt, a hundred years of unknowable things.

"Do you have the same dream?"

She shook her head. "I dream of my people, you dream of yours. That's the nature of things."

"What do you want from me?" Johnny asked.

"Nothing," she said.

But that was a lie, and Johnny saw it plain as day. She wanted something from him. She desired it in the worst possible way. "I just want my life back," he said.

"Yet some doors are hard to close."

"What do I do?"

"The only thing possible." Verdine pulled more cigarettes from a pocket in her robe. "Walk through the door," she said. "And dream this time of darker truths."

CHAPTER TWENTY-FOUR

Luana Freemantle knew weakness like she knew the bottom of a bottle. It lived in an old, deep part of her, and its birthplace was her childhood in the swamp. She'd never been the girl her mother wanted. She hated the heat and the mud, the legacy of slavery and old belief that steeped every aspect of life in Hush Arbor. She didn't like the cutting or the hanging tree or the strange prayers in a strange tongue. Mostly though, she'd been afraid. She'd feared the nighttime and the woods and the expectations of all the women who'd gone before. Worst of all were the dreams. They'd started a week after her fifteenth birthday: dark visions of the hanging tree and another childhood, the weight of earth on the day she was buried alive. And they didn't start slowly, those dreams. She turned fifteen and they landed on her like a mountain. She'd close her eyes a girl, and wake up a slave; and she knew such terrible things: how it felt to suffer and kill, the burn of betrayal.

This is our life, she'd been told. *And our burden.*

The old women had tried to comfort and explain, but Luana hadn't cared. She'd been fifteen. She'd wanted television, air-conditioning, and smooth, fine boys like she'd seen once on the road beyond the swamp. Mostly, she'd wanted to escape the terrible, crushing dreams.

Now her daughter was having them, too.

"Cree?"

Luana knocked on the door, but her daughter didn't answer. For three days, she'd hidden herself, whether on the roof or in her room. The only sounds she'd made were the screams when she slept or the sobbing when she woke.

"Sweetheart?"

Beyond the door the curtains were pulled tight, and no lamps burned. Cree looked like a bundle of rags where she sat in the corner, both knees pulled to her chest, her breathing too fast. Luana sat beside her and touched her face, feeling the heat and the sweat. Cree's eyes showed mostly white. The dream had her.

"Oh, my baby. I should have never sent you back."

A sound escaped Cree's throat, but the breathing never slowed. She twitched and moaned, and Luana lived it with her. The same fist was in her chest, the same blindness and dread. Luana took her daughter's hand, and flinched when the eyes rolled brown, and the girl screamed and fought and drummed her heels. Luana tried to hold her down, but the girl fought harder and clawed, so Luana did the only thing a mother could. She screamed her own mad scream. She held her child, and hid the tears that burned her face.

When it was done and both were quiet, Cree's head was in her mother's lap, and the housecoat was damp where her face pressed against it. "I'm going insane," she said.

"You're not," Luana whispered.

"You have no idea."

"Oh, child . . ." Luana stroked her hair because guilt stole the rest of her words. She'd sent her daughter back because the old women wanted her—that was true—but Luana had been selfish, too; she'd been young in a world of liquor and tall lights and smooth-skinned boys. "I should never have let them have you."

"What's happening to me?"

"Hush now. Just breathe."

But it wasn't that easy. She trembled and burned, and Luana knew how drawn she was. In the long fight to stay awake, the minutes were battles and the hours, wars. When sleep did come, it rarely came alone. The old women said that the strong would acclimate in time, but what did Luana know of strength? She was a runner, a quitter. "You're stronger than you know," she said, but doubted it was true. Her daughter had lost weight in three days. Her eyes were sunken. The jeans hung on her hips.

"Why are you even here?" Cree rose from her mother's lap, and crossed to the bed. "You never come in my room."

"I'm here because we're not as different as you think."

"Yeah, right."

"Do you want to talk about what's happening?"

Cree laughed, but it was more like a sob. "With you, no. Let's not pretend."

"Maybe I can help—"

"You can't."

"Cree—"

"Just leave me alone."

She sank onto the mattress and Luana touched the damp place made by her daughter's tears. "I've never been much of a mother—"

"Any kind of mother."

Luana nodded because it was true. "I'm going out for a while. Are you sure you don't want me to stay? You can talk to me, you know. I *was* your age once."

"Say hi to your friends at the bar."

"Sweetheart . . ."

"I thought you were leaving."

Luana nodded in the silence. In the hall outside, she touched the door once, then went to her room and dressed. She put aside the housecoat and worn slippers, then tidied her hair and found a dress that was modest over plain shoes. Putting what money she had into a small clutch, she looked once at the bottle, but left the apartment without it. That was hard, but not the hardest part. At the apartment next door, she knocked and waited, and tried to smile even as the neighbor frowned.

"What are you supposed to be? Some kind of church lady?"

Luana smoothed the dress, embarrassed to know her neighbor of ten years had never seen her out of a bathrobe or short skirts or sweatpants. "I need to use your car."

The neighbor frowned around a cigarette. "You're a drunk."

"No more so than you."

"That may be true, but it's my car."

"Not now, Theresa. Not your normal bullshit."

Theresa laughed once, an otherwise unflinching woman, soft and colorless except for her eyes, which glittered. She and Luana drank together in one apartment or the other, and once a week they'd meet in the local dive by the chicken shack, the two of them side by side over cigarettes and off-brand liquor. They were friends the way cellmates were friends.

"It's important," Luana said. "I need it."

"To drive where?"

"East and north. A few hours."

"No."

"It's for my daughter."

Theresa squinted until the marble eyes all but disappeared. The car was thirty years old with plastic taped where the right window should be. It was worth a few hundred bucks, but Luana was the only friend she had. "Screw it," she said. "I'll drive you."

The drive out of Charlotte was loud and unpleasant. The plastic slapped and cracked, and exhaust leaked in from a hole rusted through the floorboard. Theresa tried conversation for the first hour, but Luana didn't have it in her. "Turn here," she said. "Take the next highway east." Traffic fell away the farther they moved from the city. Eight lanes went to four and then two, a narrow blacktop through the pine and sand hills, then into Raven County.

"The hell are we doing out here?"

Theresa was on her second pack of menthols. A city glinted off to the left, but they were moving past it, back into the openness of small houses and sunbaked fields.

"We've known each other a long time," Luana said. "And you know most everything about me. The divorces. The jail time. This is different. I can't talk about it."

"Why not?"

"Because you wouldn't believe me."

"Yeah, well."

She was doubtful, but Luana didn't apologize or explain. A line of forest rose in the distance. There were hills beyond it. "There's a crossroad," she said. "Two miles or so. Stop there."

Five minutes later Theresa pulled onto the verge where two roads made a giant X in the world. Forest ran off to the left. To the right, a cornfield surrounded an unpainted house. Biting her lip, Luana looked up one road and down another. It looked the same, but she was unsure. "That way, I think." She pointed left, and they followed the forest for another mile. "Yes. Go left there." The road forked, then turned to gravel. "There's the driveway." Turning onto it, the old car scraped over the low spots, then rolled to a stop where a stream cut across the drive.

"I can't cross that," Theresa said.

Beyond the stream an old shack stood under the trees. "It's okay," Luana said. "You'd not be welcome anyway."

"And you will?"

"I'm not sure. Wait here."

"That sounds like a fine plan." Theresa reached into the glove box and pulled out a small revolver left on the nightstand twenty years ago by some man, now forgotten. "I'll be here if you make it back."

"Don't joke."

Luana opened the door, and metal screeched. The stream was shallow, but her shoes got wet and she left prints in the dust for the next twenty feet. Sixteen years had passed since she'd been here. She didn't even know if the old woman was alive.

"That's far enough."

The voice came from the shadows under the porch. Luana squinted and saw a shape in a chair by the door. "Is that Verdine?" she said.

"Who's asking?"

"Luana Freemantle."

"You can't be Luana Freemantle. I told Luana Freemantle sixteen years ago I'd shoot her next time she stepped foot on my dirt."

"That was a long time ago. I was a kid."

"You called me a crazy old hag, a jumped-up know-it-all with no right to look down her nose at better people."

"I brought you my daughter, is what I did."

"Only because you were too scared to face your mother straight on."

"Can I come up or not?"

"Are you drunk again?"

"No."

"Is this some kind of social visit? 'Cause this ain't no runaways' club."

"My daughter's dreaming."

"Not outside the Hush, she's not."

"Would I be here otherwise?"

Luana waited in the heat and silence. Verdine had left the Hush in her fifties, and that made her special. Most left early or died in the same place they'd been born. That made Verdine an ambassador of sorts, a conduit for medicines and news, for the children who'd left and the one who'd come back. Luana suspected it was those feelings for Cree that kept the rifle in the old woman's lap, and not on her shoulder.

"Best come on up," she said.

Luana climbed the steps, and endured the slow inspection. Even in the dress and plain shoes, she felt the disappointment break over her. She was the one who'd run away and broken her mother's heart, the thankless child who'd taken with her the last, great hope of those who remained.

"They're gone now. You know that." The old woman circled her. "Not just your mother and grandmother. Everybody. A way of life."

"I know that. I tried to get the land back."

"For money, I imagine."

"Don't pretend to know me—"

"And don't you talk back. I saw the greed in you even as a child. Blackberries weren't enough. You wanted peaches. When peaches grew tiresome, it was chocolate or tobacco. You still have that fine, silk scarf?"

Luana blushed under the question. She'd stolen the scarf from a tourist at the roadside stand where her grandmother sold honeycomb and dried fish. "Cree is dreaming," she said.

"Nobody dreams outside the Hush."

"My daughter does."

A hard glint came into Verdine's good eye. Few had the dreams. Most never did. For those who believed as the old women had, dreams of the past were signs and entreaties, raw communication that bound the dreamer to Hush Arbor as the soil itself was bound.

"The Merrimon boy was here."

"What?"

"Just yesterday. He's dreaming of John Merrimon and the dying wife, the fever. It's only a matter of time until he dreams the rest."

"You're helping him?" Luana asked.

"Merrimon men have always been the key."

"Cree is not a part of that. She can't be."

"You're implying there's some kind of choice."

"I won't allow it."

"The visions will only get worse. They'll break her down. She'll lose herself. Are you guide enough to see her through? Bring her to me. I'll keep her safe."

"You'll use her."

"It's what we've waited for."

"Not my daughter."

"Then go home." Verdine gestured at the car across the stream. "Go home to your broken daughter. Come back when you're desperate."

"I'm not leaving without an answer."

"Leon." Verdine raised her voice, and Leon stepped out onto the porch, big and unflinching. "You remember my Leon," Verdine said. "Leon, this ungrateful, know-nothing little shit-turd was just leaving. Help her along, would you?"

"Yes, ma'am."

Leon spread his big arms to herd Luana off the porch. "Wait," she said. "I'm sorry."

"No one talks down to me on my own porch. Go on. Get. Come back when she's half-starved or screaming in her sleep or doesn't know her own name."

"She's half-starved now. She screams in her sleep."

"Then you should have come more respectful. Go on. Get."

Leon drove her off the bottom step and into the dust. She looked back once from the stream, then climbed into the car. "Follow her home," Verdine said. "Find out where she lives."

"If she sees me?"

"I don't care if she does or not. Just find out where she keeps the girl."

Verdine watched the small car turn around, then Leon's truck as he followed. When it was quiet, she settled in the old chair and lit one of her cigarettes. In a century of living, she'd had the vision only once, but could never forget the girl with the knife, the great woman, the one who'd started it all.

A hundred and seventy years . . .

Verdine pulled smoke into her lungs.

All that time in the ground . . .

The girl was the key, at last—the girl and Johnny Merrimon.

If only he would dream again.

If only he would see.

CHAPTER TWENTY-FIVE

Johnny was up late, and his eyelids felt like sandpaper. He sat by the fire under a midnight sky, watching embers twist and rise, as if on fine black strings.

He was afraid to sleep.

The emotions were too deep and real. Nothing in life so far had prepared him.

She was his wife.

If he dreamed again, would he watch her die?

Verdine's cigarettes pulled his gaze like a magnet. They sat on the table across the fire. In spite of the fear, he wanted to see Marion again, to know if the baby lived. . . .

"She's not my wife."

But that was not entirely true. He was Johnny Merrimon, and he was John. He couldn't separate the two, and it was making him insane. Rising from the chair, he walked to the water and stared out across the swamp. He pictured the old woman and the gleam in her eyes.

Dream this time of darker truths. . . .

She was manipulating him—she wanted something—but he thought this was how an alcoholic might feel, the knowledge deep down that he would break in the end. Such was the treadmill of his night.

He wanted to hold his wife.

He knew she wasn't his.

"It's not my life!"

Johnny stumbled back to the fire and sat for long hours until something moved in the forest. It was a shimmer at first, a trick of light in a forest filling with the dawn. But Johnny's eyes came back to it. He watched across a dying fire, and when the blankness drifted, it was familiar in the way of lost friends and forgotten places. That's how it felt to Johnny, as if a dream had come at last, and he was held beneath its weight. Vines parted in the wood, and fear spread like the first touch of something neither warm nor cold. Johnny's limbs felt heavy, the air in his lungs as thick as liquid. He blinked because something solid seemed to move in all that blankness: a slope of shoulder, a tilted head.

It's okay to love her. . . .

The words rose in Johnny's mind, but were not his words. None of this was real. He told himself as much, trying to speak it aloud, but saying *go away* instead, saying *leave me the hell alone.*

It didn't go away.

It circled the fire, and Johnny heard the rustle of it, the dry rasp of a shallow breath.

I want you to love her. . . .

Johnny closed his eyes, afraid. He smelled rainwater and rotten leather; felt sadness and need and near-forgotten hope. He sank into the chair, and against his will, he slept. When he opened his eyes at last, there was nothing to see. The fire was burned out, the day at least two hours old. Johnny felt the dampness on his skin, the settled stiffness. Standing, he wondered if he'd been awake at all, or if the exhaustion of a long night had simply taken him down. Picking up the cigarettes, he stared into the forest and reached out the way he liked to do. He felt the normal things, the first, faint stirrings.

Had something come for him in the day's first blush?

Or had a dream just told him to love?

CHAPTER TWENTY-SIX

It was early morning when Jack's doorbell rang. He didn't know how early. Six o'clock? Six thirty? Rising from the sofa, he pulled pants over his shorts and ran a hand through tangled hair. He'd not left the apartment in a long time. Drawings were tacked to the walls and strewn across the floor.

"Who is it?"

"It's Leslie."

Jack hesitated. Leslie had called four times, left three messages. She was angry. He understood. "It's a little early."

"I don't care."

Sighing, Jack glanced at the apartment. The drawings were bad enough. There were also pizza boxes, beer bottles, cold Chinese. "Can we talk later?"

"You skipped Reamer's meeting. No one's seen you for days."

"What do you want, Leslie?"

"You still owe me."

He hesitated again.

"Buzz me up, Jack. I mean it."

He thought for an instant of cleaning up the mess. Instead, he pushed the button and buzzed her up. Cracking the door, he heard the clack of high heels on the stairs. She rounded the corner and held his gaze as she took the last four steps.

"You look like shit."

Jack scraped at his whiskers. In three days, he'd barely slept. When he closed his eyes, he saw the drawings, like flashes in black and white. He couldn't explain the power they had over him, but thought it was the sense of emptiness and fear, what he knew of the missing and the dead.

"Where have you been?" she asked.

"I haven't been myself."

"Yeah, no shit." She pushed across the threshold and took in the clutter. "Jesus, Jack." She stepped gingerly over drawings and empty bottles. Every wall was covered, every surface. She picked up a sketch; let it drop. "What is all this?"

"Kind of a project."

"It smells in here." She opened a window and looked at Jack with something between disgust and worry. "You understand the concept of a law firm, right? Tech-Stone is a big deal. No associate worth his salt would walk away from it like you just did. What the hell is this project of yours?" She found Jack's research on Hush Arbor, but he took the pages from her hands before she could read of any deaths or disappearances.

"Leslie, listen." He put the articles facedown on a table and guided her toward the door. "I'm sorry I blew off Reamer and Tech-Stone. I'm sorry for everything, but this is not a good time."

"Not a good time? Have you lost your mind? People are talking. Partners, Jack. The ones who hired you. Whatever this is. Whatever you're doing—" She gestured at the walls, the refrigerator, the cabinets. "—you're going to get fired."

"I don't really care."

"Then you are definitely not the man I thought you were. You were going to be the youngest partner we ever had. I *saw* something in you."

"Something's changed. I'm sorry."

"You still owe me one."

"Ah. Business."

"Don't make that face. I told you from the start it was just sex." She pulled a card from a pocket in her coat. "I want you to call this man. He's a New York editor. He wants to talk to Johnny Merrimon."

"Why should I do that?"

"There's money in it. Maybe a lot."

"For Johnny?"

"Of course."

"Why do you care?"

"Maybe I want to write a book one day. Having an editor's ear is never a bad thing."

"You're kidding, right?"

"Hey, my life is more than sex and law and money."

"How much, then?"

"A lot, I imagine. They're going big, apparently. Color photographs. A special hardcover edition. It's the bestselling true crime they've ever published. They want to send Johnny on tour with the author. Talk shows. All that. They've been trying for months to reach him. Just ask him."

"He'll never do it." Jack dropped the card on a table and steered Leslie for the door.

"He just wants to talk—"

"Goodbye, Leslie."

Jack got her into the stairwell and closed the door behind her. Moving back to the center of the room, he stood where he could turn a circle and see the drawings like a movie. There was a pattern, he believed, a sense of brokenness and malice too disjointed to easily understand. But Ms. Showalter's drawings were more than random. It was a puzzle, the broken bits of a dim, gray slate.

Removing one sketch, he replaced it with another, then shifted two more. Stepping back, he considered the puzzle with fresh eyes. Something moved in the Hush. He sensed it in the totality of the drawings. It teased in the blank spaces and streaks of black, in the charcoal worked so hard and fast that the paper, in places, was worn shiny. Whatever it was—whatever the reason so many people had died or gone missing—Johnny was in the middle of it. In the tapestry of such deceit and violence, what was Jack's responsibility to a friend who didn't want his help? Just how much did one friend really owe another?

Everything.

Jack took down a row of pictures; shifted three more.

He owed Johnny everything.

By morning the next day, even Jack had to admit that he was drifting dangerously. His career was falling apart. Johnny wouldn't answer the phone.

Maybe like this . . .

He cleared an entire wall and tacked up drawings of the cave and scattered bones. Leslie called at nine, but every thought was Johnny, the Hush, Jack's worry. At noon he had a beer, but it didn't fix the problem.

Jack was hiding in the drawings.

He was afraid.

By early afternoon, Jack knew it was time to leave the apartment. The cracks were widening. He needed answers.

Taking the stairwell down, he hit the sidewalk, blinking. People were lined up at the bakery counter, and a few stared at him through the glass. Ducking around the corner, he slipped into the car and pointed it at the Hush, making it two full blocks before stopping at the curb and pressing palms against his eyes.

"Damn it."

Unfolding a crumpled page, he studied a drawing of the frozen waterfall and the forked tree. Jack knew what he had to do, but laid his forehead on the steering wheel instead.

The Hush was Johnny's home.

Johnny didn't want his help.

Looking in the mirror, Jack saw red eyes and bruised-looking skin. "You don't have to do it," he said, then tried again.

You don't have to do it now. . . .

Jack held the stare for ten hard seconds, then looked away and twisted the mirror up. Hating himself more than he had since childhood, he phoned the office and found an assistant still willing to help. "Desk drawer," he said. "The Johnny Merrimon file." He waited while the assistant found Luana Freemantle's address in Charlotte.

It was a ninety-mile drive.

The Hush, he decided, could wait.

Charlotte, North Carolina, was like a lot of old cities grown rich. Towers rose like the tines of a crown, and wealth spilled outward from the shadows. Fine restaurants. Trendy neighborhoods. Time and neglect had driven the poverty into entrenched pockets of subsidized housing, and Luana Freemantle lived in one of the worst. GPS took Jack to a faded tower beside a cracked sidewalk and an empty lot, where he parked on the street between a shuttered church and the offices of a bail bondsman named Big Chris. People moved outside, but not really. They leaned on cars; lifted bottles and cigarettes. After crossing the street, Jack passed through a courtyard and into an elevator that smelled of urine and vomit. On the twenty-third floor, he found the right number above a heavy-gauge door with multiple locks. He knocked twice and waited. Trash spilled down the hall, and a boy on a tricycle maneuvered through it like an old pro, his eyes sliding left as he rolled past and disappeared around a corner. Eventually, locks turned and the door opened, catching on the chain. A single eye filled the gap—a young woman.

"Who are you?"

"My name is Jack Cross. I'm looking for Luana Freemantle."

"Why?"

"I'm a lawyer—"

"We're done with lawyers."

The woman cut him off, but Jack caught the door before it could close. "Please. I can pay."

"For what?"

"Information."

"How much?"

"A hundred dollars?"

"Just keep walking, mister."

"Five hundred."

The one eye narrowed. "What kind of information?"

"I want to know about Hush Arbor. Raven County. Do you know it?"

"I lived there for four years."

"Oh my God. That's perfect. I have this research—"

"You said five hundred dollars."

"Oh. Yeah." Jack dug out his wallet. He opened it, hesitating. "I have fifty-seven dollars." The door started to close again, and Jack panicked. "Please," he said. "I need to know if people die there."

"What?"

"Not now. I know about now. I mean in the past, the history. I want the old stories."

"Those stories are not for you."

"A thousand," he said. "If you have stories, I'll pay a thousand dollars."

"You don't have it."

"I can get it. Wait." Jack pushed a card through the crack. "That's office and cell on the front, personal on the back. Please don't close the door."

She studied the card, doubtful. "Why do you care about Hush Arbor?"

Jack thought about lying, but decided against it. "Johnny Merrimon is my friend. I'm worried."

"You should be."

"Wait. What does that mean?"

"Nothing." She said it softly. "It means nothing."

"Wait, wait. One more thing." He dug out the crumpled drawing and held it up: the frozen waterfall, the forked tree. "Do you know this place?"

The girl grew very still. "Where did you get that?"

Jack passed the drawing through the crack, and she took it. "Have you ever seen it?"

She looked from the drawing to Jack's face, and when she spoke, the lie was in her voice. "No," she said. "I've never seen this place."

"Are you sure?"

"I'm sure," she said, and closed the door.

After that, Cree stood for a long time, staring at the drawing even as the lawyer knocked at the door, his voice faint on the other side: *Excuse me . . . hello . . .*

He left eventually, but Cree stood even longer, childhood rising up as she remembered her grandmother and a winter's day. The sky was heavy with cloud, the first flakes falling. Cree had gone wandering, and wasn't supposed to. She was five. . . .

"Hello, child."

Cree stopped walking, her hand on a twist of vine, brambles at her feet where the trail bent left. Her nose ran from the cold, but her fingers were warm in the mittens her great-aunt had made. She'd never left the village alone, and knew in the way of children that displeasure lurked behind her grandmother's cool and careful smile. "Are you mad at me?" she asked.

"A little, yes." Grandmother stepped around the tree. "But just a little. I wandered, too, when I was young."

"I'm sorry," Cree said.

"Sorry you broke the rules or sorry you got caught?"

"Both, Grandmother."

"Tell me the rule for little girls."

"The village is safe, the woods are not."

"When can you leave the village?"

"Only when you say."

Grandmother knelt, and her knees popped, and she made an old person's face. "When you are older, it will be different."

"How much older?"

"When you know enough to stay safe. When you are stronger."

The smile was the same that sent Cree wandering in the first place. It was patient but amused, warm and somehow not.

"Would you like your first lesson?" she asked, and Cree nodded, suddenly afraid. "Take my hand." They turned away from the village, and followed a game trail through the trees. Grandmother asked, "Are you happy here?"

"Yes, ma'am."

"A well-intentioned lie. That's fine, too. Tell me what you miss most. Your mother?" Cree looked down, ashamed to say it was her toys and her bed and the little girl next door. Grandmother recognized the conflict and squeezed her hand. "What do you like most about Hush Arbor?"

"The animals."

"What about the people?" Cree lifted her shoulders. There were few people and no children. She spent her time with the old women in the single cabin. "It's okay," Grandmother said. "You make them nervous. That's all. I make them nervous, too."

"Why?"

"Because they think we know things."

"Do we?"

"Some things, yes. Also they are afraid."

"Of what?"

"Some are afraid of the world outside. It's so large and different. This is the only life they know. Others are afraid of what lives in the swamp. Some fear what's buried beneath it."

"What's beneath?" Cree asked.

"That, too, is for when you are older."

Cree considered what she was being told. Other than the old women, only twelve people lived in the village. It had been larger once. She'd seen the empty houses, the old barns. Just last week, a young man had left, destined, he'd said, for any place other than this. There'd been yelling and tears, and Cree had been afraid of that, too. The next day, though, no one mentioned the young man. People worked in the gardens and butchered a hog; and Grandmother, once, smiled sadly and winked.

The snow fell harder as they walked. Flakes caught in Cree's eyelashes and melted on her nose. "Are you afraid like the others?" she asked.

"No," Grandmother said. "Not for a long time."

"Are you the one that keeps the village safe?"

"Partly," she said. "There is also my mother. Would you like to help us someday?"

"Yes, ma'am."

The trail ended at a clearing, and Grandmother knelt again, pulling Cree close and pointing across the glade. "This is your first lesson, then. You are never to go there. No closer than this, not even when you are older. Do you understand?"

Cree nodded solemnly. "I will never go there."

"Promise me."

"I promise."

"Good girl." The bony arm squeezed her tight. "It will be dark soon. Would you like some warm milk?"

"Yes, ma'am."

"Okay, then—you and me, and warm milk by the fire. There may even be some chocolate."

"I like chocolate."

"Every little girl does."

Grandmother stood and took Cree's hand again. She turned for the village, but not before Cree looked a final time across the glade. It was beautiful, she thought.

The waterfall on gray stone.

The funny tree on top.

The drawing brought it all back. That's how perfectly it captured the forlornness of the glade in winter. The weight of sky. The empty spaces. Whatever the cause—exhaustion or memory—Cree began to cry, there on the low sofa with its stains and cigarette burns. After that day with Grandmother, life had become richer somehow. A bond had grown between them, a connection born of smiles and knowing looks and promise. *There are secrets in this world,* she'd say, *and those of us born to keep them.*

What was Cree's life now?

How much had she lost when Grandmother died, at last?

Smoothing the drawing on her lap, Cree felt the thinness of her legs. Her hands were gaunt as well. She had no appetite or energy. How much longer could she stay awake? What dream would find her if she slept?

Grandmother . . .

Cree curled on the sofa, clutching the drawing to her chest.

If only Grandmother had lived.

If only Cree could sleep.

CHAPTER TWENTY-SEVEN

The road ran empty for miles as Johnny left the Hush, and the old moped rattled along at thirty miles an hour, the bald tires slick on the pavement, the smell in the air like burnt oil and hot metal. Since the dream of John Merrimon, it was harder than ever to leave his own land, but Johnny's need today was bigger. He needed to see something, to kneel in the dirt and touch it.

Rolling back the gas, he coasted to a halt where a long drive wound through the hills and touched the county road. He saw trim pastures and manicured trees, a large house on a far hill. A stream babbled along the drive before disappearing into a culvert under the road. Johnny knew the stream, as he knew the forest trails and the hollows between the hills.

He'd walked the land a thousand times.

He'd owned it.

Such feelings lay in constant wait—the shadows of another man's life—but none of that made the sentiment less real. Johnny didn't have all John Merrimon's memories, but what he'd dreamed he knew as if he'd lived it himself: the actions and reactions, the loves and hates, small flickers of thought.

This had been his home.

The drive was paved now, but it followed the same lines.

The manor had been just there. . . .

Johnny studied the lodge, and thought briefly of William Boyd, humbled by how eternal the land remained.

John Merrimon, dead and gone.

Now William Boyd.

Johnny turned onto the drive and moved slowly for the lodge. He'd owned this once. . . .

That wasn't me.

But he passed open fields and remembered clearing them. The town was to the south, and he knew the ride on horseback, how long it would take and the best places to cross the last, large creek before it fed into the river. At the lodge, he turned off the engine and faced the views that were as intimate to him as the memories of any husband and wife. He'd buried his parents and a sister here. Far off were distant hills, a smudge of green that was the Hush.

The lodge felt empty, but he rang the bell anyway. As much as he hated trespassers on his own land, he could do nothing different, even with Boyd dead. When no one answered, he stepped back into the heat and followed a footpath through trees as old as Johnny's memory. They rose, twisted and gray, their limbs sweeping low, as if to brace themselves on holy ground.

And for Johnny, it was.

The cemetery dated to 1769, when his first ancestor died on this land. William Merrimon had been English and a retired officer before moving here under a land grant from the king. The original document was under glass in the Raven County Museum, and Johnny knew the language by heart.

> George the Third by the Grace of God, of the United Kingdom of Great Britain and Ireland King, Defender of the Faith. To all Whom these Presents shall come, Greetings . . .

Johnny slipped through an iron gate, still smiling at the memory of such childhood pride.

> Know Ye that we of our special grace, certain knowledge, and mere notion, have Given and Granted, and by these Presents

do Give and Grant unto William Merrimon, forty thousand acres of land, defined and bounded as follows . . .

The cemetery was overgrown, but Johnny found the stone he wanted in a far corner where the shade was deepest. He had to drag honeysuckle from the face of it to find John Merrimon's name adjacent to Marion's. Time had weathered the letters, but Johnny could make out the dates of birth, and beneath those numbers the words that said it all.

BOUND IN LOVE, FOREVER SOULS

Johnny touched his forehead to the stone. He'd lived alone for most of his life. He'd been with women, but never felt emotions like these. He knew the look in Marion's eyes, her gentle ways, the fullness of her lips.

It was his life, before.

She was his life.

CHAPTER TWENTY-EIGHT

Cree could not get off the sofa. She missed home, her true home, and those feelings were larger than memories of Hush Arbor or the big bed or the little stool kept by the winter stove. Young as she'd been, she'd had a people, a future. Pushing deeper into the cushions, Cree smelled her mother's perfume and spilled coffee and all the foods she ate. Everything smelled of plastic: the plates and the food, the television that sat blankly across the room. A clock ticked in the kitchen, and even that was plastic.

Rolling onto her side, Cree stared at the drawing.

They said I was special.

A mighty thread.

Looking at the drawing, she thought maybe her grandmother had been insane, after all. What did her mother call her?

A crazy old witch.

An old witch born of old witches . . .

Cree closed her eyes, but flinched when a knock sounded at the door. *The lawyer,* she thought. "Go away." Someone hit the door again. "Please go away."

"Open the door, child."

The voice was faint through the door, but like her grandmother's. No one else had ever sounded so frail but sure. No one else had called her *child.*

"Who are you?"

Through the peephole, the woman appeared small and withered, so short that Cree could see little of her face, just the forehead and hair, the creases and the black eyes.

"You can call me Verdine. Most everyone does."

"What do you want?"

"Why, to talk to you, of course."

Cree opened the door to the length of the chain. "I don't know you."

"We met once when you were very young. Your mother brought you to my house. I took you into the Hush."

Cree thought she remembered the day: her mother's hand, hard on her wrist, an old woman wreathed in smoke. There'd been yelling then, too, then her mother's car throwing gravel and dirt. "You had a dog," she said.

"That's right, child. A Plott hound we called Redmond. After your mother left, he slept on the porch with his head in your lap. He rode with us into the Hush. You wanted to keep him, and I wouldn't allow it. You grew very angry."

Cree unbolted the door. The woman was very old, and smiling. Behind her was a big man with a square jaw and flecks of white in his hair.

"This is Leon, my grandson. Is it your plan to leave us in the hall?"

It wasn't the wry smile that decided Cree, but the smell of smoke on the old woman's clothes. Even now it was familiar.

"Thank you, child." Verdine and Leon entered the apartment, and Cree locked the door behind them. "Is your mother home?"

"She's out."

"Do you have coffee?"

"I'm not sure."

"Be a good girl and check, would you?" They followed her into the kitchen, and to Cree it felt unreal. Verdine looked as her grandmother had looked, small and wiry and sharp-eyed. They sat at the table while Cree opened cabinets and made coffee. "You appear much as your mother did as a teenager, though I must say, you look unwell." The sugar jar rattled in Cree's hand, but she got the top off and pushed in a spoon. When she turned, the old woman looked sad, even with the smile. "Thank you." She took the sugar and a mug. "Milk, too, if you don't mind."

Cree pulled a carton from the refrigerator, but grimaced when she smelled it. "The milk's bad."

"Just the sugar, then." Cree nodded, but kept her back turned as the coffee perked. "Leon, would you be a dear and go on into the other room?" Leon did as he was told, and when the coffee was brewed, Cree filled the mug and put it on the table. "So . . ." A spoon clacked as the old woman stirred in the sugar. "Which dream is it?"

"What? I don't—"

"The hanging tree or buried alive? Those two are most common." Cree sat loosely. She was dizzy. She was cold. The old woman sipped and nodded. "When did it start?"

"I think I might be sick."

"Just breathe, child. We're only talking."

Cree closed her eyes and concentrated. "The girl with the knife," she said. "I've seen that one for years, but not often. The other one . . ." She broke off. "Four days, now. Four nights."

"Any others?"

"Sometimes," Cree said, and was not ready to speak of Johnny Merrimon or the gate. She was struggling with too much already. The woman. The conversation.

More sugar went in the mug, the spoon clicking. Verdine sipped, but kept her eyes on Cree's face. "Your mother had the dreams when she was young, though she'd probably deny it if you asked. Your grandmother had them until the day she died. Your great-grandmother did, too. They find the women in your family. They always have."

"Is that why you're here?"

"I'm here because no one is supposed to dream outside the Hush. In a century and a half, no one ever has. No one but you."

Cree fidgeted under the black-eyed stare. There was too much strength for such an old woman, too much fire. "How well did you know my grandmother?"

"We were cousins. We grew up together."

"And Hush Arbor?"

"I lived there same as you, but left a long time ago."

"Why?"

"A man from outside. I thought I was in love."

"Do you . . . uh. Do you have the dreams?"

"Once," Verdine said. "A long time ago."

"Why are you here?"

"To help you."

"But how—?"

"Let's talk about these dreams. What do you remember of your time in Hush Arbor?"

"Most of it, I think."

"Do you remember the story of Aina?"

The question took Cree by surprise. "It's a children's story," she said. "Grandmother would tell it to me before bed at night."

"Tell it to me now."

"Why?"

"Humor an old lady."

The request for the story struck Cree harder than anything yet. It was the beginning and the end: one of the first things taught by her grandmother, and the last story told on the day she'd died. Cree had been so small that—kneeling by the bed—her face had been level with the old woman's. She could close her eyes even now and see the tired smile and the map of her skin. She'd smelled of tea and dried leaves and dying.

"Come closer, child."

Cree pressed tightly to the bed. Wind sighed against the glass, and people were gathered outside in the cold: the whole village, all who remained. Grandmother was dying, and the village would die with her. People understood, so there was keening beyond the glass, the crying of women and the murmur of lost men. They were afraid of her death and what it meant for the larger world. Grandmother sensed them out there—same as Cree—but her eyes were for the girl alone.

"Tell me the story of Aina," she whispered; and Cree—afraid—shook her small head. "It's more important than you know. Please."

"I don't want to."

"Come, child. Tell me one last time."

Cree wept then, thinking of all their nights together and of the times she'd heard the story or told it herself. It was as familiar as the feather pillows, the woolen blankets, the warmth of the fire. Grandmother touched the tears on Cree's cheek, then nodded and closed her eyes. "It's the first story," she said. "The most important of all." Cree took the withered hand and felt how cold it was. "Go on, child. Do this last thing for me. I want to hear the story and to know you will remember it."

Cree looked from Grandmother to the window, and saw the faces there, the dark eyes beyond the glass. She was alone with the old woman, so she leaned into the bed and told the story of Aina, exactly as she'd learned it. "Hush Arbor is our home," she said. "But our people are, and always have been, of Africa. We come from the coast on the western edge, from the top of a mountain that rose higher than all others. For centuries, women ruled on the mountain, and the greatest ruler of all was named Akachi, which means 'Hand of God.' At the height of her power, twenty-nine nations bowed to Akachi on the mountain. Ten thousand spears defended her home, and her daughter's name was Aina, which means 'Difficult Birth,' which is also just, as Akachi labored for three days to bring Aina into the world. When the child at last was born, a great storm fell on the mountain, so powerful, it is said, that much of Akachi's power washed away with it, for she was sickly in the years that followed, and the kingdom fractured. War followed war, and Aina grew in a world defined by death and blood and a broken mother. By the time she was ten, Aina sat on the throne to hide her mother's weakness. By fifteen, she commanded armies of men, and was grown cruel by years of war. When the great queen died, she gave to her daughter the power that was hers by birth; yet, great as that power was, Aina was too young to wield it well, and in the blindness of her youth, the great betrayal came.

"The man who betrayed Aina was called Daren, which means 'Born of Night.' This was also a just name, as it was in the night he came with a hundred men to take Aina from the place she slept. A trusted general, he sought to find her sleeping and weak, but a servant girl saw the men coming with spears and rope, and woke Aina in time to flee the caverns that made her palace. For half a night she was pursued by this man she'd once trusted. And though she was new to the great power and weak in its use, she killed thirteen men before she was trapped and bound and carried from the mountain so that Daren, born of night, might be king.

"Knowing her death would mean an uprising from those who loved her,

Daren hid Aina by day, and in darkness carried her down the coast to a small kingdom ruled by a bitter man. There she was stripped and sold, and put on a ship so she might be brought across the ocean and sold again and taken north to a county whose very name means black as night—"

"Raven County." The old woman interrupted Cree, her smile loving but small. "Our home," she said. "This place."

The old woman was crying, too, so Cree climbed into bed and put her cheek against the failing heart. She heard it slow inside the narrow chest, and Grandmother's hand was on her head.

"I'm sorry," the old woman said. "I wanted to teach you more. I wanted to make you strong. . . ."

In the apartment, Cree was shaking her head. "I don't want to tell the story."

"But you remember it?"

"I remember," Cree said; and, looking with fresh eyes at the old woman, saw all the ways she was unlike the grandmother she'd loved. The stare was too intent, the mouth a bitter line. "Why are you really here?"

"Because you are the last of your line and because the dreams matter in ways you can't possibly understand."

"Then tell me."

The old eyes narrowed, and the woman nodded. "Your grandmother said you were special—"

"Enough about my grandmother. Tell me what you want."

Verdine nodded again, but even as her mouth opened, a commotion rose in the other room. A door slammed. Cree's mother was yelling.

"What the hell is happening here?"

Cree rounded the corner as bags hit the floor and groceries spilled out.

"What are you doing in my house? Get out!" Leon had the big arms spread, but Luana Freemantle was undaunted. A finger came up when she saw the old woman. "I told you to stay away from my daughter."

"We're just talking, Luana."

"With you there is never 'just' anything. Get out of my house! Both of you! Cree, go to your room."

"I'm not yet finished with your daughter," Verdine said. "I'll need a few more minutes."

"No. Absolutely not."

"Leon, if you would keep Luana in this room. Cree, come back to the kitchen—"

"Don't you go anywhere with her, Cree!"

"Come, child. You have questions. I have answers."

The voice was soft, the smile inviting. Cree looked at her mother and saw panic twist her face. She mouthed the word *no,* but Cree was already turning.

"She's *my* daughter, damn it! You can't have her!"

Verdine raised a hand, dismissive, and Cree fell into her wake as if pulled. She was exhausted and sick, and the moment was blurry, as if it, too, were a dream: the narrow woman and the raised hand, how small and bent she was, and how she walked as if floating. Part of Cree's mind said *exhaustion, hunger, hallucination;* but the dreaminess was fine because she wanted what was in the dream. Looking back from the kitchen door, she saw her mother in the same strange haze, but a gun was in her hand, and that, too, could not be real. But the gun spit smoke and fire. A bullet snapped into the wall, and everything froze.

"That was a warning."

The gun was small in her hand, but everyone stared at it. Verdine stood very still. Leon said, "It's just a .22."

"A .22 magnum. And I missed on purpose."

"Why do you have a gun?" Verdine asked.

"Because I'm not stupid. Now, I want you out, and I want you to stay out. Cree, go to your room and stay there." Cree didn't move. Neither did Verdine. "I'll kill you," Luana said. "I'll kill you now and not think twice about it. Don't think I won't."

"The girl should be allowed to choose, to know the truth or not. It's her birthright, just as it was yours."

"Only if I say so."

"Still the weak one, aren't you? Still the runner. Still afraid."

"I'm glad that I left."

"Are you really? Even now?"

Maybe she meant the apartment, the squalor, the lack of purpose. Cree never learned, because the big man lunged for the gun, and her mother pulled the trigger again and put a hole in his chest. It was very small with little blood. Luana thumbed the hammer. "There's a hospital nine blocks east."

Leon looked at Verdine. The blood was coming faster, as were the signs of pain on his face. He staggered, but Verdine's eyes never left Luana's. "Finally found some spine, have you?"

"Get out."

"This is bigger than you, than any of us."

"You can't have my daughter."

"A hundred and seventy years. You've felt it."

"I felt it ruin my life." She pointed the gun at Verdine, but the old woman took Cree's wrist and pulled her close with shocking strength. Cree smelled the smoke in her clothes, the skin like her grandmother's, like old leather and dried leaves. "Your mother is a coward," she said.

"You're hurting me."

"When you dream again—and you will—I want you to dream of Aina."

"Let her go, Verdine!"

But the old woman did not. "Think her name as you fall asleep—"

"Verdine, goddamn it!"

"Remember her story, and remember this, too." She leaned so close that her thin, dry lips touched the shell of Cree's ear. "She wants you to understand, child. She wants to be found."

They left after that, and for Cree the world no longer made sense. She'd always hated the apartment. Now there was blood and smoke and a smell in the air like burnt matches. Her mother was different, too. "How could you do that?" Cree asked.

"I let you go once." Luana locked the hall door and put the gun on a table. "I won't do it again."

"She wanted to talk about Grandmother."

"And the dreams, and Hush Arbor, and how only she can help you. Verdine does nothing that's not good for Verdine. Things are happening that you don't understand."

Cree sank onto the sofa. She was tired and confused, and now there was this other side of her mother. "Will she go to the police?"

"To an outsider? No."

"What about the gunshots?"

"Not the first we've heard in this building, and not the last, either."

"She told me to dream of Aina."

"You'll do no such thing."

"Sooner or later I'll have to sleep."

"So we move before that happens. Far away. Another country if we have to."

"With what money?"

Luana's face softened unexpectedly, and she sank to her knees, taking Cree's hands in her own. "Don't be seduced by the dreams or Verdine or her talk of your birthright. Hush Arbor is a cancer. It eats lives." She squeezed her daughter's hands. "Just trust me, please. That woman is not your friend."

"Was she Grandmother's?"

"Your grandmother never loved Verdine. She cast her out, banished her for her lies and greed, and her black heart. Best you remember that. Verdine Freemantle is evil. You hear me? Pure damn evil. She'll do anything to get what she wants. She'll say anything, tell any lie."

Cree pulled the crumpled drawing from her back pocket, and smoothed it on her leg. "Do you know this place?" She handed it over, then watched her mother's face.

"No, I don't."

"Grandmother showed me when I was young. She would have shown you, too."

"She didn't."

"Who's lying now?"

"Only to protect you," Luana said.

"Your lies. Her lies. What's the difference?"

"I'm not like Verdine. Don't think that I am."

"I want to know about this place."

"This place? This?" In short, angry motions, Luana ripped up the drawing and dropped the pieces. "Hush Arbor is a cancer. I'll not say it again." After gathering the fallen groceries, she straightened. "I'm going to put these away, then you and I will talk about leaving this city. Bus tickets are not expensive. We'll find the money."

"It's my childhood—"

"Have you eaten yet? I'll make lunch."

"I can't walk away from it."

"Sandwich okay?"

"I said I'm not leaving."

Luana turned at the kitchen door, and her eyes were near to brimming. "Then the dreams, my love, will eat you alive."

"You can't know that."

"I've seen it," she said. "I've lived it."

She turned, and Cree listened to the sounds from the kitchen. A cabinet opened, and she knew it was the one below the sink where her mother kept the vodka. Cree pictured the shaking hands, the long swallow. Maybe her mother would make lunch. Maybe she'd drain the bottle and forget. Either way, there would be no bus, no answers, and no fresh start. Knowing the pain she was about to cause, Cree gathered bits of paper from the floor, then unlocked the door and slipped quietly into the hall.

Five hours later, Cree was back in Raven County, on the busy streets downtown. She touched her face and thought how insubstantial it all was: the city, her bones, everything that was not the dream. She found the building where the lawyer worked, and its windows showed her a sunk-eyed girl in three-day clothes.

Too ashamed to go inside, she turned over the lawyer's card to find his home address. She stopped a dozen people before one agreed to help. When she gave him the name of the street, he pointed down the hill and left, and she found the address above a narrow stairwell beside a bakery full of sleek people in nice clothes. Fumbling at the door, she stepped into a dim stairwell that bent twice on the way up. On the landing outside his apartment door, Cree asked herself a final time if this was smart. She didn't know him. He didn't know her. But the drawing was his. Maybe he could tell her more. Maybe they wanted the same thing.

Knocking twice, she waited. When no one came, she found a spot on the floor and leaned into a corner where the old plaster smelled like old paint. She pictured Leon and the small hole that leaked such little blood. She wondered what her mother was doing, and if Johnny Merrimon was alive, and why Verdine wanted so much for her to dream.

Settling into the corner, Cree felt her eyes grow heavy. She was tired and afraid, so she pictured herself in a treetop on a vast plain. Black stone covered the plain, and the only sound was wind. It moved the treetop, and Cree moved with it. She was untouchable. She could see forever.

Aina . . .

How many times had she heard the story?

"I want to dream of Aina."

She repeated the words until they softened, and she believed them enough to drift. She was safe in the branches of her imaginary tree. They cradled her as wind rose and fell, and rocked her. There was no world beyond the blackness of her skin and the sky and the stony plain that ran forever. She imagined a world of infinite warmth, then said Aina's name a final time. It sounded in the darkness, and Cree was gone from the world. She was a traveler, a dreamer, a sailor on a broken sea.

When her eyes opened, she was on another ship and half-dead and covered in grime. She was on her side, bodies pressed so tightly against her own that she couldn't move, could barely breathe. She retched, and the bile ran down her chin to join the blood and shit and other vomit. Around her, people cried out and prayed. Twelve of them were dead, and still chained. It was night, and waves crashed against the hull beside her head. She was Cree, but only just. The rest was Aina, and she felt it all: the wounds and starvation, the old and the dead, the children too young to understand. They were in the darkness, all of them, terrified and lost and weeping.

It was too much and too real, so Cree squeezed her eyes shut and held her breath. The ship rolled, and she felt the thrum of it, the sluice of water. She focused on that because the rest was bigger than fear or pain or even death. Aina felt it all as if it were her own, all the souls and chains and abandoned hope. She felt the motherless child, half-starved and bleeding for the first time. She knew the man who'd lost his wife and was ashamed, the broken women and the raped girls; she knew hunger and hot air, the ankles rubbed to bone and smeared with grease to keep off the maggots. Cree felt it, too, and couldn't bear it. She fisted her eyes and screamed; tried to leave but could not. She was of the girl, and in her, a passenger, trapped.

For long hours the despair of so many drove her mad with pain. It was too much, like stone breaking. Cree tried to crawl away, but Aina's mind was filled with madness, too. Suffering and want and suicidal thoughts—she was the drain that drank it down, a flower in the rain. She had nowhere to hide, and that made it hard for Cree, too. She'd never known awareness like this: the power of it and the weight. In despair, she clawed into the recesses of Aina's mind, looking for the corners and quiet eddies. No such place existed, so Cree sought the stillness of memory, forging deeper and down until she found the darkness of a cave and firelight and other nights. She saw little, and felt less. She was a child afraid, skin against a naked breast; but there was love there, and peace, a gentle voice and the promise of morning. Cree knew in the way of dreams that it was Aina's childhood before—that she would walk soon, and leave the cavern and grow strong on the mountain. Cree felt all of that, and wanted to stay buried, to flow from one memory to the next and never return to the ship where people called out for water and family and lost gods.

But the dream was deep, and the ship forever. It plowed through waves; shuddered as a double crest lifted it high, stalled it for a moment, then dropped it like a building down the side of a mountain. Cree felt the crush of bodies, the slide of skin and chains and sludge. People cried out, and she knew their thirst and loss, the fear of drowning with an iron collar on her neck. The ship rose again and fell, and she lost herself in the bitter sway. She was a queen, a frightened slave; she was Aina, entire.

CHAPTER TWENTY-NINE

"Aina"

1853

Death came on a Sunday, but it was not the death people expected. It should have been the Master's wife—that's what Aina heard—that his wife was eaten up with a fever like none had ever seen. Of course, the whole world was burning. Scorched pastures. Dead cattle. Aina knew only a few slaves, but they worried at the sick children and failed crops, and what it meant for the moon to rise red. There was talk, too, of fighting in town, of brawls and blame and a white man bullet-holed in the Main Street dirt. It was the heat that did it, and every day was worse than the last. The sun rose red, and the moon followed. Even the river felt like blood. That was Aina's thought as they carried the Master's wife down the bank and tried to drown the fever that was killing her.

It wouldn't work, she knew, not that kind of fever and not as weak as the white woman was. Aina had watched them leave the house, and was in the river before them, a slip of a girl as black as night and naked behind a river birch the size of her waist. She wanted to see if white people died the same as slaves, and from where she hid, it looked like the answer was yes.

"Get her hair wet! Hold her head! Get the rest of her down deep."

That was John Merrimon, though Aina had never seen him up close. She spent her days chained to a wall or locked in a room. She was too wild to be trusted, too unpredictable and violent and African. Three weeks had passed since she'd been bought off the docks of Charles Towne, but she'd never broken, not once. She stretched her lips if they got close; she fought and cursed, and felt the rising wildness that made the other slaves look away. They were scared of her—they wouldn't admit it, but they were. The women said her eyes shone yellow in the dark. The men spoke of how she bared her teeth and made animal noises deep in her throat. Of course they came for her just the same: the yellow-haired foreman and the livery boy and the hardhanded slave, still filthy from the fields. They came because she was small and well shaped, and because she never spoke of what happened when the door swung in on leather hinges. She was weak in this place, so she hadn't killed them yet. But she knew their names, just the same. She knew their names and what they ate and where they slept.

Settling deeper, Aina glided from one birch to the next. She knew some of the words they spoke, but not all of them, knew fever *and* dying *and* doctor. *But no doctor could cure John Merrimon's wife. It would take power to do that, and there was no power in the river beyond Aina's. Curious, though, she watched the Master and his sister, the field hands, and a house slave named Isaac. She watched Isaac most intently because he was smarter than all the other slaves put together. He knew things, she thought, white-man things like marks on paper and guns and the great man they worshipped in the sky. It was because of him that Aina stayed so low in the water. Everyone else paid attention to the dying woman, but not Isaac. He watched the bank and the water; his eyes touched many things, but not her. She knew the night, and the night loved her for it. It hid her when she wept, held her as she climbed the tallest trees to stare at the same moon she'd known before the betrayal and the chains and the ship that stank of death and shit and vomit. But Aina would not be a slave for long. She was weak in this place, but still her mother's child.*

Not this person they thought her to be.

Not this slave.

Turning her attention to John Merrimon, she watched him weep, and thought it weak in a man who owned other men. He had many things—this Master—but his woman would die. Aina heard the lungs rattle; felt the heat so deep, no river could touch it. She looked at the hump of the white woman's stomach, and knew the baby would come soon if it could, but not soon enough to live. Aina could save them both if she chose, but the black-haired man owned her, and because of that, she hated his world and all things in it.

But she'd learned his secret, there in the river.

The white man was human after all.

She could use that.

The house slave came for her three hours later. She heard his step in the dirt beyond the door, and knew the smell of him, the rhythm of his breath. He hesitated, then opened the door and loomed above the pallet where she lay. She saw the large head, the giant shoulders. He shook the chain that bound her ankle to an iron ring. "You were at the river."

He spoke a language she knew, one of the lesser tribes from narrow valleys beyond the great mountain.

"Are you sure of that?"

"I'm not as blind as most."

"There is this chain," she said.

"Yes, but I know what you are."

"Then you should be running afraid or begging for your life. This will end badly for you and the man you call Master."

"John is not as bad as some."

"He owns children."

"Yet you are no child."

She smiled in the dimness, and knew he could see it. "Does your Master see so clearly as you?"

"He is little more than a child himself. His father just died. He does what the foreman says."

"The foreman." She spit that word, too, and thought the house slave understood the reason. "Are you here for this?" She spread her legs—a rattle of chain. "Or are you wise enough to know the danger?"

He nodded at the last question.

"Tell me why," she said.

"Because I know what you are."

"Say it, then." He swallowed hard, and she turned her face to show the scars put there by her mother's own hand. "Say it," she said, and he did: a word in her language, the one true tongue.

It meant "priestess," "prophet," "dark queen."

Minutes later, the house slave led Aina through brittle grass and to the grand, white house. It was like houses she'd seen on the roads of Charles Towne, and reminded her of the ship that carried her across the ocean. Six months ago, she'd not known that men could build such things. Men were for fighting and hunting and fucking. But the white men built splendid things, and crossed oceans. They worshipped a gentle god, yet were as cruel as children. It was to understand this contradiction that she mounted the broad steps and passed through tall doors. Inside was a space as vast as any cavern in the great mountains of home. She saw colors and fabrics, metals that gleamed, and wood as dark and smooth as a baby's skin.

Stepping inside, she kept her head high, ignoring the women who were not women at all, but shadows of women that cooked and cleaned and carried the white man's shit. They risked glances at Aina's face, then looked away from the scars cut like spirals in her cheeks. Ignoring them, Aina studied a square of silver glass that hung on the wall and showed her reflection as well as any pool she'd ever seen. It showed her as others saw her: the wild eyes and scars, a dirty girl in a scrap of cloth. They thought her young and ignorant and wild, but it wasn't like that, and Isaac knew it, too. No one else wore scars like hers.

Not by choice.

Not if they wanted to live.

"This way. Please." He moved up a curving staircase, and she followed at her own pace. At a great door, he paused, and Aina saw the fear in his eyes. "Please," he said. "I'm begging you."

When the door opened, Aina saw the dying woman in a wide bed, and by her side was John Merrimon holding a small, bright knife. He looked at Isaac, terrified. "She's dying," he said.

Isaac pushed into the room, and Aina watched them argue. It started slowly, then grew louder. She understood few of the words, but knew enough to smile a little when Isaac said black magic. *She'd heard the words from the mouths of other slaves, from field hands and cooks, from the old women who said the foreman couldn't break Aina, and that the fear was in his eyes, too. They said she was driving him mad, that he raped her and choked her, and that she laughed in his face as he did it.*

They said the heat came with her.

That it would leave when she was dead.

John Merrimon was no different. He looked at her, appalled; but the hope was growing in his heart. She saw it when he looked at his wife, and the big slave spoke.

The child can save her. . . .

There will be a price. . . .

She nodded because there was always a price. That was the way of things, woman or child, white man or black.

The argument grew, and she thought it was about gods and the woman and right and wrong. Aina watched until she was bored, then crossed the room in silence. No one noticed when she moved, and that was part of her gift: cunning and deceit, suppleness and speed.

They blinked and she was beside the bed.

"I fix."

The white man stopped and stared because no slave off the boat should know his language so soon. But Aina was smarter than any man. "Baby die first," she said. "Then woman. You pay, I fix."

"You can't fix her. No one can."

But Aina felt a tingle in her palms, a gathering of threads. She touched the woman's skin, and color returned. For an instant, the eyes opened.

"John . . ."

The white woman spoke, and the husband broke like a child. He dropped to his knees, the knife clattering beside the bed.

"You pay, I fix."

Aina removed her touch, and the woman's eyes rolled white.

"No! Please! Bring her back!"

Aina stooped for the knife, and no one stopped her. The white man cupped his hands, begging.

"Please, God . . ."

But his god was not listening, and neither was Aina. She walked to tall windows with a view over fields and forest. It was a new place, a new world.

"I'll pay you," he said. "I'll pay!"

Aina took her time because she could ask for anything and he would give it to her. Money. Land. His life. When she spoke, it was to Isaac and in her own tongue. "I want freedom," she said. "I want his mark on paper for all to see."

Isaac translated, and the man said, "Yes! Done!"

"Land, too."

"Anything. Please."

Aina moved from the window, remorseless. She touched the white man's face, the bend of his arm; she let him see the wildness in her heart, then offered up a smile and named her final price.

The livery boy.

The foreman.

The hardhanded slave.

CHAPTER THIRTY

Jack was in his cups again, not drunk really, but not entirely sober. He sat at the end of a dim bar at the back of a dim restaurant. The beer at his elbow was warm. The bartender, a soft man in his sixties, pointed at the glass. "Is that not working for you?"

"I'm sorry?" Jack said. "What?"

"It's been sitting there for twenty minutes. I'm asking if you want something different."

"Maybe a whiskey," Jack said.

"What kind?"

"Bourbon. I don't care."

The bartender put a drink on the bar, and Jack nodded his thanks, sipping without really tasting. The phone was in his other hand. On it was a message from the senior partner. Jack played it for the fifth time.

Mr. Cross, this is Michael Adkins. I'd like you to be in my office tomorrow morning at eight. It's time for a serious discussion about your future at this firm.

There was more, but Jack didn't want to hear it. The first two lines said it all.

He wasn't showing up.

Wasn't billing.

Draining the bourbon, he stood, fishing for his wallet. "What do I owe you?" The bartender gave him a number, and Jack dropped bills on the bar. He wobbled a bit going through the restaurant, but didn't care about that, either.

He had to talk to Johnny.

Outside, the sun was down and a hot wind licked the concrete. Jack looked left and right, orienting himself. He'd never been to the restaurant before, though it was not far from the apartment or his office. After the trip to Charlotte, he'd parked the car and gone walking along one edge of downtown, and then another. He'd worn his feet raw before finding the restaurant and dropping half-dead onto the barstool. The first beer had gone fast, the second more slowly. The whiskey, he was thinking, might have been a mistake.

"Eight o'clock." He started walking. "Fabulous."

It was twelve blocks to his apartment, up nine and over three. People were out, the better restaurants booming. He thought again of eating, but had no appetite.

How would he defend his behavior at the firm?

Did he even care?

The last question cut deep. He *should* care. God knows, he'd worked hard enough.

At the bakery, he slipped into the narrow stairwell, and drew up sharply when he saw the girl on the landing by his door. She was slumped in a corner, twitching; her eyes rolled so far back in her skull, they showed entirely white. It took Jack a moment to recognize the girl from the apartment in Charlotte. He'd seen half her face, a single eye.

What was she doing here?

"Excuse me." Jack leaned close, uncertain how best to wake her. "Um, miss." He reached for her arm, but stopped short when her mouth opened. "Hello," Jack said.

The girl started screaming.

Cree didn't know where she was or what was happening. The world was bloody and sharp, a jagged shard. She could feel the knife in her hand, the handle of it so slick and warm, it felt like something alive. There was a dark night and a dim hallway.

The men were mutilated and screaming.

She was screaming.

"Stay away from me, stay away!"

She drove herself into the corner.

"It's okay . . ."

Cree scrambled to her feet. The hallway tilted and for a hard second she felt the fire on her skin, the pressure wave of moaning as a hundred slaves rocked foot to foot and kept their eyes on the dirt. "Who are you?"

"My name is Jack Cross. We met earlier. This is where I live."

Cree saw the stairwell, the plaster walls. "There was a knife. . . ."

"No," he said. "No knife."

Cree blinked twice. She could trust or not, leave or stay. She thought they wanted the same thing—she and the lawyer—but she'd never dreamed as Aina, not like this. She'd seen the hanging tree and held the knife, but she'd never known the reasons for it, not the history or raw emotion, not the god-awful gladness as men screamed and died. "Just a second, okay." The dream wasn't fading. It fluttered someplace deep, a living thing that wanted her to know that Aina was real, that it wasn't a story. Cree forced herself to straighten, to open her eyes and be the girl she'd always been, just the girl. She dug into her back pocket and pulled out shredded bits of paper. "I'm sorry your drawing got ruined."

"This is why you're here?"

"Where'd you get it?"

"Perhaps you should come inside." The lawyer studied her face for long seconds. "You'll want to see this." Inside, the apartment was all shadows and hollow places. "Just a minute. I'm sorry." He fumbled for the switch, and paused. "Don't be startled."

Cree blinked as light flooded the room. The drawings hung on walls and cabinets and doors. They stretched over tables and the sofa, spilled from stacks on the floor. She saw the glade, as if she were five again. She could hear her grandmother's voice. *You are never to go there,* she'd said. *No closer than this, not even when you are older. . . .*

"These were drawn a very long time ago." He watched her move through the room and explained how he came to have them. "The artist drew them over a lifetime: ten in one year, a hundred the next. There's a pattern," he said. "I can't explain it. Something about the way she used the charcoal. See how parts of some are so much darker and shinier. I've been studying this for days, and almost have it. It's like a word on the tip of my tongue."

He went on like that for a while, but Cree tuned him out. The pictures stirred memories of every winter she'd known in the Hush: the short, cold days, how fires burned large and people scurried from one cabin to the next. She'd been too young to understand the fear she'd seen, but the drawings captured those feelings of stark aloneness.

"I've seen this place." He touched a drawing of the waterfall and the tree. "I can't remember where, exactly, but I've seen it and it scares me. People have gone lost in that swamp. People have died, and I'm looking for answers. I'm hoping you can help me."

"With the old stories?"

"The stories, yes. And I want to find this waterfall. Tomorrow, I'm going to look for it."

"You say people have died. You mean outsiders?" He nodded carefully. "Start at the beginning," she said. "Tell me everything."

The telling took a while, and Cree got more than she'd expected. She learned of the trapper found frozen in a creek bed, and of the surveyor who'd stumbled into a rattlesnake den and suffered thirty-seven bites, including nineteen in the face. He spoke of boys lost in the swamp, of so many people dead or missing that Cree was disbelieving. But he showed her the articles, the old write-ups.

"I've never heard these stories," she said.

"Few have."

"What about your friend?"

"Don't be bitter."

"About the lawsuit?" Cree looked away because *bitter* was not the right word, not after the dreams. She could close her eyes and see John Merrimon in the summer of 1853: his face above the dying wife, the same face yellow with fire and shadow. She knew the dream as if she'd lived it. That meant she hated him, couldn't help it. How much of that hate went down the line to land on Johnny? She wasn't sure, but saw him at the gate, his blood in the dust. She was afraid but not sorry. There was too much history between their families, too much slavery and blood and betrayal. "This was a mistake. I should probably go."

"It's the middle of the night." Cree glanced at the window, and at the city beyond. "There's just the one bedroom," he continued. "But you can take it if you like. The door locks."

The same distrust haunted Cree, but she had nowhere else to go. Not to her mother. Not to the Hush. "Maybe the sofa—"

"Stay right there." He retrieved sheets and a pillow. "I've slept on it before. It's comfortable."

Cree nodded her thanks, and when he was gone, she sat alone on the sofa, her back very straight. She studied pictures on the wall, the dark marks, the careful use of empty space.

Crossing the room, she removed a sketch from the wall, tilting it against the light before stepping back to take in as many of the drawings as she could. After a moment, she removed another sketch, then six more. Some were perfect, she realized, but many were not. Cree turned a slow circle, feeling hints of *wrongness,* like an instinct. In that first hour, she cleared two entire walls and began again. It took most of the night to find what the artist had hidden. The darkest sketches gathered in the center. Corners touched corners. In places, they overlapped. Thirty of them together formed a single picture that covered most of the wall. Cree felt cold looking at the darkness, the glints of light.

She saw the swamp of her childhood.

Saw black eyes, watching.

When light broke over the city, Cree was still awake. It was the drawings, the fear of dreams. Turning from the window, she watched pink light play on the sketches. Thirty of them combined to make the great, black eyes. Eight feet long and five feet tall, the charcoal was shiny black except where it was not: the white glints in the pupils, the crease between the eyes, and then the brows, like leaves and branches and twigs.

Sitting on the sofa, Cree folded her hands in her lap. She wanted to take down the drawings and wasn't sure why. They were just drawings.

But when she paced again, the eyes followed her, and she wanted to rip them down so badly, it hurt. When the lawyer stirred behind the door, she thought about it a final time. She had time to do it. Tear them down. Run. But when the door opened, she was still on the sofa, and she felt him behind her: the sudden stop, the deep breath.

"Sweet Jesus." He sat beside her. The shoes he wore were shined, the suit pants creased under a bright blue tie. "How . . . ?"

"I rarely sleep these days." It was no answer, but he accepted it. They sat for a long time in a difficult silence. "You're going to work?"

"What?"

"The suit."

She pointed, and he looked down, as if dazed. His hand moved to the lapel. "Just a minute." He disappeared into the bedroom, and returned in jeans and boots. The dazed look was gone, his features pale but grim. "I need to find my friend." Cree stood, and he picked up the keys. "I need to find him right now."

They rode in a car as nice as any Cree had ever seen. The metal gleamed. It smelled new. When they got to Hush Arbor, he stayed in the car as Cree opened the gate.

The same gate . . .

She watched him pull the big car through, and almost left him then and there. It was real now, all of it. They'd find Johnny dead. Maybe they'd find what killed him, or it would find them.

"You coming or not?"

Shit . . .

Cree got back in the car, and the lawyer took them deeper into the forest, then over a causeway with water on both sides. He stopped only once, at the old sign. Pointing, he said, "I was thirteen, the first time I saw that."

The sign was faded wood, half-rotted and covered with honeysuckle. HUSH ARBOR, it read. *1853.* Cree rolled down her window and smelled the mud.

"Why are you doing this?" the lawyer asked. "You don't know me. You have every reason to hate my friend."

"Why are *you* here?" She turned in the seat, defensive. "You're terrified. I can tell. What's in this for you?"

"Just my friend."

She said nothing after that, and the lawyer took them past the sign and into the gloom.

The hanging tree was there.

Just through those trees.

"We'll go to the cabin first, and get Johnny. Then you can show us the waterfall." They parked at the abandoned village, and got out of the car. He went left, but she stepped into the old church, feeling the heat and the stillness.

"Ms. Freemantle?"

Inside, things looked as they had for years: the sconces and tumbled benches, the layers of dust. The lawyer appeared in the door behind her, but was little more than a shadow himself. She ignored him, drawn instead to the stone baptismal font. It was small, on a carved pedestal.

Only it wasn't a baptismal font.

How do I know that?

As a child, she'd been kept from the weekly gathering, but she'd gone to the window once. She'd stood on a stone block and seen . . . what? She remembered her fingers on the ledge, ripples in the glass. Inside, candles burned in sconces on the wall, and Grandmother stood at the baptismal font. People were cowed and bent.

It was nighttime.

It was raining.

"Ms. Freemantle?"

"Shhh."

She'd been four or five, soaking wet and afraid of being caught as her grandmother lifted her arms to show the withered skin, the map work of fine, pale scars. People swayed on the benches, shoulder to shoulder, eyes squeezed tight.

"May I be alone for a moment?"

The lawyer stepped outside, and Cree shut the door as an image came, unbidden. She saw the bright knife and people lined at the baptismal font. They offered a hand, an arm . . .

Cree touched the inside of the bowl, which was stained and dark. She pictured nighttime and rain. She had the sense of black stone moving. . . .

"Ms. Freemantle . . ."

When she pushed on the baptismal, the stone bowl rocked on its pedestal. Lifting it from the base, she put it on the floor, feeling something very much like superstitious awe. Reaching into the open pedestal, she found the knife inside. It was unchanged from childhood: a small bone handle; a rabbit-skin sheath. Drawing it, she saw an edge as bright as ice. On her palm was a thin white scar from her first day in the Hush, her first time at the tree. How many of her people had the knife cut? How much blood had it spilled?

Outside, she said nothing about her discovery. Her past was a secret. So was the knife. "Sorry about that," she said.

"It's fine."

"Are you ready?"

"I am."

She glanced at the old church and thought of blood in a black-stained bowl. "Tell me what we're doing next."

He took her deeper into the swamp than she had ever been, and she shrank under the scale of it. She'd been arrogant, she thought, to think she knew this place. They followed trails only the lawyer seemed to see, and when the view opened up to show a cabin across still water, Cree stopped and stared. It was beautiful. The isolation. The stony hills.

"We found this spot when we were fourteen." The lawyer led her to the right, picking his way from island to tussock to dry land. "He won't be happy I brought you, so let me do the talking."

The cabin, though, was empty.

"Damn." Jack closed the door, then stared across the clearing and out into the wilderness. He called out Johnny's name, then tried the cell. "He could be anywhere."

For Cree, it was a relief. The swamp was different since the dream, and more so since she'd found the knife in the old church. Strange things moved in the back of her mind. She felt shadows of memory that were not entirely her own. She knew the knife as if she'd held it a hundred times. She saw people she'd never met, and remembered things she should not, things like power, and the blood of hanged men, and how to skin a wild pig. Stooping, she let damp soil run between her fingers.

"We could wait," Jack said.

"I can't do that."

The lawyer held his palm above the dead fire. "Still warm."

"We need to leave."

"I really think—"

"If you want to see the waterfall, we're going back now."

He didn't argue after that. Maybe it was her voice, or the way she stared. She needed to move, and needed it now. Ten minutes took them back to the first island, and Cree paused a moment to look back, feeling an ache of recognition. She knew the movement of the hills, the yellow light and broken stone.

In 1853, she'd known the land. She'd hunted it, owned it, lived it.

Cree closed her eyes, and in her mind, a fire was burning. She heard the creak of rope and felt bits of men. She knew screams and frightened slaves. A red sheen was on the same small blade. . . .

"Ms. Freemantle."

She felt the joy and satisfaction. Her arms went up and a hundred silent faces waited. Black faces. Bright, wide eyes. They swayed in the night, and John Merrimon was there, too. Blood pooled in the dirt. The bodies twisted. . . .

"Ms. Freemantle, please."

Cree opened her eyes, and the sun was shining. The lawyer was staring, his face very close.

"You went away for a minute." His hand was on her arm. "You don't seem well at all."

Cree shook off the hand, and for a while he was right. She watched her feet, and kept her thoughts rigid.

My name is Cree, short for Creola.

It's a family name.

My name is Cree. . . .

At the car, he gave her water and she kept her eyes on the ground. "Are you sure you're okay?" he asked.

She wasn't. "The waterfall is that way. Not far."

Cree took the lead, and for a while the dislocation faded. They followed game trails to a lone hill that rose as if cast off from those to the north. Cree remembered the first time she'd seen it. There'd been snow on the ground, a low, dull sky. "This is what you want."

The stone face was twenty feet tall, the waterfall loud in the silence. The lawyer shrugged off his pack and dug out one of the drawings. He held it up to make a comparison. It matched. "Now what?"

"I don't see any great, black eyes."

"Don't be flip."

But that's how Cree was when she got scared. She was dismissive and raw and rude. Otherwise, it was too real. Otherwise, she ran. "As a child, I was told to stay away from this place. Are you sure you want to be here?"

"I don't have a choice."

Cree said nothing in return, but this is why she wanted the lawyer here. So she wouldn't be alone. So she wouldn't run. They started across the glade, and he was going on about the dead deer, and how this was the place it happened . . . *the exact spot, just like the drawings and the newspaper story, Jesus Christ, exactly the same.* He was a talker when he got scared, and that was okay. They both felt it: the static in the air, the expectation.

Ten minutes later, they found the cave.

CHAPTER THIRTY-ONE

Johnny knew Jack was coming—he'd felt him for an hour—but he'd missed the girl until she actually appeared at the cabin. It was the second time he'd missed her.

No, he thought.

It was the second time he knew about for sure.

Johnny didn't like any of it. The invisible girl. Dreams of John Merrimon. A month ago, life had been as simple as preparing for winter. Now wood lay unsplit; the garden drooped under its own weight. Watching Jack fiddle with his cell phone, part of Johnny wanted to step from the trees as if it were a step through time instead. They'd open a bottle of something. Johnny would worry about the girl, but pour a glass for her, too. He'd be civil; maybe learn something about the past of this place. He'd not forgotten his manners. He could hold a conversation if he tried. But something about the girl made Johnny cautious. He wanted her off his land, wanted her gone.

Turning away, Johnny worked up into the hills, stopping at the tree where he often slept. From high in the branches, he looked down on the Hush, and had a sense of Jack making his way back to the old village. Between the two of them were miles of swamp and rough country, but Jack was his oldest friend, and Johnny would know the feel of him anywhere in the Hush. The girl remained hidden, but Johnny faced larger questions at the moment. After days of reflection and sleeplessness, it had come to this. Verdine had warned Johnny of the past.

She'd been emphatic, and he'd experienced enough to know the dangers of it. That life felt as real as this, and though there was darkness there, there was beauty as well. A wife. A child. Even now he felt the pull, and wondered if he could lose himself in all that lushness. It was the past—his family's past—and he thought maybe there were answers there.

Stretching out in the hammock, he peered through the leaves and into the same sky Marion would have known. Did she die so the child might live? Had John cut the baby out? As questions, they were worn beyond their age, but Johnny could think of little else: Marion and the child, this life that was not his own. Settling deeper, he drew one of Verdine's cigarettes from his pocket.

He stared at it for a long time.

Then he lit it.

John Merrimon was delirious with exhaustion and grief, but not so far gone he doubted word of the hanging would spread.

His foreman would swing. A white man.

John didn't care.

Kneeling at Marion's side, he smoothed her soaking hair. Her eyes were open, but unseeing. "Is the doctor here yet?"

"Word came from the river. He's at the ford. His horse is balking." Isaac hovered in the bedroom door, his big hands open.

"Send another horse, for God's sake! Drag him if you have to!"

Isaac left the room to deal with it. When he returned, he nodded. "It's done. Your fastest horse."

"And the lawyer?"

"Downstairs. He doesn't like it."

John nodded slowly. What man would? "Give him dinner and a bottle. He doesn't leave until I say."

"We have to move fast," Isaac said.

People would not stand for it: a white man hanged with slaves.

"Where are they now?"

"The foreman's in the cellar, bound and gagged. The slaves are outside, under guard."

"What's the mood?"

"People are grim. They're scared."

It was bad business, and they both knew it. Not a single name had been spoken, as if somehow that made it less real. It was the foreman, the slaves. "What about the girl? She understands the map?"

"She wants the swamp and the northern hills, the most inaccessible places you own."

It was six thousand acres, but John didn't care. He touched his wife's face, and when he looked up, his eyes were burning. "It's murder, Isaac."

"She says they raped her, hurt her."

"Do you believe her?"

"Does it matter?"

When the doctor arrived, John met him on the stairs. "I need to know if you can save her." He dragged the doctor upstairs and pushed him at the bed. "I need to know if she will live or die."

"Calm yourself. Please."

"Damn you, man! Tell me!"

"Very well." Displeasure deepened the doctor's voice, but he checked her temperature and pulse, then opened her gown and listened for the baby. When he stood, his face told the tale. "A fever this high would have killed most people by now."

"But?"

"There is no 'but.' Her pulse is weak, her breathing so thin, it's barely there at all."

"The baby?"

"Still alive, though I consider it a miracle. Have there been any changes since my last visit?"

John thought of the girl, and how she'd touched his wife, and how his wife had opened her eyes and said his name.

"No," he lied. "None."

"I can still take the baby—"

"Don't say that!"

"Mr. Merrimon. John . . ." He put a hand on John's shoulder. They weren't close, but he'd delivered John nineteen years before. He'd stood beside

John's father as he'd breathed his last. "I urge you to consider the larger picture."

"Not if it kills my wife."

The doctor sighed and nodded. "May I at least take a look at you?"

"I'm fine."

"No, Mr. Merrimon. You're not."

John knew it was true. He'd not eaten in six days. He'd not slept or bathed or left his wife's side. "Is there any reason for hope, any reason at all?"

"Are you a godly man?"

"I was once."

"Then I would pray for a miracle."

When he was gone, the girl came at last, and came slyly. "You know the land I want?" She stopped ten feet into the room, and John had a sudden insight into just how smart she was. Had she asked for the whole plantation, the county would have risen up. She wanted the dark places, the forgotten lands. "I want people, too. And tools for building."

She used a mix of English and her own language. John looked at Isaac, who translated.

"People?" John asked.

"My people, African people."

"Just heal my wife."

"There is a place your slaves worship. We will go there first."

"There is no such place."

"He knows."

She pointed at Isaac, and spoke in her own language. Isaac explained, looking ashamed. "Some of us worship in secret. She says it's the only place she will accept your . . . payment."

"Do you know this place?"

"In the swamp," Isaac said. "I know it."

She wanted the slaves to see, so they trailed behind. John looked back at the shuffling line, the condemned men on the buckboard that rattled and clanked as the path narrowed. "How much farther?" he asked.

Isaac rode beside him. "Not far." The air thickened as they neared the swamp, and when the sun set, they lit torches. "This is the place."

It was a clearing in the woods, a hollow place that smelled of mud and stagnant water. "There's nothing here," John said.

"That's always been the point."

John swung down from the horse, and held Isaac's gaze. "For Marion," he said.

"For your wife."

"Tell her to get on with it."

But the girl was already moving. She cut away the white man's clothes, then did the same to the other two. They froze as the knife moved, but the girl was not finished. She pointed with the knife and spoke in her own language.

"Isaac?" John whispered.

"She's telling them what she plans to do. She's taunting them."

She touched a penis with the blade, then an eyelid, the white man's lips.

"You can't stop it," Isaac said.

Even if John wanted to, he knew that he could not. The huddled slaves were in her thrall. They watched the foreman, the men who were like them. No one moved to help them; no one dared. "What's she saying now?"

"She's listing their crimes."

John looked at the foreman, but thought of his wife. The girl straightened and pointed at a great tree that rose from the clearing.

"She wants them hung from their ankles."

John knew what was coming; he could see it in her face. "Do it."

Men screamed as they were strung up, and John knew then that his soul was forfeit. There would be no joy in life, not if Marion died, not even if she lived. When the men were hung, the girl spoke to Isaac but kept her eyes on John.

"She says the deal is not yet done."

"Isaac, Jesus . . ."

"There will be one last thing, but you must agree now."

"This was the deal. This!"

"She says it is a small thing, a nothing."

John dragged fingers through his hair. He looked at the night sky, and Isaac spoke the sentence that was already formed and perfect in his mind. "What choice is there?" he said; and John, in his soul, knew the answer.

"No choice," he said. "I have no choice at all."

CHAPTER THIRTY-TWO

Clyde Hunt liked to drive with the windows down. He liked the smell of it, the cut grass and warm pavement—and he liked the sounds of it, too. There was something about the rattle of a mower, the crackle and fire of young men playing sports in the heat.

"Two-Allen-One. Dispatch."

Clyde keyed the radio. "Two-Allen-One. Go ahead, Dispatch."

"You have a call, Detective. Jack Cross. He sounds upset."

Hunt took a curve, saw young women arguing beneath the awning of a convenience store that had been robbed twice in the past year. "How upset are we talking about?"

"Two-Allen-One, I'd say *very upset*."

"Okay, Dispatch. Patch him through to my cell."

A minute later, Clyde was blasting east and north, the heavy cruiser leaning into the curves, sitting down on the flats. The windows were up. Otherwise, he couldn't understand a damn thing. He'd heard *Johnny* and something indistinct, and then, *he's dead, man, I think he's dead* . . . "Just slow down, son. I'm coming your way right now. Just slow down and breathe. I can barely understand you."

"Sorry, sorry. I've been running. Cell service. That damn swamp. . . ."

The connection crackled. "Jack, you're breaking up. . . ."

"You need to get here, Clyde. . . ." Static. White noise. ". . . hurry, man . . . holy shit . . . please hurry. . . ."

"Where are you now?"

"Roadside . . ."

"Roadside. Understood. But exactly where?"

Clyde saw Jack from a mile out. He rolled the needle from 90 to 110 and ate that last mile like it was nothing at all: a whisker of green, a shudder beneath his palm. Fifty yards out, he hit the brakes; the last ten, he was sliding. On the roadside, Jack was scraped and pale and bruised. "Are you okay, son? Come here."

"It's nothing. I'm fine."

"What's happening here, Jack? Where's Johnny?"

"I don't know."

Clyde let out a breath he didn't know he was holding. "You said someone was dead."

"We need cops," Jack said.

"Just breathe, son. I'm here."

"You don't understand." Jack bent at the waist, sucking wind. "We need lots of cops."

Clyde needed to see it for himself first. He drove to the church, pocketed a radio, and unlocked the shotgun from the dash. "That's your car," he said. "Why were you running?"

"Lost my keys."

Hunt pulled an emergency kit from the trunk and locked the car. "Tell me again about the cave."

Jack spoke as they walked, but didn't make a lot of sense. He was still wild-eyed and rattled. Concussion was a real possibility. "Just slow down," Clyde said. "Let's start with who's dead."

"I don't know, man. You're not listening."

"Just breathe, son . . ."

The boy's story made little sense: one man dead, another dying. Something about a waterfall, a deer, this hidden cave, and piles of old equipment. Hunt stopped when he saw the waterfall across the glade. "Where's the cave?" Jack pointed, and Hunt ducked low at the cave's mouth. "It looks shallow."

"You're wrong about that."

"What about the girl?"

"In the back, and down. There's a drop, and then it opens up. Cree's in there with the . . . uh . . . you know, with the dude."

Clyde studied the young man's face, then pushed the emergency kit and rope into his arms. "Take these," he said. "Stay behind me."

Hunt bent low, and the shotgun scraped against naked rock as he maneuvered his big frame through the narrow opening. Ten feet in, something shiny glinted in the dimness. "Your keys." He scooped them up and handed them back. Damp air stirred the deeper he went.

"Jack? Is that you?"

A voice rose from the gloom. A young woman. "Ms. Freemantle. My name is Detective Hunt. Jack Cross is with me."

"Hurry, please. I think he's dying."

Hunt slid deeper into the cave. Fifty feet in, the floor fell away, and he saw the young woman deeper and down. It looked like a man beside her, but everything was obscure in the gloom. "Give me the pack." Jack handed it over, and Hunt pulled out a half-dozen glow sticks.

He cracked the seals and dropped them.

They fell into a sea of bones.

Everything looked different under the floodlights. The stone was gray, the bones so old, they were almost black. Hunt watched technicians in white hazmat suits work across the exposed bits of rock, setting markers, taking photographs.

He struggled with the image.

The cave was not so wide as he'd thought, but deeper. The floor was littered with bones and bits of rotted cloth, an old pack, and a broken snowshoe. Farther in, he saw a brass lantern, a rusted rifle. If he had to guess at the number of human remains, he could not. They gathered in the low places. Some of the bones were cracked and chewed.

"Scavengers, maybe. Coyotes or something." Tom Lee joined Hunt at the drop. "How old, you think?"

"Some of it's pretty old, but not all of it." Hunt pointed at scraps of faded cloth. "That looks like Gore-Tex. Nineteen eighties, maybe. The rifle, though, that's a hundred years at least."

"What's going on here, Clyde?"

"Your guess is good as mine. Anything from the survivor?"

"He'll be lucky if he lives. He's sure as hell not talking."

"What about the dead one?"

"Twenty-four hours, maybe. Maybe forty-eight. You see his face?"

Hunt had. He glanced at the captain, a lean man with weathered features and a narrow mouth. Bent as he was, Hunt thought he looked coiled. That could be subconscious, though. Hunt knew what was coming.

"I'll need to talk to him, Clyde."

"Johnny had nothing to do with this."

"We don't know that."

Hunt gestured at the old bones and the old gear. "Some of that goes back a hundred years."

"Some of it, but not all."

Hunt looked back at the world outside. The day was ending. People moved in the glade. "You'll need help here. Forensic anthropologists. Pathologists. Forensic dentists."

"State police. FBI. Yeah, I get it."

"Still no sign of the sheriff?"

"He'll turn up."

Hunt picked up a pebble, bounced it on his palm. "You're not going to let me near this, are you?"

"The sheriff might say different. Until he does, the answer is no."

The sheriff was the wild card. He didn't like Hunt, but respected him. Captain Lee knew that. Then again, the sheriff hated Johnny, and that was no secret, either. "Come on," he said. "Let's get some air."

Outside, a dozen four-wheelers were parked haphazardly, mud on the fender wells, heavy cases on the racks. People weren't panicking yet, but a current was moving. Johnny had been a wild card since childhood, but it was different now, even for the harder cops. Little time had passed since William Boyd died in a way no one yet understood, and the rumors were rampant. Now there was this cave, the multitude of old remains, another fresh body.

An investigator called out from across the clearing, and Lee said, "Stay here."

"Yeah, no problem."

Hunt watched him leave, then let his gaze slide to the body bag stretched out in the dusk. After a moment's thought, he crossed the clearing and unzipped it. No one stopped him. No one said a word. Settling onto both knees, he spread the vinyl and peered down. The odor was bad, but Hunt was habituated to death smells. The face was a different matter, and Hunt leaned closer to study it from one side and then the other. The features were inflamed to the point of deformity: the lips, the tongue. His entire face was so swollen and dark, it was liverish. No one had ever seen anything quite like it. No one knew what to think.

"The hell are you doing, Hunt?" Captain Lee called across the glade, and people stopped what they were doing to watch. "No one said you could touch that body! Step away!"

Hunt did not. He had a few seconds.

"Detective!"

Hunt unbuttoned the dead man's shirt and understood why, in spite of everything, he seemed familiar. "Ah, shit." He studied the filthy skin, the scars. He looked again at the face, then stood slowly.

"What are you thinking, Clyde?" Captain Lee arrived. "Your stepson is a person of interest. You can't touch the damn body. Come on. You know better."

He bent to zip the bag, but Clyde stopped him. "You were with the sheriff in '07, right?"

"So?"

"In June of that year, he was stabbed four times."

"A meth head by the river, I remember."

"I'm sorry about this, Tom." Hunt drew back the dead man's shirt to reveal a cluster of scars six inches above the right hip bone.

"That doesn't mean . . . It might not . . ."

"I sat with him in the hospital," Hunt said. "I made the arrest."

To his credit, Lee kept himself together for the first five minutes. He huddled with his top people, and Hunt watched from his place beneath the tree with Jack and Creola Freemantle.

"What's going on?" Jack asked.

"I think it's about to get ugly."

"What do you mean?"

Hunt didn't answer. Lee was on the radio, his face pale at first, and then an angry red. He stormed across the clearing, and Hunt braced for it. "Does the name Waylon Carter mean anything to you?"

"Should it?" Hunt asked.

"He says the sheriff and a man named Jimmy Ray Hill came out here for a single purpose. Would you care to guess what?" Hunt said nothing, and the captain's eyes moved from him to Jack. The grief was unmistakable. So was the rage. "Where's your friend, Mr. Cross?"

"I . . . uh . . . what?"

"Don't screw with me, son. Where the hell is Johnny Merrimon?"

CHAPTER THIRTY-THREE

Johnny rose from the dream like a forgotten creature in a forgotten sea. Above him the sky was purple, the shadows beneath, the same. He felt police far away and, in the past, hanged men. Between them, Johnny drifted, and there was no peace in that place. Men were dying behind him, and Jack was out there, afraid. Johnny almost rose, but choice, in the end, was an illusion. He had nothing left for Jack, not even for himself. He sank back into the blackness, for that's what forgotten creatures did.

They surrendered themselves.

They faded.

John Merrimon was on his knees, the taste of vomit in his mouth. He couldn't look anymore, couldn't bear the screams. Isaac knelt at his side. "The girl says you must watch."

"No . . ."

"She says you must watch if you want your wife to live."

John did it for Marion's sake, but he watched the knife instead of the girl, focused on its movements rather than the things it cut. There was purpose in her eyes. She was playing to the crowd, showing her power. John saw it in the firelight. A white man was bleeding, same as the blacks. The blood glinted the same. The screams were the same.

"Dear God, have mercy on my soul."

It was a whisper only Isaac heard. "God is dead in this place."

And that, too, was her purpose, the killing of gods and expectation and systems. She was making this place her own, and some of the people, as well. John saw the ones who would stay. Their eyes burned, and they nodded as the knife moved. It was a line in the gathering as clear as any John had ever seen: those who looked down and cowered, those who watched.

It took a long time for the men to die, and when it was done, she drove the knife into the tree and stripped away the rags that were her clothes. Naked, she stood before the gathered slaves, and before her nakedness they bowed. John had never seen such silence in so many people. She spoke in her native tongue, her voice soft but loud enough to fill the clearing.

"Do they understand her?" John asked.

"Some," Isaac said.

"What is she saying?"

"That this is her land now, and that those who are willing and strong may live here as well."

"Tell her it's not done yet."

Isaac delivered the message. She spoke again and smiled. "She says to give her your jacket." The jacket was bottle green with gilt buttons and a velvet collar. John smoothed the front, then handed it over.

She wore it like a coronation gown.

The walk back was processional, and at the house, the crowd lingered. From the porch they were a sea of faces, and John felt the animosity. People had tasted blood. There were some who wanted more.

"Now my wife."

The girl dipped her head, and John led the way. He tried to ignore how she smiled out from his coat. He didn't care anymore, not about her bloody hands or the things he'd seen or the parts of himself he'd sold. But the girl was in no rush. She circled the room slowly, then put a palm on Isaac's chest, whispered in his ear, "She knows the power of words on paper."

"Fine," John said. "Bring the lawyer."

The lawyer came, and was disbelieving. "My God, man. You actually did it. You let a slave kill a white man."

"I had no choice."

"You'll pay for this. You know that."

"I'm sure I will. You've prepared the documents?"

"I wish now that I had not."

"The sooner we finish, the sooner you can be away."

"Very well." The lawyer opened his case. "I'll need legal names, et cetera. No woman has ever owned so much land, and certainly no slave. There will be repercussions—"

"I don't care about that. How much time to finish?"

"Not long."

They discussed names and particulars, and John sent him to the study with a warning. "If you leave before I say, I will hunt you down and kill you myself. Isaac, if you please."

Isaac took the lawyer's arm and guided him from the room. When he returned, John pointed at the bed. "Fix her," he said to Aina.

The girl did not move.

"Fix her or I'll kill you, too. I'll kill everybody."

The gun was in John's belt, and he was deadly serious. Were his wife to die, he would die with her. In some ways, that was better.

Eternity.

An escape from this shame.

"Do it."

The girl shrugged and laid a finger on the dying woman's face. For an instant the air hummed, then Marion's eyes opened, and she spoke as if she'd been awake for hours. "The baby's coming, John. I feel the baby. . . ."

John staggered for the bed, but the girl lifted her hand and Marion fell away again—the soul of her, the only part that mattered.

"Bring her back!"

"There is the final price—"

She spoke in broken English, but John understood. "Anything."

The girl rattled off in her own tongue, and Isaac spoke haltingly. "She wants a daughter."

"A daughter. Yes. Whatever she wants."

"For that she needs a man."

"What . . ."

But her intention was obvious. She cupped a palm between Isaac's legs, and when she spoke again, it was with the same satisfied smile.

"She says I will give her daughters, and they will be strong and fine."

"Isaac. Jesus . . ."

"She says you will give me to her now, or else the woman dies."

CHAPTER THIRTY-FOUR

It took Jack ten minutes to convince Captain Lee to leave him alone, and that was only because Clyde helped. "Just back off, all right! He doesn't know anything!" Hunt was yelling at the end, but Lee didn't buy it. Behind him, others gathered and watched and hated. They thought Jack knew, that maybe he was involved. "I said back the hell off. I mean it. He called this in. We wouldn't be here otherwise."

That made sense to Jack, but the anger overrode it, that sense of loss and betrayal.

"That's Willard Cline in the bag," Lee said. "Do you know how long I've served with him? How much he means to me, to all of us?"

"I don't know anything," Jack said. "I'd tell you if I did."

"Bullshit. You and the Merrimon kid go back forever. You think I'm stupid? You think I don't remember? And you!" He stabbed a finger at Hunt. "Don't pretend for a second that you're impartial."

"No one's pretending anything." Hunt showed his palms. "But you need to calm down. This is bigger than the sheriff. You know that."

"All I know is that I want your son."

"I don't know where he is," Jack said.

"Do you know where he lives?" Jack looked away from the question. "You help me with this, Clyde, or I swear to God I'll burn you down."

"You said it yourself. I have no jurisdiction here. FBI. State police. You should be making calls."

He wouldn't do it yet, not with daylight fading and the sheriff in a bag at his feet. Jack thought it was smart, though, the way Clyde reminded him that others would be watching.

Captain Lee leaned into Hunt as if some thin bond still connected them. "What if it was one of yours?" he said. "Your friend? Your boss?"

"I would do the job," Hunt said. "I would take the long view."

The stare between them held, but no one was convinced the captain would take the long view. Maybe in a day, Jack thought. Maybe tomorrow. When Lee turned away, Hunt watched him for a few seconds, then gathered Cree and Jack close. "Do you know where he is?"

"We were at his cabin earlier," Jack said. "He wasn't there."

"You need to find him and warn him. Keep him away until state police arrive or these people settle down."

"What? You mean now? In the dark?"

"I've seen what happens when cops die," Hunt said. "Revenge. The mob mentality. Here." He took a flashlight from an open case on the back of a four-wheeler. "Go to the cabin. They won't find it tonight, not in the dark. Find Johnny. Get him out of Hush Arbor. Does your phone have a charge?" Jack nodded. "Good. Keep it close. Jack, look at me. You have twenty minutes before it gets truly dark. You know where the cabin is. Johnny has to come home sometime. You need to be there when he does." Jack nodded, but was doubtful. Hunt turned to Cree. "You're not part of this. I can call someone to take you home."

"I'll stay with Jack."

"Okay, your choice." Hunt draped an arm over Jack's shoulders and squeezed tight. "Just stand here," he said. "Make for the trees when the shouting starts."

"Shouting?"

Jack asked it numbly, but Hunt was already walking. He circled the knot of county police, then knelt by the body and unzipped the bag a second time.

After that, the shouting came fast.

They went to the cabin, but Jack knew from fifty yards out that Johnny wasn't there. Ten seconds inside and a minute calling Johnny's name made the silence even starker. "Is there some other place he might be?"

Jack knew the tree in which Johnny often slept. It was on a hilltop to the north, a hard walk in full daylight. "Are you afraid?" he asked.

"We just found a pile of dead bodies. The cops are sure to be looking for us, if not now, then later."

"But other than that? You know . . ."

He meant the silence and the unusual stillness. She hugged herself, and felt the terrors of those early years. "When I was a child here, the days were special, like they could go on forever, just sunshine and all these trees, people working together for the common good. Planting. Fishing. People hummed when they worked. People laughed. That changed when the shadows got long. People moved a little faster. They watched out under the trees. I was inside by sunset and never allowed out after. It felt like something terrible, the way people talked about it, like something solid or alive. Few risked the darkness."

"Do you know why not?"

Cree considered the question. Truth was, only the old women moved freely at night, and then only two together or maybe three. "All I know is that people got edgy with the sun going down. They got their work done, then locked the doors tight."

"Jesus."

"Are we going inside?"

"Yes, God yes."

Jack fumbled around inside. He found matches, lit candles. Cree stepped in behind him, studying the fireplace, the bed, the books rowed on a shelf. "This is where he lives?"

"Sort of." Jack opened one cabinet, then another. "Let's have a fire and some food. Then we can decide what to do. I'll get wood."

He went outside, and Cree sat on the edge of Johnny's bed. This was his place, a Merrimon place. Drawing the knife, Cree tilted it against the light, then touched the edge and watched a line appear on the pad of her thumb. A drop of blood rose, and she felt a strange stirring in her chest.

Tilting her head, she listened to the sounds outside. The lawyer was stacking wood in his arms. Wind moved the trees, and when a nighthawk made its sharp, electric call, she pictured its looping flight, the long wings with a white blaze beyond the bend.

How did she know that?

She'd left the swamp as a child, and cared nothing for birds. But she knew the nighthawk laid its eggs on bare ground, that they came in summer to breed and left for the winter in great flocks. Cree spread her palms where Johnny slept, and felt pressure in her skull, like something was trying to get inside. She wanted to burn this place, to wipe it so clean, only the earth would remember.

Why?

Her head ached. She was sweating. Pressing her palms against her temples, Cree rocked where she sat and knew the moment something broke.

She was Aina.

She was Cree.

"Stop it," she said, but there was no clearing outside, no city lights beyond the wood. Her face was broader and scarred. Her heart was filled with anger.

"Ms. Freemantle . . ."

Too many memories.

Too much hate.

"Go away," she said.

"Ms. Freemantle?"

"Leave me alone. Please."

Cree was on her feet with no memory of standing. Jack was in the doorway, and wood clattered as he dropped it.

"Sit. Come on. Sit down."

Cree didn't argue. She was faint. Her head was splitting. "Take this chair. Here." Cree sat and put her face in her hands. "Just breathe. You're fine." His hand was warm on her back, but her thoughts were not fine.

She wanted to hurt Johnny Merrimon.

She wanted to make him scream.

The sky was moonless when they left. Footing was treacherous with a single flashlight, so Cree stayed close at the lawyer's back. He was solicitous, concerned.

"Watch your step. Careful, now."

Moving onto high ground, she struggled with the contradictions inside. All she'd ever wanted was a purpose in life, some calling beyond the safety of a bolted door. But all of that was gone now. She watched her feet, and struggled with the pressures in her mind. Right foot, left foot. She blinked and saw a river of blood.

"We'll find Johnny," the lawyer said. "We'll find Johnny and we'll figure this out."

He was battling his own fears, but Cree knew from long experience that those demons were not so easily slain. They found dark corners and chose words that made you weak. Such was the demon in Cree's mind. It said Aina was stronger; it said Aina lived.

"Are you okay back there?"

"Yes," Cree lied, but she didn't trust herself or know herself. When they found the right hill, they clambered up until an oak tree spread above them. Its limbs were enormous, the trunk as thick as any she'd ever imagined, thicker even than the hanging tree. Touching it, she had a single thought.

This tree was old when Aina was alive.

It was another thread that spun out in the night.

"Johnny!"

The lawyer's light shone into the branches, and she saw something high above. "Is that him?"

"There should be a hammock. . . ."

It looked right to Cree, the bend of it and the length. The lawyer called out again, but nothing moved where Cree thought she saw the hammock. "I'll go," she said.

"Are you sure?"

She ignored the eagerness that took her into the lower branches. She didn't want to hurt him, didn't want to kill him.

"Be careful, please."

Already, the lawyer seemed far below, his light shining upward as

Cree moved up into the smaller branches. When the trunk forked, she followed the larger spine, and where it forked a final time, she found the hammock and the man in it. Darkness hid the details of his face, but she knew the cheek, the slope of his jaw. He was moaning in his sleep, his eyes rolled white.

"He's here."

"Is he all right?"

Cree didn't answer. He was helpless a hundred feet up. . . .

"Ms. Freemantle?"

The lawyer called up, and it helped. "Hey." She tried to wake him, but the word came softer than she'd planned. "Johnny," she said; but the name was wrong. *John,* she heard, and the sound of it was a wind in her head. She went away for a moment, and when she returned, the knife was in her hand and against his throat.

Do it!

It was not a voice, but an echo. She touched the blade to his skin and felt want so profound, it was need. She saw him on horseback and at the river. Were his eyes to open, she would know the exact shade—a brown so deep, it was black.

Do it for us. . . .

She tilted the knife and saw its edge, the killing edge. In that moment, she was ready to open his throat, there beneath a rising moon. It was that close—the same eagerness—then she looked into his rolled-white eyes and understood the horrible truth. It wasn't a dream at all, the echo in her head.

It was a touch.

It was a taking.

CHAPTER THIRTY-FIVE

Helicopters came into the skies of Hush Arbor twenty minutes after the sun did. Hunt heard them before he saw them, a murmur as they neared, then the rattle and clatter as they thundered overhead. Rising from his car, Hunt scrubbed sleep from his eyes to watch them circle and bank. One was owned by the sheriff's department, and had the distinct markings he knew so well. The other was unfamiliar. State police, maybe. Maybe a loaner.

Squinting at his phone, he looked for Jack's number, then punched it in as the helicopters banked a final time above the old village before working off in separate directions, one moving due north, the other bending north and west. Hunt held his breath as the number cycled and the phone struggled to find a signal.

"Damn it."

Hunt shoved the phone in his pocket. He'd been up most of the night, trying to contact Jack or Johnny, trying to calm his wife. She didn't know everything, but law enforcement was a small community, and she'd been catching the whispers that something bad had happened in the swamp. Hunt had said: *Trust me, sweetheart, please.* But how long could he expect that to hold? An hour more? He doubted it. Not with the sheriff dead. Not with Johnny in the mix. It was the troublesome side of the boy's notoriety. People knew his name. The fascination remained.

Hunt considered the phone again. The nearest dependable signal was four miles away, one of them on dirt roads, the last three on old pavement. Ten minutes away. Maybe twelve.

"Where are you, son?"

As questions went, it was pretty desperate. The sheriff's department had flooded in overnight. On duty, off duty. Hunt had counted a dozen retired deputies before it grew too dark to count much of anything. They'd established a main command center in the old church, and kept a presence, too, at the cave. All night people had moved between the two. Flashlights. Floodlights.

Everything but the torches . . .

Ignoring his hunger, Hunt circled the clearing, trying to pick up information, anything. Most were steady enough, but it was clear that no one trusted him. People he'd known for twenty years, some even longer. He'd get a nod or maybe not. No one answered his questions. *Have you found anything yet? Where are you looking? What about cause of death?* All that mattered were the simple facts of the sheriff's death and Johnny's potential involvement.

They had history.

He was dead on Johnny's land.

Beyond that, it came down to the years. Willard Cline had been the sheriff of Raven County for four decades. People knew him and loved him. People owed him. Normally, that was a good thing. Not today. Today, a pair of deputies stopped Hunt as he stepped onto the trail that would lead him to the cave. "Uh-uh. Sorry, Detective."

They didn't look sorry at all. Hunt gauged the tension in their shoulders, the way both men rode the balls of their feet and watched to see if he might push back. "Are the state police coming?" he asked.

"We're not to talk to you or to let you pass. Orders."

"What about FBI? Scientists? Any outsiders at all?"

"Just you."

Hunt gave it a four-count, then turned back the way he'd come. At the car, he saw a truckload of rough, slouch-hatted men rumble into the clearing and stop beside the church. They spilled out onto the damp grass, worn-looking outdoorsmen, men with rifles rubbed shiny from years of hard use. Hunt knew one of them from a disabled-veterans fundraiser he'd put together years ago. He was big and heavy, but good on his feet, good in a fight.

"Timmy Beach." Hunt culled the big man from the group and led him to a quiet place beside the church steps. "What are you boys doing out here?"

"Tracking."

"Sheriff's department brought you in?"

"It's not like they could do it on their own."

"You're no friend of law enforcement. I'd wager none of you are."

"You'd win that bet. We're doing this for Jimmy Ray Hill."

"What about Jimmy Ray?"

"He's the survivor. They didn't tell you that?"

"Jesus." Hunt turned away, trying to process. He knew Jimmy Ray. Not well, but well enough. "Listen, Johnny didn't do this—"

"Let me stop you right there, Clyde. Okay. You see that fella there, the big one with the Winchester? That's Jimmy Ray's brother. The young one beside him—the skinny one with all the hair—he put baby number two in Jimmy Ray's daughter. Course, the only reason I'm telling you any of this is because my brother still goes on about how that money you raised cleaned up his doctor bills and bought those new prosthetics. Changed his life, he says. I think he might have killed himself otherwise. You can consider this conversation your payback."

"You can't go in there armed. Even the sheriff's department knows better."

"We're considering it a don't-ask-don't-tell kind of situation."

Hunt ran a hand through his hair. He saw the danger so clearly. "Your friend's alive, Timmy. All this eagerness I'm seeing, the anger . . . you need to dial it down before somebody gets hurt."

"Jimmy Ray lost most of one leg and half of the other. His back is broken."

"My son did not do that."

"Were I in your shoes, I might share the same conviction, but we all know Jimmy Ray and the sheriff came out here looking for your boy. That was their intent and sole purpose. My guess is they found him."

"Timmy—"

"I'm sorry, Clyde. One way or another, I intend to see this through."

Timmy walked off after that. He said a few words to the other men, then stomped up the stairs and into the church.

Things were going sideways.

Hunt felt it.

Sliding into the car, he fired the big engine and drove four miles to find reception. He'd already been there twice, a sandy verge with views of the distant city. He called Johnny and Jack first, but was shunted straight to voice mail. Speaking quickly but clearly, he explained what was happening, and left the same basic message.

If you're in the swamp, leave.

If you're already out, stay away.

After that, Hunt did something he'd never done.

He called reporters.

He called lots of them.

CHAPTER THIRTY-SIX

Johnny moved from one awareness to the next as if being drawn through a hole in a wall. Aina was grinning in the firelight, then she was above him, but the scars were gone. She had the same dark eyes but different lips. The sky beyond her was a morning sky.

"Where am I?"

She looked away, and yelled at someone below. "He's awake."

Johnny tried to rise, but was belted into the hammock. "What . . . ?"

"You spent most of the night thrashing about. I thought you might fall."

"I'm going to be sick."

"Go ahead, then. Get it over with."

"It's Cree, right?"

"Don't talk to me like we're friends."

She slipped from view, and Johnny tried to gather his thoughts. This was his hammock, his tree.

That meant Aina was long dead.

So is Marion. . . .

Johnny's stomach flipped again, and he almost lost it. He touched his face, the tree. "Jack! Are you there?"

"I'm here!"

Of course he was.

Jack.

Good old Jack.

Johnny lay still, and rolled the dream in his thoughts.

Isaac . . .

Twisting in the hammock, Johnny cupped his body around the unexpected hurt that was Isaac. Isaac had raised John and stood by his side. Johnny pictured him on the Persian rug before the bedroom fire. He saw Aina's eyes as she toyed with him, then Isaac's face as the understanding spread.

Isaac . . .

John had been speechless.

It's okay . . .

It's not . . .

For your wife, Isaac had said. *For the mother of your child, and for you . . .*

John Merrimon had wept at the kindness, the sacrifice. . . .

"Hey, man. Are you coming down?"

Johnny knew that some kind of trouble waited below. He could feel it in his friend, and in the Hush, felt cops and movement and anger. He tuned it out to think again of the life he'd never lived. Verdine had warned him of the dangers of dreams. *Life can pale,* she'd said. *This life, yours.*

"Johnny, man, come on. I want to get the hell out of here."

"All right, Jack. Keep your pants on."

Stripping off the belts that held him, Johnny descended to find Jack and Cree, the both of them dirty and sleepless. "Here. Thanks." He handed over the belts.

"You okay?" Jack said. "You're bleeding."

"What?"

He pointed, and Johnny touched his throat, dotting his fingers with blood.

"It's just a scratch," Cree said.

But Johnny recognized the lie. The line on his throat was straight and razor thin. "The hell?"

"I said it's just a scratch."

"What's going on here, Jack?"

"All right, listen . . ."

Jack spoke like a lawyer laying out the facts of his case. He kept it linear and clean: the cave, the cops, the bodies. Johnny drank it like a sponge. He ignored the feelings, the thoughts of so many dead in this place he loved. "What about you?" He gave Cree the full stare. "Why do you care about any of this?"

"You're not the only one with questions."

Johnny filed that under *half the story.* She kept her eyes neutral, but couldn't hide the dislike and distrust, the awareness so entrenched, it was animal. She looked like Aina; she had Aina's blood. Johnny's spine prickled. "Why were you in the tree?" he asked.

"Someone had to watch you."

Johnny touched the line on his throat. "What day is it?"

"You're shitting me, right."

Johnny wasn't. He could have been in the hammock for two nights, or even three. His whole body ached. The hunger was crippling; so was the thirst. "Just give me a minute."

He turned away, needing time to think. Cops were in the Hush, and Sheriff Cline was dead. Cree seemed to know things, or at least feel them. "You say they found someone alive in the cave?"

"I think he's in ICU."

Johnny looked down on the distant swamp. He wanted his life back, his home. But then there was Jack.

"We need to leave," he said. "Now."

"And go where?" Johnny asked.

"Someplace they won't find you."

"I haven't done anything wrong. This is my home."

"Trust me, J-man, as your friend and your lawyer. You don't want to go down there until things have settled."

Johnny decided not to argue. He needed food. He needed to think about the dream and Cree, and what it all meant.

"Okay," he said. "I know a place."

Leon's was empty so early in the day, but Leon was there. Johnny saw him as they crossed the field beyond the washout. He was turning meat on the giant cooker in the back of the sprawling bar. Johnny recognized the tilt of his head, the massive shoulders. Even before he turned, Johnny knew what was coming.

He looked like Isaac.

It was the broad face and deep-set eyes, the steadiness and the easy smile. Johnny saw it slide onto his face, then disappear just as quickly. He looked at Jack and Cree, then closed the lid on the cooker and wiped his hands on an apron. "What's all this, then?"

"Good morning, Leon."

"Johnny." His eyes flickered on Jack, but settled on Cree. "Young lady."

"How's your chest?"

She said it flatly, and Leon didn't smile.

"You know each other?" Johnny asked.

"We've met," she said, and after that it got awkward. Cree said nothing else, and Leon had trouble meeting her eyes.

"You'll be wanting breakfast, then?"

"Yes, please."

"Sit anywhere. I'll be along in a minute."

Johnny led the way inside, and they took a table with views of the bridge. "How do you know Leon?"

"You know how this place is," Cree said. "People go back. Everything's connected."

"That doesn't answer the question."

"Do I owe you an answer, really? You of all people?"

The anger that time was unmistakable, and Johnny didn't need a special awareness to catch the implication.

Your family owned all of this. . . .

All of us . . .

They'd met only once before, but this was something new between them. Johnny thought he understood. "Does the name Verdine mean anything to you?" She looked away, jaw twisting. Johnny leaned closer. "What about *Aina*?"

"Aina?" She said it fiercely. "You're asking me about Aina? You?"

"That's right."

Her fingers found a knife on the table. "Just order your breakfast, all right. Order your white eggs and your white toast, and don't pretend to know me."

But Johnny thought maybe he did.

"I'm going to call Clyde," he said. "Jack, can I use your phone?"

"No signal."

"Then I'm going to get some air."

Johnny walked out onto the first covered porch. When he was clear of the window, he dropped into a crouch and let himself go for just a minute. It was too much all at once: the dream and the waking from it, bodies in the Hush and this sense he had of Cree.

She'd wanted to kill him.

He'd wanted to kill her back.

That line still ran from one side of the wall to the next. Recognition. Emotion. Aina and John Merrimon.

"Jesus Christ . . ."

His palms were rough on his face, but real. What else was real? What else was insane?

Behind him, the screen door screeched and Isaac stepped out, carrying coffee. "You look like you could use this." He handed down the cup, and hooked a thumb at the door. "Bacon and eggs," he said. "How about you?"

"Throw in some pancakes and grits."

"Jeez, man. Hungry much?"

Johnny didn't smile back. With the light on his face, Leon didn't look quite so much like Isaac. He had the same shape, but was not so large. The eyes were lighter.

"Are you all right, my friend?"

Johnny looked away. Isaac. Leon. Who was he kidding? They looked the same. "I'll eat out here, Leon. Thanks."

"Your friends?"

"Make an excuse for me, will you?"

Leon went back inside, and came out later with breakfast. Johnny took it to a chair at the nearest table and ate by himself. Sunlight was bright in the east, but the day was still cool. That changed as Johnny worked his way through the eggs and pancakes and bacon.

The sun rose higher.

A cop car rolled onto the bridge.

Leon was making biscuits when Johnny ghosted inside, closing the door with a whisper of sound. "Everybody down, everybody quiet."

Leon came into the room as the other two stared dumbly.

"Cops," Johnny said.

Moving to the window, Leon watched the car roll to a stop. He disliked cops as much as anyone, but he'd never seen Johnny Merrimon care one way or another. "Sheriff's deputy," he said. "Grayson. I've met him before."

"Get rid of him," Johnny said.

"Why?"

"We're not here, okay. You never saw us."

Leon was enough of an outlaw to lie for just about anyone when it came to the cops. "Clear the table. Get in the kitchen."

They did what he said, and Leon stepped outside with a rolling pin in one hand and white flour halfway up his arms. The deputy met him under the second roofline. "Leon," he said.

"Deputy Grayson."

"I'm looking for someone. Was wondering if maybe you'd seen him."

"Nope."

"I haven't given you a name yet."

"Doesn't matter. I've been here since five thirty. You're the first person I've laid eyes on."

Grayson frowned, taking his time. "He lives back that way. Johnny Merrimon. You heard of him?"

"Most everyone has."

"Does he come here?"

"Why do you care?"

"We think he killed Sheriff Cline."

"Am I supposed to be sorry for the loss?"

Leon wasn't. Sheriff Cline had caught him once running bare-knuckle fights in an old barn five miles down the road. Gambling, assault, illegal liquor. He'd dangled those charges for ten hard minutes, then walked away with a wink and a nod. He liked to eat and drink, as it turned out, mostly for free. He liked to slum it, too: farmworkers, waitresses—the poorer, the better.

"You know, the sheriff always had a soft spot for you, Leon." Grayson crossed the last porch and peered in the windows. "He knew you stepped over the line from time to time, and chose to look the other way. You should respect that memory. You should help me out."

"Your sheriff took more than he gave."

"Maybe. Maybe you're being unfair."

Leon leaned against a post and crossed his arms, the rolling pin like a child's toy in his large hand. "You say he had a soft spot. Fine. Maybe he did. Or maybe he let me slide because of the dirt floors and rusted roof, and because I keep pickled pigs' feet on the bar. Maybe he liked eating and drinking for free, and liked young women, too. Maybe he was a white man feeling good about his whiteness. Maybe he was no friend at all."

"It could have been like that," the deputy said. "Could just as easily have been that he was a simple man in a complicated world, that he liked your ribs and whiskey, and thought you were doing no real harm with your fights and your gambling, your moonshine and your tax-free cigarettes. Maybe he talked to me about it once or twice. Maybe he explained to me that he could relax out here in a way he never could in town, that there was beauty in simplicity and that paved roads weren't always good things. Maybe he thought you and yours got short shrift in this world, and deserved a little compassion. Now—" A card appeared in the deputy's hand, and he put it on the table. "—every cop in the county is within a few miles of here, and none of us are leaving until Johnny Merrimon is dead or in cuffs, so do us all a favor. You see him, you give a jingle."

He tapped the card once, then crossed the dirt lot and slid into the county cruiser. When he was across the bridge and gone, Leon brought Johnny and his friends out of the kitchen. "Is it true the sheriff's dead?"

"It's true," Jack said.

Leon kept his eyes on Johnny. "Did you kill him?"

"No."

"Why did you run?"

"Who says I'm running?"

"You're here, aren't you? The cops are looking."

Johnny leaned onto his elbows, not smiling but almost. "There's not a cop alive who could find me in that swamp. Not a thousand cops at once, not in a thousand years. Not even you could find me."

"That's pride talking."

"Maybe."

"What about you?" He spoke to Cree. "You're what? Eighteen years old? Why are you involved with this mess?"

She shrugged, and he looked at Jack.

"I go where Johnny goes."

Leon followed the glance, and let his gaze linger on Johnny's features. He was the only city boy Leon had ever liked, the only white face. "Do you want me to get you out of here?" he asked.

"Where would we go?"

"My grandmother's place," Leon said. "She knows you. She knows Cree. Besides, no cop would go there."

"Is that right?" Jack asked.

"Oh hell yes." Leon stood, and was certain. "Not even the sheriff bothered Verdine."

Johnny kept his eyes on Cree as the three of them slid into the rusted, dirt-strewn bed of the pickup truck. Leon got them low in the bed, then drew up a tarp to cover them. "Stay down and still," he said. "It's not far, but Deputy Grayson won't be the only cop on the back roads."

"It seems over the top," Jack said.

"And yet I have no reason to lie."

He tucked the tarp around them, weighting the edges with bits of cinder block. The space beneath the tarp was blue and dim; it smelled of gasoline and old grease. Cree was curled on her side beneath the cab window. She was watching Johnny's face, and trying to conceal her emotions. For another man, it would have worked, but bits of awareness lingered, and Johnny knew two things at once: that, in Cree, the anger was winning, and that Leon did, in fact, have some reason to lie. It was a cloud on his thoughts, a flicker when he thought no one was watching. But Johnny could watch with his back turned and his eyes closed. From under the tarp, he saw Leon clear as day.

He steered the truck across the bridge.

He was unhappy about the lie.

"How do you know Verdine?" Cree asked.

"She knows things," Johnny said. "I sought her out."

"What things?"

"Stories of your family."

"That's none of your damn business."

"Stories of my family, too." Johnny watched the resentment move on her face. If emotions were color, hers would be purple-black, streaked with red. "Tell me about Aina," he said.

"Screw you."

She turned away, but Johnny saw the battle inside.

A blaze of orange, he thought.

A bonfire in the night.

Leon drove slowly, and dust rose as the old shocks complained and gravel pinged off the undercarriage. Verdine was doing things that made little sense. He humored the old lady because she was all the family he had left in the world, and because she'd been harmless, more or less. Keep an eye on the swamp, she'd said. Keep an eye on Johnny Merrimon. He'd never actually expected to meet Johnny Merrimon. He was just a name, a kid.

Leon rolled his right shoulder, feeling stitches pull where the little bullet had gone in, tumbling. It had torn through his pectoral muscle, glanced off a rib. Even now, he didn't know why they'd gone to that rat-box apartment in that rat-box city.

Six years.

That was the length of their unlikely friendship. Johnny was white. His stepdad was a cop. Then there was Leon's abiding distrust of white society. Verdine had raised him that way; she'd fanned the flames.

Look what they *have.*

Look what we *have.*

It had never been pleasant to look at straight on, but the woman had a hole in her heart that a hundred years of life had never filled. Small as she was, she was always hungry.

Bring him to me, she'd said.

Every chance you get.

Leon glanced at the tarp in the rearview mirror. Last Christmas Johnny had given him a pair of deerskin gloves he'd made himself. Before that, it was a rifle scabbard, and before that a wild hog, not just fully dressed but carried through the hills on his back besides. Leon had been hunting the deep woods for almost fifty years, and knew how hard it was to carry two hundred pounds of meat over broken ground. That was blood and sweat, serious hard work. What did an old woman want with a man like that? Leon turned the questions as he drove. She was crazy, he decided. Just a crazy old woman.

But he thought of the hunger, too.

When the turn came he took it, his truck rolling through the stream, then up the far bank. Verdine was on the porch, standing and watching.

Like she knew they were coming.

Like she was waiting.

CHAPTER THIRTY-SEVEN

The first reporter arrived at nine minutes after eight. Tom Lee learned of it from the rookie he'd left on the roadside specifically to make sure no one wandered into his crime scene.

"Uh, Captain Lee? Come in, please."

Lee keyed the mike, already unhappy. "What is it, McGreevy?"

"Uh, sir. I have a reporter here."

"What?"

"Yes, sir. Um, Ellie Pinkerton."

Lee pictured Ellie Pinkerton in his mind's eye. Late thirties. Moderately well known to the Raven County voters. She had a small overbite, and a voice too high-pitched for serious news. "Can she hear me right now, McGreevy?"

"Yes, but—"

"Walk away, son. I'll wait." He didn't want to wait; he wanted to hit something. When McGreevy came back on, he said, "What the hell is a reporter doing on my crime scene?"

"Sir, I—"

"How did she find out?"

"I don't know."

"What did she say? Wait, scratch that. Give me your cell number. We're not doing this on an open channel." The rookie gave his number, and Lee dialed it. "What does she know about my crime scene?"

"She heard there were bodies. She said there was a cave—"

"Shit."

"She has a camera crew, sir. They're filming me right now."

"All right, listen." Lee surveyed the command center. "I'm sending two more men your way. You keep those reporters on the state road. No one gets in."

"There's just the one reporter, sir—"

"Shut the hell up, son. Where there's one, there'll be more coming." Hanging up the phone, Lee shoved it into a pocket, then tracked down two uniformed officers he trusted. "Come with me." They fell in behind, and Lee banged on the top of Clyde Hunt's car. The city cop rose into the heat, and the deputy wasted no time. "Who did you tell?"

"What do you mean?"

"Don't bullshit me, Clyde. Who did you call?"

"State police. FBI."

"This is my jurisdiction. They won't come without a call from my office."

"True, but now they're waiting for it. They're gearing up."

"Goddamn it. Who else?"

"Reporters."

"Which ones."

"All of them."

Lee nodded at last, angry with himself. He should have kept Hunt close, should have seen it coming. "All right, Clyde. I understand why you did it. I'm not happy, but I get it. You—" He pointed at the two deputies. "—get him off my crime scene, then stay out there with McGreevy and keep everyone else out. Nobody gets in. Not even the state police. Not unless you call me first."

He turned away, but Hunt wasn't finished.

"People are watching, Tom. Keep your people in check."

Hunt was right, and Lee knew it. For a man as hard as Willard Cline, a lot of people had loved him, and they were worked up now. It was the way he'd died. His face. That goddamn cave. Taking the church steps, he surveyed the map tacked up on the wall inside. Thirteen teams were on foot in the swamp. Nineteen patrol cars worked back roads around Hush Arbor. Two helicopters were in the air.

"Any word yet?"

A female deputy worked the radio from a camp table they'd set up in the corner. "Lot of interference out there. Not everyone's in touch."

"What's the longest gap?"

She threw out some names and times. Ninety minutes for two of the teams. For another, multiple hours had passed. That was bad. Teams were to check in at the top of every hour. "Anything good?" Lee asked.

"Hang on."

She pressed a hand against the headphones she wore, then keyed the microphone. "Chopper Two, say again, please." A pause. "Roger. Stand by." She stripped off the headphones, twisting in the chair. "Ask me your question again."

"Anything good?" Lee asked.

"Chopper Two just found his house."

Lee took the microphone. "Put it on speaker." She flipped the switch, and static rolled onto the dial. "Chopper Two, can you confirm location?"

"Roger, Dispatch. Stand by." A second passed; then the pilot gave the coordinates. "There's a clearing. We're setting down."

"Signs of movement?"

"There's something—"

"Is it Merrimon?"

"What the hell is that?"

"Chopper Two—"

"Stand by, Dispatch." Static. "Jamie, you seeing this?"

"Chopper Two—"

"Stand by! Stand by! Jesus Christ. Sweet Jesus—"

Lee heard a scream, then static. "What just happened?" He handed over the microphone. "Get them back."

She tried for two full minutes. "Nothing. I'm sorry."

"Shit." Lee went outside, staring northward. "No, no, no. You. Come here." A deputy came to his side. "Give me a boost."

"Really?"

"Now, damn it."

Another deputy came over, and two of them boosted Lee high enough to clamber onto the church roof. It was metal and steep, but he climbed to its peak, and stopped there, breathing hard. To the north, smoke rose.

A great boil of it.

A hard, black plume.

Finding the wreckage was a foregone conclusion. They had the coordinates, the pillar of smoke. When they reached the site, everyone was sweaty and filthy, their faces streaked with blood from the switchgrass and brambles. "Oh my God." Wreckage littered the clearing. Even the cabin was burning. "How many men?" Lee asked.

"Just the pilot and a spotter." The radio operator was at Lee's side. She'd insisted. "Ravenwood had the stick—"

"The spotter?"

"Jamie Kimmel."

"Ah shit." Ravenwood was sixty-three years old, a veteran. Kimmel was just a kid. "All right, people. Spread out."

They moved into the clearing, keeping their distance from the hottest parts of the fire. It looked as if the helicopter had struck the upper branches of a single tree, then cartwheeled past it, breaking apart on impact and slamming into the cabin. The tree still burned. The fuselage was charred and gutted. Flames guttered on the inside.

Lee saw the pilot from thirty feet out, still strapped in and smoldering. The spotter was on the ground fifty feet away, half his body blistered and burned.

"Jamie!"

The radio operator dropped at the wounded man's side, and Lee remembered only then that they'd been dating for a while. "Medic!"

The medic was a retired deputy and almost seventy years old, but he'd been a corpsman in Vietnam, and hadn't lost a step. He worked hard and fast, stabilizing the boy as best he could, prepping a syringe of morphine.

"I need to talk to him first."

"He's in a lot of pain, Captain."

"I understand that."

"For God's sake," the girlfriend cried. "Give him the morphine! Get the other helicopter in here!"

"Jensen." Lee glanced at one of his deputies, then dipped his head toward the radio operator. "Please."

Jensen did his best to calm the moment, but emotions burned as hot as the fire. The second helicopter was en route back to town—Lee's call. Until he knew what caused the crash, he couldn't risk other lives or other aircraft. He asked the medic, "Can the boy hear me?"

"He won't want to talk."

Lee leaned over the boy. One eye was blistered shut. "Can you hear me, son?" A nod. Tears on the boy's face. "What happened here?"

Kimmel tried to speak, but the words died in his throat. He swallowed; tried again. "There was no tree," he said.

"What?"

"There was a blur. We were coming in—"

"A blur?"

"There was no tree at all," he said. "There was no tree at all, and then there was."

CHAPTER THIRTY-EIGHT

Johnny took the steps to Verdine's porch with more caution than the last time. He felt the years behind them, his family and hers, hanged men and the Hush.

"So," she said. "This is a fine picture."

"We don't intend to stay long."

She stepped aside to make room. Leon hung back, but Cree and Jack followed Johnny up. "Creola," she said, then glanced at Jack and dismissed him. "Does your mother know you've come?"

"Let's leave her out of this," Cree said.

"A wise choice for one so young. Come. Sit." She motioned them to chairs on the porch. "Leon, don't stand out there like a bump on a log. We need another chair." When they were seated, she reached for an old transistor radio that sat on the railing, antennae extended. "You've been busy, haven't you?" She dialed up the power, and they listened to local radio coverage of the gathering storm. Rumors swirled of dead policemen and a mass grave. Reporters were being held at bay. Further rumor spoke of manhunts in the swamp, and of potential FBI involvement. "Wait for it," she said.

Two minutes later, the reporter mentioned Johnny's name.

"Why are you smiling?" Johnny asked.

"Because knowledge is power, and you lack the knowledge you need. Because you require my help, and it's time, at last, I ask for something in return."

"I don't need anybody's help."

She turned on the radio again. In thirty seconds, Johnny's name was mentioned twice more. *Facing potential murder charges, local resident Johnny Merrimon is the subject of this very intense search. . . .* Turning the knob again, Verdine rocked, and in the silence waited.

"What do you want?" Johnny asked.

"For you to walk with me." She rose, leaning on a cane, and Johnny walked beside her in the yard. "Tell me about your latest dreams."

"Who says I'm dreaming?"

She laughed quietly, still walking. "I've known dreams and dreamers for a hundred years. Don't lie to me, son. You dreamed of John and Aina. I see it on your face, and in the way you look at Cree. How far did the dream take you? The hanging tree? The baby?"

"The baby lived?" he asked.

"Your great-grandfather."

Emotion welled up in Johnny's chest, so unexpected and strong, he had to look away. "How do you know these things?"

"All my people knew the stories. They dreamed themselves or spoke to those who did. A few dreamed more than once, and most of those poor souls fled the swamp or lost themselves in the darkness. That's the most common dream for my people, the closeness and damp, the rich, black earth."

"What about Cree?"

"Cree is the last of her kind. She dreams her own dreams."

"Dreams of Aina."

"She's a direct descendant, mother to daughter. You see how they are the same?"

Cree stood alone at the rail, watching them. She looked the same as Aina, small and narrow-waisted. She stood the same, held her head the same. "She hates me," Johnny said.

"Do you blame her?"

"She wants to kill me."

"You or John Merrimon?"

Johnny closed his eyes. "What do you know about the cave?"

"I know there are truths you must discover for yourself."

"You mean another dream." She looked away, pursing her lips. "I just want my life back, my normal life."

"There is no 'normal' in the Hush. There is only story and magic."

"There is no magic."

"Don't play with me, boy. I know truths you can't dream of, stories of sacrifice and love and horrors that will make your hair turn white. I've walked beside the great dreamers, and seen what rises in the night. No magic! Please. You have the stink of it all over you."

"What do you want from me, Verdine?"

"Your dreams. Haven't I been clear?"

"What about Cree? She's your family."

"Cree cannot dream this dream. Only you can. Only a descendant of John Merrimon."

They put a pillow on the floor because Johnny could never sleep in something as soft as a feather bed. Jack was beside himself. "Johnny-man. What the hell are you doing here? Seriously."

"Just keep an eye out, will you?"

"For what?"

Johnny didn't have an answer. He was too long from the Hush to know the thoughts or reasons behind Verdine's request. She'd said Cree could see only through Aina's eyes, as he could dream only through John's. Logically, that made sense.

Logic . . .

Johnny's lips twisted at the thought.

"The hell are you smiling at?" Jack demanded.

"Just don't go anywhere."

"Are you ready, young Merrimon?"

Johnny looked up at the old woman. Beyond her, Leon leaned against the wall, frowning. Cree was bitterly unhappy, but Verdine didn't care, and neither did Johnny. They'd closed the blinds. The cabin was dim and still. "What am I looking for?"

"Aina. I want to know where she's buried."

"How do I do that?"

"Do you remember her face?"

"Yes."

"Picture it in blackness." The old woman drew smoke; handed the cigarette down. "Picture open eyes and dirt falling."

Sleep for Johnny did not come easily or quickly, Verdine's special cigarette notwithstanding. Eyes were on his face, and Johnny felt them the way any man would. "This isn't working."

"It will. Just breathe."

Johnny tried for an hour, then imagined a curtain around him, a black cloth that rose beyond the ceiling.

The pillow was soft.

The floor was not hard.

For another hour there was stillness in the cabin; then Johnny twitched once and bolted up screaming. Jack tried to hold him down, but could not. Leon added his weight, but Johnny fought and clawed, and drew blood. He was choking and half-crushed, so he fought like a dying man.

He was not himself.

He was.

He screamed until something tore, and in the darkness he was blind.

CHAPTER THIRTY-NINE

Luana Freemantle felt forgotten and used up and pointless. It was not a new sensation. She sat on the sofa and flipped from one channel to the next. Not every station was talking about it, but three of them were.

. . . Official police sources are characteristically tight-lipped, but it's impossible to miss the feverish level of activity here on the northern edge of Raven County. . . .

Behind the reporter, an ambulance rushed by, lights spinning. Police cars followed it. In the distance, a plume of smoke rose.

. . . While dangerous to speculate, sources close to the sheriff's department indicate that multiple bodies have been recovered. Of unusual significance is the apparent age of some of the remains. With no official statement from authorities, we can only speculate as to the veracity of these claims, but the sheer volume of police indicates that something large is, indeed, happening. I've counted no less than twenty official vehicles in the past hour as men and material move ceaselessly into this vast tract of wilderness. . . .

Luana turned it off, thinking of her daughter. Before Cree, the future had been like a shiny dime far out on an empty road. She'd thought it would be so easy to walk out there and pick it up, but the dime never came any closer. She'd thought boys might take her there, and when they could not, she'd decided that men might be better suited. Somewhere along that road, she'd dropped Cree like an afterthought.

Maybe a kid would be fun.

Maybe that would keep her man close.

Four husbands later, Luana understood the painful truth. There was no dime on that road, and there never had been. Closing her eyes, she thought of her daughter. Only Cree had the shine now, and she'd run away from home, drawn to whatever place the dreams took her. She'd be in the Hush or with Verdine. Maybe she was one of those bodies found dead in a cave. Luana chewed on how Verdine had stolen Cree away with her talk of dreams and Aina and *choice*. There was no choice! How many had gone crazy from the dreams? How many had killed themselves? That old bitch had her own agenda, and it was a dark damn business. Would she risk Cree to get what she wanted? Of course she would. It's why she'd been driven out in the first place, that selfishness and greed, that heedlessness.

"And what about you, Luana Freemantle? Have you been any less selfish?"

That was an ugly question, but Luana tried to face it straight on. She'd been hungry for that shiny dime. She'd chased it blindly, and in her tireless pursuit of it had sent her only daughter back to life in the Hush. Had the old women lived, Cree would have been there still. Luana admitted that guilt. She breathed it in, then considered the pistol in her lap and rose with it in her hand.

It was time to put her child before herself.

Time, at last, to be a mother.

CHAPTER FORTY

Johnny rose up kicking and screaming. "Get away! Get the hell off!" He found his feet like a punch-drunk fighter. "Damn it. God . . . damn—"

"Johnny—"

"No," he said. "Just stay the hell away." His hands found a hard plank wall, and he pressed his face into the wood. He saw the grain of it, and beads of sweat on the edge of his nose. "What the hell just happened?"

"I don't know, man. You tell me."

Jack dashed blood from his nose; pressed it with a handkerchief. Leon had a gash on his cheek, a swollen lip. Cree's hand was at her chest, and only Verdine seemed calm. "What did you see? Tell me quickly."

"Nothing—"

"Don't lie."

"I saw nothing," Johnny said. "I was in the dirt—"

"No, you weren't."

"I was. I can taste it."

"No!" The old woman drove her cane into the floorboards with such force, it was like a shot. "You cannot have had that dream! It is born of Aina's pain, *her* suffering!" Verdine looked at Cree. "What do you have to say about this?"

"I . . ."

"Speak, child!"

"I wanted him to feel what I felt, what Aina felt. I was pushing. I wanted him to suffer."

"Why?" Johnny asked.

"Because John Merrimon is the one who buried her alive."

"That wasn't me."

"Yet I see you in the dreams. I see you both."

Verdine shook her head. "None of this is possible. We dream of our people. He dreams of his."

"Screw all of this," Johnny said.

"Johnny, wait—"

But Johnny pushed past his friend and went outside. His chest ached from dreams of choking. The rest of him hurt from Leon and Jack. No one had been soft or gentle. Johnny was bruised and bleeding. He knelt at the creek and splashed water on his face. Air moved down his throat; it came back out. Hurt as he was, nothing real had changed.

He wanted answers.

That meant he had to risk the dark again.

Johnny made it different this time. "I want everybody out."

Ten minutes had passed since he knelt at the creek, yet everyone looked the same. They stood in the same places, as if rooted. "Johnny, come on, man."

"You, too, Jack. Outside." Johnny turned to Cree. "If I wake up in a grave, I'll blame you for it."

"I'll try to think nice thoughts."

"Just get out." He watched her go, then faced Verdine. "It would be helpful if I knew exactly what I was getting into."

The old woman straightened above the cane, but seemed smaller, somehow. "Foreknowledge might affect the vision."

"I don't care."

"All that matters is the location of Aina's grave."

"Why?"

"Need you ask? Really? You know what she feels."

"You mean *felt*. Past tense." She stared blankly, and Johnny frowned. "What makes you so certain I can find her?"

"John Merrimon shot Aina twice, and buried her in the swamp. No one else was with him. The memories are his alone."

"Say you're right and I find this grave. What's in it for me?"

"I'll answer any questions that remain about the place you call home. I'll make Hush Arbor yours alone in every way that matters, all its secrets and history. You do this for me, boy, and I'll give you everything you ever wanted."

She was selling hard, but Johnny still didn't trust her. "I didn't kill anybody," he said to Cree. "Maybe John Merrimon did, but it wasn't me."

"Just find her."

"You want the same thing?" he asked. "Same as her?"

"Yes."

"Then keep your thoughts to yourself," he said. "Don't put me in some damn grave."

After that, it took a long time.

He heard their whispers beyond the door.

He closed his eyes and tasted dirt.

When sleep arrived, it came as softly as a blush. It wasn't there, and then it was. The dream came next, and it began with Isaac.

His face glistened, and it was night outside, torches beyond the glass.

"They've come," he said.

The mob was moving down the drive beyond the great porch. Fifty people. Maybe more.

"How many do we have on the front door?"

"Four."

Some of John's men remained loyal, in spite of everything. They guarded the door, rifles in hand. "How about the back?" he asked.

"Two more."

"It'll be enough."

"I hanged a white man."

"On my orders."

"It won't matter," Isaac said. "They want me to hang next."

"Yeah, well . . ."

John checked the loads in the heavy revolver he wore at the waist. They were in his study, John and Isaac and the lawyer. Aina stood at a different window, watching the crowd. The lawyer sat at the desk. "Finished," he said.

"The slaves?" John asked.

"Freed."

"And the land?"

The lawyer glanced at the girl by the window. She was ignoring them, but he lowered his voice nonetheless. "In Isaac's name alone, as you requested."

John opened the safe and drew out a stack of notes. "You should go out the back," he said. "It's safest."

The lawyer took the money and donned his hat. "I'm not sure you'll survive this. I'm not sure you should."

John thought maybe the lawyer was right. He didn't care. "Back door, Isaac. Show him out." When Isaac returned, John pushed the deed into his hands. "Six thousand acres, my friend. For you and your family. For your sacrifice."

"That's not what she wanted."

"She won't know the difference until it's too late."

"Why are you doing this?"

"Maybe it will give you some leverage in the days that follow. Maybe it will make this bearable, somehow." John lifted a rifle from the rack and laid a hand on the sheaf of pages left by the lawyer. "These are documents of manumission, one for each of our people. If I don't come back—"

"You will."

John nodded, but shouts rang outside. He spoke above the din. "Not everyone will wish to stay with her. For those who do not, I've arranged transportation north—" A window shattered as a rock sailed through, struck the fire tools, and scattered them. "Whatever happens, you stay inside."

"Are you sure about this?"

"You saved my life." John smiled. "Freedom. Land. My love and respect. How else could I ever repay you?"

John left him with the girl, and at his bedroom door, he stopped.

His wife was smiling up.

The child was at her breast.

Even in his sleep, Johnny choked at the sight.

She was alive.

She'd named the boy Spencer, after her father.

The dream almost broke then, but it moved instead. He was staring down the mob, the rifle in one hand. Stars paled above, but the dream was moving again.

He was in the swamp.

His heart was broken.

"Where is she, Isaac?"

"John, my God. What are you doing here? How long has it been?"

"Since last we spoke, three months."

Another eight had passed since the night of the mob, but Isaac had aged a dozen years. A beard covered his throat, and much of it was white. John was hardscrabble, too. His boots were worn through, his own beard ragged and long. He'd cut new holes in his belt just to keep his pants from sliding off his narrow waist. How long since he'd slept? He didn't know. All he had was the rage, the need to move and do and kill.

"Where do I find her?" he asked.

"She'll know you're coming a mile before you get there."

John stared out at the black and starless night. Beyond the water and through the trees, lights glinted where the small cabins stood. "She's truly so powerful?" he asked.

"Life. Death. The unthinkable." Isaac's large head moved. "There is no god in heaven to explain the things I've seen."

John swallowed his disappointment and fear. "How many people remain?"

"Seven children have been born. Nineteen adults remain."

"Will they help me?"

"They fear her," Isaac said. "They fear and love and worship her."

"Then I must ask a final favor."

"Name it."

"I need your help if she's to die."

Isaac bowed under the weight of John's words. "Is your life so terrible, you would risk it?"

"The house is burned, the livestock either slaughtered or stolen. People have been unforgiving. We live in fear."

"And your son?"

"He grows strong."

"And Marion . . .?"

"Unchanged since last we spoke."

"I'm so sorry."

John looked away. He could not speak further of his wife, could not think of her, as she'd become. "Aina must die, my friend."

"And if it's you, instead. What of your son?"

"I've found a woman who will provide."

"John, please—"

"Aina or me, Isaac. One of us dies tonight."

For an instant, Johnny rose above the dream. He did not know what was wrong with Marion, only that they lived now in squalor, and that the boy liked to play in the morning light: a rosy child on a narrow bed, one hand wrapped around his mother's finger.

Why was the image so sad?

The dream was moving fast, just bits and pieces now: the gurgling boy, the mother at his side. Johnny felt that note again—*sadness*—then understood as the dream took him down.

Her hand was lifeless on the bed.

It was lifeless and warm and unfeeling.

Night changed to dawn before John found the place Isaac had described: a cypress far from the water's edge, a forgotten giant with a hollow space between its roots that was large enough to hide a man. "A quiet place," Isaac had said. "A gentle place for making children. Dawn is a favorite time, and she thinks of little else. My presence will distract her."

John was folded between the roots when first light came. His view was of mist and moss and trees across a narrow glade. Licking his thumb, he cleaned dirt from the sights. Would she know his heart, as Isaac feared? Would she feel it? In secret, John had met Isaac twice before, so he knew something of Aina. She was kind to those who'd stayed, but intemperate; and the rage, once upon her, was fearsome. She demanded loyalty and love and, from Isaac, all the children in the world. Their first daughter was two months old. She wanted a second.

"She says the time between night and day is blessed, so the light will be gray when we come. If the sun rises above the trees, then I have failed, and you should leave. She owns this swamp, John. She owns it in ways you could never understand."

John had no reason to doubt. She was a giver of life, and a taker. . . .

He shied from thoughts of what she'd taken, thought instead of muzzle control and trigger discipline.

Let her come, *he thought.*

Dear Lord, if you love me . . .

And the Lord, it seemed, loved him. John saw movement in the trees, and heard a girlish laugh that ill fit his memories of Aina. She held Isaac's hand, and walked with her head up and a sway in her hips. She stopped once to draw him down and kiss him full on the mouth. It was a long kiss, and full of promise. John laid his cheek to the stock and sighted down the barrel. He, too, had promises to keep.

For Spencer, *he thought.*

For Marion.

Aina stepped onto the moss, and Isaac was a half pace to her side when John drew the hammer to full cock. She heard or sensed it, her small head snapping around, the jawline tight as her eyes moved unerringly to the place John hid. She opened her mouth to speak, but John squeezed the trigger without hesitation. She dodged at the same moment, moving fast enough to cost him the heart shot he wanted. The bullet, instead, struck her arm and shattered it. It spun her sideways, and onto moss so soft, John didn't feel his feet as he ran from the cypress and stopped above her, his revolver out and pointed. In spite of the ruined arm, she rolled onto her back, the black eyes flashing.

"For God's sake, John. Do it!"

Isaac was desperately afraid. John felt it, but his own glee was stronger. She'd lied. She'd stolen.

"John!"

She'd taken so much. . . .

"Do it now or die yourself!"

Isaac was right. There was no joy here, only justice and need and hate. Isaac opened his mouth again, but John didn't want to hear it. He crossed himself for the sake of his soul, then shot her in the chest instead.

CHAPTER FORTY-ONE

Luana took the car without asking. Her neighbor was passed out drunk, and things were bad between them, anyway. She'd accused Luana of stealing the pistol from her glove compartment. Luana had denied it, but both of them knew the truth. The end of their friendship wasn't about the stolen pistol or borrowed money or any of the little things they squabbled about. Luana wouldn't go to the bars anymore. She wouldn't wear the short skirts or fishnets or the red lipstick. She'd given that up. She was done.

"You won't last a day," the neighbor had said, and Luana feared she might have been right. Her hands shook as she fumbled with the keys. She tried to steady herself. The backseat was stuffed with boxes and bags—everything from the apartment that had any kind of value: clothing and pots, a toaster, and Cree's extra shoes. She didn't really know what else. The packing had been a blur of sweat and tears and the fear she'd get caught; but no one stopped her. A couple of boys eyed her lazily. An old woman watched from a window on the third floor.

Luana looked once at her own windows, then rattled out of the city and onto the back roads leading north and east. The route took her through small towns with liquor stores and open bars, but she kept driving. Once across the Raven County line, she felt the prickling of childhood fears. Verdine was the story told to frighten children. She was the taker, the untrusted, the one they'd driven out.

Do as you're told, child, or she'll come for you, too. . . .

Now she had Cree.

Skirting the edge of town, Luana steered for Hush Arbor, and two miles out, she felt the difference. Cars passed where there had never been cars before. Police cars. News vans. The roadblock was set up twenty yards after the last turn off the state road. A dozen vehicles waited to be let through or turned away. Luana pulled onto the verge and studied all the official men with their badges and vinyl belts and hard-edged guns. The radio said state police had come, at last, and that the FBI was en route from the field office in Raleigh. For a while, she watched a cop she knew. He was Johnny Merrimon's father—she'd seen him in court. He stood at the tree line, speaking to an older man in a uniform. Luana closed her eyes, trying to process all the energy and movement. Hush Arbor had never been about engine noise and radios and crowds from the city, and it surprised her how much that sense of wrongness bothered her. Didn't she hate the swamp? Hadn't she left? Digging in a kitchen box, she found a small, sharp knife, and tested its blade against her skin.

For her daughter's sake, she planned to challenge Verdine.

She'd need to make an offering first.

Clyde Hunt had been a cop for decades, and had connections everywhere. The media. State police. Especially the sheriff's department. Yes, Tom Lee had frozen him out, but the captain couldn't be everywhere at once. He sure as hell wasn't on the roadside.

"Talk to me, Clint."

Hunt guided an older deputy into the shade. They'd worked cases together back when Hunt was green. They went to the same church, shared a few friends.

"No one's found him yet, if that's what you're asking."

"And?"

The deputy looked uncomfortable. His boots were muddy. He'd been on his feet a long time, in and out of the swamp. "You know about the helicopter?"

"It went down, I heard."

"It crashed into Johnny's cabin—"

"Jesus."

"People are scared, Clyde. I mean truly afraid."

"Of what?"

"The way the helicopter went down. Some other things."

"I need you to be more specific." Clint frowned, and it cut deep lines at the eyes and mouth. Clyde realized, with a shock, that he was frightened, too. "Clint?"

"That helicopter should not have crashed."

"Accidents happen."

"Charlie Ravenwood has been flying for forty years. Desert Shield. Desert Storm. He was decorated twice. You knew that, right?"

"I did, yeah."

"He flew into a tree."

Clyde tried to picture it. "I don't understand."

"He hit it sixty feet up and spun off into the cabin. There's not a cloud in the sky. There's no fog, no wind. There're other things, too. Communications are breaking down. Radios work and then they don't. Men are getting bogged down and lost."

"Operational mishaps—"

"No, Clyde! You're not listening!"

Hunt was listening now. In thirty years, he'd never seen Clint raise his voice outside of an arrest or some kind of violent disturbance. "All right, then. Talk to me."

"When I say people are lost, I mean that literally. Two men from two different search parties. They're just gone, vanished."

"That's not possible."

"I don't know what to tell you, Clyde. They were there and then they weren't. People are shaken. They're spooked. But that's not the worst of it."

"What?"

"We still have teams out there. We still have people missing."

Colson Hightower knew very little about what was going on in the swamp or, for that matter, in the world beyond Raven County. He'd become a sheriff's deputy to make his mom proud, and because he'd thought the uniform might make him more handsome, somehow. He'd been right about both things. His mother forgot about his lack of will, his failures, his years as a middling student. She thought he looked snappy and fine in the brown polyester uniform; and so did Jenny Clayburn. She'd married him, after all, and they'd been together for twelve good years. They had a dog and a small house with a garden where Jenny liked to grow tomatoes and cucumbers and carrots. Watching her do that work gave Colson no small amount of pleasure: her hands in the earth, her soft, round figure in cutoff jeans and one of his old shirts. She'd put him in the shade, bring him a beer, and say, *Relax, enjoy, you've had a hard day making the world safe.* She always smiled when she said it; she smiled and smelled of warm earth and growing things, and her lips were soft on his cheek.

Colson thought of Jenny's garden as he trudged through the swamp, the last man in a line of exhausted men. This part of the job was not so fun. He liked riding in the car and doing paperwork and cleaning his gun once a week, even though he never fired it. He liked making safety presentations to kids at school, and working the football games on Friday nights, and having a beer with the other deputy once the stands were empty and everyone safely off school grounds. He liked the clean parts of the job, the safe, predictable parts, and didn't mind when the higher-ups got angry with him, or frustrated with his lack of ambition. He had the uniform and he had Jenny, and that was enough.

He held on to those thoughts as the swamp tried to break him. It was the mud and the heat, the loss of radio communication, and the fact that no one knew where the hell they were, even though the old man guiding them fought in a war and trained soldiers and was supposed to be infallible in the woods.

He wasn't.

He got turned around and lost, and led them off dry ground so many times that they twice used rope to haul out one of their party who got so bogged down in the mud, he couldn't move.

So, Colson thought of his wife as he walked. He tripped on brambles and went down in the mud; and when he rose, dripping, he was still thinking of Jenny. Her neck was red from the sun, but she smelled of that garden, and of the lotion she liked.

Lilac . . .

That was the smell. Lilac and bruised stems and soft, warm dirt.

"Jenny."

He said her name, and it did not seem strange to speak it aloud. They were crossing shallow water, and no one heard him over the splashing and the cursing. Colson slowed his pace, and when he heard Jenny singing, her voice was so clear and sweet, he stopped walking entirely. It was a song she sang in the garden, and for a long minute, Colson stood with his head tilted, trying to catch the notes that hung in the air like the last, faint peal of a distant church bell. The other men were moving away, but he wasn't worried. Softness welled in the air, a fog he couldn't quite see. Colson smiled because the sense of his wife grew, as well.

You sweet man . . .

Colson couldn't see her.

Come to me. . . .

The words were in his head, and the swamp was a mist that swirled and faded. He stood on green grass, and Jenny was on her back beneath him, the round arms up, a knowing smile on her face.

You poor man . . .

She drew him down, and put his head on her chest. He was crying, and didn't know why. It was all so big. The world, its expectations . . .

Just breathe, honey. Just breathe . . .

The grass was strange and formless and wet, but she was his Jenny, and she smelled of things he loved: his house and his yard, the garden and the memories, the lilac on her skin. She held him tightly down, and Colson had never known such completeness and bliss. In his arms was the embodiment of everything he'd ever wanted, so Colson breathed deep, and did not think it strange that his wife was so wet or that the smell of her was thick as water. He dug his fingers into the soft richness that was Jenny. He drew her into his lungs, and was as joyful as a man could be, warm and fulfilled and drowning in the things he adored.

Luana turned the car around and parked a mile away. When she was ready to go, she slipped into the woods like a runaway child, home at last. The trails were roads that welcomed. The trees made rooms, and she remembered them from those long and lonesome years. She'd had little enough in childhood, and the forest had been her life: the long walks and silent halls, the yellow light that walked beside her. When the dreams began, only the forest had time for her tears. Her mother wanted the details, to hammer out every little thing in hopes of enlightenment or understanding. Grandmother had been worse, and that was the curse that came from eighty years of dreaming. The need for an ending consumed her. Was it any wonder Luana ran or that, even now, the hate walked with her, too? She considered herself an abandoner, a recreant to a twisted faith, yet she followed the same trails and heard people far off in the swamp. Staying clear of them was not difficult. The cemetery lay south of the old church—a half mile through the trees—and she moved heel to toe, knees bent. At the stone wall, she climbed over and knelt beside a marker to stare across the garden of her people. It was quiet in the clearing, and only the blackbirds moved. They lined high branches at the hanging tree, and watched as Luana neared. At the trunk, she wasted no time.

"This is for Aina."

She used the blade to open her palm.

"Give me your courage, your will to survive."

Luana was supposed to offer *her* courage and *her* will, but her people were gone and the world had changed. Did that make her choices wrong? Luana knew only that, homeless in a cold world, she'd returned to close the circle. Her hand was on the tree, and so was her blood.

It glistened wetly, then dulled.

She watched as the tree drank it down.

CHAPTER FORTY-TWO

Johnny woke in the pages of another man's life. He felt the brush of them in his mind: an image, a word, the memory of a wife. He saw her on the pages, the way she'd held the boy and lifted him from the bed as if to say, *This is us, our life.* Johnny held that memory closest because the other pages were so terribly dark. Ten days after the baby's birth, Marion neither moved nor spoke. She didn't know John's face; didn't know their son. How many months had she stared at the same spot on the ceiling? A lifetime, it seemed. Forever.

Johnny tried to stay in that happy place, but remembered other trips into the swamp, the way he'd begged and crawled and, finally, threatened. Aina had dismissed him each time, refusing even to speak.

Maybe next time, Isaac had said.

Maybe next month.

Johnny understood Isaac's fear of Aina. Marion didn't eat or sleep. She barely breathed, yet did not fade. She was perfect in every way but the one that mattered.

What have you done with my wife's soul?

That was the darkest page of all, an echo of screams. She was alive but dead. Dead but alive.

Johnny rolled onto his elbows and knees, not yet himself or in the present. He saw Aina's eyes as her life spilled into the mossy earth. He felt her anger and fear, her closeness to death.

Bring me a shovel, he'd said to Isaac. *And then go to your daughter.*

Isaac left and returned. After that, Johnny knew the weight of her body, the place she was buried.

"Dear God—"

He sat up on the floor. It was dim in the cabin, and he was sick down in his soul.

"Who's Marion?"

Johnny peered out from bruised eyes. Jack was on a chair at the narrow table. No one else was inside.

"What are you doing here?" Johnny asked.

"You were calling out in your sleep."

"The others?"

"I wouldn't let them come inside."

Johnny dragged himself up and took the second chair. "How long was I asleep?"

"I don't know."

Johnny touched his face. The bones were his, not John's.

"What's going on, Johnny? What is all this? Why are we here? Really?"

"You wouldn't believe me if I told you."

"Try me."

"I can't."

"I said you were calling out before. That was a lie. You were screaming bloody murder."

"Jack—"

"Leon stopped me the first time I tried to come inside. The old woman said what you were doing had to run its course, that if I woke you, it would be for nothing. I threatened to call the police. It's the only reason she agreed."

Johnny leaned back in the chair. Lifting an edge of the curtain, he saw Verdine and Cree and Leon. Only Verdine looked happy.

"She said if I woke you, she'd kill me. I believed her, Johnny. I think she's dangerous."

"She wants something from me. That's all. I'm watching her."

"Have you looked in her eyes? Watching's not enough."

"Just bring her in, all right."

"Not until you tell me what's going on."

"I can't."

"Then I want to go home."

Johnny understood. Jack was a creature of logic and rules, an educated man bound to a system Johnny no longer trusted. Could he accept the truth, were Johnny to share? Not a chance. He'd see risk where Johnny saw beauty, danger rather than something glorious and grand. It didn't matter that the past was troubled and grim. They were his people, his beginnings. "Go if you want to, Jack. I understand."

"Damn it, Johnny. Don't do that."

"What?"

"That calm acceptance thing you always do. Can't you be needful, just once? Just once, can't you admit that we're the same?"

The hurt was so obvious in Jack's face that Johnny didn't need to think about it at all. "Of course we're the same," he said. "Like brothers."

"Do you really want my help?"

"You're my best friend, Jack. Who else is there?"

"The two of us, then?"

"Like old times."

"All right, then." Jack rose to his feet, grim but satisfied. "Was that so damn hard?"

When Verdine came inside, she moved sideways and slow, and looked to Johnny like a bottom-feeder searching for the scent of something dead. She wanted what he knew. She wanted to sink her teeth into it, consume it. That energy lit her face so the dark eyes shone. "Well, boy? We all heard you screaming."

"I know where she is."

The old woman shifted above the cane. Nothing else moved, but the change was hard to miss. "Tell me."

"Why do you want to find her so badly?"

"That wasn't our deal."

"It's a simple question."

"Leon." The old woman stepped aside, and Leon shouldered through the narrow door. "How did I raise you to handle deal breakers?"

"I'd rather not get involved," Leon said. "Johnny's a friend."

"I don't care about your friendships or your druthers. Do it like I told you." He hesitated. "Don't pretend to understand me, boy, and don't presume to know better. I told you what I want. Now, do it."

Leon met Johnny's gaze. "I'm sorry about this." He lifted his shirt to show a revolver wedged behind the belt. It was large and, in places, rubbed silver.

"Does that even work?" Johnny asked.

"I shot it twice twenty years ago. I'm thinking it still works fine."

"What if I don't tell her? You going to shoot me?"

"This doesn't have to be complicated, Johnny. You answer her questions. She answers yours. Everybody gets what they want. We all go home."

"All right." Johnny glanced at Jack, then shrugged because he'd known all along he'd take her to Aina's grave. He'd wanted a better read on Verdine, though, and now he had it.

Dangerous, Jack had said.

Jack was right.

They rode in the same truck under the same tarp, and for Cree it was all about the breathing: in and out, looking for the calm. She knew the difference between Johnny and John, but they were so alike. Looking at Johnny's face, she saw betrayal and pain, the black eyes as dirt rained down. She concentrated on Verdine instead. She'd come into the village once when Cree was only seven. There'd been shouting and anger. Cree had watched from the door—too young to understand the anger and movement—but the old women had talked about it that night.

Her wants are impure. That was Grandmother, at the stove.

Lustful? Great-grandmother asked.

Not just lustful, no.

Wanton?

Yes, that's the word. Grandmother's hands moved, and grease popped in the skillet. *The woman is shameless and lustful and wanton.*

Cree had been too young to understand the words, but she never forgot the disapproval in those lined, old faces.

Wanton . . .

Cree had looked up the word once. It meant many things.

Dissolute.

Malicious.

Unrestrained.

Luana knelt in the dirt by the hanging tree, humbled by the same religious awe that had terrified her as a child. The bark was dry where she'd touched it, and she felt the spread of branches above, the twine of them and the deep, cool shade. The tree was so damaged and massive, she couldn't believe it was still alive. It had been ancient when she was a child, and older than most when men were hanged from its lowest branch. It was failing at last, but was still the tree of her childhood; it still held up the clouds.

Luana wrapped her palm in a scrap of cloth, thinking of that childhood and the small knife and the dreams they'd said would come. From an early age, they'd told her: *We feel Aina as few others do, the women of our line. The dreams are our burden and our gift.*

If lives of poverty, misery, and thankless commitment were gifts, then, yes, the old women had been blessed indeed. But had they ever been happy? They'd had each other, of course, and men on occasion. Luana remembered smiles and kind looks and a million conversations by the stove. Were it not for the tree, she'd argue that they'd been benignly crazy, just crazy old women, forgotten in the swamp.

But the tree was hard to ignore.

The tree and the dreams.

Leaving it behind her, Luana sought out her mother's grave. It lay in a sunny place near the eastern wall, and the inscription carved into it was simple. A CHILD OF DARK EARTH, it read, and few would understand just how many chords those simple words struck. They spoke of Africa and Aina, of long struggles and the muds of Hush Arbor. It was too much for Luana: the sweep of time and family and endings.

"I'm sorry," she said. "I'm sorry I wasn't there to say goodbye."

She touched the stone, then spread out on the grass and lay like that for a long time. The sun set and night fell, but Luana didn't care. She was in the garden with the mothers and daughters who'd gone before. Now the line was at an end. There was just her and Cree, and they were leaving.

"Where are you, baby girl?"

Rising at last, she climbed the wall and made her way back into the woods. She thought of Verdine, who'd been driven out. That's where Cree would be, with the taker, the untrusted. Luana left the cemetery behind and turned for darker trails. She walked for five minutes, then saw it, far out in the trees.

A whisper of movement.

A flicker of light.

Hunt was on the roadside when the sun settled, and still there when something fundamental changed. A vehicle emerged from the swamp, then another, then seven more in a ragged, mud-spattered line. The men inside wore sour expressions, and looked neither left nor right as they rolled past reporters who shouted questions and trailed them with cameras. Hunt made a mental inventory as they passed. Woodsmen, volunteers, retired cops. He waited until he recognized one of the drivers, then flagged the truck down.

"Brinson. Hey."

The truck rocked onto the verge, and stopped. In the fading light the driver looked grim. They all did.

"Detective."

Brinson was a retired drill instructor who'd moved up from Fort Benning ten years earlier. Early seventies, he was still one of the toughest men Hunt had ever known. Two other men were in the truck, both younger and clean-cut. Hunt didn't recognize them.

"What's happening?" Hunt asked. "Why are you pulling out?"

"Nobody's seen your son yet, if that's what you're asking."

"It's not, but I appreciate the information." Brinson kept his eyes straight ahead. Beneath the weather-beaten face, he was pale. Hunt would swear he was pale all the way down to his soul. "You want to tell me what's going on?"

"I lost a man."

"What do you mean?"

Brinson showed the eyes at last. "I mean he's dead."

"Who? How?"

"A sheriff's deputy named Colson Hightower. Young guy. Married. You know him?"

Hunt pictured a deputy in his early thirties. A little overweight. A little lazy. "I've met him, yeah."

"He was part of my group, and got separated. When I went looking, I found him facedown in eighteen inches of water."

"Drowned?"

"Captain Lee thinks he had help."

"Not Johnny—"

"That's how the cops are calling it, but I saw Hightower's body up close. I pulled him out, and he looked as soft and peaceful as a baby in its mother's arms. I swear to God, Clyde, he didn't have a mark on him. Poor bastard was almost smiling."

Hunt strung that image into the movie playing in his head. How many dead? How many wounded? "Why is everyone leaving?"

"They've ordered out all nonessential personnel. State police are involved now, and they plan to go tactical first thing tomorrow. More helicopters. More men. Three cops are dead. You see it."

"Yeah, I see it."

"Listen, Clyde. You've always been a straight shooter, and I appreciate that, but all those men there, all those hunters and hard men—" He pointed at the line of trucks far down the road. "—not one of them was sad to leave. A good hunt, a fair fight—they love it. Hell, I do, too. But the rest of it—grown men disappearing, choppers crashing on windless days. It's not right, what's happening here, and those fellas there—" He pointed again. "—most of them are smart enough to know it."

"Come on, Brinson—"

"Eighteen inches, Clyde. You tell me how the hell that happens."

They were back in the truck, and Johnny—under the tarp—watched the light turn orange and then red. The sun was going down. "This is it." He banged three times on the side of the bed, and the truck slowed.

Rising to his knees, Johnny leaned over Cree and stuck his head into the open window at the back of the cab. "There's a trailhead on the left. You can pull the truck in and get it out of sight. That's it, right there." There was not much ditch line, so Leon powered through the cut and up into the trees. Branches scraped the metal, but he pushed in deep. No one had any illusions. They'd passed three police cars already. "This'll do."

Johnny stripped off the tarp and dropped from the truck. He was in the Hush, and opening so fast, it made him dizzy. Feeling his way along the bed, he pushed off into the green, stumbling a bit as his mind tried to catch up with the sudden flood of awareness.

Life, he thought.

So much life he was choking.

"Johnny-man, you okay?"

"Yeah, buddy. All good. Come on." At the truck, Johnny propped his forearms on the ledge of Verdine's open window. "You ready?"

"Are you telling me this is the place?"

"From here on, we walk."

"No roads?"

"Not without cops."

"Do you *know* that or just *think* it?"

Johnny studied the lines around her eyes, and wondered exactly what she knew about his life in the Hush. The question felt intimate. She was watching too closely. "Come on."

He opened the door, and she descended from the truck. "Leon." She gestured at the bed, and Leon heaved out a pickax and shovel.

Jack said, "Are you serious?"

"Lantern, too." Verdine nodded at the backseat, and Leon reached in for the lantern. "All right, then, young Merrimon. Start walking."

"Can you keep up?" Johnny asked.

"Try me."

Johnny took the long route, keeping the cops to the northwest. When Verdine lagged, he eased up. He didn't trust her, but he didn't want her to drop dead, either. "You may have to carry her."

"I'm watching her," Leon said.

"About that revolver . . ."

"Let's not, okay?"

Leon kept his voice flat, but Johnny knew he didn't want to hurt anybody. That being said, Verdine was all the family Leon knew. Johnny had to think about that, too. "Is she crazy?" he asked.

"You're the one taking us to a dead woman's grave." Leon stepped across a fallen trunk. "You tell me."

Johnny went inward after that. He tried to read Verdine, but found that the awareness dulled if he focused too closely. He felt Leon perfectly, and Jack, too. But when he closed his eyes to concentrate on Verdine, she was like a ghost. Cree was ten times worse. She vanished in the Hush, and he remembered how he'd met her that first time, invisible at the church. She was imperceptible now, too. He heard her footsteps, and saw her. He could reach out and touch her. Otherwise, she wasn't there. Johnny studied the empty place she made, then looked at Verdine. She was watching with a smile on her face. "You see it, don't you?"

"What?"

"Yeah." Verdine nodded and kept walking. "You see it."

After that, it got dark quickly. Leon lit the lantern when the old woman tripped for the first time.

"It's just a little night blindness."

"How much farther?" Leon asked.

"This is good for now." Johnny stopped, and everyone else did, too. "The cemetery is just there, three hundred yards through the trees."

"We're close, then?"

Johnny sat on the ground to show he would not be rushed. He would take her to the grave, but she had an end to keep up, too. "Let's talk first."

"There's no time!"

"I have all the time in the world."

Johnny watched the struggle at play on her face. Whatever she wanted from Aina's grave, she'd craved it for a very long time. Anger. Need. Impatience. She pushed them all down. "Very well." She gathered herself and sank onto her haunches. Beside her, the lantern hissed in Leon's hand. No one else sat. "What do you want to know?"

"Everything."

"Johnny, I don't like this—"

Jack's worry was palpable. Johnny held up a hand to silence him. Verdine was hungry. He was, too. "Talk."

Verdine settled lower, and grew still. "You love this land," she said.

"Yes."

"Do you know why?"

"Why would anyone—?"

"Shush, boy. Do you think I'm stupid? You have the stink of power all over you. You're flush with it. You think I'm greedy? Look inward, boy. You stink of hunger, too. I could smell it the first time I saw you. You'd kill to keep what you have."

"I don't . . . I'm not . . ."

"What do you see when you look at him?" She thrust a finger at Jack. "You see everything. Don't deny it. How about her?" This time it was Cree. She shrank from his gaze, but he stared for long seconds. "You see nothing. That's what you see. You see nothing because the power you love so much belongs to her, like it belonged to her mother, like it belonged to Aina."

"I don't understand."

"Take me to her grave, and I'll show you."

"No."

"Take me now, or I will tell you nothing more."

"Not yet."

"Then I'll kill you myself, you stupid, selfish child." She rose to her feet, and the rage was real, a spring so tightly wound, she trembled with it. "You Merrimons," she spit. "You thieves and killers. You fucking, fucking men."

"Sit down," Johnny said.

"No."

"Do you want to know where she's buried or not?"

"Yes." She bared her teeth, a hiss. "Yes, yes, damn it."

"Then sit." Johnny pointed at the ground. "Please."

Like all born to life in the swamp, Luana moved well in the woods, even at night. Her feet found the soft places. She made little noise. At first, the light floated, as if carried by an unseen hand. It was a will-o'-the-wisp, a star the size of a child's fist. She'd heard childhood stories of lights in the deep woods, and been taught early that to wander alone was more than childish disregard. It led to switches and hungry nights. Every child was taught the same.

But those were children's stories, and she was grown.

Besides . . .

It was beautiful, like nothing she'd ever seen.

How, then, did she feel such a familiar pull? It was evening warmth, a mother's touch. It was every good story told around every great meal. Luana knew it as she knew her own secret hopes.

The light was for her.

The light . . .

The light disappeared. It winked out, and Luana ached for this thing she'd never known.

Wholeness.

Wellness.

Luana's legs trembled. She heard voices far away, and deeper still she saw another light. For a moment she hoped, but it was an average light surrounded by average people. Police, perhaps. She didn't care. The other light was everything. It was strength, her life, her soul. What else would ever matter? What else could? If some part of her recognized the insanity of such thoughts, the rest of her didn't care about that either. She was a shell in the night, a tired, lost woman with tears on her face. She would have cried for real then, but saw the light elsewhere. It flickered and danced, far away and fading. With a stifled cry, Luana chased it. No caution. No stealth. She pounded through the forest, tripped and fell and ran again. A small voice, deep down, said, *Stop, this is madness.* But Luana didn't care. She felt her mother and better days, and hope so rich, she might never eat again.

"Wait! Please!"

Luana ran up a small hill and down the other side. She splashed through water and found the light waiting. It floated in a hazy void and was smaller than she'd guessed. The void around it was a trick of the night. It shifted; it flowed. Luana twisted her hands in indecision; then she reached out to touch it. For a moment nothing happened; then the void collapsed to show what hid beneath.

It was horrible.

Terrible.

Luana looked from the light to its hard, black eyes, and understood, at last, why children were made to be afraid. What she saw was a perversion, a corruption; yet it moved as others moved. It reached for her and touched her, and Luana felt loneliness, despair, the fear of another hundred years. It filled her mind with every kind of hurt, then showed her what Verdine wanted and why; it opened her mind to the hunger and hate, held her as the blackness filled her up, and broke her mind. It was too much for Luana, a thunderstorm inside. She opened her throat to scream it out, but the scream was not enough.

She was naked in the rain.

She was drowning.

CHAPTER FORTY-THREE

At the old church the scream seemed to be everywhere at once: above the cops, around them. Some thought it was human; others didn't believe it. It was too high and horrible, too full of hurt.

"Jesus God Almighty."

Captain Lee closed his mouth, and finished the prayer in silence.

"What do we do?"

The voice was behind him, but Lee didn't turn. The scream went on and on, then ended suddenly. For a full minute, no one moved or said a word.

"Captain?"

Looking around, Captain Lee saw the expressions he expected. Some were resolved and ready, but most were pale. He'd heard the whispers all day: the swamp was haunted; Johnny Merrimon was a ghost. "Can anyone say for sure where that scream came from? Direction? Distance? Anyone?" No one spoke. No one moved. The captain peered out into the night, past the line of frightened faces.

There was no sound at all, nothing.

In the trees, a mist was rising.

Johnny was first to move when the scream ripped through the forest. He didn't even think about it. Jack called out, but Johnny was a hundred yards away, and then a mile. He found the woman in the trees beside a trickle of water. The screams had died to whimpers, but it was enough to track her in the darkness, and that was a good thing.

Johnny couldn't feel her.

For the length of his run, he knew little more than the sounds she made in the Hush. Finding Cree's mother, then, was no real surprise. He had no idea why she was there or how she'd managed it, but only Cree was as blank as this; only Cree was such a *nothing.*

"Ms. Freemantle?"

He touched her shoulder, but her mouth hung open, the hot, quick whimpers like those of an animal in distress. Johnny had no love for Luana Freemantle, but he couldn't leave her like this, either. "Your daughter is close. I can take you." He gripped her arm, but her body was locked tight. "Can you hear me?"

Johnny was watching closely enough to see her eyes lose some of the glaze. The panting stopped; she tried to speak. "R . . . r . . ."

"Ms. Freemantle?"

"Run," she said; but it was too late. Johnny felt the gathering behind him, the movement of air and sudden cold. He spun, but the black eyes held him like a fist. A voice in his mind said, *Remember;* and that's what Johnny did.

He saw pieces of a dream.

Lost pages of another life.

John waited for Isaac to return with the shovel, and as he did, he watched the girl die. Her arm dangled, pumping blood that looked black in the dim, morning light. The second shot had punched through her chest right of center and blown out through the shoulder blade. He'd seen deer take similar wounds, and live this long. It was not normal, but it happened.

"It didn't have to be like this."

He knelt at her side, and knew she understood. The black eyes were unblinking, the lips pulled back. It was pain, John thought, and awareness. The girl knew she was dying, but Jesus . . .

The rage in those eyes.

"We had a deal," John said. "You save my wife, I give you what you want."

"Your wife lives. . . ."

Blood ran from her lips as she spoke. She was drowning on it. Her teeth were red.

"What you gave her wasn't life. She breathes. She doesn't die. It isn't life."

"The fault is yours. . . ."

"It isn't what you promised!" John's voice broke, and he hated everything about himself. "You should have met with me! You should have made it right!"

But the girl's eyes were closed. Her lungs rattled.

When Isaac returned, John was on the ground with his elbows around his knees and the pistol dangling. He looked up at the big man and said, "She's dead."

"I doubt it."

"She's dead or so close, it doesn't matter."

"You want some free advice?" Isaac slammed the shovel blade into the earth at John's feet. "Bury her so deep, no one will ever find her. Even I don't want to know."

"Why not?"

"Because I've seen things you haven't. Because these people worship her like a god." Isaac turned away, but turned back. "After this, we're finished, you and me. I see no need for our paths to cross again." John nodded. None of it mattered. "I've got the whole village working corn in the northern plots. We'll be there till lunch. Get her buried and get out."

Isaac left, and the dream blurred. John knew the smell of her blood and skin and hair. He knew the crunch of the shovel as he dug and shifted and heaved. Every time he thought the girl was dead, blood bubbled in the chest wound. John couldn't get her in the ground fast enough, but it had to be deep and not findable. As fearful as some had been of Aina, there were others who'd loved her. Worshipped, Isaac had said, and John didn't want that kind of heat should the body be found. He wanted to be alone with his wife, to stare into her empty eyes and mourn. Maybe he would lose himself there. Maybe the hatred would fade.

When the hole was deep enough, John dragged her down, and saw a glimmer of light beneath the weave of her shirt. Twitching at the fabric, he found the source of it pressed against her skin. It hung from a leather thong and looked like a stone cut with fine lines. Light shone in the cracks, and when he smoothed the blood away, he found a blue so deep and rich, it was almost purple. He touched it, and felt the power. It moved through his skin and into the bones of his hand, his heart. John was in a hole but knew the pivot of the sky, the flow of waters and saps and blood. He knew the drift of seeds on the wind, felt the pressures of life about to burst. He felt the stirrings of the world, and knew them as he knew the stars at night. Power. Movement. Inexplicable fact. Every other thought in his head felt wrong. Killing. Stealing. Stealing from the dead. He heard the scrape of dirt as she shifted in the grave. "Mine," she said. "For my people." Their eyes met, and he knew that she saw it, his intent. "It will not save your wife."

But John was on the road to hell already.

He ripped the stone from around her neck.

He buried the girl alive.

CHAPTER FORTY-FOUR

When the vision broke, Johnny fell to his knees. The dirt felt the same under his hands. The taste in his mouth was also the same.

"That wasn't me. . . ."

But it was in his heart and under his skin. Johnny squeezed his head and tried to draw the line between the man who'd been and the person Johnny was.

I'm no killer.

I'm not.

It took a minute to remember the rest. He pictured black eyes, and knew them. He'd seen them in dreams, and in mirrors, and in dreams of mirrors.

"John!"

He called out in the night, voice breaking.

"John Merrimon, is that you?"

He saw forest and sky, then movement far out in the wood, a flicker of light that rose once and disappeared.

He thought it was an answer.

He thought it was a yes.

It took time to get Luana Freemantle back to her family. She was responsive, but in the smallest ways.

"Can you step over the log?

"No, no. Like this."

Johnny would have carried her, but each time he tried, she moaned or froze; and Johnny couldn't handle that. He saw Aina in her face; heard the cries as dirt settled on her skin. When he was close to the lantern, he called out, "It's me, coming in."

He moved into the light, and Cree rushed to her mother's side. "Mom. What happened? What are you doing here?"

Luana blinked; stopped walking.

"She saw something," Johnny said. "Something big that scared her."

Verdine was studying his face. "You saw something, too, didn't you?"

But Johnny was tired of dreams and riddles and half truths. He wanted Verdine broken enough to talk, and thought he knew the way to do it. "Come on," he said. "I'll show you the grave."

They moved in a ragged line, Johnny in front with Leon helping the old woman and Cree, her mother. The line moved slowly but with intent; and even Leon understood they were going to the cemetery.

"What about cops?" he asked.

"A half mile that way. It doesn't matter. We have no choice."

And no risk either, it seemed. Stepping from the trees, they spread out and stared in awestruck silence. The cemetery was plain enough, but beyond its walls and markers, the world ended.

Jack said, "Oh my God."

A wall of mist rose, dense and straight, and pure white, a mass that towered even above the trees. Verdine was the first to step forward. "It appears that something doesn't want the police to interfere."

Johnny nodded at the cemetery. "What you want is in there."

"It can't be."

"You wanted John Merrimon's truth. That's where you'll find it."

"All right, then. Leon."

She stabbed her cane at the stone wall, and Leon lifted her over, everyone else following. At the hanging tree, Johnny stopped. Three stones marked the remains of those who'd been hanged. Aina had let them swing for long months, and it was Isaac who'd buried them at last. Johnny pointed at the first. "That's the foreman's grave."

"Yes."

"What you want is underneath."

"We checked the early graves eighty years ago."

"You didn't dig deep enough." The old woman measured him, doubting. "I was there with John Merrimon. I saw her go under the ground."

"She didn't just 'go under the ground,'" Cree said.

"I didn't mean—"

"Your ancestor shot her."

"Yes, but—"

"He buried her alive!"

"Enough!"

"I lived it! I felt it!"

"I said that's enough!" Verdine lashed out with the cane and struck the girl on the back of her legs. "This is beyond you, child."

Cree bit down on a painful cry.

Beside her, Luana's eyes flickered.

"Show me, boy." The cane stabbed out again. "Leon, you, too. Dig."

Johnny took the pickax, and Leon settled into place beside him. "Any chance you're wrong about this, my friend?"

"She's buried there."

"Do you understand what this is about? Because I truly don't."

"All I can tell you is that your grandmother is a dangerous woman. Can't you see it?"

Leon glanced over his shoulder. She hunched above the cane, both shoulders drawn up against the wrinkled neck. "Come on, boys. Kiss and get it over with or start yourselves to digging." She clapped once, and no one could mistake the zeal. She was alive with it. She burned. "Well, come on, damn it. Not one of us is getting any younger."

"May as well do it," Leon said.

"It'll get ugly, down deep."

"I'll be all right."

Johnny waited a beat, then nodded once and swung the pick. In minutes, they'd found the rhythm. Johnny broke the earth, and Leon shoveled it out: lift and fall, black dirt in the clean night air.

Luana watched from the bruise of her mind. She was trapped in that soft place, but knowing in a way she'd never been. She knew what walked in the woods and what it feared. She knew what Verdine wanted, and what she would do to get it. The old woman would dig up the grave. She'd kill Luana. She'd kill Cree. Luana tried to stop it, but couldn't move. She pictured the gun in her pocket, and used all her strength to try to speak. She wanted to call out to the daughter she loved.

Take the gun, she wanted to say.

Kill that bitch.

Johnny knew exactly how deep the foreman was buried. That meant he knew when the pickax would be a problem. "Hand me the shovel." Leon did as Johnny asked. "You might want to climb out now."

"You sure?"

"Trust me on this."

Johnny offered a boost, and Leon crawled from the hole, leaving Johnny alone at the bottom. He tossed out the pick, and took a moment for Verdine. He couldn't read her, but knew what the old woman wanted. *Life! The stone!* It was written in every gesture and glance. She was leaning out over the grave, her eyes like black holes pricked with light. "Are you sure about this?" he asked.

"Are you?"

Her lips twisted in the kind of challenge Johnny hoped never to see again. He went back to the dig, and when he struck the foreman's remains, he felt the same revulsion as everyone else. The coffin was little more than a stain in the earth, the bones jumbled in the same slick soil. Johnny saw teeth and bone and bits of hair.

"Ha. I told you. We checked that coffin when I was young."

"You opened it?"

"What was left of it, yes."

"Did you look underneath?" She drew in a hard, sharp breath, and Johnny straightened. "I want to know what it is." He made a gesture at his neck. "The stone."

"You saw it?"

"In the dream," he said—a half truth. He was pretty sure he'd seen it in the forest, too. "I'm not digging another inch until you tell me everything."

"Leon . . ."

She gestured into the hole, but Johnny hefted the shovel like an ax. "You heard her before, Leon. A deal's a deal. She said she'd answer my questions."

"Leon, get him out of my fucking hole."

"The stone," Johnny said. "What is it?"

"Leon!" The old woman barked, but Leon lifted his hands and stepped away. Verdine stared as if looks alone might kill him. "It's not a stone," she finally said.

"You're lying."

"It's hollow and ancient and more than a stone."

"Go on."

Her lips drew back, but Leon was unmoving; so was Johnny. "In the old language, it's called a *fengi*. My mother called it a soul-stone."

"What does it do?"

"Exactly what it says it does, you stupid boy. It holds a soul."

"Whose?"

"The first of us."

"The first of your family?"

"The first woman. *Massassi*. It's been with the women of my family for a thousand lives, mother to daughter, an unbroken line."

"It came with Aina?"

"Don't speak her name as if you know her."

It seemed impossible, but Johnny imagined it.

Mother to daughter.

A thousand lives . . .

"The stone's not here," he said. "You won't find it."

He thought that truth would break her, but was wrong. He saw it in the twist of her smile, the malicious glint. "Just dig her up," she said. "Dig her up, and we'll ignore your unbearable ignorance."

Johnny looked at Jack, then turned to the hole and dug slowly, carefully. Verdine loomed above him as he removed the foreman's bones and teeth, then focused on the dirt beneath. After another ten inches, he tossed out the shovel and used his hands. The soil coated his skin, and he remembered the dream: the taste of it and the pressure—how it felt to be buried alive.

"Well, boy?"

But Johnny was in a dark place, body and soul. He dragged soil against his knees, went deeper, and touched something.

"Jesus." He rocked back.

"What is it?"

"It's warm."

"It's her! Get her out!"

But Johnny couldn't move. He saw a knuckle joint, a twist of broken nail.

Verdine said, "Leon."

But Johnny raised a hand. "No, don't. You might crush her."

"Is she alive?"

Johnny looked at Cree, who was on her knees, clutching her stomach. She felt it, same as him: suffocation, panic, the horror. He held her eyes a second more.

In the dirt, a finger moved.

For Cree, it was too much. How many times had she lived the dirt in her throat, and this man's face, this man and this abysmal hole? The finger moved again, and Cree knew that it was Aina, alive.

So many years . . .

She turned, and threw up in the grass. Anger. Intimacy. The slick, red earth. "This is real. How can this be real?"

It was a whisper, but no one was watching. No one cared. On her hands and knees, Cree risked another glance.

The fingernail was broken.

Every nail was broken.

For Johnny, it was hard to tell where the body ended and the dirt began.

The body . . .

That's how he thought of it, a scarecrow of a body. The clothing had rotted off. The hair was a matted, tangled mess, a root ball choked with mud and red clay. Johnny worked the soil as a potter might, using the tips of his fingers to cull it away from an elbow, a shoulder blade, the turn of an ear. She lay on her side, and he kept his touch soft because the skin tore easily. She was wasted beyond belief, so far gone that *skin and bones* would be a generous description.

"Well, come on! Get her out!"

But Johnny kept it slow and gentle. He found a leg, and followed it until it crossed the second, which was bent beneath it. Working along her back, he felt the pearls of her spine. When the lower arm was exhumed, he found her hand clutched around a root from the hanging tree.

"What's she holding?"

Johnny ignored the question. Working with care, he removed one finger, then the next. When the last one came free, he sensed the change before he understood it.

One of her eyes was open.

Johnny fell back in the mud, staring at the wild, dark pupil, the yellowed whites. He didn't know if she was blind or not, aware or not. Half her face was still down in the dirt; so was most of her left side. Above him, Jack said, "Dear Lord, God Almighty." But Johnny ignored him. Bloodshot and dripping, the eye had settled on his face. Stripping off his shirt, Johnny cleared mud from around her mouth, then excavated the rest of her body and covered her as best he could. "Leon, let's get her out."

The big man knelt at the edge of the grave, and Johnny handed her up.

She weighed nothing at all.

A sack of twigs.

Luana watched it from the sunken place in her mind: the wretched figure, Johnny clawing up from the earth. They put Aina on the ground, and Luana saw the black tongue, the stumps of teeth. Women of the Hush had sought Aina for almost two centuries, and Luana had thought them old fools lost in a ridiculous belief.

But not now.

Now the fingers were moving. The yellow eye rolled. It locked on

Luana, and she felt a flood of hate and madness so strong, it overwhelmed her. She hated men and life, the world that had abandoned her to eternity in the dirt. It came off her in waves, pounded like a spike into Luana's mind. How could such hatred exist without consuming itself? How could Aina be alive? Luana heard the answer in her grandmother's voice. *Because she carried the stone for years: around her neck and in her hand and hidden in a place only a woman could hide it.* Luana saw it like a flash. She'd drawn on the stone, and on the tree, on all the life in the soil around her. She'd sucked the world dry, and for what? The loathing? The madness? What terrible strength allowed such a life for so long? Or had she wanted to die all along? Had she craved that ending but been unable to achieve it?

The creature's eye rolled to Cree, and Luana knew that Cree felt it, too. She was on her hands and knees but twitched and moaned as if the same spike had split her skull. "No," she muttered. "No." And Luana knew that what remained of Aina's mind was a dangerous thing to those who'd descended from her. Luana. Cree. They were reeling, the both of them. Luana was screaming inside, but knew a deeper truth, too: that Verdine wanted Aina to die.

It's why they'd come.

Why they'd dug her up.

Luana watched as if through a broken window. Verdine was coiled like a spring, but no one else noticed. She leaned on Leon, but her hand was at his belt, then on the gun. She didn't want to save Aina, didn't want to ease her suffering or fulfill the quest undertaken by so many women for so many years. The old woman wanted the stone, and had only one way to find it. The line of women needed to end. That meant Aina had to die, and then Luana and Cree. Verdine, then, would be the only one left, the last branch on the only tree that mattered. The stone would come to her. So would time and life and power.

But only if the others were dead.

Cree . . .

She was flat on the ground now, hands at her temples as if to keep out the hate. Luana reached for her daughter, and a single finger twitched. "Run," she said, but no one heard her, and the gun was moving. It squared on Aina's face, then barked and jumped, and Aina died as she'd been buried, quick and brutal and helpless. Her head came apart; the dark blood pooled.

Massassi . . .

The connection was immediate and overwhelming.

The first woman.

The first mother.

Luana opened like a flower. She was next in the unbroken line, and felt Massassi's soul far out in the night. The connection was immediate and overwhelming, and in the wake of it, she saw the line of those who'd gone before, a great awakening of women. Luana was all of them at once, a thousand lives.

"I am Massassi. . . ."

And for that moment, she was. She was Massassi and her grandmother, and women who'd been no more than names to an unhappy child. Luana knew how it felt to stand beneath the stars in Africa, to be with men she'd never met, to bathe in foreign seas. So much life and knowledge and time! Luana was more than she'd dreamed a woman could be. She was large and small; she was selfless and still, the kind of mother she'd never been. Taking her daughter's hand, she rose from all those lives to say the only word that mattered.

"Run," she said.

Then Verdine shot her in the chest.

Luana dropped from the knees, but kept her eyes on her child.

Run, she thought, and smiled as her daughter did. She was a good runner, Cree, and always had been: along the sidewalks and through the courtyards, the city, the life she was not supposed to have. She could outrun the boys and the drugs, the weakness that until this moment had defined her mother.

Verdine was yelling her name, firing shots into the forest. . . . *Creola! Creola, goddamn it!*

But Cree had listened to her mother.

She was running.

Sprinting.

At the far wall, she slipped into the mist, and Luana turned, at last, to the stars above. She'd looked at them through so many eyes and on so many nights.

Massassi . . .

She felt the stone, far out in the night, and smiled because Cree would feel it, too. Not yet, she thought, but soon. Verdine was returning, and Luana heard the words she muttered in that cold and bitter voice.

You bitch, you damn bitch . . .

There was so much anger and hate and want, but not for Luana. She was light on the blood-soaked grass. She felt her life ending, but felt her daughter, too, so fast in the darkness, so light on the balls of her feet. Luana knew her daughter's fear, but that was okay. There was strength in the line of women, and the strength would be Cree's.

Soon, child . . .

Just run. . . .

She touched her daughter a final time; then Verdine was on her knees in the grass beside her. She smelled of sweat and earth and wet cotton. Hunger made the voice shake. "Where is it?" she demanded. "Which way?"

Luana smiled as her body cooled. "Cree is next after me," she said. "She will find Massassi."

"Cree will die, and the stone will be mine."

"Not if I die first."

"You can't die yet. I won't allow it."

"Then you should not have shot me."

"I have as much right as you!"

"If that were true, *cousin,* you wouldn't need us to die to find the stone."

"Take me to Massassi!" Verdine slapped Luana once, then twice. "Take me, goddamn it! Take me to Massassi!"

Then she was shaking her, lifting her broken body, slamming it down. It was a temper tantrum, like any child's. Luana laughed at the thought, and something burst inside. She felt it in her throat, the slippery burn. Verdine put the gun in Luana's face, but there was nothing she could do. Cree was the last of her line. Massassi was for her. "You're too late," Luana said; and then, smiling like a child herself, she died.

Cree was curled beneath a tall, black tree the moment it happened. She felt her mother's passing like the cry of a hawk, and such was the nature of her opening: a sudden awareness in a vast, high place, a conjoining of lives and memory and thought. She saw the world as if from a great height; she felt the movement of land and sky, the hills and streams, the spread of time and people and the Hush. She knew her mother's regrets and loves and, at the end, her fierce, proud joy. She knew Aina's madness and Massassi's love; she knew the darkness of war, the wonders of peace and family, the stability of empire. Cree was herself and others, the thread that wove a thousand lives. It was too much at once, so she focused on Massassi, far out in the night. She felt the warmth of her and the readiness.

Child . . .

She was the word. The word was she.

Come to me. . . .

That's what Cree wanted, but was dizzy. She touched the soil beneath her hands, and then the sky. She found that place high above, and sent her awareness there, thinking: *silence, perspective, distance.* It was quiet in those high reaches, and she opened herself slowly, seeing flickers of the past and present, so much of the world. A thousand lives, and the memories were hers. So was the knowledge, the strength. A hawk cried out, and Cree was there, too.

She was *more.*

She was *becoming.*

Cree poured herself into the hawk and felt its purity of purpose. It cried out a second time, and the sounds—for Cree—were words for her mother. They meant "acceptance" and "understanding" and "love."

They meant "thank you for my life."

They meant "goodbye."

CHAPTER FORTY-FIVE

For Johnny, it was all about the run. He didn't remember the first step or even the second, but everything else was the run. It was darkness and wind, Jack's weight as he dragged at Johnny's arm. "What the hell, Johnny? What's happening?" Gunshots were loud behind them, and Jack was in the lead. He stumbled over the wall, and pulled Johnny with him. "Why'd she do that, man? Why'd she kill her?"

Johnny had nothing for him. The old creature was dead. So was Cree's mother. They hit the mist, and another gunshot *whumped* somewhere behind them. Cree was running, too. "Just keep moving," Johnny said; and for five long minutes that was the rule. Watch your feet. Don't think. They stopped where mist ended on the other side. They spilled out into the clear night air, and Jack was still lost and hurting. "The hell, man? What the hell?"

Johnny dropped to his knees, ready to be sick. The mud on his hands was slick and wet.

A hundred and seventy-three years.

Then fresh air . . .

Then . . .

Johnny dashed sweat from his eyes, and that was slick and wet, too.

Like the old creature's skin.

Like the inside of her skull.

"Johnny?"

"Not now, Jack."

"J-man."

Jesus . . .

Johnny opened his eyes in time to see the wall of mist collapse. It dropped from the top down, rolled out into the trees.

"What's happening, Johnny? What do we do?"

Johnny had no answer. He thought Leon might be dead behind them, but wasn't sure of much. Luana was dead—he felt that—but Leon was a blur, and so was Verdine. His awareness of them flickered and faded. He held on for a minute, then reached out for Cree, but couldn't find her if he wanted to. "Cops are stirring," he said, and felt their fears, like a red pulse. "They're close."

"Good. Let's go there."

But Johnny worried about all that fear.

"Come on, J-man. Cops. Guns. Right now those are good things." Jack was begging with his eyes. "What are we waiting for?"

Johnny was waiting for inspiration, but that answer would not be good enough for Jack. He looked into his friend, and saw the kind of fear Jack couldn't settle into or walk off. His world was shaken, his fundamental beliefs. "You're right," Johnny said. "It's the logical choice."

"Logic. Yes. Please, God."

"Come on, then." He draped an arm over Jack's shoulders and led him toward the church. He found a path where trees leaned back to give them room. In the distance, floodlights burned. Someone had built a fire. "See. All good. A straight shot. Do you see it?"

"What do we tell them?"

"I don't know. You're the lawyer."

"Lawyer, yes."

"Call out before you walk in. Okay? You understand?"

"Wait. What?"

There was a quiver in the muscles along Jack's spine, but the flicker of fire had given Johnny his inspiration. He nudged his friend in the right direction, then stepped off the trail and ghosted. Jack would be angry and afraid, but John Merrimon was out there somewhere, and Johnny thought he knew the place to look. It would be on the third hill in a line of hills.

It would be marked with smoke.

It would be marked with fire.

Leon stood very still as his grandmother rose from the dead woman's side. She was small and old, but the gun was in her hand, and she looked as if she might kill Leon, too. "You let those boys go," she said.

"Was I supposed to stop them?"

"No witnesses." The words were simple but horrible. She spit on the ground near her dead cousin's face. "The hell are you waiting for, boy? Put 'em in the hole."

"What?"

"You want cops finding those bodies?" She waved the pistol in the direction of the old church, a half mile away. "Be quick, now."

Leon was unhappy, but moved from long habit. His mother had died in childbirth and his father when he was only seventeen. Verdine had always been there, his only family. Stooping for the old creature they called Aina, he put her body back in the hole.

"That one, too."

He hesitated over the remains of Luana Freemantle. He'd known her. He'd been in her home. "This is wrong."

"Deal with it, boy. We have a long night."

"What do you mean?"

"I mean you need to work faster."

Moving carefully, he placed Luana's body in the hole, too. He was gentle, and sad.

"Fill it in. Let's go."

He did that, too, but felt the weight of her impatience.

"Come on, come on. Faster, goddamn it."

Sweat soaked through his clothes, and turned dirt on his skin to mud. He watched the shovel. He thought about the gun.

"That's good enough. Now we find the girl."

"Cree?"

"She won't have gone far."

"You can't know that."

"Her mother just died. What comes next takes time."

Leon didn't understand that either. Nothing made sense. "You're going to hurt her?"

"Just leave that to me."

"You're going to hurt Johnny, too?"

"You let me worry about him."

Leon looked out at the night, the tall sky. "How do you expect me to find her?"

"Don't bullshit me, son. You've been tracking since you were eight."

She was right about the tracking. His father had the skill, and he'd passed it on. The deep woods. The stony ground.

"Cree ran that way. You see the signs?" The old woman pointed, and Leon nodded. "Good boy," she said. "Now, take me to that bitch-whore little thief, so I can get what's mine."

The girl's tracks were easy enough to follow, even in the dark with nothing more than lantern light. She'd run hard on damp soil thick with forest litter. It took little time to find the tree where she'd curled. Leon put two fingers where her hip had been, the divots made by an elbow, her shoulder. "She lay here for a good long while. Scared, I guess. Hiding."

"When did she leave?"

Leon rubbed soil between his fingers, and looked at the pinpricks burning in his grandmother's eyes. He saw the same hunger, only worse. She leaned above the cane, up on the balls of her feet. "A few minutes, maybe."

"Find her."

"So you can kill her, too?"

"Don't presume, son."

But Leon did. He straightened and lifted the lantern. The tracks ran north toward the hills. He turned west. "Come on," he said. "I'll take you where you need to go."

The old woman was too night-blind to know the difference until lights appeared in the distance. They stood ghostly bright, and beneath them were flickers of movement, hints of men and machines and firelight. "That's the church."

"Yes."

"Cree would not have come this close."

"Just keep walking."

Leon stayed close beside the old woman. When she stopped moving, he took her arm and held it fast.

"Let me go," she said.

"You killed those women."

"It was necessary."

"You plan to kill Johnny and Cree."

She dug in her heels, and barked a bitter laugh. "Don't forget the lawyer."

"I won't forget anything about this night, not ever."

Verdine understood, then, just how serious he was. "Take your hands off me, boy."

But Leon held her tighter. He pulled her toward the church, and they heard shouting beyond the tree line. Cops had seen their light. They were coming.

"Let me go."

"It'll be over soon."

She cocked the revolver, and pressed the barrel against his ribs.

"You won't shoot me."

"That's ignorance talking. You've always been a stupid, ignorant boy."

"Shoot me, then. I dare you."

He stopped, and stared down. She looked unflinchingly at his face and, in the darkness, pulled the trigger. Nothing happened. She pulled it again, and Leon took the weapon from her hand. "I told you earlier. I shot this gun twice twenty years ago."

"You should be dead, goddamn it."

"Thing is," he said. "I only had the six bullets."

Johnny saw fire from the top of the sleeping tree. He smelled smoke, and found the light far out on that third hill. It wasn't like the other times, nothing small or barely there. This was a bonfire, an invitation, so Johnny came down from the tree and crossed the valleys and peaks as he'd done before. At the foot of the third hill, he worked through the boulder field and up onto the scree. A great fire burned two thirds of the way up, and Johnny slowed at last, knowing how the scree had almost killed him the last time up. This time, though, the footing cooperated, and so did the hill. None of the trails moved or faded; the fire stayed put. Johnny climbed until he found a ledge that opened into a cave whose ceiling slanted downward beyond the fire. Circling the flames, Johnny saw weaker light deep in the cave. Something moved, and a shadow flickered. "John Merrimon?" No one answered, but the yellow light brightened, and Johnny was unsure what to feel. He knew fear. He knew John Merrimon. "I'm coming down."

There was a bend ahead, and Johnny was almost on the shimmer before he noticed it. It was a blankness where the cave bent, a void he'd seen before. "John Merrimon?"

A sigh moved the air, and the voice that followed was so tired and thin, it was almost gone. "Do you see me, then?"

"I see a flicker."

"It's a trick I've learned, the deceiving of another's mind." The shimmer broke, and Johnny saw a cascade of images: an old man, a boy, then something horrible and broken and bent. They ran together—one after another—and when they disappeared, only the shimmer remained. "People are endlessly predictable. The play of light. An old love. An older fear. I rarely have to exert myself, which is good, I suppose, all things considered."

"All things?"

"Time and weariness and age."

Johnny moved closer, trying to see through the void.

"That's close enough."

Johnny stepped again without thinking, and an unseen force gripped him. It lifted him off the ground, hung him in the empty air. He couldn't move, could barely breathe.

"My house," he heard. "My rules."

"Your house, yes."

"Are you certain you understand?"

"Please . . ."

The grip eased, and Johnny fell, rubbing his throat. "It is John, though, isn't it?"

"That name means little to me now."

"But I know you."

"You know who I was. There's a difference."

The shimmer broke again, and Johnny saw the crooked figure. He was old by every measure. His legs were bowed and thin, his arms twisted. The skin of his face was mottled and gray, but not just from age. It was something deeper and corrupt: the shape of his skull, the swollen places under his skin. Johnny saw nothing of the man he knew from so many dreams.

"Is it truly so bad?" The old man faded, and John Merrimon appeared, as Johnny knew him: a little taller than Johnny, a little broader. He tried to smile, but it failed. "Which vision do you prefer?"

"I've never been squeamish."

"No, you've not." The vision of the old man returned. "Nor have you asked for anything, or taken more than was needed. I've admired that about you for some time: your sense of self, your love of this place. Because of that, I've welcomed you here. I've healed your wounds and made the Hush your home. I've given you things."

"The awareness . . ."

"And the dreams."

"Why?"

"Would you love this land as you love it now? Would you have accepted any of this without the benefit of foresight?"

He meant the cave, his existence, his misshapenness. But for Johnny, things were tilting. He thought of Aina in the mud, of John's fierce rage as he'd ripped the stone from her neck and buried her alive. "You've been here all this time?"

Both eyes narrowed, and the voice dropped dangerously. "What are you asking me?"

"I don't . . . I just . . ."

"She's not yours."

"What? Who?"

The old man turned a shoulder and looked out sideways, something angry in his gaze. Air moved in the cave, and Johnny felt power build like a storm. Small hairs stood on his arms. The smell was electric.

"It's just a question," Johnny said. "I'm just trying, okay, just trying to understand."

Hiding the fear was impossible. Madness stirred in the old, black eyes; his lips drew back, and Johnny thought of William Boyd, who'd been crushed and twisted and broken. He imagined the old man smiling as it happened. He saw the same brown teeth, the dancing eyes.

"Marion is still my wife," John said.

"Okay . . ."

"You think a few dreams compare with that?" He moved closer. "You think that means something?"

"Just settle down, okay."

But the old man did not settle. The wildness grew in his eyes, and if John Merrimon was still in there, Johnny didn't see him. He saw jealousy and resentment, a hundred years of madness.

"She's not yours yet," John said.

"What?"

"If you touch her, I'll kill you."

Johnny wasn't going to touch a damn thing. Nothing seemed real but the stale air and the stone beneath his feet. The old man was ranting about a ghost, a shadow. Now he was leading Johnny into the earth, down to God knows what. Johnny stooped as the ceiling dropped, and the light dimmed. He watched the twisted legs, the bent back, and the roll of his hips.

At the final turn, the old man stopped and put the dark eyes back on Johnny. Strings of greasy hair fell across his face, and the madness still simmered. "I'm not insane," he said.

"I believe you."

"No, you don't."

Understanding came the moment they rounded into the chamber. A second fire burned, and in its light Johnny saw . . .

Marion.

She lay on a bed of pelts and skins, and was utterly unchanged: the shape of her, the lines of her face. Johnny buckled under the flood of unexpected emotion. She was the crossroad of past and present, a flicker of dream; but Johnny remembered a childhood together, the glint in her eyes when she'd said they'd marry one day. She'd worn a blue dress and a flower he'd picked beside the river. He remembered her parents and sister, the ring he'd bought on a trip to Boston. The memories were John's, but it didn't matter. Johnny knew her hopes and dreams, the secret smiles and promises, a thousand nights of passion.

She was his, and she was not.

It was too much.

"You see now why I brought you?"

"I can't do this."

John shuffled closer to the bed, and smoothed her hair. "Do you not love her?" he asked. "Do you not know her as I do?"

Johnny struggled for words. Her chest rose and fell. A flush was in her cheek. "Why am I here?" he finally asked.

"Because I'm dying."

"But the stone . . ."

The old man shook his head. "No man was born to hold Massassi's soul. I owe you that much truth, at least."

The old man drew the stone from beneath his shirt, and the last tatters of illusion fell away. He wore clothing made of ragged skins, and was more decayed than even Johnny had suspected. His skin was breaking down, and his eyes were cloudy. He was failing. He was dying as Johnny watched.

"Do you not love her?" he asked again. "Would you not pay any price to keep her safe?"

Johnny looked down on Marion, whose hands were pale at her sides. He thought of his childhood, then of the lives of his parents and grandparents, the march of history. All that time they'd been here, the two of them together.

So many years . . .

So much loneliness . . .

"Take the stone."

Johnny shook his head.

"You must."

He pushed the stone at Johnny, and even at a distance, Johnny felt the power of it. His fingers tingled; his senses sharpened. He smelled the rot beneath the old man's skin, the warm flush in Marion's.

"I've watched you," John said. "I've *given* you." He pushed the stone closer, and the madness was back in his eyes. "You owe me this."

But Johnny looked deeper into the old man. The bones were eaten through with cancer, and the power in him was terrible and dark. It filled his veins like poison; it was killing him.

"I wasn't always like this," John said. "You'll have decades before you're like me, a hundred and fifty good years. You'll have the land and Marion and all that life. Take the stone. Keep her safe." Johnny took a step back, and the old man crept forward. "You can't imagine the power, the things you'll be able to do. You think you know the Hush now. You know nothing. Take it."

Johnny shook his head.

"Just touch it."

"No."

"I won't let her die over your weakness."

"Stay away from me."

"Your cowardice and intransigence."

"I said, stay the hell away!"

But Johnny was too slow. The old man lunged forward, unbelievably fast. He held Johnny's wrist in an iron grip. "She's more important than either of us." Johnny fought, but the old man was impossibly strong. He squeezed until Johnny's hand opened; then he pressed the stone against his palm. "Quiet now," he said; but that was impossible.

The world was exploding.

Johnny was exploding.

He felt the corruption first, and the old man's madness; but that was a blip, a fraction of a second. Johnny lived decades in the moment that followed. He felt John's love for Marion, so powerful and rich, Johnny knew then that his own ideas of love were as pale as the dew. So many years of sacrifice and want and care! Johnny lived them in an instant: a world of wars and change and threat; and all the while, John was here with Marion, keeping her safe and alive, keeping the world out. Johnny knew his thoughts, and drowned in the oceans of his loneliness. He felt the turn of years, and saw the changes through John's eyes: the first airplane in the sky, the first car beyond the Hush. He saw the people John had killed, and those he'd left alive to spread fear of the swamp. He saw the cabin through John's eyes, too: the way he came at night to peer down on Johnny's face and think of Marion, alone. There was affection there, but not love; and hope, though it was forlorn. Johnny felt it all: the fear John had of the old women in the village. One alone, he could manage. But two together might take the stone and his life, and Marion's, too. John hated the old women for that strength, but his guilt was never far behind. What he had was theirs: the stolen years, Marion's unfading perfection. That was a swirl of color and heat, but Johnny lived the larger fear, too: the knowledge, early on, that the stone would kill him, in time. The burn of it was in his veins, too, but so was the power.

Dear God . . .

Johnny had never known such a thing, never dreamed it. He loved the Hush, and so he was the Hush. Not a creature here or there, but all of it, every plant and beating heart, every vibration in the soil. He knew the place Jack stood, and the color of his thoughts. If he focused, he could find Leon and Verdine, and know the color of their thoughts, too: the red of the old woman's fury, the faint, pale gray of Leon's sorrow. If Johnny knew a thing, he could touch it. Such was the power of the stone, and the power went beyond mere knowledge. He could be a deceiver, as John had been. He could heal and he could kill.

Are there limits?

He turned his attention to John, feeling the tumors in his bones and liver and lungs, the will it took to hold Johnny as he did, to draw another breath. He was beyond dying; he was all but dead.

Enough . . .

He heard the word in his mind, and knew it was John's. The old man was trying to draw back, but Johnny felt the scars of 1853, the wounds of loss and the rage, the desperation as he'd taken the stone. He watched him live angrily and bereft, then find his way, at last, to the land. He loved it as Johnny loved it, and for more than a century, he'd tended the great trees and the creatures he loved most. In this they were the same.

Yes, yes . . .

He thought Johnny might yet be swayed, and used the last of his will to drive the point home. The Hush would be his in every way. He could nurture it as John had done; protect it in ways he'd never imagined—and not just the Hush.

I was bound to this land as Aina was bound. It can be different with you.

Now it was Johnny's turn to draw back. The temptation . . .

You can go anywhere, be anything.

Johnny saw that, too: the far mountains, the great forests.

Care of my wife is the only price.

But that was a lie, and Johnny felt it. The stone was bound to Cree. She was the last and the strongest.

You'll have to kill her.

"No."

Johnny tried to pull back, but John's strength was immense, a dying man's final abandon.

She will feel Massassi. She will come.

"She's just a girl."

She wants what's mine!

Johnny tore himself away from the visions of anger, greed, and resentment. He stumbled back and almost fell. The bond between them broke, and John Merrimon wept. "She will die if you say no." He cupped his hands and begged with a tearstained face. "Don't you understand? Don't you see?"

"I can't kill an innocent girl."

"Yet you want what I can give you."

He was right, and knew it. Johnny was smaller without the stone. Everything was smaller. He stared at it, remembering the heat of it on his palm, the explosion. Looking at it, he didn't care about time or even Marion.

But the Hush.

That connection.

"Yes," John said.

"I can't."

"Take the stone. Take my wife."

"I need . . ."

"You need what? Time to decide? Don't be a child. Cree is coming. You must know that."

"I don't feel her."

"We can't feel the children of Aina. That's what makes them so dangerous. Take it now, while you still can."

It would be so easy, Johnny thought. *The stone. The power.*

The old man leaned closer, the stone in his open hand. The eyes clouded further as Johnny watched. Every breath was a struggle.

"Please . . ."

He took his wife's hand. Johnny looked at the gnarled fingers twined into the smooth, pale ones. It was unnatural, and pitiful and sad. "I can't do it," he said.

"You mean you won't."

"I won't kill for you."

Johnny took a step back, and the old man found strength enough to follow. His steps were halting, but electricity charged the air, thickened it in Johnny's throat. "Then I'll do it myself," he said. "I'll kill the girl and force the stone down your throat. I'll *make* you love her."

"Marion would not want that."

"Don't you say her name. You're not strong enough. You're not worthy."

"She wouldn't want an innocent girl to die, John. Not for her."

"Yet dozens already have. Old people. Young people. I'll kill as many as it takes! *Do* whatever it takes!"

"She never asked for that."

"Take it!"

He pushed out the stone, and Johnny took two more steps back. "She shouldn't be alive, John. She shouldn't be here."

"Don't make me hurt you, son."

"Her life is no gift."

"Shut your mouth."

"It's a curse—"

"I said to shut your damn mouth!"

Something broke, then, in the old man's heart. The last of his patience burned, leaving nothing but the rage and madness. He lifted Johnny, flung him against a wall. He pinned him on the stone floor, squeezed his heart, his lungs. "I gave you the Hush." He squeezed harder. "I saved your life." He hung Johnny in the air, arms spread. Johnny tried to speak, but could not. The old man coughed, and blood burst through his lips. He didn't care. The hope was burnt. Marion would die. He turned his fist, and Johnny's arms twisted. So did his legs. Johnny screamed, but the old man wasn't finished. He made Johnny suffer. He buried him in the pain and screaming, the small releases and the awful pressures. "You'll be the first to die," John said.

"Please . . ."

"First before my wife."

"Stop . . ."

"First before me."

"Stop, please . . ."

But John did not. He dug for strength, and twisted bones until Johnny screamed. The old man fell to his knees, but kept the pressure on Johnny's joints, his ribs. When Johnny found a breath, he said the only thing left to say. "You're not doing this for her. . . ." More pressure, more screaming. Johnny bit his tongue and tasted blood. "You're afraid to be alone—"

"Shut up!"

"She'd rather die than be like this."

"You can't know that!"

"You made me know that! You showed me! She would despise what you've become!"

"No. . . ."

"It's true. Look at her face."

The old man did. He looked at her face and wept and, at last, was dying. Johnny saw it from a red place in his mind. The old man collapsed, and Johnny fell with him. He tried to move, but hurt as if every bone had splintered. Beside him, the old man lay on the stone. His eyes were white as milk, and only his lips moved. "She was the only innocent. Don't you see that? Don't you care?" Tears tracked a seam in his face. He coughed more blood, then opened his hand to show the stone. "Take it. Save my wife."

"I can't."

"Kill Cree, and the world is yours."

"She's just a girl."

"She is the final price."

"Where have I heard those words before?"

The old man blinked, and coughed more blood. "Isaac . . ."

"You loved him," Johnny said.

"I did."

"He paid a final price, too. So did the men you hanged. So did Aina, who was younger even than Cree. What about your son?" Johnny tried to move, but was broken. "What became of Marion's child?"

"I had to let him go."

"What price did *he* pay? No father. No family."

They felt like last words, but John was shaking his head, his voice the barest whisper. "She wanted to be a mother and a wife. I wanted her to have those things."

"She had them."

"Not for long enough."

"Don't you see?" Johnny found another swallow of air. "There will always be another final price. Isaac. Your son. I won't kill an innocent girl. Marion had her time. So did you."

"Please . . ."

"No."

"Johnny . . ."

"It stops here. Now. No more killing."

The old man closed his eyes, and Johnny saw all the ways that he was broken, too: the last of his will, the last of his hope. "There is a grassy place on the hill. . . ."

He was dying; Johnny understood. "I'll find it."

"Side by side . . ."

"I promise."

"This is all I have left."

He closed his eyes, and the air around them stirred. Johnny felt power and warmth, a dark moment that was a shadow of the old man's death. He touched Johnny's arm and poured the last of himself into the link that bound them. Johnny burned and hurt, and, in time, was healed. When it was done, the stone rolled from the old man's palm, his voice failing at last. "I wanted her to have those things." Johnny opened his mouth, but had no words for such a moment. The old man nodded blindly, then crawled into the skins beside his undying wife. He took her perfect hand and held it. He kissed the beloved cheek. He breathed his very last.

Johnny sat for a long time after that. The stone was near his hand, but he had not yet touched it. He thought of John and Marion, and all their long years together. He thought of his own life and of the stone, and was still there when Cree appeared. She stepped into the chamber, and Johnny watched her in the firelight. She moved with confidence and calm, and Johnny had the strange thought that he knew nothing about her, that she had changed in some magnificent way. "He said that you would find me."

"I can see you with my eyes closed."

"And the soul of Massassi?"

"She is the sun rising."

Johnny studied her face and the deep, still eyes. She shone as if the sun had risen, indeed. She looked older, wiser. She moved to the bed and looked down on the dead man, his still-breathing wife. Her gaze moved from Marion's face to John's, to the twisted limbs and distortions. "I could have told him it would end like this."

"How could you know that?"

"I've lived a thousand lives before my own." Cree sat on the floor, but not so close Johnny couldn't reach the stone first. "I knew John Merrimon when he was young. I knew his wife when she was burning with fever."

"He asked me to take the stone."

"Will you?"

"Marion will die if I don't."

"Then she should die."

Johnny swallowed past an unexpected pain. Dream or not, he knew Marion in intimate ways. Some part of him loved her. Not as John had, but still . . .

"That life was never yours," Cree said. "The power is not yours, either." Johnny said nothing, but felt the stone beside his hand. He felt the life it offered, all the things he could be and do, the knowledge of all things that were first in the world. Cree tilted her head as if she saw the struggle. Perhaps she actually did. "Do you know," she asked, "that John Merrimon was the first to break faith? That but for his actions, Marion would have lived a full and normal life as Aina promised?"

It was an ugly truth to which John Merrimon never confessed. But Johnny had seen it in his dreams, and understood. "He gave the land to Isaac instead of Aina."

"He broke the deal first."

"He loved Isaac, I think."

"Yet betrayal comes at a price, does it not?"

Johnny looked at Marion, thinking, as he'd done before, about that final price. "I'm sorry about your mother," he said. "I would have stopped Verdine if I could."

"My mother was at peace when she died. At the end, she understood."

Cree smiled serenely, and Johnny thought again that she was changed in some powerful way. She had not yet looked at the stone, though it sat on the ground between them. "It's time to do the right thing," she said.

"What will happen to Marion if I do?"

"She will die, in time."

"When?"

"John Merrimon projected the power of Massassi onto the things for which he cared. It is steeped into this place, as it's steeped into her and even into you. She'll last a day or a week, but not long. Life, after all, is the largest of things."

Johnny's hand moved closer to the stone. He wanted it and feared it. The conflict frightened him even more. "What if I take this right now?"

"Then we will struggle, you and I."

"To what end?"

"I am the last of the line, and the strongest. You would lose."

"And if I did not?"

"Massassi is the soul of women. In the end, that is the only truth that matters."

The stare between them held. She remained at peace. "Where would you go, if I agreed?"

"The world is wide, and the sufferings of women are many. Massassi will guide me."

"And this place?"

"Hush Arbor means little to me now."

"What about us, our families?"

"Do the right thing, and there is no us."

Johnny looked at the stone, and thought about all that power. John had used it to keep Marion safe, to intimidate and kill, to preserve Hush Arbor at any cost. Was it the stone that drove him mad, or was it something as simple as loneliness and time and grief? All Johnny knew for sure were the words he'd said to John. There would always be a final price, one after the other. But that was not his only concern.

"Are you a good person?" he asked.

"I am what God and my people have made me."

"This stone can change the world. It's dangerous."

"That depends on the person holding it." Cree smiled for a second time. "Aina was made hard by war, and harder still by slavery. Others are gentle and kind. You must have faith."

In that, she was right. What else did Johnny have besides faith in himself and his judgment, the faith that, after everything, the universe made sense? A thousand lives, she'd said. Johnny had no wisdom to compete with that. Worse, he had no right. Even John Merrimon had known as much.

No man was born to hold Massassi's soul. . . .

"I'm sorry for what John did to Aina, and to your family."

"Some people are weak," Cree said. "I will try to be otherwise."

It was a fine answer, Johnny thought. He watched her face for long seconds, then passed his hand above the stone. He felt its warmth and power, but Cree did not flinch. She remained at peace, he thought, and that was the finest sign of all. "Take it," he said; and rising gracefully, she did. She placed it on her breast, and seemed older and taller and splendid. Turning as a queen might, she left the cave without looking back, and Johnny followed, but slowly. He stood at the fire and stared across the Hush, which was purple in the night. There was no sign of Cree, but he felt Jack in the distance, and cops, and Verdine and Leon. Would he feel as much tomorrow? He didn't know, but Cree said that he was steeped in the power of Massassi, and that the Hush, too, was steeped.

Was he ready to live without it?

Could he?

EPILOGUE

It took Marion a full month to die, and Johnny rarely left her side. The first time he did, it was to bury John on the hilltop above the cave in which he'd lived for so long. The grassy place John mentioned crowned the eastern edge where land fell away, and Johnny dug the grave so the sun would touch it early. Even then, it was hard to leave John alone in the earth, and Johnny sat with him for most of that gentle day. He spoke little, and when he did, it was to describe the view or the breeze, or to explain the choice he'd made. There was no point belaboring it, so Johnny kept it simple.

It was the right thing to do.

John wouldn't understand, but Johnny was at peace with the decision. Every day, Marion lost a little color, yet every morning the same slight smile was on her face. She was a statue, fading; and that, too, was the natural order of things. Even the hardest mountain yielded in time, and so it was with Marion. In a week, she'd aged. In three, she was old. But Johnny held her hand when he could. He spoke to her of John and his faithfulness and all his lonely years. He promised her a place on the same sunny slope, and told her John was waiting. If she heard or understood, she never gave a sign; but Johnny had reason to hope.

The bloom faded.

The smile remained.

Once a day, Johnny sat at the cave's mouth to follow the search below. Thirty or forty people usually looked, but sometimes it was more.

They stayed in groups of six, and moved slowly from one part of the swamp to the next. They were determined to find him, and for a while it was amusing. But Johnny tired of people on his land. He tired of helicopters and reporters, of the distrust and fear that rolled like a fog up the hillside. When Johnny left Marion the second time, it was to meet Jack near where the old cabin had burned. It was not the first time Jack had come into the swamp, looking for Johnny. He stumbled around—just as determined as the cops—but he was always followed, as if Johnny might wander blithely in to say hello.

That wouldn't happen, of course.

Not while Johnny *felt*.

But the question haunted. Cree had said the magic was *steeped* into Johnny, but that was an imperfect word. It didn't mean *owned* or *attached* or *forever*. So Johnny lived with worries of blindness and loss and amputation. He watched Marion fade, yet feared his own dissolution. Did that make him insincere? Possibly. He couldn't help it. Life in the cave was like that—two worlds—so that when Jack appeared alone, Johnny set off beneath a sky that was low and white and hot for late September, so close to fall. He wanted a touchstone to his old life, and Jack was there to deliver it. "They're not filing charges," he said. "They're calling off the search."

Johnny reached out, and saw that it was true. People were pulling back. The old church was empty. "Why? How?"

"Jimmy Ray Hill is off life support. He's talking." Jack seemed calm, but touched Johnny on the shoulder. "He doesn't know what killed the sheriff, but he swears it wasn't you. Tom Lee pushed, but Jimmy Ray wouldn't change his story. And that's not the best part." Jack waited, but not for long. "James Kirkpatrick is talking, too. He's not entirely rational, but whatever he thinks it was that killed William Boyd, he won't say it was you." Jack made air quotes. "'He was floating; he was crucified.' Don't you get it? Don't you see?"

Johnny did, but then again, he'd never really worried. Maybe he'd never truly cared. "Will I have to speak to the police?"

"Captain Lee has an agenda," Jack said. "But they're not charging you, so what can he really do? He'll ask his questions. You answer or you don't."

Johnny doubted it would be that simple. Strong people were afraid, and that made for dangerous business. *No charges, though.* He smiled, as Jack wanted, but his relief was a muted thing. He'd not thought about life for weeks, not this life. "Listen," he said. "I have to go."

"What? I just got here. Don't you get it? The bodies in the cave are old, too old. You're off the hook for the new ones. People in town—now, that's another matter. You wouldn't believe the stories floating around, the speculation about you, this place. Point is—it's all good. Let's celebrate. Dinner! Drinks! The cabin burned, but we can go into town, my place. We can go anywhere. It's over."

He wanted more, but Johnny was looking north. Marion was aging faster now. It wouldn't be long. "I need a couple of weeks," he said.

"Weeks? Are you serious?"

Jack's disappointment was hard to see, but Johnny had no choice. "Tell Clyde I'm all right, would you? Tell my mother, too."

"Of course, but—"

"Thanks, Jack. You're a good man."

Johnny started to turn, but Jack wasn't finished. "Listen, buddy. I hate to mention this, but taxes are due in nine days."

"Jesus, Jack." Johnny had forgotten. In all the other worries, he'd lost this one. Would he lose the Hush after all, and for something as stupid as money? "Why are you smiling?"

"It's more of a smirk."

"Damn it, Jack—"

"Do you trust me?"

"Of course."

"Then say I'm your lawyer."

"You're my lawyer."

"Excellent. Good."

"What's happening, Jack?"

"Don't worry about it. But dinner can't be in two weeks. Eight days, all right? Eight days at the cabin. I'll bring everything."

The lawyers met five days later at three o'clock, four of them in the big conference room on the top floor. Jack came in wearing jeans, a linen shirt, and boat shoes worn white at the tips. The men from his old firm were serious in their expensive suits. Leslie was beautiful, as ever. "Gentlemen. Lady." Jack breezed across the room, and took a seat at the middle of the table. He dropped an old law-school backpack on the surface, and met every gaze in turn. The smile never wavered.

Leslie was the first to speak. "Private practice seems to suit you."

"It's great when you have the right clients."

Michael Adkins laced his thick fingers, leaning forward. "Don't you mean 'client'?"

"Quite right." Jack unzipped the backpack, pulled out a file, and slid across four copies of the same document. "Our settlement demand. Non-negotiable."

Adkins looked at it without touching it. "One million dollars."

"Only if it's paid within three days. After that, it triples." Adkins scoffed. The other lawyers looked blank, and Jack smiled more broadly. "You represent the county. Am I not in the right office?"

Leslie was the only one to return the smile. It was still dazzling. "I think you're ahead of yourself on this, Counselor."

"You flew a helicopter into my client's home—"

"A cabin, I believe."

"A cabin built with his own hands, a labor of love."

"Yet, liability has not been established," Leslie said.

"That will come at trial, of course. Destruction of private property. Excessive force. Intentional infliction of emotional distress. Malicious prosecution. Don't get me started."

"Please—"

"Your sheriff's department has been harassing my client since he was a child. The pattern is well established—"

"Your client has a criminal record," Adkins interrupted. "What you call persecution I call law enforcement."

Jack looked at the senior partner, and his smile took a bitter edge. "Captain Lee used civilians—"

"Civilian *trackers,*" Adkins interrupted.

"*Armed* civilian trackers."

"What? He wouldn't!"

Jack slid more documents from his file. "Sworn statements," he said. "Timmy Beach. Bob Brinson. A few others." All four lawyers flipped through the pages. "Two guards at the jail have confirmed that my client, when confined on suspicion of William Boyd's death, was held in unduly coercive circumstances, and that Sheriff Cline actively conspired to deny his right to counsel. Their statements." He slid over more pages. "I've not deposed Bonnie Busby yet, but she's aware of the sheriff's long vendetta against my client. She's a good person. I think she'll tell the truth, once subpoenaed. Bottom line, if this goes to trial, the county will lose a fortune. You know it. I know it. Let's not even discuss the bad publicity or the political fallout."

No one spoke the deeper truth, but it was there nonetheless. Juries in Raven County drew heavily from the rank and file of blue-collar workers, men and women who lived outside the city limits. To people like that, Johnny was a hero; and county government, the enemy. Jack smiled every time he pictured himself in front of that jury. Michael Adkins seemed to understand that reality, too. "A million dollars . . ."

"You're getting off easy."

"This is all very fast." Adkins waved a hand over the documents as if to conjure them away. "Very unusual."

"Indeed." Jack stood, and zipped up the pack. "You'll want time to discuss. I'll wait outside."

It took less time than Jack imagined. They sent Leslie to find him by the large window with views down onto the city. Her skin was the same as always, perfect and pale and slightly flushed. Her eyes shone when sunlight struck them. "Nice job, Counselor." Jack shrugged. It wasn't over yet. "They want you to take half."

"Not a chance," Jack said.

"I told them you wouldn't. I'm supposed to be playing hardball."

"So, we're good at a million?"

"Adkins won't shake your hand on it, but yeah. A million, plus the normal bells and whistles."

"Nondisclosures, waivers?"

"The usual."

"I need the money in three days."

"I'll have the paperwork tomorrow."

Jack nodded. His first real client. His first case. He started to turn, but Leslie wasn't finished. "Have you seen him since . . . you know?" She touched his hand, but Jack said nothing. She moved closer, and brought the usual smells. Perfume. Her hair. "What happened out there, Jack? I mean, what really happened? All those bodies. The stories? People say it goes back a hundred years or more, that even now no one knows for sure how Boyd or the sheriff died, how Colson Hightower drowned in eighteen inches of water." Jack shook his head, but her color was up, and she was even closer. "They say there are things not even the coroner will discuss. They say the place is haunted, that Johnny is not like the rest of us—"

"Come on, Leslie."

But she moved even closer. "I know people in the sheriff's department, some in the state police, too. A few of them have spoken to me about Verdine Freemantle and what they found in the bottom of that old grave—"

"Leslie . . ."

"They say that whatever was buried with Luana Freemantle defies explanation, that there's good reason the coroner won't discuss it. Grown men are scared, Jack. They don't know what to believe."

"What are you suggesting?"

"These are seasoned officers, men too hard for fairy tales or children's stories."

"That's all they are, Leslie, just stories."

"But who could live in a place like that? Who would? Come on, Jack. Whatever happened, you were there. You saw it."

Jack looked down on the city. She was right. He'd seen things.

"I'd love to pick your brain," she said. "You know. Once all this is done."

Leslie squeezed his bad arm, and Jack thought about that as he drove a dozen blocks to buy bourbon and cigars. He thought about their nights together, those eyes in the dimness. She was a mercenary soul, but lived the life without regret. Maybe he'd see her again, or maybe not. Whatever the case, the choice would be his.

At his apartment, he thought about the money he'd won for Johnny's future. His next job would be to convince Johnny that a conservation easement made sense. It would cut his taxes to pennies on the dollar, and Jack smiled, thinking of the argument he'd make. It's why he'd gone to law school: to have the answers, to help people who mattered.

Pouring a glass of bourbon, he took it onto the roof and stared north toward the Hush. In two days, he'd have dinner with his friend, where he'd ask about the bodies and the cave and all the other things on which the people in town had fixated. He'd want to know about the deaths and the fear and the stories told by those who'd survived. He'd present the darker questions, too, the private ones about what he'd seen and heard that night, disturbing ones about the old creature they'd dug from that muddy ground. He'd ask about Verdine and Johnny's secrets and all the things that made the Hush matter so damn much. But Jack would get few answers, and he was okay with that. They'd come later, or not at all. All Jack knew for sure was that Johnny Merrimon was the best friend he'd ever had, and that he'd been exactly that since they were boys. They had years for those questions, a lifetime.

Jack could be patient.

He'd get there in the end.

Tipping back the glass, he finished the bourbon, then stooped for a pebble that was white and smooth and small enough to sting without drawing blood. He bounced it on his palm, then put it in his pocket.

Marion died in the last hour before dawn, and Johnny was with her when it happened. He cried about it more than he was proud to admit, but John's memories remained his, and it seemed sad to him that she'd had so much life and so little living. Fifteen months of marriage. An eyeblink with her child. By noon, the second grave was dug, but Johnny lingered with the shovel. It was still hot in the Hush, still windswept and vast. The hillside was a good place for Marion, too, he thought. She'd slept belowground for so many years. Was this really any different? John was with her. The earth was the same. When the grave was smoothed above her remains, he thought of markers for the first time. Their old stone still stood in the family cemetery where the manor house had been. BOUND IN LOVE, FOREVER SOULS. Those were the words Johnny remembered, and thought few could be more fitting.

Maybe he'd bring the marker here.

Maybe he'd carve the final dates.

Johnny spent two more days in the hills, and when the sun was low on that third afternoon, he went to the cabin at last. It was basically gone; the helicopter was still there. None of that troubled him, though. He'd build another cabin. He had the cave. Righting one of the camp chairs, he brushed off the seat and then the table. He turned his face to the warmth of the sun, and in the stillness thought at last of his future. Until that moment, he'd thought mostly of Marion and John, of the past and of Cree, who was out there somewhere. Only late at night had he worried for himself, only when he was at his weakest.

What if he faded?

Breathing deeply, Johnny reached out for the Hush, and felt so much of it. He knew Jack was a half mile from the church, and whistling. He knew rain would come tomorrow, and that stone was cooling in the shade two miles north. Cree had said the land was *steeped* in power, and that Johnny, too, was *steeped*.

Maybe that word was bigger than he thought.

Maybe nothing would change.

Johnny kept his face to the sun, and though his eyes were closed, he followed Jack's progress as he wound through the swamp, slipping and cursing, but undeniably eager. Maybe this would last forever, Johnny thought. And maybe it would fade. Right now, though, just now, he was as happy as he'd ever been. He had the Hush, and his friend was close. They'd drink bourbon and smoke cigars and tell the old lies. They'd stay up too late, but have coffee in the morning, and fish the dark waters. Johnny felt it all, an eddy in the current. He saw the pebble move from Jack's pocket to his palm. He waited until the arm went back, then, smiling, said, "Don't do it, old friend."